The Last Viking

The Mercian Ninth Century
Book 8

MJ Porter

Cover and map design by Flintlock Covers

ISBN: Ingram paperback 978-1-917374-11-8

ISBN: ebook 978-1-914332-97-5

ISBN: paperback 978-1-914332-98-2

ISBN: hardback 978-1-914332-99-9

❀ Created with Vellum

Contents

For EP. On your 50th birthday.
*You old b*******
Love you.

GWYNEDD
POWYS
DYFED
GWENT
WESSEX
MERCIA
EAST ANGLIA
KENT
CHESTER
GAINSBOROUGH
TORKSEY
BARDNEY
LICHFIELD
REPTON
TAMWORTH
PETERBOROUGH
THETFORD
ELY
WARWICK
NORTHAMPTON
GRANTABRIDGE
WORCESTER
OFFA'S DYKE
HEREFORD
PASSENHAM
KINGSHOLM
GLOUCESTER
LONDON
WINCHESTER
MAP OF EARLY ENGLAND
0
50 Miles

Prologue

Gloucester, Summer AD875

We follow a trail of destruction to Gloucester. It's easy to see where our enemies have come this way. We warned the people who make their living along the riverbank. They did their best to leave, but it seems the bastards have torched anything that was left behind. Small wooden buildings, used when the ships need to be brought ashore for repairs, blaze in the summer air.

'They didn't exactly arrive with bloody stealth,' Gardulf complains at my side. I eye him. He's holding his left arm tight to his body. I can see no sign of blood, but that doesn't mean he's not wounded. Bruises can be even more painful than cuts.

'We didn't exactly fucking want them to,' I counter quickly. Rudolf's strangely quiet. I turn and eye him, confident I don't need to watch Haden's every step. He knows how to avoid impediments to our progress.

Rudolf's nose still runs with blood, and his face is too pale for my liking.

'That should have stopped by now,' I call, indicating his nose with a tilt of my chin.

'Well, it hasn't,' he scowls. The words are muffled, but I know what he meant.

'Shove this up it,' Pybba offers, extending a dirty rag. I wouldn't want to put that up my nose, but Rudolf does so, eager to stop tasting his own blood.

'That wasn't as bloody easy as we thought,' Wærwulf comments sourly. He also has some injuries. Not on his face, but I saw him limp when he mounted Cinder. One of his legs, perhaps the right, is hurt. I don't know if he's knocked it or cut it.

'No, but these things rarely are,' Pybba murmurs. He's sitting well in his saddle, Brimman taking his commands easily as he follows Haden. Pybba is much recovered from his illness, the bruises finally fading away from the beating he took. His flesh is filling out once more. Not that he was ever a fat man.

'We're nearly fucking done,' I assure them. I detect the cries of Mercians as they hear our thundering approach.

'Peace,' I shout, but the single word streams behind me because Haden's speed is so fast. In no time at all, I can see the bridge over the River Severn and hold out half a hope that Icel won't have reached it yet. I narrow my eyes. I can't bloody see well enough to know one way or another, but I can see smoke hanging over the settlement in a grey pall. Whether Icel and the other half of my warriors have arrived or not, the enemy is here, and they've set fire to something. I hope it's not the fucking bridge. I endured enough getting the bloody Welsh to rebuild it after the arseholes burned it down. I won't suffer that again.

As we get closer and closer, I sense my grumbling warriors and fleet-footed horses, forgetting all that we've already endured today. My aunt's here. Bishop Wærferth as well, and as we get even nearer, I see the two Viking raider ships at the quayside that we allowed to pass at the pinch point further south from here. Their sails are raised. The emblem of our enemies, the one-eyed raven and the owl, are easy to see against the bleached linen.

I growl low in my throat. The fucking bastards.

'Remember the strategy,' Pybba reminds me roughly as I allow

Haden to pick up pace. Not wanting Pybba to realise I'm reining Haden in because of his caution, I slowly pull my horse back to join the other animals. I don't look to Pybba. I don't want him to see my suppressed fury.

'Remember the plan,' Pybba reiterates, but I don't think it's directed solely at me, even though I lead my warriors.

'Remember the fucking intention,' I call to my men. My words are rough, filled with suppressed fury. I know where I need to direct it.

Gloucester's east gate is open, and we stream inside. I remember when we came here and found the Welsh trying to retreat. I'm reminded of all the other times I've been to Gloucester, as well. All the occasions I've prayed at the church, haggled in the market, or found a tavern to quench my thirst. Those days are long gone, but Gloucester's a special place. I'll bloody protect it just as I will the rest of Mercia.

Gloucester's warriors rush towards us, relief on their faces that we've finally arrived. I exchange rapid words with them as we dismount and hand over the horses. The animals are led away. These warriors know what they have to do, and that's to get the animals to Kingsholm and protect the royal settlement with their lives. I won't allow anyone to wound Haden. Not again. Never again. I won't permit Kingsholm to be overwhelmed. Kingsholm must be held secure. That's where most of Gloucester's inhabitants have gone for protection from the events about to unfold here today. Including my aunt, young Æthelred and Bishop Wærferth.

Choking on the grey smoke wafting inside the walls, we walk as one into Gloucester through the open gateway. With my warriors at my side, my exhaustion is banished. All we've accomplished today has led us here, and we will prevail.

Smoke billows from the quayside. The crackle of flames can be heard from close to one of the water mills. I hope the bastards haven't torched it. I know how complex the mechanism is to line up and put in place. I don't want the miller to bitch to me about it for the next three years, or however long the memory stays fresh in his mind. He's a grouch of a man but a good one.

Again, a flash of memory has me turning as though to find Edmund beside me, his face filled with fury at finding the bastard Welsh inside the market site. But he's not there. Neither is his horse, or indeed mine. Instead, I catch sight of the bastard Viking raiders ahead.

The shipmen have surrounded the long hall that dominates the settlement. Inside, transactions are completed, and law is dispensed, and right now, that's where the bastard, Jarl Guthrum, is. The man who took Edmund from me. The man I fucking hate.

'With me,' I urge my warriors, Rudolf and Pybba, closest to me. I amble to a run, feeling every ache in my body from the long battle we've already endured. My chest is too tight, my arms too heavy, and my head unsteady. We've already undertaken a bloody, long fight, and we've only just started. I wish Ealdorman Ælhun and his warriors were here, but they're not. I left him and them at Northampton. Equally, there are fewer men here than there should be on any given day, especially when facing a Viking raider attack.

'My lord,' I turn and see Icel emerging from the drifts of smoke at the quayside. I eye him, noticing his greying beard and broad shoulders, the firmness of his stance, and the ire that flashes in his familiar eyes.

'It's good to see you.' I find I mean it.

'A bloody nasty fight,' Icel mutters, but his lips are thin with determination. I look behind him and see the rest of my warriors. Some limp, some bleed, but they're all there. That fills me with renewed resolve.

I turn to those with me. I hold the gaze of some, Pybba and Rudolf the longest. Rudolf's nose has stopped weeping, but I doubt it'll ever be straight again. His breathing is nasally, and he winces and coughs. I've half a mind to tell him to get his arse to Kingsholm.

'Don't even bloody think about it,' Rudolf reads my mind. His defiance is fierce. Pybba nods just once. A sign that he's content for

Rudolf to continue. Not that any of them would know when they'd reached the limit of their skills. I can hardly argue with him about it. I'm not capable of that either.

'Remember the bastard plan,' I urge my men instead. I see Gardulf gripping his seax. His face is dirty and etched with fury. Hereman's perpetual good humour is missing. This is too personal for the pair of them. It's too personal for me.

'Aye, yes, get on with it,' my warriors growl or call to me. I sense a smile on my lips as I absorb their desire to stand beside me, no matter what I bloody order them to do. I am nothing without my warriors.

'Stay the fuck alive,' I command. More and more of them meet my eyes. Fire burns within them all, not just Gardulf and Hereman. Goda growls. Sæbald runs his hand over the trace of the cut that's permanently divided his beard into two halves. Wærwulf, with his familiar, if lopsided face from a long ago wound. And more of them. These are my warriors, and losing Edmund has reminded me that I love every single one of the damn bastards.

'Stay the fuck alive,' I repeat more forcibly, fearing my voice might break with emotion. Without further thought, I turn and run. The great hall's smoking. On feet that abruptly feel lighter, I dash towards the scene of the fighting. Not to the front door of the hall, though. I do catch a glimpse of combat inside and hear the shrieks of wood being moved over floorboards but veer aside to the rear of the building. There's another entrance here. Few know of it. It's for the servants, not for the king of bloody Mercia and his warriors.

The Viking raiders don't even seem to notice our arrival. They certainly don't see us moving away from the entrance. Instead, smoke cloaks our passage. We're not exactly quiet, with shields, byrnies and our weapons, but there is no cry of alarm. I think this has always been their weakness. The thirst for blood, revenge, and triumph. It blinds them to anything the Mercians can do to rebuff their attacks. This time, I'm bloody relying on that.

Ahead, I see a figure I don't want to meet. Not here. Not outside the bloody hall within which the Viking raiders are knocking the shit out of the Mercians under the command of Kyred.

'Aunt,' I glower. She looks at me and, in one swoop, takes me in from my feet to my head.

'At last,' she offers, as though I'm late for a church service or the witan and not to deal with the bastard enemy.

'Why are you here?' I huff, amazed I don't say something far worse.

'To show you the entrance, of course.'

'I know my way to the entrance,' I glower darkly, but she shrugs a shoulder. I eye her then, really taking her in, while Icel bends to peer inside the lower doorway. It's not actually that small for people who don't have a warrior's build.

'Why are you wearing a bloody byrnie?' I realise what it is that's caught my eye, and now I can't stop myself.

'To be safe,' she offers, shrugging again, biting back a comment on my language. I open my mouth to argue, but Pybba interjects.

'Come the fuck on, my lord.' More and more of my warriors make their way inside, following Icel. My aunt winces at Pybba's turn of phrase despite the imminent threat. At least it's all she does. If it had been me, I'd have probably had my ears boxed.

'How many of them?' I ask her, realising I may as well make use of her close proximity to the fight.

'Too many, not enough. It doesn't matter. Just do what must be done.' A clatter of a horse and I look up, expecting to see one of my warriors come to take my aunt to Kingsholm, but instead, I meet the gaze of Bishop Wærferth. His clothing is askew, and his face flushed, but I think he also wears a byrnie. He moves to dismount.

'Don't even bloody think about it,' I caution. 'Either of you. Don't make me leave some of my men here to guard you.' A wounded look crosses the bishop's face, and my aunt opens her mouth to reply. She also wears a weapons belt beneath her cloak. When did she bloody get that? I look closer, and my blood runs chill. She has Edmund's sword. Damn her. And damn him. And damn Hereman and Gardulf, who've no doubt known about this all along.

'Of course, nephew,' she demures, but I don't believe her for one moment. However, the sound of fighting from inside the long hall draws my attention.

'Bloody hurry up, my lord,' Rudolf pokes his bloodied nose back through the door, and there's no time to argue.

'I'll contend with this shitshow later,' I promise. I don't miss the look of relief that passes over both of their faces. They'll defy me. I know they will. 'I can't be bloody everywhere at once,' I shout over my shoulder, hoping they'll hear the caution and heed it for once in their lives. My aunt's wounds have not long healed. I can't believe she invites more.

Inside the hall, it takes a moment for my eyes to adjust to the gloom beneath the eaves of the building. I can sense there's a battle taking place, but I can't see it. I grip my shield and seax, prepared for anything, only to be jostled by someone in front of me. For a moment, I'm not sure who it is. But the wild strikes and breadth of his shoulders ensure I realise it's bloody Hereman.

Although smoke billows in the air, I can see more. Someone's distributed the fire from the hearth, or something's burning. It's acrid, and I cough. It's not the usual smell of sweet herbs and apple wood. It reminds me of events in Grantabridge, and my rage blooms once more. Everywhere I look today, memories of Edmund plague me.

The Viking raiders battle against Bishop Wærferth's warriors. They know what to do, and they're doing a bloody good job of it.

Icel, Pybba, Hereman and Gardulf are absorbing the brunt of the fight. They're slowly moving their way towards our enemy. The Viking raiders seem determined to overawe us. They have enough men to meet our attack, even as they try to overwhelm Kyred. In the press of the huge space, I realise it would have been better to stage this outside. Here, it's too cramped and too liable to end poorly.

A blood-curdling cry from a Mercian warrior elicits a judder down my spine. I don't want my warriors to die here. Not for this.

'Come on,' I urge my men, adding my weight to Hereman's back. His furious face turns my way.

'There's bloody nowhere to go,' he growls low in his throat. 'The bastard floor's on fire, and we'll burn alongside it.'

'Bollocks,' I glower, abruptly appreciating the problem. The acrid smoke is being caused by the bastards trying to burn us out. Or if not, by a lucky happenstance that makes it difficult for us to use the back entrance to our advantage. Perhaps they did know of it, after all.

'Jump it,' I mutter. But Hereman shakes his head.

'If you want to lose the bloody hair on your legs, then yes. And probably on your head as well.' Only then do I recognise that the sharp, caustic stink of the flames is caused by burning hair.

'Bloody hell.' I look around. My warriors have their shields ready and prepared, but it's as though yellow, flaming fingers hold us back, pushing us further and further towards the doorway through which we gained entry. We fight flames, not the fucking Viking raiders. I look up, eyeing the wooden struts. The rafters here are already blackened, and in places, the flames leap up to meet them. They'll be weakened. They might even crumble to ashes. Bollocks.

'Lay your shields over the bastard flames,' I order. But, in front, Hereman makes no move to do so.

'Lay your shields over the bastard flames,' I repeat, trying to shoulder my way through. Hereman turns to glare at me. Gardulf does the same.

'They're fucking wet enough,' I remind them of our previous fight. It's not taken us that long to return to Gloucester that they've dried out from the dunking they received.

Hereman relents. I glance at my Mercians being overawed and then drop my shield as I ordered. For the briefest moment, the flames extinguish before the wood and fabric of the shield starts to smoulder. I step over the shield, not allowing myself to consider what I'm bloody doing. It's either this or work my way to the main entrance and then have the enemy trapped between mine and Kyred's force. I don't want to bloody do that.

I jump over the shield, wincing at the flash of unwelcome heat. At least my feet are warm again. I bend and bat out a single flame on my left boot with damp gloves.

'Bloody hurry up,' I urge my warriors, repeating Rudolf's demands to me earlier. I'm where I want to be, but now I've no shield because I won't risk gathering it back into my hand. There'll be nothing left of it soon.

I wait long enough to ensure the others follow my lead and then rush to join the skirmish. That bastard, Jarl Guthrum, has disappeared from view. The smoke's too dense to see the main doorway. Instead, I focus on what I can bloody do: reinforce the Mercian warriors fighting on my behalf. Behind me, I hear shields falling and the outraged shrieks of my warriors as they forge a path over the flames, but at least they're bloody following me for once.

We need to end this quickly before Gloucester's main hall is little more than a smoking ruin.

Chapter One

Kingsholm, Two months earlier

Tears stream down my face, and I don't fucking care. I'm not embarrassed by my sorrow at losing Edmund. He was my friend, almost my brother, and without him, I don't know how I'll go on with this ridiculous masquerade. I'm Mercia's king, but I don't bloody want to be.

Hands gripped tightly within Jethson's coat, I know the horse feels as I do. I expected more from my aunt. I thought she'd grieve her lover, and yet, it's as though Edmund is merely missing and not dead at all. I'd hate her, but I know what grief does to people. One day, and I pity her when it arrives, the full fucking force of her sorrow will buckle her. I don't wish to be with her when that happens, although I must be. Not supporting her would make me a coward, and while I might rant against being Mercia's king, I know I'm no bloody coward. I'll kill the man who killed Edmund. I'll tear him limb from limb or stab him through each of his limbs. I'll make him suffer. I'll relish his death. I'll watch him bleed his last and spit on his shuddering corpse as his final breath leaves him.

Only I can't do that.

Damn Jarl Guthrum.

Fuck the bloody Viking raiders.

I'll kill every single one of the damn bastards and luxuriate in my triumph.

Only I can't do that either.

Frustration thrums through my clenched hands. Jethson shuffles forward. I step back and try to calm myself. Jethson's fractious enough without me being here. He'll let no one near him. He'll not eat. He'll not move. He'll not leave his stable. Returning him to Kingsholm has been a heroic effort. Since he carried Edmund's lifeless body from Grantabridge to Northampton, he's been inconsolable. I bloody fear for him. And I can't lose him as well as sodding Edmund.

I think back to Edmund's final words to me. He named me as a fine king. How little he knew about the effect his death would have on me. Or perhaps he did know. I loved him as a brother. I grieve for him as my friend.

At my feet, an inquisitive nose shuffles against my lower legs. I look into the eyes of my aunt's surviving hound. Berhtwulf knows more sorrow than my bloody aunt. He lost his mate as well, poor Wiglaf, dead and buried within the woodlands close to Northampton. Berhtwulf has been healed, but whether he would sooner be dead, I find it impossible to know.

'Sorry, Jethson,' I mouth, only then becoming aware Rudolf's also within the stables.

'My lord?' he questions. I glower at him. He shrugs his growing shoulders. Rudolf's so far from the boy I first met all those years ago, yet the passage of time is no comfort to me. He might be a man-grown, but I'm a man weakened. Am I too old for this shit?

'How is he, Coelwulf?' Rudolf tries again, naming me as I demand when there are no bastard bishops and ealdormen to show outrage for our familiarity with one another.

'I don't bloody know. He won't eat, but he doesn't resent my presence.'

'Unlike Haden,' Rudolf's tone drips with wounded pride. Haden has treated us all poorly recently. No doubt because we show too much concern for his old rival, Jethson.

We've been forced to pull the two horses apart. They've always been fractious with one another, but now Jethson's refusal to acknowledge my mount has led Haden to kick through the wooden stall to incite a fight. That it didn't work has frustrated my horse and me. For once, I wouldn't have quailed to find them biting and kicking one another. I might even have wept joyfully to know that Jethson couldn't deny his nature despite his debilitating grief.

'Aye, well, he's no good to us in this state,' I turn to leave, only for Jethson to bend his magnificent chestnut head and eye Berhtwulf.

'Perhaps the hound might help?' I offer. I'm no man of herb craft, but this animal isn't ill, merely heart sick. I understand his feelings only too well. Perhaps being heart sick is worse than being ill. There's no hope of a cure for what ails me and Jethson.

'The witan,' Rudolf reminds me. I snap back my angry retort. The other cowards have sent Rudolf to do their fucking dirty work for them. The bastards. He always gets lumbered with speaking to me of matters the others don't wish to face my wrath over.

'What of it?' I huff, still watching Jethson and Berhtwulf, who's curled up beneath the chestnut mount. He's braver than I am.

'If you're going to arrive in time, we need to leave.'

The emptiness of the stables suddenly makes itself known in a gust of wind that picks up a stray piece of hay, bringing it to rest in my groomed blond beard.

'I bloody know,' I confirm. Haden's waiting for me. Fuck it, all of the horses are waiting for me, and yet I linger all the same.

Rudolf huffs softly. Not with annoyance, just to make a sound.

'What?' I question.

'I don't want to bloody go either,' he offers, as though that'll make it all better for me.

I try to crack a smile at his plaintive complaint, but it hurts my cheeks. I've not smiled for a long time.

'Well, in that case, let's not go,' I try, but he shakes his head with a knowing look.

'Icel says you come now, or he'll boot you up the bloody arse, and you won't sit down until Christ's Mass.'

I shake my head. The thought's unappealing, but I'd like to see Icel perform the task. I'm not a weak man. I could run from him. I doubt he'd have the force to shove his foot far up my arse. And I'd make sure it stank when it came out.

'And Pybba says he'll hold you down while he does it.'

I shake my head once more. Pybba's missing a hand. He's not as fit as he once was after his captivity at the hand of Jarl Sigurd's widow and the illness before that. I can't imagine either him or Icel managing to carry out their threats. It amuses me that the old men think they can better me. I almost smirk.

'And Hereman has assured them both he's the man for the job.'

Now I do crack a smile. My warriors. I don't know what I'd bloody do without them. Icel and Pybba have been a part of my life for as long as I can remember. Hereman as well, although, younger than me, I've truly been a part of his life since he can remember. And Rudolf? Well, Rudolf is just as important, even if he's only been a member of the Kingsholm warriors for a decade. He was a young scamp then. Look at the man he's becoming now. His face is all but recovered from the beating he took within Grantabridge for starting the fire that destroyed the settlement. I've still not asked him how he did it. Talking about the events that occurred in Grantabridge is still too hard for me. I'm not sure the terrible sorrow will ever leave me.

'Bloody come on then,' I sigh, running my hand along Jethson's long back in parting. The horse makes no indication that he's even aware of my touch. I pity him again, but at least he can stand here and sulk. It seems I've got a fucking kingdom to rule, whether I want to or not.

'Let's be sodding going,' I take a deep breath and sigh, leaving the stable door open. Should Jethson think to leave, the inhabitants of Kingsholm will tend to his needs. After all, I can't leave Berhtwulf locked up in the stable beside him. I know Werburg will keep watch over the horse and the hound. My aunt has decreed that Berhtwulf not be allowed to leave Kingsholm again. I've half a mind to tell her the same.

'He's bloody coming,' Rudolf's youthful cry echoes from outside, where he's gone to prove to the others that he's a better man than them.

'He's coming,' I mimic, trying to release the tension in my shoulders and make myself more comfortable in my riding tunic and byrnie.

'I heard that,' Rudolf ducks back inside to complain, an arched eyebrow assuring me he really did.

'I heard that,' I mimic again while Rudolf growls low and moves to Dever. He's another bloody old horse.

In the bright sunlight, I eye my warriors, meeting Icel's unhappy face with one of mine. He sits astride Samson, and I consider how old the horse is. Not as old as the man, but certainly well into its third decade. I know Icel's had many horses throughout his life, but this animal is special to him. I consider why that might be. Not that the old bastard will ever tell me.

'Hail,' I call to my warriors, making my way to Haden's side. My horse eyes me with a stamp of his hoof, showing his impatience and perhaps his fury that I was talking with his nemesis, Jethson. 'I'm bloody coming,' I glower at him.

'About bloody time,' Hereman complains. I can see his face is pinched with cold. It's not the warmest of days, but we'll be warm soon enough.

'I had things to do,' I mutter, ensuring my balance is good before placing one foot in the stirrups to mount my tall horse. Taking the time to settle myself, I attempt to shake the feeling that every single member of my war band's watching me. Damn the fuckers. They know this is hard for me. Or they should. If they don't, they don't know me at all well.

When I'm ready, I slowly appraise my warriors. Gardulf eyes me with some sympathy. As Edmund's son, he's shown his sorrow. His uncle, Hereman, is all bluff, but I know he mourns his brother. Wærwulf nods as he notes my gaze. Lyfing offers me a knowing look, wrinkling the scars to either side of his nose, while Hemming struggles to control his mount and doesn't notice my attention. I wish they were all as oblivious as Hemming.

It falls to Pybba to say what they're all thinking.

'Let's get this bloody over and done with,' his words are caustic. 'And then we can get back to doing what we do best. Killing the bastard Viking raiders and the damn Welsh.' His words thrum with fury that we all feel. Edmund hated the bloody Welsh. Icel has no love for the damn West Saxon warriors, and I'd happily kill any who dared step foot on Mercian soil. But as so often the case, before we can do any of these things, we need to face the Mercian witan and their damn demands regarding our bloody captive, who, by rights, should be as dead and buried as sodding Edmund.

I doubt the witan will request we kill him for his part in destroying so much of Mercia.

No, I imagine they'll demand we exchange him as a valuable hostage. And that we accept the request of an alliance from Wessex and their double-dealing bastard of a king, Alfred. Now that we have one of the Viking raiders under our control, with absolutely sod all thanks to them, and perhaps despite them, Mercia remains an appealing ally for the West Saxons. I'm still wary of who was directing Bishop Smithwulf's actions with the Viking raiders of Grantabridge. We might have ensured Smithwulf had a timely burial within London, and we might have suggested the enemy killed him to any who asked, which they did, but those who were there know Bishop Smithwulf was meddling in affairs that were none of his damn concern. If he were alive, I'd kill the fucker. And I've not even mentioned Archbishop Wulfhere of York and his useless turd of a king in Northumbria. I can hardly fucking wait to hear the demands of Mercia's witan.

'To Worcester,' I order my warriors, and not one of us cheers, even as I feel the appraising gaze of all those who live within Kingsholm, Werburg commanding there in my aunt's absence. We're a sullen bunch, and they're sullen as well.

Mercia isn't yet safe. Edmund's dead. And the bishops can go fuck themselves, alongside Alfred, king of Wessex, if they think I'm going to agree to all of their damn demands.

Chapter Two

Worcester

'My lord king.' Bishop Wærferth speaks to me as I'm seated before the witan. I didn't want this to be a discussion, but there's no way I can avoid it. If I wanted this resolved to my bloody satisfaction, I should have killed Jarl Guthrum outside Grantabridge and had done with it. That I didn't is because Ealdorman Ælhun knew me well enough to remove Jarl Guthrum from my care. Edmund would curse me for a fool for allowing that to happen. I'd bloody agree with him.

'Speak,' I urge, wincing at my sharp tone. I don't need to catch my aunt's eye to know that I must watch my temper with the bishop. After all, none of this is, strictly speaking, his fault.

Not that the bishop immediately does so. Indeed, I think he allows a moment for me to calm. I nod at him, half an apology and half a hurry-up. The weight of my royal-helm is as crushing as the responsibility I feel for Mercia.

'This matter of Jarl Guthrum is a vexing one.'

I nod again. I bloody know that. I bite my lip, wishing I was more skilled at hiding my true thoughts on the matter.

'He's a powerful prisoner to have at our command,' he continues.

I bloody know this. I wish he'd speed up and tell me his opinions instead of labouring the point. 'We can use him to rid Mercia of the Viking raiders.'

I grunt because I'm fed up with nodding, hoping he'll realise I want him to speak more quickly.

'How?' another voice calls. I gaze into the crowded room, hoping to pick out who speaks. It'll be someone from eastern Mercia, I'm sure of it.

'It's not as though he has anyone who'll pay to have him back. No, we should kill him and end his life.' Ealdorman Aldred speaks. I'm unsurprised. Aldred isn't the deepest of thinkers. Not that I'm one to condone his words. I wish Jarl Guthrum were bloody dead as well. At least I know Ealdorman Aldred's thoughts on the matter.

'There are always ways,' Bishop Wærferth mollifies. I clench my hand tight to stop myself from urging him to fucking hurry up.

'We'll not ally with the Viking raiders,' Ealdorman Aldred argues. I wince at that. Not for one moment has the bishop suggested such a thing. 'They should all be dead, the bastards.'

I'm pleased Jarl Guthrum isn't within the hall inside Worcester. He'll suspect the nature of our discussion, but if he were here to hear these words being spoken aloud, he'd be fearful as he should be. He's lucky to still live. It's a pity the double wound his foot took from the archer and the dropped seax blade didn't get wound-rot and kill him.

'I suggest no accord,' the bishop resumes, trying to retain the smoothness of his delivery despite the interruptions. 'He can merely be our means of securing what we've been fighting for all these years.'

'Sounds like a bloody alliance,' Ealdorman Aldred spits back. Once more, I feel the heat of my aunt's gaze and know I need to intervene. I can't have them fighting within the witan.

'This is to be a discussion, not a tirade,' I urge my loyal followers in a raised voice. I'm not comfortable in my position as Mercia's king. I doubt I ever will be.

'Then you agree with the bishop?' Ealdorman Aldred shrieks. I seek him out amongst the audience. He glitters in the light from the hearth and the candles. He's a man keen to show his wealth. In the past, he caused the death of many because of his love of riches. I've not forgotten that even if, temporarily, he seems to have done so.

'I agreed to listen to everyone's opinions,' I retort, first allowing silence to fall within the room and then talking softly. This is how I speak to Haden when he's being a shit. I'm sure it'll work better with rational men and women. At least, I hope it bloody will.

'Ealdorman Wulfstan allied with the Viking raiders,' Ealdorman Aldred counters, not to be stopped.

'As did King Burgred,' I allow those four words to settle in the room. It's been many years since these men and women had a warrior for a king. It's about time they remembered I didn't abandon them to the Viking raiders. Indeed, many men in this room were complicit in that terrible accord reached between King Burgred and the Viking raider leaders at Repton. It was they who wanted me dead. They named me the only viable threat to the Viking raiders, and since then, I've done nothing but fight the bastard enemy. First for my life and subsequently for Mercia's freedom.

'My lord king,' Bishop Wærferth's the first to break the silence. He does so with no wince or hitch to his voice. His words remain reasoned. It's his damn fault I'm the king of Mercia. And my aunt's. I won't forget her place in all this. Equally, they must bloody remember it as well. The onus is on them to contend with my fury.

'As I was saying,' Bishop Wærferth continues when I nod to show he should, attempting not to drum my fingers over the arms of the chair I sit within. 'Jarl Guthrum is a valuable hostage. He must be used to secure Mercia's freedom from the Viking raiders.'

'So, you mean a negotiated settlement, as with the Repton jarls?' It's not Ealdorman Aldred who speaks, but another of my ealdormen, Ælhun, his beard rimmed with frost. We've not always been allies, but now I grudgingly accept him, and he me. He's been forged into a warrior, even though he didn't wish to be one. Perhaps that's why he understands me. I don't wish to be a king, yet I'm one all the same. Ealdorman Ælhun has been Jarl Guthrum's goaler since his capture.

'Perhaps,' Bishop Wærferth concedes. 'If we can secure the borders, then Mercia can rebuild.'

'It's always about rebuilding,' Ealdorman Aldred interjects angrily. 'We should be on the offensive. We should chase the bastards far from Mercia's shores.'

'And how would we bloody do that?' I feel stung into saying. 'We've no ship army to rival theirs. We have only so many warriors to protect Mercia and her people. We're a limited quantity. We can't be everywhere at once, despite the fact the Viking raiders can do precisely that.'

This has long been a problem. The Viking raiders are innumerable. Should some die in battle, there is always more to replace the dead bastards. It's not the same within Mercia. There are only so many warriors and so many men of the fyrd. There's a limited number of swords, seaxes, shields, and spears. Not to mention horses and wealth from the land to feed these men who must train and their horses who are so picky with their food.

Ealdorman Aldred's face is mutinous. He's a damn arse, although I confess, I wish I could agree with him. I should like to kill Jarl Guthrum. If not for him, then Edmund would live. Damn it. I don't want to think of that. I risk looking to my aunt. She sits to my left, not far away. Her face is marbled and cold. I wish I could endure as she does.

'King Alfred of Wessex,' the bishop resumes.

'Is no friend to Mercia,' I interject, despite saying I would listen. I can't help it. For too long, Alfred has been a thorn in Mercia's defences. Wed to a Mercian woman, he should think more of Mercia, but I understand him all too well. He sees Mercia as a buffer between the Norse-held enclaves to the north and east and his precious kingdom. I'd like to speak to his brother-by-marriage about that, but I won't allow the argument. Ealdorman Æthelwulf isn't to blame for Alfred. I have my thoughts on the subject. I'll hold firm to them. I'm very suspicious of King Alfred's intentions.

'And what of Archbishop Wulfhere of York?'

'The archbishop means us to fight his wars for him, but first, we must fight Mercia's.' It's my aunt who speaks. Her words are the most reasoned, even more so than the bishop's. I'm glad she interjects.

'Then what do you plan?' This question comes from Bishop Wærferth. It's not tinged with anger but curiosity. I yearn to have an answer for him. Silence falls. Perhaps, as so often the case in the last two years, they mean for me to solve everything for them. I only wish I bloody could.

'Jarl Guthrum is a valuable hostage,' I eventually acknowledge. 'We must consider all suggestions and use him best.' I swallow heavily and look down at my hands, white where they're both fisted in my lap. 'His death doesn't serve Mercia well. Alive, he can do more for us.' Those words are forced from me like a bladed edge at my throat. I bleed to admit the truth of them.

I don't wish to reach an accord with the bastard enemy. I want to kill them all and then kill them all over again. I hunger to make Mercia free.

'My lord king,' my aunt doesn't face me but instead fixes her gaze somewhere over the heads of those in attendance. Her words are sharp as iron and edged with resolve. 'We have a unique opportunity thanks to Jarl Guthrum's capture at Grantabridge.' I can barely breathe as she speaks. I can feel her hurt, anger, grief, and sorrow for Edmund, yet she talks around it. 'We must use it. If the situation were reversed, Jarl Guthrum would do the same.' So spoken, she turns to face me. I gaze at her familiar face. She's been more of a mother to me than any other. My mother died birthing me. I never knew her. Lady Cyneswith has been the most constant presence in my entire life. Her resolve has been stronger than my father's. I respect her. She bloody knows it.

I nod along with her, encouraging even though I don't wish to do so.

'Bishop Wærferth's correct. An accord, with the Viking raiders, which will see Jarl Guthrum retained as our hostage in exchange for an agreement with the remaining Grantabridge jarls. If they strike against Mercia, Jarl Guthrum will die. They'll pay us to keep him safe, and we'll treat him with respect for the next twelve months, after which the terms can be renegotiated.'

A roar of disapproval rushes through the room. My aunt speaks over it, almost as though the only person she needs to convince is me.

'Jarl Guthrum will convert and become a Christian. King Coelwulf will stand as his godfather. He'll be like a son to our king. Should he be freed after a year, everything he does will be for the good of Mercia and against his base nature.'

I hear Ealdorman Aldred denying the words loudly, as though if he shouts the loudest, his opinions will prevail. I close my eyes against the wash of rage and fury. I don't bloody want this. I don't want to be any fucking relative to Jarl Guthrum, even if it's only through a shared religion. I also understand that my aunt has thought about this. She's probably done nothing but consider this since Edmund's death. Some good must come from the murder of my friend, my ally, my brother. And her lover.

I recognise that my aunt will have the support of Bishop Wærferth, and probably all of Mercia's bishops, and many of the ealdormen. I'm not sure she has mine. She knows that as well. That's why the words have been spoken here, before everyone within the witan. She means to hound me into a corner and make me accept the unacceptable. She intends to use her grief for Edmund against me, as though it's my fault that Edmund is bloody dead and I yet live.

I hold her gaze, trying to see through her glacial eyes, her rigid stance, and her elaborate clothing.

Damn her.

Fucking damn her. And damn bloody Edmund for dying like that. It wasn't a good exchange. It was never going to be a bloody good bargain that he struck.

'An accord with Jarl Guthrum and the remaining, free, Grantabridge jarls. To last twelve months, and to secure the eastern Mercian border using the rivers and other landmarks as guides.' She continues to speak. The audacity of her plan slowly reveals itself to all within the hall. Silence falls, unwillingly at first and then more and more fully, as the shuffling of feet and coughs of those in attendance are stilled and stifled.

'We'll show these Viking raiders what it is to be honourable, and with the promise that should they step one single foot inside Mercia, Jarl Guthrum will pay with his life. He'll be returned to them in six separate boxes, his body carved up in mockery of the payments they must make to us to keep him alive.'

The callousness of my aunt's words astounds me. I watch Pybba wince. I see Rudolf's mouth fall open in shock. I even see young Æthelred returned to us from Hereford, looking aghast at the words from a woman he now knows to look upon kindly as his great aunt after Edmund admitted the truth of his parentage.

As though a spectre or ghost, I imagine I see Edmund behind them, nodding along in support of all his lover has just proposed, his familiar lips cast into a scowl of approval, his one green eye watching all avidly.

Damn her.

Bloody damn her.

Chapter Three

'Well, that went bloody well.' It's Pybba who speaks, his tone filled with dismay. The ealdormen and those attending the witan have left the hall, retiring for some fresh air in anticipation of the feast being prepared for them. I linger, sulking, I admit, and enjoying the silence. My warriors remain with me. So far, only Pybba has had the stones to speak.

'Indeed,' I murmur. I'm angry. I'm furious. And yet, a sneaking respect for my aunt's tactics stops me from reneging on the agreement reached in the witan. I am the king. I am the figurehead. There are others with just as much right to an opinion as me. Not that I welcome having to explain all this to an angry Ealdorman Aldred.

I eye my warrior-helm. I've yanked it from my head, but as of yet, Bishop Wærferth's cleric hasn't hastened to return it to its place of concealment somewhere within this hall.

'When will this damn baptism take place?' Hereman questions. 'And where?' This is a problem. Jarl Guthrum is at Northampton, under the watchful eye of Ealdorman Ælhun's warriors. Better to keep him to the periphery of Mercia's holdings, should the two remaining Grantabridge jarls decide to win him back. Not that I think they will. I imagine when they hear the terms we propose, they'll bloody wish he'd been killed just as much as I wish I'd ended his life.

'I'll leave that to Bishop Wærferth,' I confirm. I'm perplexed how such a position of strength against the Grantabridge jarls has become a noose around my neck. If this fails, it will fall at my feet, and I'm not the one who demanded it.

'And when will it happen?' Rudolf questions.

'I'll leave that to Bishop Wærferth,' I reply again. I hear his huff of annoyance and snap my mouth shut on an angry retort. My warriors and I include Rudolf, in that, know me well enough to understand I don't bloody like this. Not at all.

The tap-tapping of feet over the wooden floorboards, and I look up to see my aunt. Her face is more open now. The ravages of speaking before the witan have bled from her tight lips and cheeks. But she's pale in the glow from the fire. She huddles inside her cloak. I consider what this has cost her as opposed to what it will cost me.

'My lord king, nephew,' her words are firm. 'Your presence is requested.'

I grunt and walk towards her, taking her hand in mine and trying to offer her some warmth. She's as cold as death, and that worries me.

'You're cold,' I complain.

'I can't get warm, no matter what,' she counters. I turn to Icel as he overhears our conversations.

'A warming tonic,' he offers. 'Ask the monks for a filling pottage.' He doesn't mention grief or sorrow, but we all know that's what ails my aunt. Even if she won't admit it. I wish I knew Icel's secrets, but although there are hints, every now and then, he's more likely to poison us these days than cure us with his lacklustre knowledge of how to heal.

'Perhaps,' she acknowledges. 'Perhaps,' she repeats. After all, she is skilled in herb law. She should know how to cure herself.

'Was your suggestion a wise one?' I ask, walking towards the doorway, her arm looped through mine so that I try to warm her and keep her steady. I realise she has Æthelred with her. While a formal announcement on his parentage has yet to be made, his closeness to my aunt and me, has occasioned some discussion. I'm not going to hide that he's my brother's son, even if the identity of his mother is known only to Icel and Æthelred. I think it should probably stay that way.

'It was the only way,' she counters quickly. 'I thought long and hard about it. This is the first time Mercia has had one of her enemies within their grasp. We must be bold and also sensible.'

'Sooner he was dead.'

'And you allowed the Grantabridge jarls to resume their fight with Mercia?' She arches an eyebrow. 'Better this way. Mercia has known nearly a year and a half of war. She needs peace.'

'And what will twelve months allow Mercia to do?' I question. I'm a man of war, not politics. What does she intend to do with this hard-won peace she proposes?

'Mercia will grow strong and powerful once more. Mercia and her ealdormen must gather weapons and warriors. Mercia must have a bountiful harvest and the wealth to keep herself Mercia. Mercia, nephew, must do more than simply endure.' Her voice thrums with conviction.

'We've not been doing too badly,' I counter, frustrated to have the risks my warriors and I have endured somehow trivialised. Not, I realise, against my grumpiness, that I was fighting for anything other than Mercia's freedom. I don't like to hear my endeavours spoken about like this.

'No, not at all. If you call racing from Kingsholm to Repton, to Torksey to Repton to Northampton, to Worcester to Hereford, to Warwick doing not too badly. You've lost men,' and her voice hitches. I wince. 'This is our first solid gain so far.'

I open my mouth to argue but snap it shut once more. I can't argue that the personal cost has been too bloody high, and not just for my aunt.

'The Viking raiders have been expelled from Mercia,' I eventually offer, aware my voice is small, as though I'm a child scolded for stealing the honeycombs.

'But they must remain away from Mercia.' Now, she stops and turns to me. 'Coelwulf, this isn't a complaint against all you've accomplished. You must look beyond yourself and see what Mercia requires instead of what you need.' The words are softly spoken. The heartache in them almost causes tears to well in my eyes once.

'Damn the fucking bastards,' I explode, unable to help myself, and she nods, gripping my arm tighter.

'Damn them all, Coelwulf. But we must triumph against them. You'll not be Mercia's last king.' I swallow against my shock to hear her say that. I'd not even considered that could happen, and a sad smile plays on her lips, as she nods. 'You've no son, no heir, no one to leave your kingdom, but you can fight and make her strong and, in time, nominate your successor, who could be Æthelred, your brother's son. It's been done before, after all, especially in Mercia. Your namesake succeeded his brother to the kingship over fifty summers ago. But that can only happen if the Viking raiders leave Mercia alone. There'll never be a warrior like you, Coelwulf. Not again. Ask Icel. He'll speak to you of the past and the men he's fought beside. He'll tell you of those who fell beneath blades, and their bravery before they did so, but none have done all that you have, not even Icel.' As she speaks Icel's name, her voice is filled with sorrow. 'And you know full well that your brother and I named our hounds for Mercia's ineffectual previous kings. But it was also a promise that we would never gain the poor reputation they hold.'

'And so, this is a means to protect me as much as Mercia?' I query, trying to decipher the intent behind her words.

'This is a means for me to protect you, as much as Mercia, yes. I've,' and her words break. 'I've lost too much already,' she manages to choke. I grip her arm tighter. 'I've lost too much already, Coelwulf, and I won't lose you.' With that, she speeds her steps, hastening me onwards to once more face those of Mercia who help rule. I want to bloody argue with her. I want to tell her that I'm not indispensable and that there will be someone who can fight as well as I do in the future. That there's hope for Mercia and her future, but words fail me. I can think of no single person who could do so, not even amongst my warriors, and that, more than anything else my aunt has said to me, assures that her intentions, as much as I bloody hate them, are correct.

Mercia needs peace. I need bloody peace, even if I don't want it to come at such a cost.

Chapter Four

Northampton

'My lord king,' I eye Bishop Wærferth. He allows a tight smile to touch his lips.

'A good day for Mercia,' he offers. I only grunt in reply. I'm far from convinced. We're at Northampton. The small church there has been cleaned and made magnificent, my aunt working to ensure that the Grantabridge jarls will be overawed by the wealth on display. I can't help thinking it's contrary to the Christian ideals, but I hold my tongue. I'm not about to complain about that. My faith has been tested, and today, I must stand as though it's the most precious thing to me in the world. But it isn't.

That bastard, Jarl Guthrum, will be baptised. He'll take a Christian name and become my godson. I would laugh at that. He's older than me. How can he become my son?

The two other jarls will be welcomed into Northampton under heavy guard just before the ceremony is conducted. They've been informed of the terms of this peace accord. They've unwillingly accepted them. All the same, I've tripled the watch inside Northampton, and Ealdorman Ælhun has half of his men in the woodlands to the north and south. I suspect treachery, but have to pretend I don't.

Goda has command of some of my men in the hinterlands north of Northampton, opposite to where the Viking raiders have been camping since they arrived yesterday. I didn't venture outside to welcome them. I allowed Bishop Wærferth to speak to them alongside his fellow bishops, Eadberht of Lichfield and Ceobred of Leicester, although Mercian warriors protected them under the command of Wulfsige. Bishop Wærferth's face when he returned wasn't the most reassuring. But of course, he's met the men before when King Burgred negotiated his way out of Mercia. Admittedly, no one was talking about baptisms then. The only thing on King Burgred's mind was escaping from Mercia with his life. The fucking coward. The nithing.

'What did they say?' I ask.

'That you had their agreement, for now, but threaten violence should anything befall Jarl Guthrum.' I hiss at that. I've done nothing to Jarl Guthrum. He's been housed in more luxury than I've enjoyed since becoming king. He even has new clothes for the ceremony. And his wound has been healed, and I'd like people to realise it was his own damn archer that first skewered his foot to the ground. Admittedly, the second might have been the fault of the Mercians.

'That's good to know,' I counter. I'm standing on the battlements, eyeing the collection of tents and canvases that the Viking raiders are using. My double-headed eagle banner flies from Northampton's battlements, the colours bright, whipped by the brisk wind. It might be aggressive, but I don't bloody care. Northampton and I have greatly endured in the last year.

'I don't believe either man capable of retaliation alone,' I argue. 'It was Jarls Guthrum and Halfdan who led, not Oscetel and Anwend.'

'I think you're correct,' the bishop concedes. 'Let's hope they're all hot air and little else. Admittedly, Guthrum's oathsworn men are most aggrieved.'

'It'll be them who present the threat. They won't think to be contained by the terms of the treaty,' I concede unhappily.

'Perhaps, but Anwend and Oscetel are content with the borders agreed. They'll hold what little remains of Grantabridge. And they assure me there is very little left since the conflagration.' I smirk to think of that. Rudolf did a bloody fine job.

'It wasn't really Mercia's to give away,' I concede.

'No, but there's no king of the East Angles to argue either way any more.'

I accept that without argument. The reminder of what befell King Edmund of the East Angles is perhaps one reason not to deride King Burgred's decision to leave Mercia with his life. All the same, my eyes narrow, seeking out Jarls Anwend and Oscetel in the encampment. I remember meeting them at Repton. I remember it very bloody well. Then, it seemed that Anwend was the stronger of the men, alongside that bastard Halfdan, while Oscetel and Guthrum were more minor. But Anwend ran away with his son. It was the others who stood their ground.

I see it all before me. I can feel my naked feet, cold and protesting beneath me. I can sense the panic of knowing I was entirely under their control. And I remember Edmund and how he kept me bloody safe after a fashion.

The situation has been reversed, and yet I'm wary. I've used guile to beat them. I certainly used that at Repton. I hope they don't have anything similar planned here today, but I'm alert. I'd be a bloody fool not to realise they'll try anything to get their hands on Jarl Guthrum. Perhaps they would have held onto their erstwhile ally if Anwend and Oscetel had been at Grantabridge when we attacked it. I'm grateful they weren't

'We've warriors on guard and prepared to intervene if necessary,' I comment. Bishop Wærferth remains silent. Whether he approves of this or not is irrelevant. In this, I have the command of Northampton. I am Mercia's protection. Mercia's religious conviction falls at his feet.

'Let us hope we achieve peace, not war,' but his eyes glitter. Despite today's peaceful intentions, I'm far from unconvinced he wouldn't welcome a bloody big fight, given half a chance. I know I would.

I turn then, surveying the preparations for this ceremony. Northampton's heavily guarded. Should it be needed, the bridge and its tricks will protect us. They'll maroon everyone on this side of the river if it means Mercia remains free from attack. The ships have also been cast to the far side, brought ashore and laid out on the river bank. There'll be no easy access to Watling Street for our enemy. They might believe they know Northampton and Mercia as well as we do, but we always know more and can prepare more. I even have a contingent of men close to Icknield Street to the southeast. Whatever the remaining two Grantabridge jarls have planned, we'll counter it.

'Come, my lord king,' Bishop Wærferth indicates it's time to descend to street level. As I move to the stairs, I see movement in the camp. The Grantabridge jarls are coming to Northampton, and I will make them welcome. Well, as welcome as shit on my shoe. I growl and hurry down the wooden stairs.

I recognise both men, obviously, and note that the squat and ugly Anwend is accompanied by his son. Jarl Anwend's a small man hiding behind a long nose and elongated chin. If anything, it's grown longer since I last met him. His son is no prettier. Oscetel is as ugly as ever. The curling snake tattoo on his face has weathered poorly. Its teeth no longer seem as sharp. It lacks all menace. If anything, he looks like an old man trying to prove he's still young. As I thought, the slackening of his skin with age makes the snake look wrinkled, not terrifying.

'Welcome, Jarl Anwend and Jarl Oscetel, and your son, Anwend Anwendsson,' I don't bow, but I try and flood my voice with something other than the cold menace I feel. It does me no disservice to remind Anwend that his son only lives because I didn't kill him. Why else would I know his identity?

'If we can call it a welcome when you have our fellow warrior as your prisoner.' I'm unsurprised it's Oscetel who speaks first. Wærwulf's translating his words for me. The jarls have their own interpreter as well. While I listen to Wærwulf, I watch Oscetel's snake head moving unnaturally with the rage of his words. Oscetel thinks much of himself. Behind him, I detect a wince on Jarl Anwend's face and appreciate he'd rather this went more smoothly than Oscetel intends. Anwend Anwendsson watches me with unease, not straying from his father's side.

Mercia's warriors protect my hall within Northampton. It's impossible for Anwend and Oscetel not to appreciate my strength when they're so outnumbered. I realise how similar this situation is to the day I first had the joy of meeting them in Repton. I hope I've not overplayed my hand as they did there. I wouldn't wish this to bloody fail before it's even begun.

'I think it's a welcome,' I reply slowly. 'You have no blades at your throat?' The soft tone I use belies the threat. Both Wærwulf and his counterpart mirror it.

'Indeed, King Coelwulf,' Jarl Anwend interjects before Oscetel can say more, Wærwulf hurrying to repeat the words. 'And where is Jarl Guthrum?'

I nod my head. Icel and Hereman escort Jarl Guthrum into the room. In the time he's been our captive, his bruises have faded, although he will probably always limp. There is a faint pink line across his throat, where Edmund held a blade to it. Other than that, I realise, he looks hale and hearty. Perhaps we should feed him less. He's clothed far too well.

'Anwend, Oscetel,' Guthrum greets his fellow war leaders before gazing at me. There's no fury in his eyes. Not at the moment. He's banished it from his face just as I try to remove mine.

The three begin to gabble in Danish. I turn to Wærwulf. I've been trying to learn it. I suspect Icel knows far more of it than I might have thought. How could he not, with all the years of fighting our enemy?

'They speak of Grantabridge and the men and women who died there,' Wærwulf says loudly enough that all can hear. 'He asks after Jarl Halfdan as well.' If the three men object to having their words translated so we understand them, it's only Oscetel who reveals it. His face is furious, and he lowers his voice. That only makes Wærwulf step closer. I lower my head to hide my smirk. Oscetel is a bloody arse.

'Bring food and drink,' I instruct those of my warriors who'll serve as servants today, Hiltiberht, Hemming and Rudolf most prominent. The actual servants are elsewhere. I won't risk them with the Viking raiders, even if my warriors carry no weapons. At least I know they could better them if it came to fists and kicking.

A table is brought forward, a small one, just enough that they can rest drinks and plates on its surface. A bench is also brought. The men can sit and watch me. I don't hold Jarl Guthrum in ropes. He's free to move around with his allies. He's not free to leave Northampton, though.

'This treaty,' Jarl Oscetel begins, now prepared to take advantage of Wærwulf's translations. 'How will you ensure the Mercians don't attack us?' While Wærwulf tells me Oscetel's words, I keep a firm eye on others I know who speak Danish. It's not that I distrust Wærwulf, but they might detect something that Wærwulf misses. Bishop Wærferth's cleric is close. The woman who is so often found recording the actions of the witan, has a good grasp of the Norse tongue as well. Not that she indicates this.

'If you're within Grantabridge, then no Mercians will come close,' is my smooth reply. 'If you venture without Grantabridge, then yes, the Mercians might attack you.' I allow Wærwulf to repeat my words. I can decipher every other word. The jarls don't need to know that.

'And the jarl? What will happen to him?' The conversation is stilted and uncomfortable, reliant as we are on others to convey our intentions. It amuses me, for I'm not uncomfortable.

'He'll be kept as a guest of Mercia. You need not know where.'

'Then how can we be assured of his safety?'

Jarl Guthrum's face lights in a smirk as Jarl Oscetel demands answers that Guthrum's not been allowed to voice. No doubt he's hoping that Oscetel will somehow win him his freedom. That's not going to happen. The damn fool should know that. Surely he knows that as the man I hold responsible for the death of Edmund, it's very unlikely I will ever allow him to be free, despite the treaty terms.

'Are you safe? Here, with us? Inside one of Mercia's strongholds?' I counter, far from aggressively. While Wærwulf translates my words, I don't truly think it's needed. The intent is easy to determine.

'Well,' Oscetel's gaze flicks nervously around the room. He's not alone. As Anwend has his son, Oscetel has been allowed to bring others with him. All told, there are seven Viking raiders within Northampton's walls. It's more than I'd like and far fewer than Jarl Guthrum demanded. 'Yes, I suppose we are,' he capitulates. I don't miss the swift flash of fury that covers Guthrum's face as Wærwulf tells me his response. Jarl Guthrum evidently expects the argument to go on for much longer.

Jarl Oscetel meets my eyes.

'You think you've won?' he questions aggressively. Wærwulf's words lack the bite, but I hear it all the same. The Danish tongue, when spoken by these men, always sounds aggressive.

'I don't think I've lost,' I reply. His eyes narrow as Wærwulf repeats the phrase. I can see where his hand shakes around the elaborate drinking horn, fashioned from a cow horn or some such but polished to a high sheen and then festooned with circling threads of silver. Such a response reveals his fear and weakness.

These three men, alongside Jarl Halfdan, who brought Mercia to its knees, are far from as sure of themselves here, even though they once held Northampton themselves. Jarl Guthrum has been a prisoner of mine for some time now. Well, he's been Mercia's prisoner. I've been kept away from him, probably for the best. I don't fear the jarls. I don't understand why King Burgred dreaded them, even with the knowledge that King Edmund of the East Angles fell beneath their onslaught.

They're bloody nothing. Well, they're not nothing, but they lack what's needed to rule. They're men who've taken chances and gambled the lives of others to enrich themselves. I feel my lips curl in displeasure and work to keep my thoughts from showing on my face.

'You haven't won either,' Jarl Oscetel grumbles. His eyes tell me the truth of his words, although it aids me that Wærwulf mutters them to me in my language.

'And neither have you,' I incline my head towards them. I didn't think I'd enjoy meeting the other jarls before the baptism. But I'm not objecting to it any more. I only wish every Mercian was here to see these Viking raiders cast so low. Admittedly, it cost me Edmund and the devious Bishop Smithwulf to get to this stage.

'This baptism,' Jarl Anwend interrupts before Oscetel can speak again. 'It'll make my fellow jarl a Christian?' He speaks in halting English, and I incline my head towards him respectfully.

'Yes, he'll welcome the word of God into his life,' I intone. I don't bloody believe that. I don't believe any of it, but we all know what these bastard Viking raiders are like with their gods. They have many. We have one. Somehow, we must make them believe our Christ God is greater than theirs.

'And what will happen to him?' Anwend's using his son to ensure he says what he means. His son speaks our language much better than his father. The two mutter one to another, but Wærwulf is listening to everything. He'll tell me if I should be concerned.

'Happen to him?' I feel my forehead furrow at that. Another gable of conversation and Anwend Anwendsson elaborates. 'Will he change?'

'Not physically,' I counter. I don't want to dismiss my thoughts on the baptism. I don't believe it'll change Jarl Guthrum. I don't think it'll do anything to him. Honestly, I'm more concerned that it will bloody do something to me to accept him as my godson.

'But his mind?' Anwend Anwendsson persists.

'Perhaps,' I mollify. I imagine Bishop Wærferth would have more to say on the matter.

Jarl Guthrum laughs then. It seems he's learning my language better as well. 'It will do nothing to me. I will accept their Christ God and keep to my own as well.'

'Then you'll face the wrath of our God. He can do to you what he sees fit.' The menace in my voice is impossible to ignore. All the more enjoyable for me because I don't believe a bloody word of it, but if these jarls do, then that'll help us keep Mercia free for long enough to build a force to counter theirs.

I notice the flicker of unease on Jarl Guthrum's face at the prospect of upsetting another God and try not to enjoy it. Before more can be said, the door opens, and Bishop Wærferth enters the room.

'My lord king, jarls, the ceremony will begin shortly.' He speaks expansively. Compared to Jarl Guthrum, he looks like a strutting pheasant. His holy robes are bright and intricately stitched. They must have taken many, many days to produce. The vibrant red of his robes is as bright as blood and as menacing. I consider if the choice was intentional.

Quickly, my warriors return to the Viking raiders, Icel and Pybba taking command of Jarl Guthrum. At the same time, Rudolf, Hereman and others ensure that Oscetel and Anwend and his son are closely escorted.

'I'll be a Christian soon,' Jarl Guthrum intones as he's led away. I hear the wobble in his voice and pretend not to do so. If I'd known enacting a miracle or something similar close to the Viking raiders would instil such fear in them, I'd have bloody done so long ago—no need for blades and shields. No, a little water might well have done the trick.

My aunt joins me as we leave the hall. She's wearing an elaborate gown, and her hair is threaded with priceless jewels. She certainly looks the part of the king of Mercia's aunt.

'Well done,' she offers without inflexion.

'I did nothing,' I counter quickly.

'Exactly,' she replies with satisfaction. We fall silent as the sound of prayers and humming fills the interior of Northampton. The church here is small and haphazardly built, the wooden tower that now crowns it at one end looking uncomfortable and unstable. But the bishops and my aunt have ensured the interior looks as magnificent as the royal church at Repton and others of a similar ilk. It will shimmer with gold and silver, and the number of bishops and priests in attendance will outnumber the congregation. If the jarls weren't already fearful of the power of my Christ God, then they bloody will be after this farce of a baptism.

Chapter Five

The ceremony is tediously long, unnecessarily monotonously elongated. Even I'm struggling to stand still as Bishop Wærferth and his fellow bishops take turns using Latin to flood the space beneath the high thatched roof. I can only imagine what the jarls think of all this. Not that we don't all know when to add our 'amens', but much of the rest is gobbledygook. I wasn't raised to be a king. I've not had the education æthelings might have had. Not in terms of book learning. No, all I've learned has been of my doing. My battle-prowess is all mine. Admittedly, my morals might have more to do with my aunt than I care to consider, and she is a devout woman.

'Will this never end?' I hiss to Rudolf, standing beside me. He smirks, shifting his weight from his right to his left leg. If someone as young as him is feeling the ache in his bones, then it's no wonder I am as well.

'Shush,' my aunt turns to me, eyes flashing dangerously. I'd roll my eyes at her, but even that small sound has drawn the eye of bloody Jarl Oscetel. I incline my head towards him in a kingly manner. I can't allow him to see how thoroughly bored I am.

Finally, we're at the part of the ceremony that involves Jarl Guthrum. He stands to the front, wearing only a bleached linen tunic and his boots. I've said he should be allowed his boots. I know that having bloody cold feet can make even the most placid of men furious. His elaborate tunic has been cast aside. His beard and moustache have been trimmed, his hair cut short, and the trinkets and sigils removed. I'm sure even his ears are clean. Not that anything can be done about the owl markings on his arms.

Bishop Wærferth is beside him, escorted by Bishops Ceobred and Eadberht, as well as priests who all seem to hold onto one thing or another concerned with the service. The tediousness of the ceremony is perhaps to be laid at the feet of the doddering Bishop Ceobred. He is bastard old, after all, and seems incapable of remembering his own parts in the ceremony.

I'd have liked to dunk Jarl Guthrum in the River Nene, as I'm told happened when the disciples lived, but this is our way now. A touch of holy water and a mumble of words, and suddenly, I realise I should be beside him. Indeed, Bishop Wærferth has paused the proceedings while he waits for me. I shoulder my way forward. Others have forgotten that I must also be close and smile benignly as I look at Jarl Guthrum.

I'm surprised by the fear in his eyes. Perhaps this is something we should have considered long ago. Maybe the Viking raider jarls should have forced King Burgred to their religion instead of allowing him to leave. I'll bloody think about that in my future dealings with the bastards.

'Will you renounce Satan?' Bishop Wærferth demands while Wærwulf translates these words for the Norse in attendance. I know Guthrum has been undergoing instruction about the baptism. Bishop Wærferth insisted on that.

I glance to Jarls Oscetel and Anwend, seeing they're also uneasy. Although not as apprehensive as Jarl Guthrum.

'I will renounce him,' Jarl Guthrum stumbles, forced to use the language of Mercia.

'Do you believe in God, his son, Jesus Christ and the holy spirit?' The rumble of the Danish is a counterpart to this part of the ceremony, which is conducted in our tongue as all need to hear and understand the vows being taken.

'I do believe in God, Jesus Christ and the holy spirit,' Guthrum mumbles, his words so soft I almost have to lean forward to hear him. I'm tempted to force him to repeat them, but Bishop Wærferth shakes his head once, assuring me there's no need.

'Will you be baptised in the faith of Christianity, and do you do so willingly?' This really is the crutch of the baptism. Even now, Guthrum could say he does so unwillingly, and this would all be for bloody nothing. Then, I could kill the bastard. Perhaps he will say this is unwillingly done. I almost grip my hand as though around the hilt of my seax.

Silence falls within the church, not even the cry of the many crammed inside or those that spill outside it into the street heard. I dare not take my eyes off Jarl Guthrum, although I'd welcome seeing the expressions on Anwend and Oscetel's faces.

'I do so willingly,' Guthrum eventually announces, and as one, everyone begins to breathe once more. I think a foul word. How much easier if he'd not said that?

'What baptismal name will you take?' Bishop Wærferth asks Guthrum. I'm unsure about this aspect of the ceremony, but it has been the same for many years. A baptismal name to use alongside his given one. I have one. I don't use it. I'm not bloody telling anyone what it is, either.

'Æthelstan,' Guthrum announces, a name that surprises me, for there are precious few Æthelstan's and none of them, as far as I know, have ever done anything particularly saintly.

'Æthelstan,' Bishop Wærferth acknowledges with a dip of his head as he drips water onto the jarl's forehead, having already used holy oil to make a mark. Now, I look to Jarls Anwend and Oscetel. I witness them shudder at the implication behind this act. Will they believe that Guthrum or Æthelstan, is different to them now? Will they still accord him the same respect, or has the step into Christianity opened up a void between the conniving threesome? It was always a fraught alliance, working because it had to as opposed to because they wanted it to do so.

I step aside, returning to my place beside Rudolf and my aunt. I've played my part and need do nothing else. And, I confess, I'm starting to truly appreciate the artifice my aunt has put into motion here. I'd not realised how unsettling the jarls would find it.

Throughout the rest of the ceremony, as prayers are intoned, I watch the three men. Of them all, I'm surprised that Oscetel eyes the candles and shimmering silver and gold ornaments with such trepidation. When they took Repton and turned St Wystan's into a part of their defences, they showed no such fear or reticence. But then, they perhaps didn't realise what they did. Now, maybe Oscetel is fearful of the desecration they committed and the monks they killed inside Repton.

Eventually, the service grinds to a halt. I eye Bishop Wærferth, who inclines his head towards me, and wonder whether he's enjoyed protracting the service. Or whether, like me, he regrets the inclusion of Bishop Ceobred. There was no need for it, but undoubtedly, he and my aunt decided on that.

'My lord Æthelstan,' I offer to Jarl Guthrum, watching him visibly judder with a suppressed smirk. What has my aunt done to this man? I'd almost pity him, but I can't. If not for him, then Edmund would live, and perhaps so would the treasonous bishop of London. Not that I'll miss Smithwulf and his split loyalties to King Alfred in Wessex.

'My lord king,' even Guthrum's stance has altered since he was touched with holy oil and water. He seems almost bloody deferential. The part of me that understands men and warriors knows it won't last. The part of me that's kingly respects the bishop and my aunt once more.

'Come, we'll feast and celebrate our accord,' I offer, indicating he should walk ahead. Instead, he waits for me, so I'm the first to make their way from the church back into Northampton. Unsurprisingly, the day has moved on a pace, and my belly rumbles. I'm hungry and thirsty and could do with a piss, but some of those needs will have to wait. First, I must ensure all see Jarl Guthrum in his new guise as Æthelstan. If we're to make much of his conversion, I need to safeguard that as many witness it as possible. The men and women of Northampton and Mercia, who've long hated him, will need to view him with more forgiving eyes. And if they manage that, they'll be doing bloody better than me.

Jarl Guthrum says nothing further, his eyes ablaze with the majesty of the ceremony he's undertaken. If he's playing at this to make us believe he believes what's happened to him, then he's doing a good job of it. That makes me think he isn't pretending. I'm genuinely astonished that a man such as him could be as moved by his baptism. I consider when Jarls Oscetel and Anwend might ask for the same treatment.

Inside the great hall, a feast has been laid out, rich smells enticing me, but all I can think about is my need to piss. I escort the three jarls to the front, catching Rudolf's eye and wishing I could send the lad to piss on my behalf.

'What's the matter with you?' my aunt whispers harshly in my ear. 'You look like a child needing to relieve himself.'

'And what if I do?' I glower. She surprises me by laughing.

'Go,' she urges me. 'We can't have Mercia's king relieving himself before our new allies.'

I hasten to do as she suggests, weaving a path through the swell of people and leaving the jarls in the safe hands of her and Bishop Wærferth. They're certainly safer with them than they are with me.

Finally, able to relieve myself in the latrine, I exit the small building, and walk into Rudolf. He eyes me sullenly.

'What is it?'

'I don't bloody like it,' he mutters. I'm surprised when Icel, Pybba, Hereman and Gardulf join him. None of them look happy. The rest of my men would also be here, but they're all on various guard details. Easier for them to complain out of my presence, but I know they'll be bloody complaining. I wish I could do the same.

'Do you believe this shit?' Gardulf growls. His face is white with fury. His fists are clenched. This must be hard for him and even harder because it appears as though his father's lover is instrumental in forcing the baptism of Jarl Guthrum. My aunt will need to make her peace with Gardulf.

'If it gives Mercia what she needs,' Icel interjects, but his tone is half-hearted, and his words left hanging. Even he's not invested in this. I snap down on my immediate response. I'm not going to argue with them. I don't believe this shit either, but it wasn't my decision. Perhaps, as Mercia's king, I shouldn't abrogate responsibility like that. All the same, I know I bloody will.

'What Mercia needs is for those bastards to be dead,' Gardulf cries. Pybba and I both glance around, hoping none of the Viking raiders overhears his words. I don't wish to rehash this argument from the witan with the whiff of the latrine strong in my nose. Or when I know my aunt will be waiting for me inside, as will Guthrum and the two other jarls.

'It is what it bloody is,' Pybba tries to console. 'Coelwulf might be the king, but this decision isn't all his.' I don't expect to find him arguing for me, but Pybba knows the way of politics well enough. I'm pleased he's here, with me, and not still recovering from his wounds. There has been news of his granddaughter and her father. Bishop Deorlaf's men have been as good as their word, and found them. Pybba's family have been reunited in his absence. I'm pleased for him. Some good must come of our trip into the borderlands with the Welsh kingdoms.

'But he's the bloody king, and he's the one who has to stand in the bastard shield wall and face these fuckers.' Spit flies from Gardulf's mouth, and not even Hereman moves to console him. I remember being so young and filled with rage. I wish it had been directed at the Viking raiders, not my father and brother.

'I am the bloody king, yes,' I confirm. 'And I need to return to the hall and speak with these jarls.'

'Stab 'em more like,' Gardulf continues, his words growing louder, not softer.

'Speak with them,' I reiterate, holding his gaze for a moment too long. It hurts me to see Edmund peering through those furious eyes. I miss him with almost every breath, not that I'd ever have told the bastard that.

'Rudolf, take Gardulf and find Hemming. The three of you can find some mischief to get into that doesn't involve the Viking raider jarls.' I hear Rudolf's huff but I've turned my back and scamper through the street towards the hall. It's not far, but it's still thronged with people, and I find it difficult to force a path. Not even Icel's arrival helps me. He's a big man, or he once was. Now he's smaller, his age settling on him like a heavy winter cloak, but he still strides like he fills the space he once did.

'They'll be bloody trouble,' he rumbles. I nod. I know it as well.

'Keep an eye on them,' I urge. Unlike Rudolf, Icel takes no offence at being called upon to watch the younger members of my war band.

'And watch what you bloody say,' Icel instructs me before moving aside. 'Those bastards will take any excuse to start a fight. Jarl Guthrum's fear will wear off soon enough, and then he'll be busy plotting.'

With more effort than I think the king should need to make, I find myself back inside the hall, and here a path finally opens up for me to join the jarls, my aunt, and Bishop Wærferth at the front. Ealdorman Ælhun is also there. Inside, the atmosphere is more tense than outside. The men and women here don't strain to see the Grantabridge jarls. They already know what they look like. For these people, the jarls aren't to be gawped at. No, I imagine many of them are either devising the means to kill them in revenge for the loss of a family member or trying to decide how to profit from this accord. There'll be some, and I have some suspicions as to who they might be, who'll think nothing of working to break apart this pact reached between the captive Guthrum and his two allies.

'Apologies,' I murmur to my aunt when she eyes me as though I'm a naughty child, late for church or a lesson in political statecraft. 'There was a queue,' I voice a feeble excuse and work myself to my position at the centre of the table. Once there, I turn to eye the men and women of Mercia. They watch me, some as sullen as Gardulf, others as flushed with wine as though this were a feast day. I hold the gaze of one or two, acknowledging others and thinking of all that's happened in this hall. I've murdered men here. I've slipped in their blood here. I've retrieved Werburg from her terrible captivity, and now it's to play host to a harmony reached between men who are enemies. Bloody wonderful.

'Fellow Mercians and our honoured guests,' my voice stretches into the furthest recesses of the hall, and even the noise from outside quiets down. Everyone wishes to hear what I say. 'Today is a momentous occasion. Jarl Guthrum, now known as Æthelstan, has joined our faith, and his brother jarls honour that and pledge a year of peace between us all. After today, Jarls Oscetel and Anwend will not allow their warriors to attack Mercia. In exchange, we'll keep Jarl Guthrum safe, teach him our ways, and we can renew our agreement in twelve months if all is as it should be.' There's no sound, not even the hush of acceptance. I suppress my annoyance. These men and women demanded a peaceful resolution, not me.

'And so, now we feast and celebrate. To the future of Mercia and her ongoing friendship with the Grantabridge jarls.' I raise my drinking goblet to a splattering of applause and turn an appealing look on my aunt and Bishop Wærferth. Belatedly, they both raise their drinking goblets, as does Guthrum and then Oscetel and Anwend. I'd welcome Edmund's presence right now. Whether he agreed with this direction or not, I could at least rely on him to be a noisy bastard when needed.

Slowly, a few stand and raise their drinking cups. Even slower yet, more and more stand, and so does Guthrum. He arches an eyebrow my way. I mirror his perplexed expression. Out in the crowd, those who accompanied Oscetel and Anwend also take to their feet, and eventually a ragged cheer reverberates through the hall.

It's far from my finest moment, but then, as I keep saying, this wasn't my bloody decision. But that doesn't mean I won't abide by it. I will until Oscetel and Anwend show themselves to be false to their oaths. Or, until I can be assured of Guthrum's involvement in something he shouldn't be involved with. This time, I'll ensure the bastard is dead and that no one else gets their hands on him before the deed can be accomplished.

I welcome peace. But not like this. The only way I can resolve myself to it is to assure myself that Mercia will benefit from this and become stronger, far stronger than she is now.

We'll banish the Viking raiders, and it won't be by tricking one of their numbers into believing that our God has more magic at his fingertips than their collection of bickering Gods.

I can hardly bloody wait.

Chapter Six

'My lord king,' cursing softly under my breath, I eye Ealdorman Aldred. His face is mutinous. I'm far from surprised. He doesn't like what's happening here. I wish I could tell him that I bloody didn't either, but the events from Gainsborough stick in my mind too vividly. The damn fool allowed Mercians to die so he could keep his wealth. He almost allowed the Viking raiders to overwhelm him.

'My lord,' I reply, standing once more on the walkway over-looking the rear of Northampton. Jarls Oscetel and Anwend are gone from inside Northampton, but their camp remains. I don't know if the two jarls have left or if they linger alongside some men most loyal to Jarl Guthrum, or Æthelstan as I should get used to calling him. If they were so damn loyal, they shouldn't have allowed him to be bloody captured. They should have fought harder. I'm glad they didn't. Enough damage was done within Grantabridge.

The ealdorman's lips curl on seeing the campsite. He so mirrors my thoughts on the matter that I cannot berate him. Rudolf and Icel are with me. The two move aside to allow the ealdorman some time to speak with me alone.

'York,' he begins. I shake my head, but he continues speaking. 'It would be good if we aided them,' he announces, surprising me. I feel my eyes narrow. I know his holdings are to the north, but what has Archbishop Wulfhere promised him? I know that Bishop Burgheard remains at Lincoln, watching the situation there carefully.

'It's no concern of yours,' I counter quickly. I need to stop him before he arouses my suspicions further.

'It's everyone's concern if we can keep the Viking raiders at bay,' he presses.

'It is, but first, we look to Mercia.' Ealdorman Aldred's face clouds with fury at my obdurate tone.

'The archbishop has much to offer,' he persists. I'm about to tell Ealdorman Aldred exactly what I think of Archbishop Wulfhere when I hear cries from below inside Northampton. I peer over the interior wall and see a flurry of activity at the gate closest to the bridge. It can't be Jarl Guthrum. He's been escorted to Worcester with Bishop Wærferth and a small collection of my warriors under the command of Tatberht, as well as some of Ealdorman Ælhun's men, led by Wulfsige. Who, then, is this?

'What now?' I query, cursing my inability to see as well as others.

Ealdorman Aldred responds quickly. 'Whoever they are, they carry the Wessex wyvern.'

'Bloody hell,' I explode. Icel and Rudolf join me in hastening down the steep wooden steps. Whatever Ealdorman Aldred wished to say is forgotten about. I'm not expecting a delegation from the Wessex king. I certainly don't welcome one. The words are already on my lips to deny everything they might request from me. If I won't aid Northumbria and York, then I sure as shit have no interest in helping Wessex. They've provided no assistance to Mercia in recent years, and I don't bloody want any now. My suspicions regarding who was the power behind Bishop Smithwulf's actions with the jarls persists.

'Coelwulf,' my aunt intercepts me before I can move further than the main hall. Her eyes are hard and edged with flint.

'What do you know of this?' I ask. She shakes her head at my tone and hurried footsteps. I stop beside her. She's right. I need to wait. I'm the damn king. I shouldn't barrel my way through to the gate.

'They're being allowed entry,' she informs me. She's made the decision without me, or so it seems. How else would this delegation be allowed inside?

'King Alfred?' I question, just to be sure.

'Not in person, obviously.' Her tone is caustic, taking me back to when I was a small boy and deserved a telling off for something foolish I'd done or said.

'Of course,' I murmur. My thoughts once more lingering on Bishop Smithwulf. He turned out to be worse than a two-headed snake with a foot in every encampment. I'm glad he's bloody dead.

I stand and wait impatiently, Icel and Rudolf joined by Pybba and Hereman. I've had to be careful who I sent to escort Jarl Guthrum to Worcester. Many men would sooner he was dead. I'm bloody one of them.

'What's this?' Pybba questions.

'Wessex,' Icel growls. It's hardly surprising. I know he hates the West Saxons. I don't know all the details of why, but I'm sure there's a bloody good explanation for it, should Icel ever think to tell me. I don't miss a look that passes between him and my aunt. The pair of them have more secrets than a trader of fine spices or a whore.

'My lord king,' I eye the man being escorted towards me by warriors wearing Mercia's eagle emblem. The man is dressed well; a fine cloak flung over one shoulder, the Wessex wyvern visible on the silver brooches holding the cloak in place, and the banner hanging limply over his head, held there by a man with the bulk of a warrior. He shouldn't be wearing that. His allegiance doesn't belong to Wessex.

'Ealdorman Æthelwulf,' I greet. I know him well. He's the worst of all Mercians. A man who cowers at the court of King Alfred with his sister wed to the Wessex king.

'My lord king.' His voice is firm but warm. I distrust his presence.

'Come inside,' I beckon, hopeful that my aunt has considered everything that should have been prepared for such an occasion.

Ealdorman Æthelwulf steps lightly. He's probably of a similar age to me, a man in his prime. But he doesn't have the build of a warrior. Neither is he priestly. He's somewhere nondescript in-between, with dark brown hair skimming his neck and a moustache and beard that almost, but not quite, cover his uneven, chipped front teeth. I consider what he sees when he looks at me. My aunt and her women had been busy producing clothes for me. My tunics must be wide in the shoulders and tapered to my waist. It seems when I look at my flat tunics before I wear them that my arms are very long.

My hair's longer than Ealdorman Æthelwulf's, still blond, I hope, although I fear there is some grey starting to thread it. My face, I know, is a collection of scars and bruises. I don't look like a court politician, as Ealdorman Æthelwulf does. No doubt, my reputation as a bloody warrior speaks more of me than my appearance. I've no memory of him before his sister was wed to the Wessex king.

Inside the hall, a fire burns, emitting pleasant aromas, no doubt aided by some herbs. I see that, indeed, my aunt has considered everything. Ealdorman Aldred is there already, standing to the side, surrounded by those who must be his loyal adherents. He's come to see what's distracted me from our conversation on the battlements and what I consider more important than listening to him argue for an alliance that will never happen.

I sit at the table, encouraging Ealdorman Æthelwulf to do the same. He does so with a keen look in his eyes, appraising all he sees. I'm grateful that my aunt decorated the hall so elaborately for yester-day's celebration feast. It gleams with cleanliness, even the smell of spilt wine and ale banished beneath the herbs added to the flames that scent the air with an appetising aroma. I feel my belly growl.

'A fine hall, and I admire the defences,' Ealdorman Æthelwulf offers. I realise he's actually saying, *'Perhaps you could show me them,'* but without the stones to do so.

'I could show them to you if it would be of interest to you.' I reply, because I'm a contrary bastard, and why not?

'Anything interests me when it involves halting the grabbing ways of the Viking raiders and defending Mercia.'

'Is that what brings you here?' I question. As a Mercian, he should always be welcome in Mercia. After all, the River Thames is no impediment, provided you know the correct routes. All the same, the fact that he's walked through Mercia without being stopped infuriates me. He can't be two things. He's either a Mercian or a West Saxon. Not both.

'I've come on the orders of King Alfred. I believe you might be aware of his overtures of friendship to Bishop Smithwulf. God Rest His Soul.' Somehow, I keep my lips from curling at the reminder of Bishop Smithwulf and his betrayals. 'I'd hoped to be here to witness Jarl Guthrum's baptism, but believe I'm a day too late.' How he knew of this I don't ask. Again, I'm frustrated. Does Mercia have no secrets?

'Yes, and he's no longer here. He'll be kept inside Mercia and not on her periphery.'

'A wise choice,' he murmurs, taking the time to drink the wine before him. I notice his hand shakes a little, the fluid in the goblet threatening to slop. Is he nervous, or is this some injury gained in battle? Or a sign of his age. I banish that thought. I wouldn't want anyone to think I was old and infirm.

'Bishop Smithwulf was not all he seemed,' I add quickly. I don't want to have to say pleasant things about that lying snivelling turd. Equally, the decision has been made to portray him as a martyr to the cause.

'No, so it seems, which is why I am here in person in place of him. King Alfred wishes me to assure you of his good intentions towards Mercia. He desires you to know that Wessex is Mercia's ally.' I don't miss the irony that Alfred has sent a bloody Mercian to speak with me.

'Is she?' I question before I can stop myself.

'Yes, she is,' Ealdorman Æthelwulf's voice has grown firmer. 'And in that regard, King Alfred once more extends the possibility of an alliance, between Mercia and Wessex, as has stood for many years, or it did until King Burgred's somewhat hasty departure for Rome.'

Those words mask many others. I'm forced to snap down my response or start a war of words here and now.

'Lady Ealhswith, the king's wife and my sister, is eager to ensure the safety of her birth-land.'

'I'm sure she is,' my aunt interjects without warning. Ealdorman Æthelwulf glances at her, and recognition flashes.

'Lady Cyneswith. How wonderful to see you looking so well.'

I watch the exchange between them. My aunt's almost as consummate at not revealing her true thoughts as Ealdorman Æthelwulf.

'It has been some time, but yes, I remember you well enough. Lady Ealhswith is well?' I suppress a shudder at her saccharine tone. My aunt doesn't like Ealhswith. Not one bit. I find myself seeking out Icel. He stands before the fire, able to hear but not a part of the conversation. His expression gives away none of his thoughts on the matter, but his fists clench slowly, revealing all I need to know.

'Lady Ealhswith is indeed well. A son, born last year. Edward. A healthy child. It's to be hoped he thrives like his older sister.'

There's a threat there, but I can't truly decipher it. I understood that while they have a daughter, Lady Ealhswith has also some suffered some losses. I believe the daughter is a child of about nine winters old. No doubt, the birth of a son has Alfred and his wife considering his future. It would be better if they focused on the Viking raider threat, but some people have the wrong priorities. In the past, such alliances have been used against the wife's family. Admittedly, it is sometimes against the husband's family as well. There are many ambitious bastards out there.

'That is welcome news.' My aunt continues. I hardly know where to look as these two exchange what seem to be pleasant words but are evidently anything but.

'This friendship,' I remind Ealdorman Æthelwulf when the silence has grown too uncomfortable for me to stand.

'Ah, yes, one of mutual assistance, perhaps with some show on Mercia's part that she respects all that Wessex has accomplished.' I can't help it. I choke on my mouthful of water, grateful that Rudolf's there to whack my back to help me clear it. I don't struggle for breath for that reason, but the audacity of the man's words astound me. Mercia owes Wessex nothing. Wessex owes Mercia a great deal. And fucking Ealdorman Æthelwulf should know that.

'There's much to discuss there,' my aunt helpfully interjects before I can say something I might regret.

'There is, my lady, there is, and King Alfred would welcome meeting King Coelwulf in person to discuss the details more fully. Perhaps in London? A neutral location.'

London isn't neutral. London is Mercia's—thoughts of Bishop Smithwulf ring in my mind.

'Perhaps somewhere inside Wessex,' my aunt counters quickly. 'Close to the river crossings. I'm sure there's a suitable location. Lechlade, perhaps?'

'Or London,' Æthelwulf repeats more firmly.

'Or not at all,' I interject with finality. 'Mercia has won a respite. And we mean to take full advantage of it.

Ealdorman Æthelwulf's expression falters momentarily. He opens his mouth to speak and then snaps it shut again.

'Well, something to think about,' he concedes unwillingly. I sit back and drink more carefully this time. 'Perhaps you could show me your ramparts and how they were constructed.' I imagine he means to win me over by being awed by the stout defences that protect Northampton. But, at least if we're discussing that, I needn't respond to this proposed meeting with King Alfred. I've no wish to meet with him. I've no wish to aid Northumbria or Wessex, not until Mercia is secure. Some might rue that decision, but it's the correct one. Northumbria is all but overrun by Jarl Halfdan and his bastard warriors. Despite how Ealdorman Æthelwulf hides away in Wessex,

Alfred is far from as secure in his kingship as this little discussion might have anyone believing. King Alfred wants Mercia's battle-hardened warriors. I'm sure of it. I'm not about to let them go anywhere.

'Indeed, my lord. I'll happily show you Northampton's ramparts. I'm sure you saw the ditch and high walls you entered through. They encircle the settlement. Northampton can only be accessed via the bridge from the south.' I stand as I speak, wary of the silent exchange between my aunt and Icel. I'd like to ask them for their personal thoughts, but first, I have Ealdorman Æthelwulf to show around Northampton. His acquisitive eyes are already making me reconsider my decision. Perhaps it would be simpler to cast him to his death over the side of Northampton's steep ramparts. Maybe that's what I should have done to bloody Jarl Guthrum as well.

I take the Mercian defector to the ramparts despite my misgivings. His eyes are wide, taking in all there is to see. These are Mercia's secrets, but it would be best to share them with Wessex. Easier if they defend themselves than try and involve us in it. Provided they don't share them with Mercia's enemies.

'It's high,' Ealdorman Æthelwulf gasps in surprise when we finally crest the top of the steep steps. I see the enemy encampment below us and appreciate that it's growing smaller every time I look. Yet, some, I imagine, won't ever bloody leave, even with Jarl Guthrum removed from Northampton to Worcester. Not, I realise, that these people will know he's gone.

'Better to look down on the enemy,' I offer with a smirk of pride. The Viking raiders might have started this defensive structure, but we've honed it and made it much better than anything they thought to build.

'And you really do look down on the enemy.' I turn in surprise to gaze at the man. He's green, and I can see how he tries to control his breathing.

'We can go down,' I find myself muttering. We could. It would be no problem for me, but he grips the wooden sides and stays firm.

'No, I'll see it all,' he puffs through pale cheeks.

'Shall we walk around?' I counter, enjoying him shudder at the thought of moving from this spot. I know some who don't like to be so high up. It doesn't feel natural, but then war isn't natural. Fighting for my kingdom shouldn't be the normal way of things, even if that's what it's bloody become.

'No, here is fine,' he splutters.

'Very well.' I rest lightly on the top of the rampart. I've been here many times before. Some of those visits were a test of my strength and recovery. I run my hand around the scar that mars my throat from where I nearly lost my head in the woodland. I nearly died not far from here. I was forced to stand here and show Jarl Guthrum I was far from dead. I don't plan on allowing myself to be so fucking vulnerable again.

'Haven't you climbed the old fort's walls in London?' Icel questions Ealdorman Æthelwulf. I quirk an eyebrow towards Icel. The old walls are far from ruined. Are they, I question, as tall as these walls? Are they taller? I don't recall ever having used them before. The Viking raiders haven't thought of taking London for many long years. The threat has come from Wessex. Although. I squint towards Icel, but he shakes his head. It's just another story about which I'm never to learn the truth.

'No,' Ealdorman Æthelwulf admits. 'Although there are some within Wessex who've told me about it. They've used the walls themselves. I believe my sister's husband's grandfather was there. He once held London.' Silence greets those words. I'm unsurprised to find Icel looking pensive as he gazes towards the Viking raider encampment. I don't understand why Ealdorman Æthelwulf needed to remind me of the family connection. Damn arsehole.

'Yes, Wessex once made the mistake of trying to gain London, or Lundenwic and Londinium, as they were known in my youth.' Again, I want Icel to say more, but Ealdorman Æthelwulf startles at his deep, gravelly voice. No doubt the lackwit has realised his mistake of mentioning Wessex's failed attempt to claim London when his intention here is to ask for help.

'Are those walls as tall as these?' Ealdorman Æthelwulf mumbles, undoubtedly trying to turn the conversation aside.

Icel's silent for a moment. I see his fists once more clenched to the side of his body, but when he speaks I allow a smirk to touch my lips.

'You can see almost as far as Winchester on a good day.'

I shake my head, smiling broadly while looking down so the ealdorman doesn't see my amusement. That's an outright lie, but Icel means to toy with Æthelwulf. I don't object to that. I would sooner he was less confident. King Alfred has been forced to fight the Viking raiders for his kingdom. His brother died in one of those battles.

'Shall we go down?' I question Ealdorman Æthelwulf. But he shakes his head, holding firm to the wooden railing. He's still green. If he's not careful, his elaborate cloak will be stained with his vomit.

'No, I will stay and see more. Tell me, how did you build this? How long did it take? How many men.'

I remember last year. When we all sweated and strained to lift these ramparts from the mud of the surrounding landscape, and to block the tunnels, and also, to remake them. It was an effort. It was bloody worth it.

'Last summer,' I state. I don't honestly recall how long it took. 'There were some foundations already in place. We elaborated upon them.'

'And now you build similar elsewhere within Mercia?' I'm surprised he knows this. I probably bloody shouldn't be. If he knew of Jarl Guthrum's baptism, he probably knows everything that happens within Mercia.

'Yes, Worcester and Hereford, amongst other places. The settlements on the peripheries need the most protection, as I'm sure you can imagine.' Icel gives the impression he's not listening to the conversation, but I know he is. His stance is too tight. He wouldn't be here with us if he didn't want to listen to this stilted discussion. I know his thoughts about Wessex well enough. Icel has lived enough in his long years to endure much hardship from the West Saxons and the Viking raiders. His determination sometimes astounds me. His belief that we will one day triumph keeps me going, no matter the setbacks and the loss of our friends and allies.

'I'll speak of this to my brother-by-marriage,' Ealdorman Æthelwulf murmurs. 'But tell me, how do you guard the walls?'

'With the people from the local area. So many men for so much wall,' I offer. It's really not that difficult to work out how it must be done.

'And so many men and women to build it?'

'Indeed, and of course, the ditches must also be kept in good repair.'

'But what of the land to the east of here? The kingdom of the East Angles?'

'That's where the remaining Grantabridge jarls keep themselves. They killed the king of the East Angles and now think of taking their land, too. We banished many of them, but the bastards have come snivelling back. Grantabridge itself is in need of a complete rebuild.' I grin as I speak. It pleases me to know how much damage was done.

'And you'll build another of these defences to the east?'

'Perhaps,' I offer. 'It'll depend if there is anything to defend. Much of the kingdom of the East Angles is almost an island, even on a good day. My concern is for Mercia's borders, not the holdings of others who are no longer here to protect it.'

All of this he absorbs, and I fear I've said too much. But, it's nothing to me what happens beyond Mercia's borders. I'm determined to protect those borders and only those borders.

'I'll tell my brother-by-marriage about all of this, but he still wishes to meet in person to discuss an alliance. After all,' and his smile is honey-sweet. 'Mercia and Wessex have long been allied through the marriage of my sister and, of course, King Alfred's sister as well.'

'And kept apart through bloody war,' Icel grumbles, unable to help himself.

I'm pleased I agree with him on all this, but I don't miss the sharp look that Ealdorman Æthelwulf throws his way. Icel isn't the man to have close by when discussing any sort of union with Wessex. Pybba would be better. For all his lost hand and lack of hair, he's the most skilled in politics.

'Mercia and Wessex have the same enemy, I don't deny,' I offer. I don't want to diffuse the situation, but I'll acknowledge that much.

'We do, yes,' Ealdorman Æthelwulf is too keen to agree.

'But, the enemy doesn't attack as a unified force. We can be engaged in war with one Viking raider army and Wessex with another. The solutions are, no doubt, different.'

'Or the same,' Ealdorman Æthelwulf almost bites my hand off with his eagerness to get that in. 'Unity can go a long way to resolving the problem.'

'Mercian warriors will never fight for Wessex,' Icel's words are dark and laced with experience. Not for the first time, and certainly not the last, I wish I knew more about him. Perhaps my aunt? But no. She and Icel keep their secrets so well that I sometimes wonder if they remember them all.

'I don't ask them to,' Ealdorman Æthelwulf snaps. He's still uncomfortable so high up, but his words are sharp.

'Perhaps we should descend,' I offer. Perversely, I don't enjoy seeing him so discomforted. The knowledge surprises me. His legs are stiff when he moves, as though made from wood, not flesh and blood.

'Here,' I hold out my hand as he wobbles precariously. I don't want him to fall. It would be his death, and I don't really want that argument with his 'brother,' King Alfred of Wessex. I can't see that Alfred would accept it if his brother-by-marriage fell to his death in Northampton. He'd think we were involved. I don't have the time to smooth over that fractured relationship.

The man's grip is tight, his face laced with sweat. A fine warrior he must make. Not, of course, that most fights take place from so high up.

Together, Ealdorman Æthelwulf's grip on my hands far too tight, we slowly descend. As his foot touches the ground, he pipes up.

'A fine means of defending the settlement, even if it does block out the sunlight.' His voice no longer shows any fear. I grimace at Icel, but his eyes are elsewhere. Whatever he sees isn't visible to me. I wish I knew more about all he's witnessed in his long life.

'The walls are a good beginning,' I acknowledge. 'The rest is to ensure my warriors are well-trained and have the equipment they did.'

'Well, of course, the West Saxon warriors are the best there are,' Ealdorman Æthelwulf is all bluff and confidence. 'We've already overwhelmed the enemy on many occasions.' I'm tempted to punch the cocky fucker, even while I remind him of how King Æthelred met his death. Does he forget his Mercian roots?

I notice Icel's shoulders flinch. What is it he understands? I might be forced to ask my aunt. I know she's known him since before I was born.

Ealdorman Æthelwulf's eyes stray towards the part of the rampart where we tricked the Viking raiders. Has he heard the story of that? I suspect he has from the way his gaze lingers on the filled tunnels. I turn him aside.

'Come, we'll walk the periphery,' I suggest. Unwillingly, he follows me.

'Are there no walls surrounding Winchester?' I feel I should know this, but I don't.

'Not like these tall walls,' Ealdorman Æthelwulf acknowledges. I confess this surprises me, although, of course, not everywhere in Mercia is surrounded by walls. There was no need for it when Mercia was ascendant, and now there is. They should, I feel, have been built many years ago, but Mercia hasn't had the most far-thinking of kings in the last few decades.

'Winchester's an old settlement. Or at least parts of it are. But whatever they were doing there, it didn't involve having walls this tall. And, in the intervening years, some of the stones have been repurposed. But now, we must return to the reason for my visit. King Alfred wishes to meet you as warrior-brothers and kings.'

I don't miss the rumble of displeasure from Icel, although I think Ealdorman Æthelwulf does. He's either very good at not seeing things or astute at realising some things should not be seen or heard. He's either a consummate politician or a bloody fool. I wish he were a bloody fool, but I don't think he is.

'King Alfred's a man with a young family and a kingdom under constant threat. He'd welcome an alliance with Mercia, although I'm unaware of all the details.' This time, I sense Icel's gaze resting on me. The subject of who will rule Mercia after me isn't one for everyone to discuss, although clearly, they are doing so, even in Wessex. At least I understand why Ealdorman Æthelwulf has been given this task. Fucking cock.

'And Mercia has fought hard for this brief respite, agreed with the Grantabridge jarls. While there's nothing to prevent Mercia from allying with one of her neighbours in that accord, it's still not some-thing to be considered lightly. It's not a matter of my brother king inviting me to play with him, as it were. There are many implications. It would never be easy, and at this moment in time, it's not something I've even considered. My focus is on Mercia and only on Mercia.'

'Then you forgot all that Wessex has done for Mercia in the past.' His tone is light. His eyes reveal his true feelings on the matter. I'm tempted to slap him. He's more West Saxon than Mercian. Fucking arse.

'And what would that be?' I don't object to Icel interrupting. I'm curious to see how Wessex views their interference in Mercia throughout the last five or six decades.

'Why Wessex has reinforced Mercia, both with the blood of their women through marriage, my sister, and the blood of their men in battle. Surely you know your history? Your aunt? She has lived through much of this.'

'As has my lord King Coelwulf,' Icel interjects. 'And his brother, Ealdorman Coenwulf, before him.' Something flashes in Icel's eyes, and some far-distant memory tugs for my attention, but I can't grip it. I feel my mouth open to ask the question, but Ealdorman Æthelwulf continues.

'And West Saxon warriors restored Nottingham when the Viking raiders claimed it. Wessex has lent Mercia its strength, and now it merely asks for the same consideration.'

Icel's rumble of fury is too easy to detect this time, and even Ealdorman Æthelwulf is forced to notice it. I consider if Alfred thinks so little of Mercia that he believes sending Æthelwulf will have us bending over backwards to assist them. If he does, he's a fucking arse as well. Ealdorman Æthelwulf should ensure his people and possessions are secured, and not be hob-knobbing with King Alfred.

'What's the matter with you, man?' Ealdorman Æthelwulf demands. Icel falls silent. What can be seen of his face beneath his greying beard and moustache, pale with fury, his hands clenched once more.

'I've lived a good long life, my lord,' and the way Icel bows his head is so close to pure insolence, I'm astonished. This isn't the man I know. 'I understand the truth behind those lies you sprout, and if those are the lies which King Alfred thinks to use to make Mercia an ally, then he's the biggest fool of all the spawn of King Ecgberht of Wessex.' Icel's lips curl in fury. 'I'll advise you, and my king and his aunt will certainly agree, that the only way forward for Wessex and Mercia is for the West Saxon king to take a good, long, hard look at himself, and his predecessors, and then come here and grovel for Mercia's assistance. It might then be given grudgingly.' I confess, my mouth opens in an 'O' of shock as Icel concludes his speech. Neither is it spoken in petulance but rather with surety.

He holds Ealdorman Æthelwulf's gaze, daring him to deny those words. The ealdorman doesn't attempt to do so. 'Decisions have been made to the detriment of Mercia in the past, but with the royal helm on the correct royal head, they won't be any more.'

I might not know all I should regarding relations between Mercia and Wessex throughout my lifetime, but Icel does. At that moment, he appears more kingly than me. His defiance is astounding to behold. I wish all had been here to witness him bring the Mercia ealdorman to his senses. I'd certainly watch it again.

'Now, my good man,' Ealdorman Æthelwulf splutters.

'I'm not your good man, Ealdorman Æthelwulf. I'm Icel, one of Mercia's warriors. I've fought my whole life for Mercia, against Wessex, against the Viking raiders, against the Welsh and on occasion, those from Northumbria. I'm not a fool to be blindsided by your honeyed words. Now, get your arse back to Winchester and tell your damn fool of a king, and his Mercian bitch of a wife, that most of us have far longer memories than that. Your sister, Lady Ealhswith, is accorded so little respect within Wessex that she's not even named as queen. It almost behoves my lord King Coelwulf to ride to her rescue because you certainly won't.'

Ealdorman Æthelwulf's words die on his lips. I can see him thinking hard. I'm doing the same. I must learn more about the circumstances surrounding the marriage. And also about past battles between Wessex and Mercia. Wessex thinks to make me believe Mercia is weak, but I know the truth of that. Mercia has never been weak, but weak kings have served her, and I'm not bloody one of them. Still, Icel's mention of past kings has me thinking.

'Well, my lord king,' Ealdorman Æthelwulf eventually falters. 'I take it you agree with this jumped-up warrior's words.' How Ealdorman Æthelwulf can speak with such derision about Icel astounds me. Icel wears the wounds of every battle he's fought. I can see them etched on his skin, like a spider's web in the early morning light, only they don't shatter and move aside when I brush past them. They're just as much a part of him as his skin and bones. I know Icel has done much more for Mercia than I can claim to have done. Much more than Ealdorman Æthelwulf could ever pretend to have done.

'I suggest, if you return, that you show some respect to Mercia and her finest warriors. A man who can live such a long life as Icel, fighting almost yearly to protect her, is no 'jumped-up' warrior, as you pronounce him. Respect should be shown where respect is due. Even I would never say as such to a Viking raider warrior. Between men who fight and bleed for their kingdoms and what they believe in, there should only ever be respect, not derision.' My words rumble from me with conviction. I'm grateful my aunt isn't here to overhear them. I doubt she'd be pleased.

With his face looking as though he's just eaten the last of the summer apples and found a dead worm coiling around its heart, Ealdorman Æthelwulf, a man who should be Mercian but is clearly West Saxon, stammers for more to say. Only then he bows sharply.

'I will leave you today and return to my brother, my lord king, and Wessex. My thanks for your hospitality, such as it is.' And without another word, Ealdorman Æthelwulf marches onwards, no doubt to where he thinks his men are being feted in the hall.

'My lord, it is this way,' I eventually call to him just before he turns from my sight. I'd like to allow him to make more of an arse of himself, but he's right. He needs to leave here. I've more important things about which to worry. But, I must ask my aunt about Lady Ealhswith, Alfred's wife. She's a Mercian. Should I discover the union was against her wishes or that she's harshly treated by her husband, as well as her brother, then I'll certainly demand better conditions for her, perhaps even her return to Mercia. I'd enjoy doing that. Not that I wish to cause unnecessary discord between Mercia and Wessex, not when we have the Viking raiders to contend with. But perhaps it might be worth shaking the tree, as it were, and seeing what bloody falls.

King Alfred of Wessex isn't the man I thought he was, and I've not even met him yet. If anything, he sounds worse than I already think of him. I don't respect men who rewrite history to serve their purpose. And, I'd not truly appreciated that Lady Ealhswith isn't accorded the title of queen of Wessex. I might start by demanding that be bloody set right.

Chapter Seven

'Well, that went well,' my aunt mutters after the Wessex delegation has left in a huff of cloaks and a cloud of dust.

'Indeed,' I murmur, my distracted thoughts trying to recall much that I might have forgotten over the last decades of my life, especially the events of my childhood. Icel stands beside my aunt. The two haven't spoken. As far as I know, they've not even looked at one another. I wonder if she'll berate him, but somehow, I doubt that. Looking back and thinking of specific events, I realise that my aunt and Icel have always been close. I know she sent him to keep an eye on me when I refused to have anything to do with my brother. Faintly, I recall he might have paid me out of a few bills in taverns and such. Perhaps I owe him even more thanks than I thought.

'Aunt,' I ask when we've returned to the hall, and I'm warming myself before the fire.

'Nephew,' she responds, the single word conveying so much more than it should.

'Tell me of Lady Ealhswith?' I think this is the easier one of my queries.

'The wife of King Alfred and Ealdorman Æthelwulf's sister?'

'Yes, I know little about her or the circumstances of her marriage to Alfred.'

A brief look passes between her and Icel, but she settles on a bench close to the fire and beckons me to sit beside her.

'The union between the two was agreed by King Burgred. He was married to Alfred's sister. I confess Lady Ealhswith and I were not fond of one another. I certainly thought little of her mother. Her father wasn't a bad man but was easily swayed and had half an eye to the future.'

'So the union was a Mercian suggestion?'

'No, it was orchestrated by Wessex,' her lips curl at that admission. 'It should never have been agreed upon, but as we know, King Burgred wasn't the king that Mercia needed at that time.'

Now my forehead furrows.

'I didn't think you liked him.'

'I didn't, but others did, and alas, alternatives were lacking other than you and your brother, and your brother didn't wish to be Mercia's king and wouldn't have won the support that you have. He was a good man, a loyal man, but Coenwulf's eyes didn't extend to the whole of Mercia.'

I bite back my retort that I didn't bloody wish to be Mercia's king. Even though it was only last year, it feels like a long time ago. Much has happened in the last eighteen months, but one thing is a certainty, and I don't speak with arrogance when I think this: Mercia wouldn't have survived if her king had been a weaker man than me. Or even if her king hadn't been prepared to kill as many bloody Viking raiders as possible.

I want to ask more, but at that moment, Rudolf rushes into the hall, his eyes bright as he seeks me out.

'My lord,' he calls, huffing before me, 'you need to see this.'

'What?' I question. I've barely gotten warm, and now he wants me to go outside again.

'The Viking raider camp. It's growing.'

'Bollocks,' I exclaim, not even noticing my aunt's wince, as I surge to my feet and stamp my way back onto the ramparts. I don't expect Rudolf to lie to me, but I want to see it as he demands.

I'm not alone up there. Icel and my aunt join me, as do Pybba and Hereman, the wooden steps creaking and groaning under the passage of so many feet. Hereman isn't the same man his brother was, and yet I find myself enjoying his company, perhaps more now that he can cast aside the shadow of his brother's personality. God, I miss bloody Edmund.

Little time has passed since I stood here with Ealdorman Æthelwulf, watching the temporary settlement being dismantled, but now it's certainly grown and grown closer to Northampton's walls. I see figures scuttling around, ensuring ropes hold and tents stay upright.

'What the fuck are they doing?' I growl. 'They should be leaving, not returning.' I seek out Jarls Anwend and Oscetel, but of course, I can't see enough to pick out individual men. 'Who is it?' I demand. Rudolf's expression is pensive as he seeks out a familiar face amongst the campsite. But then there's no need for him to do so because a blue banner with a wolf's head emblazoned on it is raised, revealing who's come to stand guard against Northampton's walls. I confess I'm not happy about it, and yet, at the same time, I am. I should have known Jarl Halfdan wouldn't be able to accept the accord forged between Mercia and the other Grantabridge jarls.

'What the fuck does he want?' Icel snarls, but none of us reply. It seems quite obvious he's come for Jarl Guthrum. But he's not about to find him here. My aunt makes no comment to the coarse language Icel and I employ. She must be unsettled by what's happening below us.

'Double the guard,' I call to Pybba. He nods and hastens down the steps, his voice shouting to those within Northampton who he needs to obey his instructions.

'Ensure the entranceway is guarded well and secure,' I instruct Hereman. He's just as quick to obey.

'Make sure we have sharpened blades and shields enough to beat this bastard,' I murmur to Icel, before turning to my aunt. 'Ensure we have supplies should we be marooned inside Northampton.' Even she hurries away, already calling instructions to her women.

With Icel, Rudolf and Wærwulf, I stand and watch the encampment grow. I hunger to see that bastard, Jarl Halfdan, with my eyes. I want to know that he's there. And arrogant cunt that he is, he soon steps forth and waves at me.

'Fucking bastard,' I grumble.

Mercia was to have peace for twelve months, but it barely lasted half a bloody day.

Chapter Eight

'**K**ing Coelwulf,' his sharp-edged words reach me despite the wind tugging all sound from my lips.

'Jarl Halfdan,' I counter. I'd sooner not shout from the ramparts, but perhaps it's better if that's all that bloody happens.

'I believe you have one of my men,' he roars. 'And I'll have him back.' I don't need Wærwulf beside me to translate what he says. I understand it well enough.

The words don't surprise me. Mercia has gone from the potential for peace to war in the beat of a heart. Now I wish we'd killed Jarl Guthrum all over again. It's going to make sod all difference, so what was the point in allowing him to bloody live.

'He's his own man. He and the other jarls made the peace. Not you. Sod off back to Northumbria.' Wærwulf repeats my words in Danish. But Jarl Halfdan has someone at his side. No doubt he murmurs the translation as well. Something swift covers Jarl Halfdan's face. I wish I knew what it meant. Perhaps he's lost Northumbria? I can't see any other reason for him being here. The alliance between him and Jarl Guthrum wasn't that strong. I've realised that it was more that Halfdan needed Guthrum's men than because of any great friendship between them. He won't want to fight to the death for Guthrum's release. Will he?

'Bring him outside, and I'll leave you in peace,' Jarl Halfdan quips, a smile on his face so wide that I can almost see his teeth in the flickering sunlight. He's an ugly bastard.

'I think not,' I counter. More and more of my warriors have joined me, summoned by Pybba. While Jarl Halfdan stands alone apart from his translator, I have my men to either side of me. I hope my aunt doesn't reappear. I don't want her to face Jarl Halfdan. I don't truly want her ever to see another Viking raider in her life, but that's unlikely to happen. Perhaps I should say I never wish her to see a living, breathing Viking raider.

With an imperious wave of Jarl Halfdan's hand, Viking raider warriors appear from behind the growing encampment. They're well-armed as blades flash in the sunlight. They growl menacingly.

'Are the other jarls amongst them?' I question Hereman. With Edmund gone, and despite only having one remaining eye, he could see far better than I ever could, I need someone else to be my eyes.

'Not as far as I can see, my lord, no,' he quickly replies. Rudolf nods in agreement.

'Then he's alone. How many men?'

Rudolf's answer doesn't fill me with fear.

'About two hundred, my lord.'

'Not many, four ships,' I know it's how these men reckon the size of their force. It does perhaps slip from me too easily. I don't wish to become tainted by their bloody ways.

While I murmur to my warriors, Jarl Halfdan doesn't move but stands his ground, arms hanging to either side of him, his stance relaxed. The bastard believes he's won already, and he's done fuck all.

'I have more men, King Coelwulf,' he taunts. 'Many more men than you. We'll overpower you.'

I smile and shake my head. I don't feel I need to point out the defences I stand upon. Or how many others have failed to take Northampton from me. It would be churlish, surely.

'As do I,' I retort. He nods as though expecting that and once more waves his arms imperiously. This time, four bowmen emerge from hiding, all with arrows nocked and ready. I make no movements. I won't run from him. I'm pleased my warriors also stand firm, even when, one after another, the arrows are loosed. Not, I realise, that the twang of the taunt bowstrings and the whoosh of the flying objects are actually aimed at me. Or if they were, Jarl Halfdan needs to get himself some new archers, perhaps the man who killed Edmund and wounded Jarl Guthrum within Grantabridge. Although, I know that man is dead. I have Cuthwalh to thank for that. The four arrows fall uselessly to the ground, far out of reach of Northampton and much lower to the ground than I now stand.

'You have until tomorrow,' Jarl Halfdan calls casually, ordering his warriors aside. 'Until tomorrow, or we'll take Northampton from you and your damn life as well.' He turns his back on me. The arrogant fucker.

'Goda, Sæbald and Wulfhere, you have the first watch.'

A smirk on their faces assures me they're pleased to take it.

'Tell me everything they do,' I instruct. Not that I need to issue the order. This isn't their first watch duty. It won't be their bloody last, either.

While Jarl Halfdan already seems to have given his orders, some of the warriors taking an aggressive stance in front of the makeshift camp, I need to do the same.

'The rest of you, with me.' I'm thinking as I hurry down the steps. Is it a coincidence that Jarl Halfdan reappeared on the very day the Wessex delegate came here? I don't trust the West Saxons. I know they're devious bastards, and it seems there is much about the last forty years of which I'm ignorant. Icel's persistent and consistent hatred of them assures me that something isn't right in Wessex. They don't view Mercia as an equal. I consider whether they ever have. And I'm still perplexed by why Alfred has a Mercian wife when he seems to think so little of Mercia.

'We need the gates reinforced,' I inform Hereman. 'Take who

you need, and ensure the river is devoid of boats and that we have control of the bridge.'

We've fought around Northampton many times and know it well, but the same precautions must still be taken. We might know how to win Northampton back from the Viking raiders, but I don't want to have to fucking do that again. Northampton is Mercian. It will remain as such.

In the hall, my aunt watches my approach, an unfathomable expression on her face.

'So soon?' she offers, trying to make light of the words. I nod. I still can't decide how I feel about all this. My overriding feeling is that I'm just bloody pissed off that I didn't kill Jarl Guthrum when I had the chance. I wonder if she's starting to wish that as well. No one would have blamed her for demanding his death. It was she who concocted this bloody peace accord.

Not, I realise that having Jarl Guthrum dead would have prevented Jarl Halfdan from trying his luck again. His involvement was detected at Grantabridge, after all.

Have the Northumbrians overwhelmed him, or is he just here to cause trouble? Does he truly care that we have Jarl Guthrum? I realise that it doesn't bloody matter. All that's important is how we get him off Mercian land and, preferably, buried beneath it as well.

'Jarl Halfdan's,' I murmur, 'come to take back Jarl Guthrum.'

'With the other jarls?' She questions immediately.

'No, alone, as far as I can tell.'

'Then this has nothing to do with Jarl Guthrum and all to do without whatever cock-up he's made of Northumbria and his excursion into the land of the Picts.'

'Perhaps,' I agree. 'Or maybe King Ricsige has managed to evict him.' I offer more hopefully.

'With what army?' she counters. 'No, this is Jarl Halfdan making a powerplay. How will you counter him?'

'I won't. We'll stand a guard and see what the daft git does next.'

'It might be a good opportunity to take another of the Viking raiders hostage,' she offers, eyebrows high. I confess I scoff at her audacity. She truly should have been born a man.

'What, you think we should infiltrate his camp?'

'I do, yes.'

'It's not very large.'

'Yet. It will grow. These Viking raiders have a strange fascination with Northampton. Almost as bad as with Repton. They've been here before. No doubt they think it should be theirs.'

The thought's appealing. I want Mercia to have peace for twelve months, but what if we can win Mercia's freedom for longer and merely by risking my loyal warriors? I know none of them would fear losing their lives if the prize was so high. We took Jarl Guthrum more by his bad luck than anything else. His involvement in Edmund's death, perversely, was how he became our captive. We won't be able to do the same with Jarl Halfdan. No matter what I think of him, I won't deny he's clever enough to understand that. Or he should be.

'I'll think on it,' I muse, running my hand through my beard and moving my head from side to side to alleviate the ache in my neck. I know that if Edmund were here, he'd grumble and bitch, but he'd probably be in amongst the Viking raiders by morning. We'll need to employ more stealth. We've tried many tricks on the Viking raiders in the past. Well, not tricks, but tactics. We tricked our way into Repton and Northampton and, indeed, inside Grantabridge. Jarl Halfdan will be alert to the potential we'll try something again. Does he know all my warriors, though? Yes, he knows who I am, but I'm sure there are others he's never fought.

But do I want to send them? Should I risk another of my loyal men? Too many have fallen beneath our enemy's blades. I'm lucky that Icel somehow came back to me when I thought him dead. I've been much less fortunate with Edmund and Siric, Eadulf, Athelstan, Hereberht, Eoppa, and Beornberht.

'We're once more on a war footing?' my aunt asks conversationally. I'm unsure how long I've been silent.

'We must be,' I confirm. 'Would you like to be removed from

Northampton? Taken to Kingsholm or Worcester.' She grimaces at my words.

'No, I'm safer here, with my king, who is my nephew, and his warriors,' she affirms, with no trace of weakness.

'Then, I'll keep you safe,' I offer, lifting my beaker of water high. She toasts me with a small beaker of ale or perhaps mead. The smell is sweet and cloying.

'I know you will, nephew. And you'll also keep Mercia safe. We all understand that. A pity that you can't bring the Viking raiders together in one place and just cut them down. A pitched battle, like in the stories of old, Hædfeld, Maserfeld, perhaps not Winwæd, for we know the truth of that battle, despite the monks who like to peddle the story of Oswiu stopping Penda in his prime.' I smile again, feeling the tension draining from my body.

Mercia, the land of the people on the borders, has always been beset by enemies. My aunt is correct in reminding me of that. But, in time, Mercia will triumph, and peace will reign. I wish it didn't take the shed blood of my sworn oath brothers to accomplish it. But it will. And they'll give it willingly.

I eye them, those that haven't been dispatched to guard duty, or the few who've gone to Worcester alongside Tatberht. From the young to the old, Rudolf to Icel, these men would do bloody anything for me and Mercia, and it's probable, once more, they'll have to fucking do so.

Chapter Nine

'A quiet night,' Rudolf informs me as I stride into the hall. I'm astounded I've slept so well. I feel reinvigorated. I suspect I thrive on the potential for a bloody good fight. I'm not convinced that makes me a worthy king. I might say I want peace, but what if I don't? Is it somehow my fault that these bloody Viking raiders keep attacking Mercia? I clear my mind of the thought. It's not my fault. I know that. And all the better if I do enjoy it once it comes. I'm not forcing them to fucking fight me. I must remember that.

'Has the camp grown?' With a swirl of cold water in my mouth, and stealing a boiled egg from the collection beside the fire, cracking the shell as I go, I hasten to the walls and the steep steps. I feel the burn in my calves and thighs. I need to expend some pent-up aggression, but I needn't fear. It won't be long until I'm fighting again.

'Somewhat,' Rudolf's tone says much, so I'm not surprised when, wiping my hands on my tunic, having eaten the boiled egg, I gaze down at a veritable market scene beneath Northampton's walls.

I smirk. The camp's grown. I don't deny that. But if Jarl Halfdan means to make me believe that there are truly as many men as shelters, then he's failed spectacularly. I can easily see where some of the shelters are less than well-constructed, but the biggest giveaway is the lack of cookfires. To feed that many people, there'd need to be more than just five plumes of smoke lifting into the air in the chill morning.

'A few more,' I offer, turning to meet the eyes of Eahric, Osmod and Cuthwalh, who've kept guard all night. They yawn and stretch. Cuthwalh still walks with a limp after falling from the roof inside Grantabridge, but at least he killed that bloody archer. Eahric grins widely, accentuating the bent tilt of his many-times broken nose. Osmod smiles as slowly as he walks, revealing his jagged rows of teeth.

'There was a lot of movement during the night, but I think it was just the same people moving around. There'll be some tired and niggly men today,' Eahric offers. I smirk at the picture that forms in my mind of men shuffling forwards and backwards, as though the pieces on the tafl board during the darkness.

'We're not the people of the East Angles or the Northumbrians to be made fools of,' I confirm. 'Keep alert today,' I instruct those who've come to replace Eahric, Osmod and Cuthwalh. 'We plan nothing, not yet. We're just going to watch and see what happens.'

Those replacing the night guards nod and yawn as much as my tired men who've been awake all night. Cealwin, Oda, and Wulfhere are wrapped up warmly against the chill wind so high up. It might be a long day, but at least they'll have something to watch. Of the three of them, only Wulfhere, as young as he is, looks keen to begin his duties. His grandfather would be proud of him. I might send Rudolf up later to give Cealwin and Oda a bloody prod.

I seek out Jarl Halfdan in the mass of tents below, but fail to do so. Wherever he is, indeed, wherever any of the force are, they're slow to rise this morning. Perhaps they've merely put up their tents and canvases and left, thinking to undermine us with such a show of strength. Either way, I'm unconvinced that this threat will amount to anything. Perhaps I won't get to bloody fight soon. That doesn't please me as much as it should.

While the people of Northampton wake below us, Rudolf stands beside me, Icel joining us as well, although he huffs and puffs his way up the steps, unlike Rudolf, who skips up them, making me feel old and earning a scowl from Icel. Hereman's sleeping. Gardulf's at the main gateway by the bridge.

Dawn has long since broken by the time I see one of the Viking raiders emerge from his tent to release his stream into the grass close to the campsite. I watch him, but not because I'm desperate to see a bloody man piss, but rather to determine what he'll do now. Will he rouse the others? Stoke the fires? Prepare food? Tend to the horses? There aren't many horses. I consider whether they've come by boat or used oxen to haul their supplies so far inland, perhaps from Grantabridge. A canvas isn't a light piece of equipment to encumber a warrior's horse. Maybe there are more people, but they're hiding away in the nearby woodlands, further to the east. I've spent more than enough time within them. I don't want to do so again, but it's rich with wood for fuel and, no doubt, small animals to be caught and fed to the men. But the horses? The horses will need hay and oats if they're to stay here for a long period of time. Horses such as Haden need time to eat and rest. They don't always get it, but anyone who knows anything about horses will realise that they can't be used relentlessly, or at least not on many occasions, or they'll grow lame, weak or simply refuse to take the weight of a warrior. Why, then, are there so few horses? It's as telling as the lack of fires.

I watch through narrowed eyes. What is Jarl Halfdan's intention? It's evidently some form of trick, but how bloody sophisticated is it? Is it merely that he doesn't have enough shipmen? Is it that, or does he, but they're hiding elsewhere, determined to attack Mercia in a different location? Or is it something else entirely? Something that I can't bloody determine right now.

'What do you think?' I question Icel. He watches with a frown, and in the early morning light, it reveals all the scars on his face. If we could see his entire body naked, would the story of Mercia's last forty years be etched all over it? I imagine much of it would. It would be good if he shared it with me. I also notice the chain around his neck. It's always there. He's never lost it. I consider once more who gave it to him.

'Bastards,' Icel growls. He tilts his head side to side, running his hand through his grey beard. The old, faded scar on his hand, which he thinks I don't know about, also reveals itself in the spider-web-like etching of lines. I wish I knew more than the few things I do about him. I find it astounding that I've known him all my life and yet grasp so little about him. Not even Rudolf has managed to extract all of the details of his life. If Rudolf can't do so, then no bloody man can.

'I think we may have a worthy enemy,' Icel announces slowly. 'I believe Jarl Halfdan has subterfuge planned. I doubt it involves only Northampton. He'll be reinforcing Grantabridge, and rebuilding it, whether the jarls there want it reinforced and rebuilt, or not. He'll also be doing something else. He means to engage your attention here and threaten Mercia elsewhere. Somewhere with a river close by. Perhaps London. Perhaps not. It's not the correct season to attack London. He would need to wait until later in the summer. I don't believe he'll go to Worcester to look for Jarl Guthrum because he doesn't know he's there. If he does, then we all know the Viking raiders have had some very bad experiences in the west, with Mercians and the Welsh arseholes. They won't want to repeat them.'

I open my mouth to ask more, but Rudolf gets there first.

'What happened at Worcester?' he questions.

'Wouldn't you like to bloody know,' Icel rumbles in his usual forbidding tone. The slight curve of his lips makes me even more desperate to know what he's talking about because I'm convinced it's not anything we've done, even with all those we killed on the borderlands.

'It could be as simple as he's reinforcing his claim over the kingdom of the East Angles because something has forced him to give up Northumbria. Perhaps he overextended in attacking the kingdom of the Picts?'

'But that wouldn't concern me,' I counter. Icel surveys me firmly.

'I think it bloody should,' he murmurs but offers nothing further about the broken kingdom of the East Angles. I know they once tried to defeat Mercia, but only after Mercia had taken control of it. It's little and nothing now. There's no king. I don't know if the ruling family survived the killing of King Edmund. I've never thought to find out. I'm not sure I need to find out now.

'So, Repton again? Or Torksey?'

'No, Jarl Halfdan will be keen to stay away from the places where he's been defeated.'

Hereman joins us, yawning widely, his footsteps loud on the wooden walkways.

'What do you think?'

'I think they're all shits and deserve to die.'

I hold my smirk in place because he speaks with his lips curled upwards.

'They mean to make us do something rash and stupid,' Hereman concedes, and now I laugh, as does Icel, even Rudolf grinning widely. It's Hereman who's rash and stupid. We all know that. 'So, don't bloody ask me. I concede to those who know better and think beyond the end of their nose.'

Rudolf's the next to speak.

'The Viking raiders and you have fought in many places, and you vanquished many of those who might think to seek revenge against you – you've almost died,' he concludes with a grimace. 'If Jarl Half-dan's any battle commander, he'll intend to do something entirely different. What do they say, 'the very essence of stupidity is doing something over and over again and expecting a different result.''

'When did you get so bloody wise?' Pybba glowers, drawing level on the steps. He looks old and tired, but his eyes are bright and alert.

'I have a suggestion, my lord, and you won't like it, not at all,' the way he repeats my oft-thought phrase puts me on edge, and somehow, I know what he's going to say. 'Pursue an alliance with Wessex. Let's give the bastard a lot more to worry about that just Mercia and Jarl Guthrum.'

Pybba's words don't fall like stone, but the silence after them ensures I can hear my breathing and even my heartbeat.

I don't want Pybba to be fucking right. Equally, and as unappealing as it is, he might not be entirely bloody wrong. That stings even more.

Chapter Ten

My aunt's lips purse as I tell her of Pybba's opinion, and indeed, of our bafflement about what Jarl Halfdan plans next.

'He'll attack, won't he?' she questions.

'Not here, or so it seems.'

'So, he's toying with you.'

'It would appear that way.'

'But what if he's toying with you, means to drive you away and then assaults Northampton?'

I know I'm frowning as she offers me that suggestion. We all think something different.

'If only we could ask the bastard,' Hereman complains, grinning at his use of the word, which we all know my aunt can't abide. She doesn't even flinch. If I'd said that, she'd be berating me within an inch of my life.

'Well, we can't,' she announces. She's in the main hall. I'm not entirely sure what she's doing but she's overseeing something. There are herbs and even some precious spices spread over one of the tables, but on the other, there seems to be little more than pieces of twigs and grass. There are also two cauldrons over the fire. The smells coming from them are enough to make me want to vomit.

'So we must do something else. Pybba, your suggestion is to trick them by allying with the Wessex king and repay their intentions to do the same?'

'Yes, get them involved. I know they've been attacked of late. They've made overtures of friendship on more than one occasion, and if not with us, they might decide to ally with the Viking raiders.'

'They have, but there's a huge difference between the honeyed words of diplomacy and their intentions. Icel and I know not to trust the West Saxon ruling family, or indeed, any of the b,' and my eyes are just about popping from my head as she almost says 'bastards.' With no more than a brief hesitation, she offers, 'buggers' instead. 'Who'll be our lead on this? It can't be Coelwulf.'

'Why not?' I argue.

'Because you must stay here and make Jarl Halfdan believe you'll fight him, or at least whoever is there in his place.'

'No, I think I have to be the one to do it. I'll certainly have to be seen by Alfred and the West Saxons.'

She doesn't call the enemy names, but the sneer is impossible to ignore. 'Yes, but send someone, an ealdorman, as your spokesperson. And then go in person.'

I consider this. I don't want to leave Northampton. I don't want someone else to agree on terms with King Alfred. But I can't be everywhere at once. My aunt's correct about that.

'Pybba,' I know better than to ask Icel. 'Can I send you, Rudolf and Ealdorman Ælhun to treat with the Wessex king.'

Pybba visibly shudders at the thought but snaps down on his reply. It was his bloody idea and now he doesn't want to be involved.

'Of course, my lord king,' he replies formally.

'Why me?' Rudolf pipes up in annoyance.

'Because you get into everything, and you'll be able to find out what everyone in Wessex thinks of Mercia.'

Rudolf smirks with pleasure at my response. I shake my head at him. His grin widens.

'I don't think we need to find that out,' Icel counters with some heat. 'There'll be unease in Mercia if word gets out that you've sent people to Wessex.'

'Perhaps,' my aunt agrees. 'But the Mercians trust their king. They know he'd die for them. If he thinks some of the answer lies within Wessex, they'll understand.'

Icel's eyes blaze into mine. If he'd tell me what he's thinking that would help. Instead, I have to make this decision which goes against everything I've ever thought.

'At least it's not the damn Welsh,' Hereman offers with a sad smile. And now we all fall silent. Talk of the Welsh would have sent Edmund into a screaming rage. Again, I wish I knew more than I do about him. I know why Edmund hated the Welsh so much, but there are other things I wish I knew. Hereman won't know. Edmund and he didn't always see eye to eye. Not that I'm one to cast aspersions. I was the same with my brother.

'Then we must move on this. For now, I'll remain here while my embassy seeks out the Mercian ealdorman and the Wessex king. Make no apologies for what we discussed here,' I caution Pybba and Rudolf. I'm not looking forward to having to tell the ealdorman of this. I'm sure he won't appreciate being forced to travel to Wessex. He's been used badly of late – and not just because he had to protect Jarl Guthrum from my rage.

'And what of London, Repton and Torksey?'

'We deploy the ealdormen and their warriors,' I confirm gruffly. There are still some that I don't trust, Ealdorman Aldred foremost of them all, but better to have those locations protected by men who profess to be loyal than have them exposed once more. It helps that he remains at Northampton. I'll be able to send him north with my commands.

'Ealdorman Aldred can protect Torksey. Ealdorman Beorhtnoth can take Repton, and Æthelwold can reinforce London in the absence of a bishop there.' I try not to growl at the memory of bloody Smithwulf.

I thought I had time to reinforce Mercia. I don't have that bloody time now, but maybe these decisions are best made in the heat of the moment anyway.

Time will fucking tell.

* * *

I take Pybba to the lookout, gazing over the Viking raider encampment. We're both silent for a long time, the men on guard duty, Cealwin, Oda and Wulfhere, moving aside so we can talk in some privacy. I almost expect Icel to appear to resume his argument. And Rudolf, just because he's a nosy shit. But they leave us alone. I hope that means Icel understands what's at play here. We don't necessarily have to make this alliance, but we do need to pretend to do so.

'What would you have me say?' Pybba asks eventually when I offer nothing.

'As with Ealdorman Æthelwulf, find out what you can about Alfred's intentions. See if he truly has the numbers to counter the enemy. I've a feeling he's as beleaguered as we were last year. His enemy might not be the Grantabridge jarls, but it'll be someone else. I confess, Mercia was lucky enough to lose its king because he was weak and fled. King Alfred lost his brother in battle against them. That's got to hurt a man.' My brother died from a wound taken while fighting the Welsh. I know what it is to lose a brother. Not that I was always loyal to him. But, he was an arse on occasion, and I was a shit. As much as I hate Alfred, I have some sympathy for that loss.

'What if we're captured?'

'You won't be,' I reassure. 'Perhaps you should take one of the holy men with you? Travel with his entourage.'

'The Viking raiders hate holy men more than they do warriors.'

'Then don't,' I stamp down my irritation that he asks the question and then dismisses my resolution so easily. 'Travel as you are. The ealdorman will have his warriors with him. They should keep you safe.' That, I realise, is more reassuring. Ealdorman Ælhun has become a wise and just member of my close adherents. We've not always agreed, but now we do more often than we don't.

'But what to say?'

I huff at this. I'm minded to remind Pybba again that this was his bloody suggestion. 'Just tell him we've reconsidered and would like to discuss an alliance.'

'Cemented with a marriage?' he asks with a twinkle in his eye. I growl at that.

'No, not cemented with a marriage. Well,' I reconsider. 'Not with my fucking marriage.' The twinkle in his eye dims. He opens his mouth to argue with me.

'I don't mean it,' I growl, realising perhaps I shouldn't have tried to beat him at his own game.

'What if they mention London?'

'Tell the bloody fool that when he can be assured of defending what he already claims, we can talk about other requests. For now, he can barely keep the wolf from the hens.'

'What if he requests military assistance?'

'The same. Mercia can only provide assistance when the Viking raiders don't threaten her. We can work together to drive them from the shores of our island, but little else.'

'What if they mention their assistance at Nottingham?'

'Bloody hell,' I explode. 'You can't be told the answer to everything. That's like me telling you how to fight and counter every move. It'll be instinctive, like fighting the Viking raiders. You know that, Pybba. You really do.'

For a moment, I think Pybba might refuse the command, but then he relaxes and grins.

'I was testing you to see how much you were invested in this and how much bloody responsibility you gave me.'

'Did you need to fucking do that?'

'Probably not,' Pybba offers, with a shrug of his shoulders. 'But why not? You'd do the same.'

I rumble low in my throat.

'And keep Rudolf under control,' I caution. 'You know what he can be like when given too much freedom.'

'Don't worry about him. I'll ensure he doesn't do anything you wouldn't bloody do.'

'That's not very reassuring.' He grins, revealing his line of teeth, not all of them straight or white any more.

He leans towards me. 'Don't worry, my lord. Those who know you will understand your actions, and those who don't, well, they can fuck off, can't they.'

I acknowledge that and jut my chin towards the encampment below.

'What's he up to, then?'

'Being a bloody arse,' Pybba menaces. 'He doesn't want you to feel safe, even here.'

'But what would he do with Mercia if he held it? It's not as though they did more than hunker down inside Repton when they forced King Burgred to abdicate. They pretended to keep hold of Torksey, but again, it was only a temporary encampment.'

'They don't know what they're doing, do they? They want land, wealth, and pretty women to bed, but when they have all that, they'll be complaints from those they rule, they'll find that wealth is fleeting, and pretty women will not always be pretty, and they'll lumber a man with a herd of bickering children. They're just playing at all this. It means they'll bloody trip over their own feet. We have to wait for that to happen.'

'And the other jarls?'

'Will be as fucked off with him as we are, I promise you.'

'Jarl Guthrum's the real menace, not Halfdan. Guthrum can think with more than his seax. While Halfdan distracts us, you need to be mindful of what Guthrum has planned. He'll be watching and learning everything you do and how Mercia works. He might not want to be your prisoner, but he's not fool enough to dismiss your achievements as insignificant, unlike Halfdan.'

'I want to kill Jarl Halfdan as much as he wants to kill me,' I menace, thinking back to the time I nearly managed to kill the fucker. If only that ship hadn't come to rescue him on the River Trent.

'And hopefully, one day, you'll get your wish. And then we can all be happy, safe and secure once more. But until then, it's better to ally with Wessex than Northumbria. Northumbria's weak unless it has succeeded in expelling Jarl Halfdan, which I strongly suspect isn't what's happened there.'

'Make sure Ealdorman Ælhun understands all that,' I urge him, watching as a handful of Viking raiders make much of leaving their canvases and bending to retrieve their weapons. They form a makeshift shield wall, five men against another six, no sign of Jarl Halfdan.

Their shields are painted with Halfdan's blue wolf emblem, and they seem well provisioned, but the first man to cast a blow against another almost falls with the weight of the shield and sword combined. The second is little better, and in no time, more and more of my men clamber upwards to discover while Pybba and I are crying with laughter.

'They really are fucking useless,' Hereman roars as two men, who've exchanged their seaxes for spears, tangle them and end up falling on their arses, the one knocking his chin with his own weapon as he does so. I look along my row of men, pleased to see that even those once held captive by our enemy are laughing. Ingwald, Eadfrith, Cealwin, Wulfred, Osmod and Oda were badly beaten by the enemy, but none as bad as Beornstan. It's taken him some time to stop glowering at me in anger. Seeing him smile now fills me with confidence that one day, he will stop blaming me for what happened and take his revenge against the Viking raider bastards.

'They don't know how to fight,' Rudolf's outraged words, make Pybba and I double up with laughter once more, having almost managed to control ourselves.

His wide eyes and open mouth reveal his complete outrage. 'Is this display meant to make us fear them?' he quibbles.

'No, young lad, no,' Icel is amongst us, his words lacking all humour. His dry voice has me struggling for composure. I imagine the look on his face. 'They mean to show how little they regard our threat. While we stand here, protected by ditch and rampart, they play at war like children who've never been taught to lift a blade before. It is funny,' and here he arches an eyebrow at me and Pybba as though we're to blame for bringing all our warriors to witness this shit show. 'But it's them who'll be laughing the hardest. No, we should ignore this, concentrate only on what needs to be done to protect Mercia.'

'And that doesn't involve watching our enemy?' Lyfing questions, his words dripping scorn.

'Not when those down there aren't our true enemy. No, they're planning something else, and we should be deciphering their intent instead of being side-tracked by this show of bloody incompetence.'

Sobering, I realise Icel's correct and also wrong.

I nod towards him with thanks but speak all the same.

'Icel's right to caution us, but we're right to laugh at them. We should recognise the subterfuge at play but also ensure they think we're fooled by it all. If not, Jarl Halfdan's plans will grow more elaborate. So stand here, laugh and watch them make tits of themselves. We have the gates guarded. We have word being sent to every corner of Mercia. We'll watch them and counter whatever they throw at us. But for now, jeer. Make those warriors down there feel more foolish than if we'd caught them with their arse hanging over the river, shitting themselves.

Icel unwillingly agrees, a rare smile splitting his lips as he turns to me.

'Watching them reminds me of when our lord king, Coelwulf, learned to fight in a shield wall. He was an utter arse that day, and for many that followed, right enough, but now he's one of the fiercest warriors I've ever fought beside.' That memory comes unwelcome to my mind, and I grumble low in my throat. I was taught with my brother, and for all Coenwulf's faults, I'll say one thing for him: he was a much better warrior than me from the very beginning.

'Do you remember,' and Pybba wipes tears from his eyes with his remaining hand, 'when Coelwulf asked us which way round the spear went.' My lips tighten, but even I find a smile tugging on them.

'I never said I was a born warrior,' I call over the thrum of laughter. 'I never bloody said that at all.'

'Which is good,' Pybba confirms. 'Because Icel would sure as shit put you in your place if you tried to argue for that. And we all know the men listen more to Icel than they do you. If there's one amongst your number who shows himself as more kingly, then it's certainly Icel.'

I detect a flicker of unease covering Icel's face and consider what all that's about, but I raise my hand as though to ward off my warriors' laughter.

'And we all know that all of you knew which spear end to hold to get the best grip, don't we?' I join in the good-natured conversation. These are my warriors. They've not always been my warriors, and perhaps it's good to remind them and me that with time, boys will become men, and men will become lethal bastards, and then they might die. But hopefully, only after they've taught all they know to those who must continue the fucking fight after them.

Chapter Eleven

I watch Pybba, Rudolf, Ealdorman Ælhun, and his warriors ride south the following morning and turn to Ingwald, Lyfing and Leonath.

'You know what I need you to do?' I question them. The three nod solemnly, although Leonath offers me a toothless grin at the same time. They have their horses ready. The animals look well rested and need to be for what I have planned for these men.

'Yes, my lord, we know,' Lyfing offers with a jaunty tone, almost rolling his eyes, but not quite. 'And we assure you, we'll be a little more careful than when you made those woods your home.' I grin in response to that. I shouldn't have expected anything different from bloody Lyfing. My warriors keep me grounded. They remind me of just how many mistakes I've made. Almost having my head severed from my neck wasn't my finest moment. I find myself running my hand along the vibrant scar.

'Make sure you bring back his head if he does fall foul of a Viking raider blade,' I urge Ingwald with a wink. He nods solemnly. Of all my men who were held captive by the enemy inside Grantabridge, Ingwald is to the one who's shaken off any fear the quickest.

'Mind, he's an ugly fucker, so perhaps not.' With that, the three mount up and ride through the gates in the stinking leavings of the earlier men, green horse shit liberally splattered over the sturdy wooden bridge. I eye it. I can see where work has been undertaken to ensure we either hold the bridge or dismantle it to stop our enemy from getting close. I had hoped such tactics were in the past, but Jarl Halfdan has ensured they must remain.

My men are to scout the woodlands on this side of the river. They'll walk in the steps of our many adventures beneath the spreading boughs, and might even find themselves close to where the hound, Wiglaf, is buried.

From beneath the trees, they'll be able to keep me informed of whatever Jarl Halfdan is up to, if anything. I'd prefer to send men to infiltrate the camp, but while it looks large, we've seen so few of our enemy I know it would be impossible to trick Jarl Halfdan and his few warriors in such a way.

The next person I encounter preparing to ride is my aunt. She eyes me from above, the horse gently moving beneath her. The animal is placid enough, but the area's crowded. It would rather be on its way. The animal was wounded by Jarl Guthrum as it fled Grantabridge. But, with my aunt's care, she's recovered quickly enough to be ridden.

'Are you sure about this?' she questions one final time. She doesn't like what I have planned for her but has accepted it's to be her task.

'I am, yes. And you understand my intentions.'

'I do, nephew, yes. I also fear you mean to get me out of the way so you can have a great big fight in my absence.'

'I don't think you need to fear that,' I chuckle. 'It's likely to happen whether you're here or not.'

'Hum,' her lips narrow. I think she's about to berate me, especially when she calls me closer to her. Instead, she places her hand on my chin and pulls my head upwards.

'Take care of yourself, nephew,' the words are murmured, and for a moment, she arrests my gaze. There's much in her expression that I don't understand. 'Men have died to ensure you lived, and men have tried to kill to ensure you died. We've got you this far, alive. Don't make it easy on any of the b...buggers.' By the time she's finished talking, her words thrum with menace, and she almost misspeaks once more. I feel a lump in my throat. I don't recall all of my early years. I know I endured events that others would never have forced upon a child.

'I never make it easy, aunt; be assured.' I gently lift her fingers away and instead grip her firm, warm hand. 'You do the same. Stay well, and stay alive. If anything befalls you, I'll come for you.'

She nods. Resolve settles on her face.

'I know you will, nephew. Ensure you do.' Without another word, she too makes her way towards the bridge over the river, escorted by another four of my warriors. Gyrth, Hemming, Ordlaf and Wulfstan ride as her guard. They, too, have a long way to go, only north, not south, and for some of that time, Ealdorman Aldred will ride with them. I must know as much as possible to ensure we overpower our enemy. The only way to do that is to send men and women to discover the truth, and that means my aunt must seek out the bishop of Lincoln, who will be more honest than Ealdorman Ælhun could ever be.

With a resounding thud, the gate's firmly closed, and a handful of the Northampton warriors take up position close to them. We're not yet on a full war footing, but now isn't the time to believe it won't happen. While I infiltrate the enemy, I'm sure Jarl Halfdan will be doing precisely the same. I go to the viewpoint on the rampart and watch the activity in the campsite below.

Wærwulf is there, watching and listening. As are Hereman and Gardulf. I nod towards the three of them. They nod back, and we settle in silence. I consider everything I should be doing and realise that standing here, watching our enemy, is perhaps more pleasurable than listening to legal disputes, as I might be if I'd followed Jarl Guthrum to Worcester. It's impossible to make everyone happy where land and money are involved. I don't wish to be grateful to Jarl Halfdan for anything, but it's a warm day, the wind gentle on my face. I'd far rather be outside than in.

'Did more come in the night?' I direct this to Hereman, who's actually on guard duty. Wærwulf's just being nosy while Gardulf, I imagine, was talking to his uncle. The two have always been close.

'No, the night guards saw nothing and heard even less. It makes me suspicious, but there are no more horses or tents, so if they're here, they've learned to mask it well.'

'There are still only five fires,' Gardulf reminds me.

'They're either not here or being fed cold rations,' I muse.

'Do you truly believe Jarl Halfdan would be this bloody devious?' Gardulf persists.

I incline my head from side to side. 'In all honesty, I don't know that he would be. I'm only thinking about what we would do in the same situation. We'd be underhand. I'm convinced brute force hasn't won him all he's taken from Mercia. Admittedly, he lost it all as well. But he had some skills to accomplish what he did. We must remember that the Repton jarls ousted King Burgred from Mercia. They knew enough to offer him his life in exchange for his kingdom. They either had no desire to continue the war or understood it could be won differently.'

'It almost makes us sound like we're the bloody thirsty bastards,' Wærwulf murmurs with downcast lips.

'I don't,' I reject, but perhaps he's right. The Viking raiders have fought and battered their way into Mercia, but once there, they only wanted to kill me. If we'd not gathered our forces to drive them from Repton, perhaps Mercia would have known peace, albeit under a different type of ruler.

'No, you don't,' Wærwulf apologies, his hands lifted before him in surrender. 'I meant nothing by it. It's just the way you presented the argument. You're right to be cautious. Gyrth, Ordlaf, Wulfstan and Hemming will discover what you need to know about events in Northumbria with the aid of Lady Cyneswith. Rudolf and Pybba will make Wessex our allies, and then we can defeat our enemy once and for all. I grow tired of the constant warfare, and yet I labour on. There'll be an end. We have to ensure that we're the ones bloody winning.'

'Don't you fancy sneaking through the tunnel?' Hereman asks, a mischievous grin on his face. 'We could steal into their encampment, slit their throats and have bloody done with it.'

I watch him, noting the rare smile that turns his lips upwards. He mourns for Edmund. Like him, I'd like to kill as many of the murderous bastards as possible.

'I don't want to do anything, not until we know more. But perhaps then we might,' I offer, eyebrows high. I'll sit and wait and watch, but I can't deny it lies uneasy on me. I want bloody Jarl Halfdan dead. Only then will I feel some contentment.

And, if we can kill Jarl Halfdan, and bind the other jarls to us with a treaty, then perhaps, just perhaps, Mercia might enjoy some hard-won peace with which to rebuild.

Chapter Twelve

The passage of time is tedious. Jarl Halfdan makes no attempt to take Northampton, and we don't endeavour to drive him and his few men from outside the walls. Little happens. The Viking raiders cook food, eat, sleep, shit and piss. We do the same. The news from Ingwald, Lyfing and Leonath is slow to arrive but tells me nothing I can't see from my vantage point. If there's guile at work, it's being done well enough that we can't determine what it is. The number of men we see doesn't increase, and the flood of tents being erected ceases.

I hear nothing from my aunt, although Bishop Wærferth sends word to assure me that Jarl Guthrum, or Æthelstan as he calls him, seems content with his new faith and endures his captivity well. While Tatberht remains with Bishop Wærferth, others of my men return, as do Ealdorman Ælhun's men, under the command of Wulfsige. They're surprised to find Ealdorman Ælhun missing.

'Æthelstan doesn't complain or demand to be set free,' Wulfsige informs me. 'He doesn't even try to escape.' I narrow my eyes at that news. I can't believe his baptism has caused such a huge bloody change in him. Like Jarl Halfdan, Guthrum is up to something. I just don't know what it is yet.

The summer moves on apace. I grow as restless as though near-darkness coats the land like winter. I feel the need to ride Haden and banish the fatigue that trails me everywhere I go. My sleep's disturbed, and I appreciate it's all caused by grief for Edmund. But knowing what causes my agitated state and being able to banish it are two very different problems. This time last summer, I was fighting for my life. No doubt I still am, but this slow march to war sits uneasily on me. And then, eventually, Pybba and Rudolf return with Ealdorman Ælhun and his warriors.

I watch their progress from the south, wondering what news they bring. I regret my decision to send them to Wessex, but I'll have to live with whatever agreement might have been tentatively agreed. I'm pleased my aunt isn't here to watch my frustration with the idea.

'My lord,' Pybba greets me in the stable yard. His words reveals nothing. I eye him. He does seem to be gaining strength after his ordeal on the Welsh borderlands. Knowing his family has been reunited, has aided him, I'm sure of it.

'Pybba,' I counter. He quirks an eyebrow. Neither of us wishes to give anything away.

'Not here,' he mutters. Rudolf follows him as we make our way out onto the bridge that closes the gap over the River Nene and allows access to Watling Street to the west. Ealdorman Ælhun watches us go and comes to join us.

'Tell me,' I urge them, looking from one to the other, my eyes for my warriors and not Ealdorman Ælhun.

Pybba grimaces. Rudolf jumps in.

'King Alfred's a fucking arse,' he exclaims. I nod, pleased to hear that. 'But, he's very keen to ally with Mercia. His terms, I confess, are strange.' I watch Rudolf. It's becoming difficult to see the young boy he once was in the tall man he's becoming. He almost has a beard.

'What are they?'

This is like getting blood from a stone or gold from a sodding churchman. A churchman is quick to take everything and slow to relinquish his tight fists. Even the prayers that should be spoken more often than not come with a stipulation.

'King Alfred wishes to be treated as your equal and repeats his desire to have his face beside yours on a coinage that both Wessex and Mercia will use.'

I roll my eyes at this oft-repeated phrase. I've only just had the Mercian coinage reissued.

'And he offers his daughter in marriage, which is just plain wrong,' Rudolf shudders at those words.

'Wait. How old is his daughter?'

'Too young to wed Rudolf, let alone you,' Pybba grimly agrees. 'I tried to dissuade him from such a suggestion. Lady Ealhswith looked revolted at the idea as well.'

'Is that it?'

'No, he wants an assurance you'll support one another in war, and you'll share the profits from keeping London safe.'

'Why is he so obsessed with bloody London?' I glower. 'London's Mercian. It's sod all to do with him.'

'I know, my lord, I know,' Pybba mollifies.

'So what's the worst of his requirements? I can tell there's something else.'

'He demands you send Mercian warriors to protect Wessex.' Pybba speaks tonelessly.

'In exchange for what?' I explode. 'Will he send West Saxon warriors to Mercia?' Not that I want them. I trust my men and my warriors. The West Saxons, it's said, don't know how to fight, even when their lives depend on it. They're about as much bloody use, it's said, as a shield made from leaves. I'm disinclined to argue with what these people say. I don't say it aloud. Well, not very often.

'In exchange for nothing but the alliance.'

'Wait, he means for me to denude Mercia of her warriors?'

'Indeed, my lord, indeed.' Pybba nods slowly as I realise the import of what he's saying.

'Is he half-cracked?'

'He's certainly a man who doesn't understand the current situation, yes.' Pybba's well-versed in politic. Perhaps he was the right man to send. However, I can see that he's spent his time trying to maintain some composure. Now rage pours from him like rain from the sky because he can finally speak his mind. Rudolf's little better.

Ealdorman Ælhun offers no opinion, which surprises me. I thought he'd be filled with tales of how wonderful Wessex is, how rich it is, and how her king is a man of honour. His silence informs me that whatever ideas he once held about Wessex have been long since banished. It can be that way. Meeting someone can reveal they're not the person you thought they were.

'How did you leave it?' I eventually ask. Pybba's expression cracks at this.

'Perhaps not as well as we could have done. I made no real assurances of anything. I told the king only that I'd inform you of his demands.'

'I should probably have devised some impossible terms before I allowed you to venture south,' I grumble, fists clenched. I'm watching the water pass beneath the bridge. The flow is fast. The weather's been pleasant, but we had a terrible storm last night, and lightning temporarily split the black sky. The river will run a little high for a day or two. I wish it could overflow and send the Viking raiders running away. Not, I realise, that they probably fear water. They have their ships somewhere. They'll find it easy enough to leave this place if they want to.

'A meeting has been agreed,' Pybba speaks into the silence. 'For a month's time. For you and Alfred to meet in person.'

'Where?' I glower. I don't believe I'll attend. I'll send my apologies, or whatever it is a king sends to another king when they've changed their mind.

'Just south of the River Thames, close to the ford opposite Lechlade.'

'At least it's not in London,' I mutter.

'And he asks that prayers are said for Bishop Smithwulf. He sent this to ensure it was done.' Pybba pulls an object from his weapons belt, hidden deep within his seax holder, and I squint to see it.

'What the hell is that?' I demand.

'Fuck knows. But they all made out it was worth a lot of money and would ensure prayers are said for a very long time.'

He hands it to me, and I feel the object's weight. It must once have been a silver Viking raider armband, I'm sure of it, only it's been twisted and distorted, perhaps by fire. There are twirling patterns along its length, and I can see how deeply they've been engraved onto the metal. But it's the weight of the metal that astounds me.

'He thinks this is silver?' I question. Pybba shrugs his shoulders.

'He made out it was silver, but it's not. It's too damn light.'

'It's iron, with a very thin covering of silver. So thin that in some places, the engraving reveals the iron beneath it.' I shake my head. 'A king should know the bloody difference between iron and silver. Fucking fool.' But I don't hand the object back, but stare at it, considering this new puzzle piece. If Alfred doesn't know the difference between iron and silver, then how is he to rule well? How will he pay his warriors? Alternatively, if Alfred does know the difference between silver and iron, why has he sent me this piece of shit? Is he bloody testing me? Does he mean to deride me? God. I hate the fucker even more now.

Chapter Thirteen

'My lord,' the cry comes from the rampart, and I find myself running towards the steep steps, Icel joining the rushing procession alongside Pybba and Rudolf. The ealdorman can be heard labouring in the background as well. He's a warrior. But he's also a man of the witan and politics. I'm amazed he manages so well. Perhaps I could suggest he spends more time training with me and my warriors. That would aid him at moments like these. The gate slams shut behind us.

With loud footsteps, I rear up before Goda and his bushy beard. I turn to see why the usually calm warrior has urgently summoned me from one end of the settlement to the other.

Below us, the Viking raider encampment is in turmoil. There seem to be men and women everywhere, and a great trail of more people arriving can be seen in a snake from the woodlands that I've spent more than enough time within. They come down the slope over which Haden once raced his heart out, only for me to fall and for him to continue without me. I nearly died that day. No, I thought I'd die that day, but I didn't. That's what I need to remember.

'What's bloody happening?' I demand.

'Fuck knows. They just started arriving. A trickle to begin with, and then more and more of the bastards.' Goda's words are filled with unease. I turn to him. He straightens, holds his breath and slowly releases it. I offer him a firm slap on the shoulder. Being fearful isn't a problem, but we should never reveal it to our enemies, even if they are far beneath our feet. Goda is always calm-headed. I remind him of that.

'From the ruins of Grantabridge, I suspect,' I say with lips down-turned. We cast out all who inhabited Grantabridge, leaving only one ship upon which they were all supposed to leave, but we couldn't hold what remained of the ruins. I didn't want to hold it. No doubt, these people have slunk back to it, like a wounded bear to its lair. What perplexes me is why they now come to Northampton.

'Are Jarls Anwend and Oscetel with them?' I confess I'm bewildered. If these people are from Grantabridge, then why have they come here? Are they no longer safe there, or have they been slowly making their west since our attack on the settlement at Easter? They don't owe allegiance to Jarl Halfdan, but Jarl Guthrum. Why then would they join Halfdan outside Northampton? Why are they even still on this island?

My confusion grows as the day advances. A throng of people are arriving. They're not coming for a short stay, either. They bring sheep and goats, even an ox slowly comes into view as the summer sky turns pink with the sunset. I don't see Jarl Halfdan greeting these people. I can't even tell if they're warriors. They might have weapons, but I see little evidence of shields strapped to horses or carts. What, then, is happening here?

Just as I'm about to stand down for the night, confident that there's no malice involved, at least for now, a cry reaches my ears.

I turn and peer down. A collection of men and women stand within easy arrow shot of the ramparts. They appear to be unarmed. But others behind them might have weapons pointed at those who shout for my attention. Or so it seems as I squint into the dying light of the day.

'My lord king,' the voice that calls is respectful and heavily accented but speaks my language well enough for me to understand what they say. 'My lord king, Coelwulf.'

'What of it?' Pybba rumbles in response. I'm grateful for his quick thinking as all eyes turn to him on the ramparts, backlit by the dying daylight. It'll be impossible to see that his right hand's missing or that he lacks my height. And hair. I don't miss Rudolf's groan of frustration that his mentor is so quick to place himself in danger. Those with spears won't be able to throw them upwards, but there's always the chance of a lucky bow shot.

'My lord king.' The assembled men and women sink to their knees without thought of the damp grass from the storm of yesterday evening. This is most odd. A muffled voice emerges from the depths of the spokesperson's chest, but I can't hear anything.

'We can't hear you,' Hereman roars, startling even me. I glower at him, and he grins. It's good to see that whatever these people are up to, Hereman is entirely unmoved by it.

'My lord king,' a shocked voice emerges, head snapping up. I can't see the facial expression, but I can imagine it. 'My lord king, apologies,' the man continues. His words are pitched to reach us, even at such a height. 'We've come from Grantabridge, seeking the word of God, as Jarl Guthrum has received it. We beg you to allow us entry into your kingdom and your faith. There's nothing left for us at Grantabridge but ruins. We didn't know Jarl Halfdan would be at Northampton. Now he threatens us because of our faith.' The man must look behind him because his words fade away, but I can't see enough to be sure that's what happened. I wish they'd made this request earlier when they first started to arrive, and it would have been light enough to see more.

I'm glad Pybba and Hereman pretend to be me because I can't deny the news bloody stuns me. I step back, almost falling down the wooden steps, and turn shocked eyes on Rudolf. His expression is as alarmed as mine. What bloody trick is this?

'We'd welcome a priest to attend upon us and a bishop to baptise us all, as Jarl Guthrum received. And your protection as well. We're Christians now. We repent of our past sins and a love of the Norse gods and seek forgiveness.' The voice is plaintive.

Hereman glances at me, his eyes hooded in the growing darkness. Pybba manages to maintain his amazed façade more easily, holding firm and peering down at those below. They stand within sight, not as close as possible, no doubt because of the deep ditch surrounding Northampton. Not for the first time, I'm grateful for the deterrent.

'Tell them to come back in the morning when it's light,' Icel rumbles beside me. I find myself nodding. I don't know what else to say. Ealdorman Ælhun hasn't spoken. I imagine he doesn't know what to make of this, either.

'Do it,' I urge Pybba. 'But make it bloody flouncy. Like we'll agree to it.'

'My good people,' Pybba begins, as Icel shakes his head at Pybba's conciliatory tone. 'Thank you for coming here today. Please return with the sunlight, and we'll listen to your petition when we can see you.' I detect a babble of voices from below. I'm not sure what it means.

And then the voice speaks once more, filled with desperation. 'My lord king, Coelwulf, holy king of Mercia. We fear for our lives if we remain here with Jarl Halfdan. He has no love for us or our new faith.' There are squeals and shrieks, rough voices, and even the crash of a war axe on wooden shield. Now, I understand that those behind them are armed warriors—the bastards.

I sigh. I should have realised what this bloody trick would be. It's clever, and my heart sinks with the understanding that I can leave these people to die, as the sound of weapons suggests, or allow them entry into Northampton. Only, I know full well that these men and women won't all wish to convert. Jarl Halfdan's not foolish enough to be ignorant about this. He'll take advantage of it. Indeed, he's probably encouraging his warriors to hold weapons close to the recent converts, to threaten them, and perhaps add a cut or two. Maybe they even open wounds along their arms and hands. This is why it's taken so long. These people might have come here to ask for a bishop and to convert to Christianity, but Jarl Halfdan has determined on a means of ensuring it enables him to put some of his bastard shipmen inside Northampton.

I can sense the gaze of my warriors on me, even though I don't look at them.

I know what my aunt would say. I know what Bishop Wærferth's response would be. I can sense that Ealdorman Ælhun has his thoughts to share. But I know what I need to say.

'We'll allow them entry,' I confirm in a soft growl. 'Pybba and Rudolf, stay here and watch for any sign of attack. Ealdorman Ælhun, have your men support my warriors. The rest of you, get your warriors' garb on. We need to root out the traitor or traitors amongst the would-be Christians.'

'But where will we put them?' Goda complains.

'In the bloody church, with the doors shut and guarded.' I don't even need to think about it. 'We'll summon a bishop to speak with them. In the meantime, the priest should be able to tend to them.'

I consider the priest who normally conducts the services in Northampton's church. I don't know him well. I've seen him on many occasions and been assured by Bishop Wærferth that the man is loyal.

We're about to discover the truth of that. I don't bloody like this.

Not at all.

* * *

We open the secret tunnel, allowing entry from the east. Ealdorman Ælhun's warriors stand there, armed, Wulfsige glowering at them to ensure they don't let down their guard. My warriors are also present and alert. I've sent word for the priest to attend upon me. He arrives in a flutter of robes, his face white, as he hears the creak of the huge door opening that seals the outer tunnel facing onto the plain where Jarl Halfdan and his men are waiting to attack us. There's some light from the five cookfires, but not much. There are brands within Northampton, but in the flickering light, it's hard to truly see everything.

'My lord king.' I sense the priest's scrutiny as his eyes flash from the open gateway to me.

'We're welcoming converts into Northampton.' He nods, eyes wild, and I hear him swallowing his horror. He's tall and thin. A gust of wind would send him sprawling to the ground. But he has a kindly, long face, his nose thin and narrow like the rest of him. His lips appear almost bloodless, while his twisting fingers seem overly large in the flare from the brands lighting the entranceway which is so rarely used.

He looks from me to the armed warriors, his forehead wrinkled in confusion.

'Viking raider converts.' He stumbles backwards. I almost think he'll fall, but quickly recovers his composure.

'From Jarl Halfdan?' he asks in a horrified whisper.

'No, from the ruins of Grantabridge, or so they say. They wish to follow in Jarl Guthrum's footsteps and seek the word of our God.'

'My lord king,' his gasp is part outrage and genuine shock, his wide eyes trying to take everything in, the whites visible in the gloom.

'They're threatened, or so they say, by Jarl Halfdan. There's no choice. I know that. You know that. But I don't bloody trust them.' I lower my voice. 'They'll be taken to the church. You'll tend to them with the aid of some of mine and Ealdorman Ælhun's warriors. They're to be kept inside or under guard, and we watch them. We watch them carefully and determine who amongst them are traitors. I'll summon the bishop, maybe even Wærferth, for a new bishop for London has yet to be found. You won't be alone with them, but you'll be the only one who can instruct them in the teachings of your faith.' I could say many things about his God and my disregard for him, but now isn't the time. If there's a God, and many would have me believe there is, then I think he's a bastard. He allowed my brother and my friend to die. I can't say that he's a generous soul.

'I,' the priest stutters. I try to remember his name. And shake my head.

'What's your name?' I question quickly.

'Wilfred, my lord king.' I nod in recollection. I do remember now.

'My aunt speaks highly of you,' I offer, in what I hope is a reassuring tone. 'And Bishop Wærferth. He'd told me you're reliable and fervent.'

'My thanks, my lord king. I didn't know Lady Cyneswith spoke so well of me.' A glimmer of pride touches his pale cheeks in the dancing flames of a passing brand. But it's quickly banished as the soft murmur of scared Norse voices permeates the interior of Northampton, echoing through the tunnel and emerging before us.

'If you need anything, ask one of my warriors. They'll get word to me straight away. I've asked for food and drink to be provided and spare blankets as well. It'll be crowded in the church, but it's that or the hall, and we all know the hall has too many easily accessible hiding places within it.' I'm thinking of where the bastards kept Werburg captive.

'I'll do my best, my lord king. Will you attend Mass in the morning?' I wrinkle my nose at the request but nod along. I'm sure I was only in the bloody church yesterday, but I must show willingness.

'I will, yes,' I reassure, although there are any number of tasks I could be performing that are more enjoyable than that.

The hum of conversation grows. I don't miss that Icel and Hereman stand close to me, fully garbed as warriors, their expressions menacing. Rudolf's there as well. While Wærwulf walks amongst the converts, offering a soft word here and there. I'm curious to see what he'll have discovered when we get a chance to talk once more.

With a resounding thud, the doorway blocking the tunnel closes once more. Ealdorman Ælhun orders his men into position to ensure it's well guarded. The enemy might have seen where the entrance is, but there is no way through it for them. That's only possible from within Northampton.

I eye those before me. I find it hard to believe that any of this collection of frightened men, women and children are here to kill me, but I know how to trick my enemy. I've done so before. I clear my throat and begin to speak.

'Welcome to Northampton,' I pause then, unsure what else to say. 'This is Priest Wilfrid. You will go with him to the church and spend the night there. We'll provide food and drink. He'll help you decide if you wish to convert to our faith in the morning. And if you do, he'll offer instruction as to how to do so.' I can hear Wærwulf speaking my words in Danish. I hope they understand them. Clearly, the spokesperson could speak my tongue, but how many more of them can, I'm unsure.

'Anyone who's found to mean Mercia ill will be sent back to Jarl Halfdan, and not necessarily alive or in one piece.' That news is greeted with a great shudder of indrawn breath. I wince at the harshness of it all, but it's necessary. I can't have men and women within Northampton who mean me harm.

'Now, go with the priest and my warriors. They'll keep you safe.'

A few nod heads. Others don't even raise them. Most look exhausted and downcast. I don't miss the collection of random animals they've brought with them. If this is a deception orchestrated by Jarl Halfdan, he's gone to a great deal of effort and thought long and hard about how to make it appear genuine.

'Rudolf, summon the stable hands. See if you can corral the sheep and goats into the stable. And the ox. We'll find them somewhere to graze tomorrow.'

Rudolf's eyes blaze with fury at such a menial task, but then a hen lurches towards him, screeching loudly, and he runs away for fear of being pecked. I watch him go with a wry smile as more of the animals shriek or baa, looking as confused and tired as the people who've brought them here.

Our exiles stream past me, Hereman and Icel never blinking, watching everything with resolve. These people know who I am. They incline their heads respectfully as they clutch small hands and encourage their children. I feel like a complete bastard when they have all gone to the church. And yet, the inhabitants of Northampton who watch the procession are sullen and mistrustful.

'Leave them be,' I order, lifting my voice. 'We'll determine the truth of their request tomorrow and over the coming days. Stay alert, but remember, our true enemy is camping outside Northampton. These people wish only to follow their leader in converting to our faith.'

'Horse shit,' a voice calls, encouraging the complaints of others. I sense Icel shift, his attention now on the Mercians, not the Norse.

'I didn't say I trusted them,' I hiss under my breath, but I can't say that to these people who've endured so much at the hands of our bloody enemy.

'Perhaps it is,' I admit. 'Perhaps it isn't. But we're good people. And we want to encourage the Viking raiders to live peacefully with us. This might be a way of accomplishing that. Or it might not be. For now, stay alert and keep your wits about you. If you suspect anything, seek out one of my men or one of Ealdorman Ælhun's. No one is to fight these people, not unless I order it. Is that understood?' My words echo with almost as much menace as I employed against the Norse converts. The Mercians are not happy about it. Fuck. I'm unhappy about it. But for now, this is what we must do. I can almost hear Jarl Halfdan's delighted laughter from here.

Chapter Fourteen

M ass the following morning is tedious, not helped by my lack of sleep and the press of too many people inside the small church.

There are thirty-four Norse Christians, comprising eleven small children, ten husbands and wives, and three elderly relatives. After contending with the goats, sheep, ox and hens last night, Rudolf spent the rest of the time riffling through their possessions and informed me of what he found.

'Unless they're all good with their fists and feet, I doubt many of them are warriors,' he offered, eating hungrily, having missed most of his meal because of his investigations.

'They're all scared but fervent,' Gardulf added. 'As soon as they entered the church, they took to their knees, sobbing and wailing. Poor Wilfrid didn't know what to do, so he got to his knees and began to pray. That soon had them quieting down. Bloody fools.'

I confess to sharing Gardulf's thoughts on the matter. I'm not sure I'd give up everything just to pray to someone different. It's not as though I ever get a bloody response.

Now, listening to Wilfrid, assisted by two youngsters I've not really noticed before but who must also be learning to preach as he does, I find myself eyeing these men and women.

The children are mostly small. I can't see even one who's older than ten winters. I'm sure they mean no harm. Their eyes are wide as they take in the church and the few pieces of gold and silver on display. Northampton's church isn't wealthy. I should probably ensure it has some better vestments and silver candlesticks. That sounds like the sort of thing my aunt can arrange. I assume the ones displayed when Jarl Guthrum underwent baptism have been returned to Worcester alongside Bishop Wærferth.

The men and women are different to the children. Some weep and clasp their hands together in prayer throughout the service. But not all of them. At least three men seem distracted, their eyes taking in everything they see. They don't appear to know what 'Amen' means. I suspect them already. The three oldsters. Well, I can see why they might wish to die as a Christian and not a pagan. It's better to go to Heaven than be excluded from Valhalla because they won't die in battle holding their weapons. Not unless we end up with a fight in Northampton.

Throughout the night, the guards have reported nothing from Jarl Halfdan's camp. It was moonlit, and it was possible to see much. None of Jarl Halfdan's warriors came to explore the secret entrance-way. If this was all a ruse, I've yet to determine how it will play out. Unless, of course, they mean to fire the settlement. In that regard, my warriors have filled every bucket with water since before daybreak. I won't allow Northampton to burn. Water surrounds the settlement. But, it'll just be my luck now that it'll bloody rain again and make it all irrelevant.

'He's a shifty bastard,' Pybba nudges me and directs his chin towards one of the three men I've already noted.

'And him,' I murmur. Pybba nods in agreement.

I'm sure Icel will tell me what he thinks of all this soon enough. He's been surprisingly quiet. That's not a good sign.

Priest Wilfrid speaks clearly, even though his words are in Latin.

I don't understand them. I doubt our guests comprehend them, either. Yet, they listen attentively. I wish my aunt were here. She'd know what to do with these people. In the cold light of day, I realise I can't keep them locked up in the church. Perhaps I should send them to Worcester and Bishop Wærferth. He'd be able to help them.

'She's shifty as well,' Pybba draws my attention to a tall woman beside a short man. Just from their height, they seem poorly matched. Perhaps she's the one leading this. Maybe she's the warrior here. Does Jarl Halfdan have sisters? I know Jarl Guthrum had at least one, but she's dead now. I wish I knew if there were others.

'A strange couple,' I smirk. It shouldn't be, but it is. No doubt the man's a fine warrior. Perhaps the woman is also. The fact their heights are so different makes no difference at all. But I note it as incongruous. Others will do the same.

Eventually, the ceremony comes to an end. Priest Wilfred has done well. I've sent an early morning messenger to Bishop Wærferth, but it'll be days until I hear back from him. What then am I supposed to do with these people in the meantime?

They turn, murmuring, one to another, when they realise Wilfred will say no more. Some still have tears in their eyes, but not all of them. They incline their head towards me. That only makes Icel tense. His hand doesn't rest on his seax, but I imagine he can have it to hand in the time it takes my heart to beat. And if not him, then Hereman and Gardulf.

'My lord king,' Priest Wilfrid appears before me, a smile on his long face that makes him look horse-like. 'They listened attentively. Some are already determined on baptism. A few have questions. I believe within a week they'll all be fervent Christians.'

I nod. Of course, that's all he worries about.

'With the assistance of Wærwulf, some of them have asked if they can help within the settlement. They're not all bloodthirsty warriors. A few possess other skills. A baker. A fisherman. Even a woman who can melt down silver and recast the shapes into something more pleasing to the Norse.'

I nod and turn to Wærwulf, who's joined us. His task was easy: to speak to those who came through the wall and determine who they were before they decided to become Christian. We'll amalgamate what they say with what they brought with them. It's still liable to be wrong, but it'll give us some idea.

'I'll let you educate your people. Some of the warriors will remain with you and them to ensure you're not threatened.'

'My lord king,' he holds his hands up, horrified by the idea that people who wish to be Christians might think of wounding him. Has he forgotten how many years the Welsh and Mercia have been at war with one another, and the Welsh were Christian long before Mercia was if I was taught the truth?

'We must be wary,' I caution him. Not that I truly doubt all of the Norse. Many of them are probably earnest. But not bloody all of them. 'They'll be allowed outside and to access the wider settlement, but there'll be guards to prevent them from leaving and causing any problems. None of them will have access to the ramparts.' I've already discussed this with my warriors and those important people within Northampton who've been beating down my door to complain about last night's events. 'Don't encourage them to do anything out of the ordinary. I don't want the baker or fisherman anywhere near the food. I don't want the blacksmith anywhere near the weapons, either. We can be welcoming but wary.' I instruct Priest Wilfrid, who looks like he wants to argue with me.

'If there are problems, you can escort them to the encampment again and continue their conversion with Jarl Halfdan watching on.' The words are cruel. Intentionally so. I wouldn't truly do it, but Wilfrid must realise I mean what I say.

He nods, arguments dying on his lips as he bows and turns back towards his new flock. He's in an unenviable position, but so am I.

I leave then, but not before crossing myself and bowing low, as I should. If these Norse are to become my subjects because of their faith, I should show myself to be respectful, even if the church is filled with people making it their home for the foreseeable future.

Outside, I go back to the ramparts, glaring down at Jarl Halfdan, while Wærwulf and Rudolf murmur to one another. I don't listen to their words. I need only hear their conclusions, not their ruminations. I fucking hate this. I feel like spiders crawl down my back, their touch light and gentle but menacing. I know that spiders mean me no harm if I mean them no harm, but they make me itch all the same. In the woodlands, or even between two buildings in the morning, their webs can snare me easily, and I must fight free. The same applies here.

I thought I was in a position of strength, albeit unwillingly in one. I believed Mercia had time to rebuild and protect itself, but so far, I've done little but wait and see what will happen next. This wasn't what I bloody intended. Not at all.

Chapter Fifteen

'I suspect six of them. Rudolf and I agree on that,' Wærwulf draws me into their conversation. I step back from the ramparts, from where I'm observing Jarl Halfdan's encampment, and allow Sæbald, Beornstan and Ælfgar to resume their watchful gaze. People are on the move but only doing the usual thing. Waking, pissing, feeding themselves and their animals.

'Six of them, is that all?'

'Yes, six of them came with some sort of weaponry other than an eating knife and who couldn't adequately account for what they did in Grantabridge. Most of them are merely camp followers; some might have been warriors once, but not the women or children. Apart from one.'

'Were they in Grantabridge at Easter?' I'm curious to know their experience of my warriors and me. If they were then they would have watched us kill and then eject many of their number. Obviously not all of them. We couldn't hold it. My warriors were needed in Mercia.

'Yes.'

I absorb that and continue my questioning. 'Is it the tall woman?' I want to show I've been paying attention.

'Yes. She has two seaxes with her, as Rudolf found. She told me her position was clothesmaker, but her hands lack discolouring, and she has no marks on her skin to show where she's skewered herself with a needle. If that's truly her profession, I'd expect her hands to show signs of staining from some of the darker dyes. She also has callouses on her hands, no doubt from holding those seaxes. That's not what I expect from a clothesmaker. She should have hands softened by the time they spend handling soft cloth and furs.'

'What's her name?'

'She called herself Begga,' Wærwulf informs me. 'The man she's with is called Ake, and he's also one of the suspected warriors.'

I consider the man. He's short and squat but broad-shouldered, with long, twisting hair down his back. I can't say I noticed the front of him.

'And the others?'

'Their names are Pedr, Leif, Mundi and Bragi. They were standing close to Ake. You might have observed them. It's a collection of men of all shapes and sizes, although Rudolf suspects some of them hide their true physique behind oversized tunics. He found a lot of huge tunics in their baggage.'

'They all had weapons?'

'All of them had some sort of weapon, from a cutting knife to a war axe, but those six had what I'm going to call 'proper' weapons in their baggage or on their person,' Rudolf offers. I consider that. Five men and one woman shouldn't overpower us, but if they're devious and move around at night, they could do much damage to Northampton. They know the way inside now. They could potentially open the tunnel for Jarl Halfdan. Not that it would be easy. It's always guarded. More fiercely than the main entrance from the River Nene side of the settlement, if I'm honest.

'We keep a close bloody eye on them. Ensure everyone knows their description.' Only then, because I'm a distrustful bastard, just as the Viking raiders are, I go further. 'Keep an eye on all of them. These six could be the decoys while the others are working against us and for the good of Jarl Halfdan. Did any of them speak of missing sons and daughters or parents?'

Wærwulf shakes his head but then stops, a puzzled expression on his face.

'One man and woman were mourning a lost child, but I don't think that's important unless their child was an adult or if that child isn't dead but held in captivity by Jarl Halfdan.' I consider that. I'm pleased my warriors are thinking carefully. We've been placed in an awkward position, which I'm not enjoying. We can't accept these new Christians are truly who they say they are.

'My lord,' Pybba calls to me, beckoning me back towards the front of the rampart where Sæbald's also standing.

'What is it?' I question, but he doesn't need to reply. I can see well enough.

'My lord king.' Jarl Halfdan has returned. He sits upon a fine black steed, and behind him stand his men in their warrior garb. 'How are the Christians?' he calls, his voice loud and filled with loathing and mocking, only for the man next to him to shout the words in our tongue, for those who can't understand Danish, 'I take it they have made themselves comfortable amongst your people?'

I try to detect the truth behind his words. He means to cast them as traitors, but I'd do the same if the situation were reversed. It doesn't mean they are. His language is a barrier, one I wish I could over-power, but I can only detect some of the words. It's another cloak he wears to obscure the truth from me.

'They're welcomed into our faith,' I reply, wishing I'd thought of something better to say. Jarl Halfdan laughs at the translation, turning to his fellow warriors to ensure they join him in being amused by my words. I can't pretend not to be me here. Jarl Halfdan and I have met too many bloody times before.

'I imagine they are, yes, you Christians are always happy to take converts. You think you steal them from our God, but our Gods are more than happy to give you the weak fools. They've had their fun with them. But, to more important matters. When will Jarl Guthrum be released from his captivity? I have been patient. I won't always be.' For this long speech, I incline my head to Wærwulf, who tells me all the jarl says, even though I've gathered the intent behind the words.

'Jarl Guthrum's my hostage. He'll not be released until the year is at an end.' I realise that Wærwulf's shouting my words to the men outside Northampton, just as Halfdan's man is. I consider if the two use the same words to explain what I'm saying. I'll have to ask Wærwulf about that.

A flicker of fury touches Jarl Halfdan's cheeks, illuminating his scar in the bright daylight. He knows much of our language. I should make the effort to have Wærwulf teach me all of Halfdan's. I know some words. Not the kindest words, admittedly. I should know more than how to name the bastards as bastards. It's not as if many of them are truly so different. I know Bishop Wærferth has spoken to me of this in the past. I confess it wasn't the most intriguing of conversations. He assures me that the Latin of the church makes it easy to understand the languages spoken in West Frankia and beyond. But it's different with the Danish language. It's not always the same. That intrigues him. It doesn't me.

'Then we will attack Northampton and take him back.' With that Jarl Halfdan turns, giving no indication of when the attack will come. I watch his wide back as the horse beneath him sways. He's learned how to ride well. He's become as Mercian as I am. Damn the bastard.

'Tell your new Christian friends that they will be the first to die, after you, of course, King Coelwulf,' he calls over his shoulder. With a clatter of weaponry, the warriors move to follow their leader back to the encampment.

'Eighty-seven warriors,' Rudolf announces quickly. 'Eighty-eight if Halfdan's going to fight.' That's not the two hundred we initially thought they had. I consider where the others have bloody gone?

We'll outnumber them easily if I summon more warriors to Northampton. If I can't, then we hold the walls. How do they expect to gain entry, if not through the tunnel? Should I double the guard over the Norse Christians? Shit. I wish Edmund stood at my side. I wish my aunt were here as well.

I watch Jarl Halfdan until he disappears amongst the lines of tents. Even now, only five fires burn. There are still not that many horses. When Halfdan moves out of sight, I turn and summon Icel, Wærwulf and Rudolf to my side.

'Wærwulf, stay with our new arrivals. But first, the man with Jarl Halfdan, does he translate my words as you would?' Wærwulf considers this. It's obvious he's not thought of it before.

'Just about, my lord. A few words are a little different. I suspected, until now, that it was a dialect I didn't know. But, well, perhaps there's more malice to him.'

'It doesn't surprise me,' I admit. 'Be alert to it.' Wærwulf bites his lip in thought, but I've not finished with my instructions yet.

'Rudolf, go into the woodlands and find Ingwald, Lyfing, and Leonath. I need to know everything they've seen. Icel, check the guards watching our new arrivals have all they need, as well as those on gate duty. Double-check everything with your eagle eyes. Ensure there are no weaknesses that can be exploited for the Viking raiders to get inside Northampton or the Christians to escape from here, leaving the door wide open.'

All three incline their heads and hasten away. I turn to Pybba. He looks as uneasy as I'm feeling.

'Fucking bastard,' I growl. He smirks and nods.

'Aye, we need to kill him,' Pybba agrees.

'We bloody do, yes.'

I think of my warriors in the woodlands, my aunt chasing down the truth of what happened in Northumbria, and King Alfred. Alfred would do fuck all to help. I'm not sure what my aunt can do, but my warriors? I hope they have something important to tell me, and if not, well, it's about time I left the comfort of Northampton and found a few Viking raiders to kill.

* * *

I'm armoured and ready for whatever happens next. Only, now his intentions have been shouted, Jarl Halfdan makes no immediate move to fulfil his threats. It doesn't surprise me. He believes the act of anticipation will be our undoing. Fucking cock.

'The walls are firm. The guards have all they need. They know what to do.' Icel's rumble is almost reassuring. 'Wærwulf has no worries with any of the Norse other than those he's already indicated.' I nod. I didn't ask Icel to check on Wærwulf. I'm grateful he has.

Rudolf's barely gone, and already, I want him to return. I eye the Viking raider encampment. There's still something about it that isn't right. It's not what they did to the Norse Christians. It's something else.

'Have the horses been prepared?'

'For what?' Icel questions. I realise I've been thinking my intentions and not speaking them aloud.

'We wait for Rudolf to return, but I want to leave Northampton from the west, swim the river and ride toward the fuckers.'

'Why would you leave Northampton?'

'We'll face them and kill them.'

'Why? They can't get inside. They can't get across the River Nene without us knowing about it. Here, my lord, we're protected.'

'I don't want to be fucking protected. I want them to be dead.'

Icel's silence is telling.

'What?'

His face is lined and old, but in the quirk of an eyebrow, he looks half his age, younger than me.

'In the reign of King Berhtwulf, I knew a man as foolhardy as you, my lord king. It didn't end well for him.' The caution has me grumbling.

'What the fuck happened to him?'

'Well, he didn't die, I confess, but it didn't end well, all the same.'

'So it didn't end well, but he didn't die. What the fuck happened to him then?'

'You'd have to ask him,' Icel counters. I'm about to snap back a reply when I pause and look at him.

'Tell me, what happened to you that was so terrible.'

A flash of respect touches Icel's lips, but he shakes his head.

'If I told you, you wouldn't believe me.'

'You can't say that,' I glower. 'You can't caution me against being fucking foolish and then not tell me what happened when you were foolish.'

'I was never a king,' Icel retorts.

'What does being a king have to do with being a foolish man?' This seems to perplex him. I can see him trying to decipher what I'm saying and how he's caught himself with another of his riddles.

'What did you do that was so bloody foolish?' I capitulate.

'I. Well. I mean. Well I took on an enemy that seemed ineffectual but wasn't.'

'And you lost?'

'You could say that, yes. I lost something I held to be valuable.'

'You're still talking in bloody riddles. You should have cautioned me to be patient, rather than tying us both up in bloody knots.'

'It wasn't my finest word of caution, I admit that.' Icel announces decisively.

'I wish you said what you thought. I don't need all these words of doom and gloom with no real bloody substance.'

'Then don't ask me for sodding advice,' he retorts. He doesn't sound angry.

'I didn't ask you for bloody advice,' I splutter. I might not have done so, but his calm words have worked on me. I no longer feel the urge to ride into Jarl Halfdan's encampment. Not yet, anyway.

'I'll wait for Rudolf to return. Unless Halfdan does something.'

'Jarl Halfdan can do nothing. He's a bag of bloody wind. That's all.' Icel stalks from my presence. I watch him with an amused twist of my lips. He's a funny fish. I can't deny that. Still, the time I thought him dead was miserable. I'm grateful he came back to me. I wish Edmund could do the bloody same.

I consider Icel's parting shot. What can Jarl Halfdan do? He's on the other side of Northampton's defences. He's scared his Christians inside, but even if they all turn on us, we have the fighting power to overwhelm them, and we're not exactly welcoming. We have eyes on them all.

So, what is he up to? King Alfred of Wessex wishes to ally with Mercia, not the Viking raiders. Jarl Guthrum is in Worcester, and as far as I know, Halfdan doesn't know that. So, why has he brought these warriors here and set up an encampment? And not even a proper encampment. We can all see it doesn't contain enough warriors and horses, as the number of tents implies.

Does he mean to distract me and keep me in Northampton? If he is, what's happening elsewhere? Where are Anwend and Oscetel these days?

Is Jarl Halfdan doing something in Northumbria? That wouldn't affect me. Does he mean to attack London? That would affect me, but would he have enough men to pretend to stake out Northampton and take London? Is he just trying his bloody luck? Does he have nothing else to offer?

I wish I knew more about how the Repton jarls captured Repton. I've never really bloody asked. I blamed King Burgred for being weak and ineffectual. I still would if he appeared before me. Could that be it? Has Jarl Halfdan invited King Burgred back to Mercia? Rumour has it he's in Rome, enjoying himself in the English quarter where men and women bow and scrape before him as though he were still the bloody king of Mercia.

Or is this something else?

Considering King Burgred makes me recall something. It's about kings still living while others are king. Is there some Christian rule against that? I consider calling for Priest Wilfrid, but I don't. I could ask Icel, but he's left my side. Pybba has since replaced him.

'Pybba,' I ask. 'Tell me. If King Burgred still lives, does that mean I'm not really Mercia's king?' If my question surprises him, it's not apparent from his reaction.

'As King Burgred abdicated, it wouldn't matter.'

'Even if it was under duress?'

'All abdications happen under duress, as I understand it. Although, no, I'm wrong. If I remember correctly, some people just give up the kingship and become monks.' I grimace at that, while he smirks. I don't want to be bloody king, but if the alternative is to become a monk, I certainly don't want that.

'No one would take King Burgred back, especially if he came with a party of Viking raiders to enforce his right to rule. I don't think you need to fear a return from King Burgred. He's gone. He'll never come back.'

I find that comforting, but I'm still perplexed by Jarl Halfdan's intentions. Why has he left Northumbria? Why is he here now? I wish I knew.

The day drags. I want Rudolf to get back quickly, but he doesn't. Indeed, not until darkness falls does he rumble over the bridge, his horse stepping jauntily beneath him. Wherever he's been, Dever hasn't been sorely tested. That animal seems to be getting younger, not older. Dever confounds me.

'My lord,' he grins on seeing me rushing to meet him. 'Patient as ever,' he mocks while I growl.

'Bloody tell me.'

'I will, but not here. Let's go somewhere that our words won't be overheard.' I realise in my impatience that I've forgotten the Christian Norse amongst us. I've had no further reports of concerns. I'm anticipating them, though.

I trail Rudolf to the bridge. The guards watch us in surprise, keen to secure the door for the night. Icel and Pybba join me.

'Well, bloody get on with it,' Icel's temper is as short as mine.

'Ingwald's well,' Rudolf says meaningfully. 'Lyfing has hurt his hand but is hale. Leonath has been badly stung by some wasps. Thank you for asking.'

I take the chastisement with a grimace. Icel inclines his head by way of an apology while Pybba smirks. He's been teaching Rudolf all the tricks that make me question my right to lead these brave warriors of Mercia.

'And the Viking raiders?'

'I doubt they're Viking raiders, from what they've seen. Yes, Jarl Halfdan might be there, but the majority aren't warriors. Admittedly, they've been garbed as though they are, but they've seen no one training or fighting. Neither have the bastards been pissed as farts every night. Whoever is with Jarl Halfdan, they're not Viking raider warriors.'

'Then why is he here? And threatening us?'

'Now, they do have a theory about that.'

'Bloody get on with it, Rudolf,' Icel has lost all pretence of an apology for being so abrupt.

'They've been able to get close enough to hear some of their conversations, and they were often spoken in our tongue. Just as with us, Jarl Halfdan believes the river protects from being overheard.'

This is like pulling bloody teeth. Rudolf flashes a smile, enjoying himself too much. I've half a mind to cuff him over the ear.

'Your men think Jarl Halfdan knows where Guthrum is. They're planning to rescue him from Worcester. Keeping you here is part of that.'

'Why didn't they tell me before now?' Already, I'm considering that I should be sending my warriors to protect Bishop Wærferth and the eastern part of Mercia. I can't allow Jarl Guthrum to be taken from me.

'I'm telling you. They only just learned this yesterday. It was good timing that I went to find them.'

'Will they ride through Mercia to get to Worcester,' but Rudolf's shaking his head.

'No, the task falls to Jarls Anwend and Oscetel. They're not in Grantabridge. They're to descend upon Worcester using their damn ships.'

'Shit,' Icel speaks for all of us. Rudolf's nodding, but there's a gleam in his eye.

'We need to take advantage of this. Ingwald's adamant. Jarl Halfdan's so busy toying with you that he's not watching his rear at all. We can cross the river and attack them. Sandwich them between our warriors and Northampton.'

'But Worcester?'

'Bishop Wærferth has his own warriors. We know Kyred knows how to fight well. He's not a fool. The town has its walls, as well. This is the opportunity to finish Jarl Halfdan once and for all.' Rudolf's words are passionate. I feel myself swept up in them, even as unease settles on Icel's old and lined face. He doesn't like the suggestion. I didn't, but it's growing on me.

'It'll take them time to get to Worcester?' I question. 'They'll also have to navigate the River Severn, and we all know she's a bitch.'

'Yes,' Pybba agrees, the word elongated. I can imagine what he's thinking. The last thing we need is for the Viking raiders to ally with the bloody Welsh. But they have to get there first.

'I don't bloody like it,' Icel grunts. 'It's too dangerous. Why should we risk it all to kill Jarl Halfdan when we already have Guthrum, provided we can hold on to him?'

'Jarl Halfdan's brother started all this,' Pybba counters quickly. 'If not for fucking Ivarr, we wouldn't be in this situation. Killing Halfdan would be a way of countering the continual threat from him. He's an arrogant bastard who thinks he's invincible.'

'What of your aunt?' Icel turns on me.

'What of her?'

'She's out there, heading north.'

'So she's nowhere near Worcester, or Northampton.'

'She's been a captive once.'

'And she won't be one again. We need not worry about my aunt. I think she's proved how well she can look after herself, and those with her, will not allow her to be captured or harmed. Gyrth, Hemming, Ordlaf and Wulfstan aren't fools.'

Icel's lips thin. I know he's unhappy with the suggestion, but I think it's a good one. It has the advantage of allowing me to leave

Northampton. I'm not enjoying the cloying sensation of being trapped. It'll also enable me to get away from the Norse who wish to be Christian. Not that I can leave Northampton unprotected.

'Ealdorman Ælhun can hold Northampton,' I decide. 'We'll send word to Worcester as well. We've already sent a message about the converts. We might be lucky and our messenger will meet the bishop coming back this way. I'll send Ælfgar and Eadfrith. It'll get them out of the fight here.' I nod, happy with my decisions. But Icel's not finished bitching yet.

'Your aunt has only four warriors with her.'

'Are you saying my men aren't up to the task of protecting her?'

'No, that's not what I'm bloody saying. I believe you need to be careful with her. She's still suffering after the death of Edmund. She might be rash if an enemy is encountered.'

I can't help myself. I chuckle at that.

'She might be rash, Icel. Do you know my aunt? Do you know me? Did you know my brother?'

'I did, my lord king, yes, and I do, my lord king yes. Why the fuck do you think I offer caution.' This brings me up short. Icel does know me and my aunt. Very well indeed.

'She won't fight them?' I rebuff, although my voice is far from certain.

'Only if she realises there's fighting taking place. If she comes this way and doesn't know what you have planned, she might do anything.'

'Bollocks.' Now I glower.

'Then we'll send someone north as well.'

'Who?'

I hold his gaze. I know he's old. I know he's tired. I realise he perhaps has no desire to face Jarl Halfdan again.

'You,' I announce before thinking myself out of it. 'You'll find my aunt and keep her safe while we deal with Jarl Halfdan.'

Icel subsides, then. I wish he'd just told me he had no heart for another fight. I wouldn't have forced him. He should know that.

'At daybreak, we'll leave Northampton. Ealdorman Ælhun will hold the settlement. Ælfgar and Eadfrith will ride to Worcester, and Icel will find my aunt and ensure she doesn't do anything stupid.'

Icel nods unhappily. Rudolf, damn the bastard, hasn't finished yet.

'And who'll stop you from doing something bloody stupid?' The question remains unanswered as we stroll back to the gates, hearing them close behind us with a resounding crash after we've entered, much to the relief of the uneasy guards on duty.

I'll be pleased to escape the bloody confines of Northampton in the morning.

Chapter Sixteen

'Hello boy,' I greet Haden. He kicks the wooden wall of the stall and eyes me with a fiery expression.

'Hello to you as well,' I mimic, reaching over the closed half door to run my hand along his nose. He doesn't jerk his head from my touch, which is a good sign he might not actually be in such a foul mood. 'We're leaving,' I speak to him, moving inside the stall now, reaching for his saddle and reins. I'm pleased to see they gleam. Undoubtedly, Hiltiberht has been cleaning them because Rudolf ordered it. He's a mouthy git sometimes. I'm grateful all the same.

I eye the reins. They're not notable for being comprised of priceless gems or delicate goldwork. They're the same ones I've had ever since Haden was his current size, long before I was king. Some would think to embellish them with rubies or garnets. I don't want people to think Haden's equipment is more valuable than he is. I also don't want to draw attention to myself. If my horse's harnesses marked me as a king, then every bastard Viking raider would know to try and kill me. Then, none of my attempts at misdirection would work. No, I'm content with them.

Murmuring to Haden, I slip the saddle over his back and work to secure it before moving to the reins. He stamps his hooves but not on my feet, for which I'm bloody grateful.

The sound of the rest of the horses being made ready can be heard in the soft shuffles and occasional outbursts of anger when horses nip their riders. I smirk. Rarely, I'm not the one doing that. I decide to enjoy it.

Ælfgar and Eadfrith left before first light, determined to be on their way as soon as possible. They know they're being let off a fight. Like Icel, they don't seem to mind. I wish my warriors weren't getting so old. I don't know what I'll do if they all decide a warm arse and a comfortable bed are preferable to sleeping under the stars with nothing but a cloak to keep the rain off.

Ealdorman Ælhun has his orders, which he agreed to unwillingly but did accept. He's to ensure the Norse Christians are kept carefully watched. I thought to leave Wærwulf behind, but he complained, and one of the Norse Christians can speak English. It's just unfortunate that we won't know all they say. But it's better to have Wærwulf with me in case we need him to translate some other Viking raider's words and taunts beyond what my men have already determined. But, it's what we know, and I must act on it. I'm tired of sitting on my arse and doing sweet fuck all.

With a sliver of lightness to the sky, we ride over the bridge that crosses the River Nene. Ealdorman Ælhun watches us leave, and I offer him a final caution.

'Keep alert. If we hear from King Alfred of Wessex, then tell him he can go fuck himself. We don't need his help.'

With a grimace on his grey-bearded face, the ealdorman chuckles.

'Go well, my lord king,' he inclines his head, and I consider what he's thinking behind his bland smile. Does he believe I'm making a mistake? Perhaps, but fuck it, I need to be doing something.

I breathe deeply of the damp air once over the bridge and take the shortest route into the woodlands. It holds many memories for me, but I dismiss them. This isn't about what happened in the past but the future.

We must banish the Viking raiders from Mercia, or at least die trying to do so. Not that I plan on dying any time soon. Edmund's death has been enough of a blow. Mine would be catastrophic. And I don't say that because I believe I'm irreplaceable. No. Mercia, without me, would suffer. I know of none who could ensure everyone behaved, considered Mercia as a unit, and were prepared to shed blood to keep her whole. The idea of finally killing Jarl Halfdan spurs me on. I thought I had the opportunity before, but he evaded me and escaped into Northumbria. Damn the fucker.

Beneath the trees, cold tendrils streak across my face and back. Spider webs shimmer in the early morning damp. I allow Haden to pick his path. Rudolf leads. He knows where to find Ingwald, Lyfing and Leonath. I listen carefully, but I can hear nothing beyond the confines of the woodland. Not even the murmur of the river is audible. We could be alone in the world. I like that thought.

I consider the past, despite my decision not to do so. Was there a time, before the Viking raiders, when Mercia's kings could enjoy such peace, or has she always been at war with one enemy of another? The Welsh have long been a pain in the arse. Northumbria has often been far from an ally. The kingdom of the East Angles was another bloody problem, and then, there's always been Wessex. Thinking itself more than it is, it's constantly wanted to be associated with Mercia. It might not have always liked it, but Wessex has often been weak and served by poor kings. Mercia hasn't often suffered that fate. Well, not until Burgred, and of course, the years of trouble following the death of King Coenwulf, my father's uncle.

The sound of hoof falls, and soft breathing fills the air. The further we delve into the woodlands, the more my shoulders relax. I should be more concerned, the threat of a fight looming, but this is what I do. Sooner this than sitting in a room listening to men and women argue and bicker about the smallest of problems. We should all be focused on defeating our bloody enemy.

The day progresses as we go deeper and deeper. The woodlands stretch a long way, I know that. But I'm beginning to worry just how far we must go when Rudolf stops ahead. Dever bends his head, keen to pick at a tendril of stray grass and then Lyfing's before me—a welcoming grin on his face.

'You need to bloody shave,' I greet. His grin widens.

'I'm becoming a woodsman. I'm going wild,' he continues. For all that, he looks hale and well fed. He might have been out here for a while, but it's doing him no harm.

'This way,' he leads on even deeper into the woodlands. I can hear the burble of the river to the east but little else. The murmur of the wind is muted beneath the stretching boughs overhead. There's some birdcall, but not much. No doubt the birds are wary of us. The small animals as well. I don't blame them for hiding away.

The campsite the three men have created is small, nestled beneath some close touching boughs so that we would have ridden past it had Lyfing not been there to find us.

'Where's Leonath and Ingwald?' I question, dismounting.

'By the river, watching the fuckers over there.'

'It stretches this far?' We've been riding for much further than I believed it would take us to reach the end of the Viking raider encampment.

'Yes, and also no. I'll show you. But be quiet when we get close to the river. Sound travels over it, despite our best attempts. The rest of you are fine here. There's still a way to go to reach the lookout.'

Removing Haden's reins and saddle, I leave him to nudge at the ground beside the other horses. Rudolf scampers at my side. Gardulf strides beside me. Hereman matches me. I can see I'm not to do this alone. Sometimes, these men forget that I can bloody look after myself. Pybba sits himself beside the fire. At least he's not coming along.

The trees grow more and more sparse as we walk. Eventually,

Lyfing urges us to the side. The river is much louder than even inside Northampton. I clamp my lips together. I'm not going to give us away.

Moving in Lyfing's path, we step from tree trunk to tree trunk, using the branches and leaves to mask the movements, and then I'm brought up short, Ingwald stood before me, blade to hand. He relaxes and smirks on seeing me.

'You always were a quiet fucker,' he whispers, urging us onwards.

I bend low, and then even lower, the unpleasant sensation of a fir tree running over my head, but now I can see the enemy. I don't step free from the tree to see how far the encampment runs, but it's a long way from here. It covers the river bank on the other side. Tents and pavilions cover the space. Some of them open, none seeming to have anyone inside them. I turn a quizzical expression to Ingwald.

He nods, sensing my confusion.

'They come at certain times of the day. It's as though they've been told to move from area to area, no doubt to make it appear that there are more of them than there are. Jarl Halfdan spends almost all his time behind the first row of tents and open pavilions. The horses are stationed behind them. We sent Leonath up a tree to get a good view. He says the encampment is long and narrow and the number of men and women small. Whatever Jarl Halfdan's up to, he means to accomplish it with as few warriors as possible.'

I nod, absorbing the information. Watching Jarl Halfdan's tents from inside Northampton is one thing. Seeing them here, the dirty canvas and dirtier lines of clothing hanging on tent ropes or drying on the ground is another. My hand slips to my seax. It's with some effort that I release my grip. Today isn't the day to start a fight. But it will be. Very soon.

To begin with, we believed he had two hundred warriors. That number dipped to eighty-seven when Rudolf last counted. Now, it appears, those eighty-seven are being put to good use, trying to make it appear as though there are more of them.

I hunker there until my back grows stiff, my legs start protesting, and only then stand. Gardulf's long since gone back to the main camp. Rudolf stays with me. Mind, his back won't hurt like mine, and likely his legs won't either. Hereman and Lyfing are deeper in the woods, talking softly to one another.

'And you heard them talking about the rescue of Jarl Guthrum?'

'There was an unholy argument,' Leonath confirms. 'Some of them spoke our language with a dialect, perhaps from Northumbria, some of them didn't. We put together what we could. Wærwulf might be able to confirm more of what we've heard. Some of it was in Danish. They don't even train those who are here. It's evident they don't intend for there to be a fight at all.'

'So, you believe they're not warriors?'

'A few might be. The rest, I'm not convinced. Those who spoke our language were outraged about Jarl Halfdan's intentions. They must have joined with their leader from Northumbria. They've been promised wealth or something more valuable than that. They're not going to get it.' He grimaces. I nod. Leonath's correct. They'll only meet their death trying to battle us.

'We've found a way across the river, as well, at a fording point. They're not being as clever as they think, stretching their encampment so far along the river bank.' He smirks. I find myself nodding along, caught up by his enthusiasm.

'What do you plan?'

'In the morning, before dawn, we cross the river at the fording point. Then we can run them down while their arses aren't even in their trews. Damn fuckers,' he announces. 'I'll kill those bastard Northumbrians first. Their bloody archbishop demanded assistance from Mercia, but some would fight for the enemy. I don't like that at all.'

'And the others are agreed with this?'

'I've had to hold them back to stop them going on their own.' His grimace tells me that was an unholy argument as well.

'Good. We'll eat, rest and end the bastards tomorrow.' I nod, happy to know I'll get to eliminate some of our enemies soon, as opposed to having to listen to them pray and exhort our God on their bloody behalf. I'll kill the Norse and any Northumbrians who think to ally with the enemy of Mercia.

Chapter Seventeen

It's barely light enough to see as we reach the fording point Leonath found. I've rested well, the shush of the leaves overhead allowing me to drift into a deep sleep that eludes me when I'm beneath thatch. I almost want to stay there, but the knowledge that today I'll work some of the tension from my body spurs me on. I've killed no one since Edmund died. I've had to play politics instead when all I wanted to do was sever Jarl Guthrum's head from his neck. I won't get to kill him today, but Jarl Halfdan is just as much a target. If I finally manage to end his life, the conniving bastard will not be fucking missed.

Ingwald and Leonath lead the way. I've refrained from asking how often they've made this journey while on guard duty beneath the sheltering trees. I'd sooner not know the risks they've been allowed to take while I've been locked up in Northampton.

Lyfing hasn't complained about his hand, but Leonath's covered in stings which make him itch and irritable. He's more desperate to kill our enemy than I am. We should have thought to bring him something to treat them. Icel might have known what to do. My aunt would certainly have had something to ease the huge, pulsing lesions that cover his back. I don't want to know how he got them. Shitting in a bush, no doubt.

Haden, of course, bucks at the thought of going through the knee-high water. He's quick enough to do so when Rudolf and Dever overtake him. He doesn't like to be beaten by the old horse. I'm not surprised, but Dever is astonishingly sprightly these days. I wonder whether Rudolf would welcome Jethson as his new mount. I know Hereman and Gardulf don't wish to ride him. But Jethson is a complete change from Dever. How the lad would take it, I don't know. Perhaps it would be better if Rudolf had Siric's horse. But a horse such as Jethson shouldn't be stewing in the stables. He should be ridden. It's another bloody problem I don't wish to consider.

The river here is wide, but shallow. Haden kicks up water in the gloaming, and I feel the cold spray soaking into my trews. My men are as ready for this coming fight as I am. Well, the younger ones are. Some of my older warriors seem less keen. No doubt they'd welcome not having to ride out this morning. But they'll do it all the same.

Petre shakes his tail on reaching the other side, dislodging water, as he slithers through the reeds and river plants, Leonath directing him. Haden hurries, surging past Dever, making Rudolf give a muffled oath in shock. I'm just grateful he wasn't tipped into the water. Rudolf's had more than enough trips into the water.

I ride to Lyfing.

'Is it always this low?' I'm concerned there's easy access into Mercia from the western side of the River Nene.

'No, it's not. It's been growing lower and lower, but as soon as there's rain, it fills up again. And, as it's rare to have a day without rain, I'm not concerned. I don't think the lazy fuckers have even thought to look. We've seen none of them so far north.'

I feel better knowing that, but a niggly concern remains. We might have to bloody do something about this. What, I'm unsure. Could we make the river deeper, or should I station warriors here to look for our enemy?

'This way,' Lyfing waits until we've all crossed in a slosh of water and sharp clips of hooves. While I've winced and growled at every noise, we've disturbed no small animals from their nightly hiding places. The sound mustn't travel as I fear it might.

'You know what we have planned?' I check with my warriors. The men nod or glower, depending on how they feel. I miss the terrified look Edmund might have given me and also the thundering growl from Icel, who would already be preparing to tell us how he overcame three hundred men singlehandedly, halfway up a hill, in a bloody blizzard and with only a stick for a weapon. I sigh softly. It feels as though something monumental has happened to my band of loyal men. Some are missing permanently. Some won't ride with me at this time. I miss all of them, even sparing a thought for my brother. What would he have made of this? I doubt he'd have been so keen to wage war on our enemy, but perhaps he would. He was no coward, even if he preferred peace to war. I should have been a bloody better brother.

I try to clear my thoughts as I follow Lyfing. Now isn't the time to be filled with sorrow and regrets. Or perhaps it is. I can use my grief and unease to overpower the bastard enemy.

We've not truly come far north of the temporary Viking raider settlement. In no time, as the first etchings of colour appear in the sky, we dismount, leaving the horses with their reins tied high and tightly, so they won't tangle their legs, and with a complaining Hiltiberht to keep an eye on them.

'If the bastards come for them, take them home,' I urge him, half an eye on Haden. If there's one horse here who won't take the instruction, it's bloody him. I slap his rump and force his long nose to meet my eyes.

'Do as you're bloody told,' I instruct. A wiffle of hot breath assures me he thinks poorly of such an idea.

I turn aside, all misgivings cast aside. Thoughts of my brother and Edmund dismissed, for now. I'll seek revenge for Edmund's death, and then, one day, I'll hunt down the bastards that killed my brother as well. Fuck 'em all.

'This way,' I whisper meeting the gazes of my warriors. Rudolf's keen. Pybba less so. Lyfing and Leonath both grimace, the thought of finally killing these bastards a balm for their souls. Others don't meet my eyes. I nod at them. I'd say their names one more time, just to hear them, but in my mind, I hear the words of the scop song instead, which tells me of men lost in other battles.

"A man of the Hwicce,
He gulped mead at midnight feasts.
Slew Raiders, night and day.
Brave Athelstan, long will his valour endure."

"Beornberht, son of the Magonsæte.
A proud man, a wise man, a strong man.
He fought and pierced with spears.
Above the blood, he slew with swords."

"A man fought for Mercia.
Against Raiders and foes.
Shield flashing red,
Brave Oslac, slew Raiders each seven-day."

"Hereberht was at the forefront, brave in battle.
He stained his spear, and splashed with blood
A thousand and more before Halfdan's men
His bravery cut short his life."

"A friend I have lost, faithful he was,
After joy, there was silence

Red his sword, let it never be cleansed
A friend I have lost, brave Eoppa."

'*A blood bath and certain death for his foes*
Brave Siric's bravery will endure forever
Although he was slain, he slew
And he will be eternally honoured.'

'*Swift in the struggle*
It grieves me to leave brave Eadberht
He was foremost in battle
The enemy feared him, and in turn, he shamed them.'

"*Sturdy and strong, it would be wrong not to praise them.*
Amid blood-red blades, in black sockets.
The war-hounds fought fiercely, tight formation.
Of the war band of Coelwulf, I would think it a burden,
To leave any in the shape of man alive."

'*Bitter in battle, with blades set for war*
Attacking in an army, cruel in battle
He slew with swords, without much sound
Edmund pillar of battle, took pleasure in giving death.'

I imagine I'm not alone in hearing the rumbled words of Icel, when he turned that scop song composed by Edmund upon him. Or of hearing Rudolf's voice as he recounted the beginning of the scop song. If men should die here today, who'll sing of them? Rudolf? I don't know if he'll have the heart to do so.

'Don't fucking die,' I instruct, my throat tight. This time, looks of understanding meet mine. I said this to Edmund, and my rage that he didn't heed me burns brightly. My men are ready, and so am I. Their nods are more convincing this time.

Lyfing skips onwards, the lines of tents and pavilions opening to us. Not that we run through them. We're not fucking idiots.

Lyfing and Leonath bend low, slitting canvas; a sharp shriek in the silence, grunts and thuds greet the action, but I'm moving to the next tent. My warriors are paired up. I have Wærwulf at my side. He's not the same as Edmund, far from it. His resolve is fixed. I'm grateful he offered to take this role. The others all looked fucking terrified when I asked them to fight beside one of their allies. No one wanted me as a partner.

A wave of precision follows. One by one, my warriors slit each canvas, forcing the fabric aside, to stab those inside without thought. Whoever these men are, they must all die. Today.

Wærwulf and I have the furthest to go—a position I chose. Hunched, we bend low, but my eyes are everywhere, and not just on where my feet should be placed. They're on level ground, but the river at our back is a threat. We could trip and fall. The guide ropes are a fucking mess. I'm ready to be discovered, for someone to be awake beneath the canvas, but there's no response. Not even a frantically stifled cry. Pybba and Rudolf duck into the canvas next to the one that belongs to Wærwulf and me, and still we're succeeding. Lyfing and Leonath have moved to the next row along.

The enemy is strung out, as my scouts assured me. Damn fools.

I bend and slip my seax through the fabric, muscles tense. The material gives far too easily. I step inside despite Wærwulf's huff of frustration. He wants to get there first. He should have known that was never going to bloody happen.

The air's rife with the smell of pork-flavoured farts and bad breath. Wærwulf also enters, his movements furtive in the darkness beneath the canvas. It's becoming light outside, but those inside are still slumbering. I reach out, feel nothing, take a step and kick the fucking bedpost instead.

An ouff of pain escapes my mouth. A figure jerks upright before me, a cry on his lips.

'Fuck it.' It's always me that gives us away.

Wærwulf's ready, his blade slicing into the man's open mouth. The scent of hot iron fills the canvas. I want to hop and rub my throbbing toe, but instead, I bend and find the other warrior asleep in the tent. His body's hot to the touch as my blade slices his chest, deep, to where his heart would beat. It doesn't any more. He wouldn't have even felt it.

'Happy?' Wærwulf hisses angrily. I shake my head.

'No, actually. My foot fucking hurts.' He growls and reaches towards the entrance of the canvas. But there weren't just two people asleep in there. I feel the movement in a rush of air. I'm before Wærwulf, protecting him from the fucker who means to kill us. My bloodied seax connects with flesh, and a cry of pain rips through the silence of the new dawn.

'Bloody hell,' I growl again, aware of Wærwulf trying to get past me. But my other hand snakes out and grips the person's throat and squeezes. It's not a good way to die, but it'll stop the noise before my blade can finish the rest of the work. Not that I get the chance. An arm reaches through the canvas doorway, a spear on the end of it, thrust with so much force through the man's chest, I have to release my grip and dance into Wærwulf to avoid the sharpened stake.

Wild eyes meet mine, hands reaching to wrap themselves around the wood.

'There's no getting out of that,' I offer, slashing the man's throat as I pass him. Rudolf's outside, the weight of the dead man on the spear's length almost pulling him off his feet.

'Drop it,' I urge him. 'The fucker's very dead.' I'm surprised that Rudolf had the strength to skewer the dead man, but rage will do strange things to a man.

Rudolf does so with evident relief as Wærwulf emerges from the stinking interior of the tent. Daylight's growing, and I can see my warriors, some of them as much as three rows over, while I've still only contended with the first of my targets.

'There aren't many warriors,' Rudolf informs me. I knew that anyway, but now it becomes clear that even more of the tents are empty as my warriors converge, a few blades dripping with blood. To the right, I can just see Northampton's tall walls, the banner of Mercia's double-headed eagle flapping in the gentle breeze as a slash of white linen. I can't see what the banner depicts from here, but I know it well enough.

'We continue,' I encourage. 'We'll bloody find them,' I urge. I look to Pybba, and he nods in agreement. Without Icel here, he's the most honest of my warriors. He'd tell me if I'm acting only to salve my bloodlust.

'We're exposed,' Goda murmurs. 'We'll have to swim over the river if we can't return to the horses.' I wince. The thought of a cold bath is far from appealing.

'We're always bloody exposed,' Pybba interjects. He still hates the fact he wasn't there when Edmund died. I nod, and the others who've sought reassurance move out again. We're light on our feet, quieter than if we had the horses. I'm content we'll get almost to Northampton's walls before the real warriors even notice what's happening.

In the far distance, I hear a cock crow and wish the creature had been muffled. I don't want light sleepers to be roused, although I'm perplexed by the lack of guards within the camp. Are they so bloody supremely confident?

Nowhere else did the Viking raiders fail to place guards. At Repton. At Torksey. Everywhere we've been. Even at Grantabridge. It took all Rudolf's courage to enter and set fire to the place.

Wærwulf stays close. Rudolf and Pybba as well, as my warriors head towards Northampton, the width of the encampment meaning there are four warriors to every row. The campsite's surprisingly neatly laid out. It wasn't just flung up. No, this was planned. A flicker of unease jolts me, but my allies have been watching Jarl Halfdan and this fake campsite. They know what they've seen, as do we. There are few men here and even fewer warriors. If they meant us to think there were more of them, they should have tried harder than making a few straight lines of tents.

Ahead, Ingwald and Gardulf duck into another tent, the noise of their actions overly loud. I'm sure someone must wake up to counter it. Did they all get pissed last night? Is no one sensible to the fact they're under attack?

The sound of the cock's crow once more fills the air. That damn creature. It's all well and good he wakes us each morning, but today, we don't need his assistance. We're already bloody awake.

On silent feet, Wærwulf and I move forward, but once more, my eyes are drawn towards Northampton's walls. I can't tell why.

I'm not alone. Rudolf's distracted as well. I beckon him to my side.

'What is it?' I hiss. He squints along the encampment, his eyes narrowed.

'Something's not right,' he comments.

'The banner?'

'No, not the bloody banner. Something else?'

Fear constricts my heart. Have the recent converts taken command of Northampton? Was I foolish to leave? I had misgivings. I really bloody did.

'Has Northampton been taken from us?'

'No, not that either. He steps forward and then back, angling his head to one side. And then turns to look at me.

'Did you have men executed on the walls?'

'You know I bloody didn't.' I'm hardly able to breathe. Abruptly, my warriors are running through the camp, the sound of their voices too loud in the still morning air, which promises to be a pleasant day. I'll not forgive myself for this. I really bloody won't. Bad enough Edmund and my other warriors, but if I've lost all of Northampton as well?

'No, you didn't. But someone has,' Rudolf confirms, his voice filled with foreboding. The cries of my warriors fill the air, but more as well. From the east, I hear the thunder of approaching hooves and the shriek of warriors determined to kill.

'Bollocks,' I huff. 'Retreat,' I lift my voice and call. I'm not about to be trapped between the walls of Northampton and the fucking Viking raiders. I thought to kill the bastards, but I was right to be suspicious. I can only hope I don't live to regret it. Or die because of it. My aunt would be bloody furious.

Chapter Eighteen

Hiltiberht saves us. While my men look at me aghast, blood-drenched weapons to hand, I urge them to follow me back to the horses.

Northampton's under attack. There are bloody dead Norse hanging from the battlements, and that only means one thing.

'Retreat,' I order once more, Wærwulf adding his voice to mine so that it rings through the suddenly thronged air. Rudolf's quick to head back, Pybba beside him. But, only when Hiltiberht and our horses thunder through the remnants of the campsite do the others realise I mean it. Haden hurries to me, head up, allowing me to mount quickly using the stirrups.

'My thanks,' I call to Hiltiberht, face pale but determined. He nods but continues to encourage those horses that don't yet have a rider. Chocolate rushes past me, eyes focused on Beornstan. Petre isn't far behind him. Billy shudders to a stop before Hereman, while Kermit catches Gardulf. And so it goes on. Ahead, I can see the Viking raiders rushing towards Northampton. As of yet, they've not seen us. I'm unsure who these people were that we killed, but Jarl Halfdan was playing a game with us. He might have bloody won, but we can still escape from here before he realises how far I've taken us from Northampton.

'Retreat,' I call one more time, eyes on the enemy.

'Two hundred, at least,' Rudolf huffs, reaching me.

'Go on,' I urge him. I can't follow until I know all of my warriors are safe. Leonath mounts labouriously, but it's bloody Osmod who worries me the most. He's slow, so bloody slow. It takes him an age to mount at the best of times. With the threat of a bloody death looming, he seems to be taking even longer.

'I'll go,' Wærwulf assures me. I bite down on my lip. I don't want him to go alone. That's not how this bloody works.

'My thanks,' I murmur. 'Retreat,' I reinforce to those close by. 'Hiltiberht, lead them back to the ford. Get across it, and then hold it until we're all there.' He nods, resolve on his face. 'Rudolf and Pybba go with him.' I think Pybba will argue. Unlike many of us, he's not battled a Viking raider since his capture in the Welsh borderlands. He hungers to kill men and women who murdered Edmund, but he nods all the same. I listen to the heavy hoofbeats rushing away from me. And still more of my men dash past, but Osmod remains slow, although Leonath has finally turned his horse.

I wish Edmund were here to assure me that my men were mounted and on their way back to the ford, but he's not. I squint against the brightening day, trying to see more, to check everyone is obeying my command. Leonath's to the rear of Osmod and Wærwulf. The three of them don't look behind them. I almost relax. The enemy hasn't seen us, but they will if we're not bloody careful.

Osmod stumbles, falling from his horse with a cry of dismay. He ambles upright, Leonath threatening to dismount and push him into his saddle. But that's not the problem. No, Osmod landed heavily on one of the canvases, and now I can smell smoke from the nearby cookfire.

'Fuck.' The damn thing was little more than ash, but with the cloth fallen into it, it begins to smoulder, the goose fat used to rain-proof the structure, giving the impetus to burst into flame.

'Shit,' I glower. Sæbald's beside me now. Aside from the other three, he's almost the last of my warriors. He scents the air like a hound. I do the same. Any moment now, the enemy will realise what's happening. Impatiently, I watch Osmod's efforts. Finally, he's seated and turns his horse to amble towards us. Wærwulf follows behind, as does Leonath. I clamp my lips together as they weave an unsteady path through the campsite. The scent of spilt blood touches my nostrils but it's the smoke that'll be our downfall.

'Hurry the fuck up,' I mutter time and time again until they're close enough to me that I can talk to them without shouting.

'Hurry up,' I urge. 'Back to the ford.' Grunts greet my words. Leonath, I realise, has been wounded. How, I'm unsure, but his chin drips with blood, landing on Petre's long neck. He doesn't notice.

'Osmod, good of you to fucking join us,' I taunt. If he hears me, there's no sign of it.

For a moment longer, I focus on Northampton, my fears running wild. What's happened in my absence? I thought the Viking raiders wished to reclaim Jarl Guthrum, not attack Northampton. I believed they were going to Worcester. But they're not.

I linger a moment more, another two. Rudolf could be right about the number of men running to assault Northampton's walls. Already, fire arrows blaze from the ramparts. That gives me some comfort. Ealdorman Ælhun must still hold the command if he's fighting the attack, but why are bodies dangling from the ramparts? It's not my way to kill. Men should die honourably, blade to hand, or fighting their enemy, not choking their last around a bit of fucking hemp rope.

'Hurry up,' Wærwulf orders me. I turn Haden, eager to follow my warriors home. I can't believe we'll escape without being seen. It's a long way to Northampton from here.

Bollocks. This has been a complete fuck up.

Haden eats up the ground once we're free from the ruins of the campsite. I catch sight of a sprawled body as he leaps over the obstruction. I wish the dead could speak. I'd know who they were and why they were here. Why weren't they preparing to attack Northampton?

Ahead, I see my men and their mounts picking a path over the ford. The water's up to the horse's legs. It's much deeper than when we crossed. I'm perplexed as to why, because it's not raining as I guide Haden into the surging water. I wince as my feet dip into the cold current and pull them higher.

I turn towards Northampton, but I can see very little. I can't hear that we're being followed, which pleases me. If we can escape from here without being chased, we might make it to Northampton to be some bloody use.

Not that I get my wish. As Haden crests the river bank, the water swelling ever higher, from what source I'm unsure, the shout of someone arrests my attention. I peer across the river's wide expanse and meet a Viking raider's snarling face. I don't recognise him, but it's easy enough to determine his Norse ancestry. His face is inked, although I can't tell if it's an animal or just a random pattern, his long hair tied with trinkets, blowing in the gentle breeze. He's not alone.

There are more of them than there are of us.

I smirk, taunting them, hoping they'll not think to swim the river. They disappoint me.

The first five men, eyes on my horses, rush down the slope.

'Goda, Leonath, Wærwulf, Sæbald and Wulfred, get your arses here.'

I don't summon Osmod. His face remains flustered from his tardiness to retreat. I need to ensure he makes some headway on his horse should the Viking raiders overwhelm us.

'Rudolf, Pybba,' while my men hasten to protect the ford, Rudolf brings Dever closer.

'Get to Northampton,' I command. 'Take Pybba with you. Find out what's happening. Take half of the men with you.'

'My lord?' he squeaks.

'Don't fucking argue with me, Rudolf. You need to do this.'

'You'll be overwhelmed,' he argues all the same.

I offer a mirthless smirk in reply.

'We'll bloody prevail,' I counter quickly, hoping I'm correct.

Pybba, forehead furrowed in thought, nods, although he's far from happy about it. If one of the bastards tells me to run for cover, I'll kill them myself.

'Fucking cocks,' Wulfred mumbles, reaching for his seax, watching the enemy drop into the water. The first man loses his footing, tumbling with the current, flailing with the weight of his weapons belt and byrnie. He'll be dead in no time. And they call themselves shipmen!

While the six of us watch, preparing for the coming fight, I can hear Rudolf and Pybba picking off the men they'll take with them. I listen to the names Osbert, Hereman, Osmod , Gardulf and Cuthwalh. I don't hear enough names to be content, but now two Viking raiders have crossed the ford, arms held above their heads, the water almost up to their shoulders. Behind them, more of the enemy take a chance. The swept-away man can no longer be seen or heard. The current won't take him to Northampton. Even his dead body will serve no purpose to his allies.

I can hear some of my warriors arguing with Rudolf and Pybba, Gardulf's most vocal.

'Get the fuck out of here,' I shout over my shoulder, menacing the bastards. Hereman and Gardulf join the men I've already positioned. My lips twist, but I understand what drives them.

Wærwulf encourages his horse forward to meet the enemy. They emerge, dripping wet, one shaking himself to dislodge the water, bending to run his hand over the few tall grasses in the hope of drying his hands. He dies with a flung spear through his neck. I hear the huff of Hereman and know he was the one to let loose the shot. He's a lucky bastard whose aim was true from Billy's back.

Wærwulf strikes low to attack the remaining man who, eyes flashing, surges upwards with his war axe to meet the blow. The wooden handle slips in his hand, dropping low and avoiding his foot. He dies with a whimper of pain as Wærwulf stabs down into the gap between his byrnie and neck.

A howl of outrage issues from those still advancing on us. I can't help thinking they're foolish bastards to take such a risk.

'Isn't this the very definition of fucking stupidity,' I growl, Sæbald barking in laughter. But the Viking raiders don't give up.

'What the hell?' Now, there are another eight or nine of them, one behind the other, balancing precariously on the lip of the ford. I can see the thick pieces of stone that run at a certain point across the river. I should have realised sooner. With the water rising, the ford's becoming uncrossable. Not that it's putting off our enemy.

'*Skiderick*,' the next man to rush from the river shouts, war axe to one hand, shield to the other. Water pools down the wooden object as he pulls it from his back. Hereman has no spear for this warrior, but Wærwulf has no intention of letting him pass.

The warrior, eyes flashing dangerously beneath his dull helm, hair spilling below it in a parody of a neck and shoulder guard, pivots into Wærwulf, aiming for his horse. Goda jumps from Magic's back and strides towards our enemy. The two engage.

Wærwulf realising he can't risk his horse, dismounts as well, and sends Cinder back amongst the trees.

Lyfing calls for the horse, to prevent him following Wærwulf. We all hasten to dismount. We'll not be losing horses today, or warriors, for that matter.

Haden, abandoned once more, nudges me with an obstinate nose, but Lyfing shouts to him as well, and he leaves quickly, the stink of shed blood as Goda's foeman screams in pain, no doubt encouraging him to move aside.

We form a semi-circle, preventing our enemy from doing more than meeting our blades. They'll have to risk the much deeper water if they want to step closer to this side of the river. None of them seem keen to do so.

Those who've not heeded Rudolf and Pybba's instructions to leave form a circle behind us. Ordheah's close to me, his breath almost in my ear. I'd tell him to fuck off, but the Viking raiders are finally thinking with more than their seaxes.

As narrow as the stone shelf is, six of them stand, holding their own in the rising waters, forming a makeshift shield wall. They emerge as one beast, teeth gritted, hidden behind their shields. We can see legs and feet. I note one of them wears strangely brightly coloured socks, visible over the top of his boots. For a moment, I can't tear my bloody eyes away from them.

They rush in, shields hitting ours. Lyfing must have stayed mounted. His voice rises above the heave of wood and weapons. 'More of them incoming,' he informs, with no inflexion to his words.

'Kill the bastards,' I urge my warriors. 'Kill them all.' There's a similar conversation taking place behind their shield wall. I pick out one or two words.

'They know who we are, my lord,' Wærwulf roars above the ruckus. The news doesn't surprise me. But I do nothing to indicate who leads here. With Lyfing mounted and shouting the orders, these fools might not know who I am, even if they know we are the king of Mercia's warriors.

My shield slips against the slickness of my enemy. Gripping it tighter, I lift it again, but only after my enemy reaches out with his seax to try his luck. The blade looms close, but it doesn't cut me. With my shield replaced, I look down.

Hereman might have used his spear, but not all of my warriors have. Spears snake beneath shields, their points aiming for the legs of our enemies. I hope whoever wields the weapon isn't distracted by the bright socks, as I was.

I grimace, lashing out with my seax. I want to push the bastard enemy shields down, but it's hard to get any purchase against the wood because they're wet. I'll have to do it with my seax hand.

Growling low in my throat, I reach over again, elbow over my shield. The seax is held firm in my hand, but I put all my weight into my arm, attempting to make it heavy enough to move the enemy shield. I feel it giving, my foeman distracted, but then he realises my intention, and the shield rises again.

'Bastard,' I mutter. The small shield wall is firm.

'Hold,' Lyfing calls. I'm pleased he's had the wits to order our small fight. There are so few enemies we should be able to overpower them easily. But it's taken more effort than I thought it would.

'Fucking bastard shit-heads,' Wulfred calls. I'd crack a smile, but I want this done.

'Attack,' Lyfing orders. I've only just bloody 'held', but he can see more than me from the back of his horse. I lower my shield and lash out with my seax, scoring along the rim of my enemy's shield. Sparks fly, and the man veers backwards. I press the advantage, taking Sæbald beside me as well. He does the same to his foeman, and the Viking raiders are being forced back, closer and closer to the water.

'Keep it up,' Lyfing encourages. I hear outraged shrieks from our adversaries. Those yet to stand on this side of the ford are undoubtedly caught up in the retreat.

Shouts of pain and anger reach my ears, but I keep my gaze on my foeman, all of my strength in my shield-holding hand and shoulder. I'll overwhelm them. I almost feel as though I could do it alone— fire courses through my body. I want them all bloody dead.

And then my feet are getting wet. The Viking raiders are in the water. Some have fallen, some are standing, and some are waiting to see what the others will do. The water's higher now. It's only three steps along the ford, and it's almost above head height. It must have rained somewhere close by to bring such a sudden change in the water levels. I can't think what else might have caused it.

'Hold,' Lyfing shrieks. I realise why. The other end of the shield wall, where Leonath, Goda and Gardulf fight, is almost in the water. If they go in fully armed, the current will take them, just like the first man, and not towards Northampton.

'Hold,' I echo the cry. I won't lose men to the watery depths, not when we can better our foemen just by standing here. The splashes of men struggling to stay upright are audible over the roaring of my breathing. 'Hold,' I repeat, lashing out with my seax. My enemy swerves to avoid the blow, and his feet go from beneath him. I follow him down, trying to find somewhere to end his life, but the lucky fucker has held onto his shield. It covers him.

'Bastard,' I growl, staying low and pushing with my seax hand. If I can shove him into the water, in that position, with the shield above his head and covering his body, he'll struggle to get upright. My eyes are caught by movement from behind as one of his allies struggles to get to his aid. A shush of something over my head, and a spear reaches for his neck. He flails, a strangled cry on his lips. His feet go from beneath him as well. Another one lost to the force of the river.

I watch him being sucked along by the current, even though I should be killing my enemy. I push with my seax hand as the man becomes entangled with his allies, all trying to stay clear from the deeper water. He reaches out and grabs onto one of his fellows, and now both have lost their balance.

'Damn fucker,' I growl, concentrating on what needs to be done. The shield continues to cover the man. I push him. He holds. I push harder. He still holds, and then the spear which skewered his friend snakes beneath the shield, forcing it upwards. I stare down, frightened eyes greeting mine, but they don't see. His legs are tangled beneath him, his belly almost flat to them. He's gargled his last breath.

I dismiss him from my thoughts with a contemptuous kick and turn to aid the rest of my men. They're not alone—Gardulf's out of the water. Goda has one leg in and one leg out while Wulfred is beside Leonath. They face three men, ugly fuckers, all of them, with scars on what's visible of their body. Why the Viking raiders like to fight with their arms uncovered, I'll never know. If they think looking at snaking creatures or depictions of wolves and ravens will scare us, then they're bloody crazy.

I suck in much-needed air as Lyfing turns his horse. I know what he's going to do. The enemy realise as well, but there's nothing they can do. My warriors are stretched along the river bank. We won't allow our opponents to access dry land, and they can't go back either because the river's too full.

Lyfing, using his reach from the back of the horse, stabs with his seax, roundly knocking the man who fights Leonath and Wulfred. His shield's raised, but it's not enough to stop the power behind the blow. Lyfing aims for his exposed shoulders and back, and while the man roars his fury, Leonath steps in as well, scoring across the man's belly which overhangs his weapons belt.

The water turns pink. Lyfing kicks him, using all the force of being above him. With the shield covering his head, the foeman loses his balance, toppling backwards, his injuries making him shriek with pain as the water closes over him.

Now, there are only the warriors whom Goda and Gardulf fight. I glance behind. There are three men left on the other side of the river bank. I bark at them, furious eyes meeting mine, but their terror gives way, and they run. I turn to Hereman. He hums happily, another spear to hand, and it scythes through the air, hitting the man in the middle so that he falls forward, lifeless, his allies running on without him, not even noticing.

'Another,' Hereman demands, hand outstretched, as though we have the time and inclination to stand there and do what he demands. I wait. I think the men are too bloody far away.

'No fucking chance,' Wulfred taunts. Hereman doesn't even flinch; his focus is on the enemy. Wulfred should know better than to wager against Hereman. The man buckles, and he's down while Hereman smirks at Wulfred. But the remaining warrior is too far away.

'Leave it,' I urge Hereman before he can mount up and ride Billy through the river's flood. 'Leave it. It's best if one should bloody live.'

'But they'll know of this ford.'

'They will, perhaps, but do you think he ever wishes to come here again? I doubt it. Without Rudolf to pilfer the dead, it falls to those keen to get wet again to drag the bodies from the surging water. Some bodies are lost, rolling along with the water, limbs flailing as though they swim with the current as it turns them.

'Someone's going to have fun finding them in their bloody fishing nets,' Hereman offers conversationally.

'They'll get some good weapons,' Gardulf complains, drawing in deep breaths, recovering from his exertions.

But I'm looking at the ford. Do I need to leave men here to guard it? I look towards Northampton. I want to rush back through the woodlands and ensure all is well there, but this is a problem that needs solving. I turn to my warriors. They've all fought hard. Some carry small cuts, and all of them will be bruised tomorrow. Even I can feel the sting of something along my lower arm, above my gloves. I touch it but feel no dampness. A cut or a bruise. If it's a cut, it's stopped bleeding, which will suffice.

'I need four of you to remain here,' I determine, looking from one to another. 'Well, not here. Close by, so you can watch to see if our enemy returns. I don't believe they will.'

My warriors nod, looking at one another. There are only so many of us as it is. When no one offers, I shake my head and eye them as though they're weapons to test for keenness of edge and strength.

These men are all good warriors. I want them at my side. But I must be wary as well.

'Cealwin, Leonath, Sæbald and Wulfred, you stay here for the remainder of today and tomorrow. I'll have others sent to replace you.' What goes unsaid but is understood all the same is that I'll send some of the ealdormen's men to keep a guard. I want my warriors with me. I don't wish to divide my force of lethal, loyal warriors.

Leonath grunts. He was part of the original force sent to watch the area.

'The pottage will be bloody ruined,' he growls, mounting up to lead the others back to the campsite they made. 'The fire will have gone out,' he keeps up his mournful dirge while Wærwulf and I bend to drag the two bodies floundering on the river bank above the surge of the water.

'They need burying,' I remind the four who'll remain behind. Leonath turns Petre, with a furious expression that dies as he sees my grin.

'Right, we'll fucking do it,' is his reply, but his lips are lifted in a smirk. 'Get back to Northampton, and we'll kill any of the bastards that try to cross,' he confirms, and with that, I mount Haden and encourage him back through the woodlands. Here, in the peace and quiet of the opening beneath the trees, it would be pleasant to linger, absorb some welcome warmth from the sun, and forget about the cares of running a kingdom. But Northampton is under attack. I must make haste.

'Stay the fuck alive,' I growl, kneeing Haden onwards.

'And you can do the fucking same,' Wulfred instructs. My grin stretches wider.

Chapter Nineteen

The closer we get to Northampton, the quieter it gets, or so it seems. The woodlands are a mess of reaching branches and too-close tree trunks. I allow Haden to lead. I've done little but fight my way to dead ends, causing us all to return the way we've come. Without Rudolf to lead us, I'm making an arse of this. Winning free feels like a triumph. Getting closer to Northampton, unease growls in my belly. I'm blood-stained, and the exertion of fighting at the ford has fled my body, leaving me cold and in need of food and drink. But I don't pause. I need to know what's bloody happening.

Gardulf and Hereman strike on ahead. Their desire to kill every single fucking Viking raider leaves them without fear. I'm not fearful. Fear isn't the word. Furious describes my feelings better. My mind's in turmoil about what's happened in my absence, which I banish as soon as I see Northampton. The smell of smoke reaches me first, hands tightening on the reins, but the settlement doesn't burn, not from what I can see. It might be the smell from where Ealdorman Ælhun sent fire arrows into our enemy. Or from where we unintentionally set fire to the almost empty tents. The wind's picked up enough for it to reach us, even here, to the west of the settlement.

'Open the gates,' Gardulf demands as we clatter over the bridge. The gate guards hasten to do so, recognising us quickly.

'My lord king,' the one cries on seeing me. 'We're under attack, from within and without,' he hastens to add. He's not precisely fearful, either. A collection of ten guards protects the gateway and the bridge. I glance around me. The people of Northampton don't run hither and thither in panic. It's too quiet.

'Where is everyone?' I demand.

'Ealdorman Ælhun ordered us to protect the gate and the bridge for your return, and now we need to bring the bridge inside,' the guard continues, almost as though I've not spoken. 'When the first body was found, we doubled the guard.'

'Body?' I question, although I have my suspicions.

'One of the Norse Christians,' he continues. 'Killed by their people.' He says this with a twist of his lips, fury pouring from him. I rein Haden in, watching as the men quickly disable the bridge and once inside, others bar the gate after us, adding more than just the single wooden bar. This time, they add all of them. It's unusual. I note it, looking for Rudolf, Pybba and the rest of my men.

'Have my other men returned?' I interrupt his explanations, eager to know they're here, or else the gate guards will be removing the bars to allow them entrance shortly.

'Yes, my lord king. They're with the ealdorman.' The man hurries to assure me.

'So, the Norse Christians were killed by their people?' I resume my questioning once I'm assured of the safety of the others.

'Six of them, my lord king. They were killed in the night, the priest knocked out cold to prevent him from raising an alarm, and then they were flung over the battlements to dangle on the ends of hempen rope. It looks like we killed them,' he adds the unnecessary explanation. I nod quickly. I can decipher this easily enough.

'Where are the killers?' I feel my hand reaching for my seax and force myself not to grip the familiar handle.

'Still within Northampton. Hiding somewhere. They've not been found.'

'Fuck,' I growl, a brief look running over the gate guards. These are all Mercians. I recognise them, even if I don't know their names.

'Continue to hold firm,' I order. 'You're doing well,' I offer quickly. Not all of the men look frightened, but some of them do. 'Stay the fuck alive,' I murmur towards them before taking Haden onwards. We don't go to the stables as much as my horse would dearly love to do so. Instead, I take him through the street, heading towards the steps to the rampart. As we pass the great hall, I hear a voice from within.

'Who goes there?' a fearful cry.

'The king,' I reply quickly. 'Stay inside.' I realise this is where many of the residents are hiding. I'd expect to find them in the church, on their knees, but if it's been tainted by murderers, then I'm unsurprised to find the people of Northampton elsewhere. It's probably easier to defend the hall, and it's much bigger as well. They won't be crammed like eels in a pot inside there.

The eerie quiet of Northampton finally gives way to the cries of battle rage and angry Viking raiders and Mercians. Haden flinches but then resumes his forward momentum. Ahead, I see the horses of the men I sent back before me. Dever and the other animals are still sweating. They've not been here long, despite my ability to get lost.

With long strides and a smile encouraging those who wait beneath the rampart close to the concealed and sealed tunnel, I rush upwards, leaving Haden beside the other horses.

'My lord king,' Ealdorman Ælhun greets me, his face white with fury, his fists clenched, his words a harsh bark. 'The bastards,' he intones. 'We've not found them yet, but we will. Every possible exit is being watched. I'm glad you survived. I feared for you, although I shouldn't have done,' he offers as an afterthought. I allow that with a tight smile. He's not the only one to have forgotten to greet his allies before launching into a summary of events.

'Could you see us from along the River Nene?'

'No, we couldn't,' His reply makes me feel better about leaving my men by the ford. I must send others to relieve them. But first, I need to counter this, and we might need every available warrior not to defend Northampton from without but to ensure it remains whole from within.

The viewing platform isn't filled with warriors. I see Rudolf, and he skips to my side.

'The others are looking for the enemy. The fight here is all bluff and little else.'

'They're still trying to get inside?' I question. The smell of burning is stronger here, and I smirk at the remains of the tents. It must have been half a day since they started their attack. The fact they persist assures me they're anticipating something, although what that might be, I don't know. Again, I have my suspicions.

'Yes, they've retreated twice but came back twice as well.' Ealdorman Ælhun confirms, his face furrowed in thought. 'They're waiting for something.'

'They're expecting the tunnel to be opened?' I surmise quickly.

'Yes. I suspect our enemies inside are giving some signal, but we can't determine what it is.'

I feel uneasy about having these Norse Christians amongst us. I should never have agreed to it. I knew it was a bloody trap, and it's been sprung.

'Hereman and Gardulf, get your arses by the eastern gateway. Reinforce the men already there.' They rush to do my bidding. They suspect that's where the fighting will be. I speculate it will be as well. 'Do any of them yet live? We could question them?'

'Yes, some live. All of the children and the elders. Six were killed and strung up over the battlements. We've managed to haul four of them in, but the Viking raiders tore the other two down. They used arrows to cut through the ropes that held them and then grabbed them and dragged them amongst the warriors. It was quite a show,' the ealdorman confirms, face twisted. 'Jarl Halfdan came forward to pick up the dead, weeping, wailing, and inciting his warriors to greater efforts. We got the other four, though, before he could arrange for their capture.'

'Show me,' I demand. For now, I can hear little from the other side of the rampart. I can see the enemy. I imagine they're sitting or standing, eating or drinking, but no one is assaulting the walls. They still wait. For what, I don't know, but I'm not foolish enough not to doubt Jarl Halfdan's intentions. His callousness towards his fellow men and women astounds me. He allowed men to die in the encampment just as a rouse. He's permitted men and women to die here, killed by their fellow warriors. I'd never do such a thing. I must protect all of Mercia, not just part of it. For a moment, my thoughts flicker to what might be happening in Worcester and where my aunt might be to the north. I've taken what precautions I can. This was meant to be a time of peace and rebuilding. Jarl Halfdan has determined that's not to be the bloody case. Damn the fucking bastard.

Ealdorman Ælhun leads me down the stairs. The group of warriors close to our secret gate has grown. I catch the eye of Pybba. He speaks with Hereman. I can well imagine what that conversation is about. I beckon him to me. He's a kind man with a sharp mind. I need his help with the few surviving Norse Christians.

I'm led to the church by Ealdorman Ælhun. Throughout Northampton, I hear the harsh cries of my warriors and the ealdorman's men seeking out our enemy. One head appears beneath the raised grain store, Oda taking no chances that an enemy might be there. I eye that with a wry smirk. He should have sent Hiltiberht, or even Rudolf to perform such a task. Now he struggles to get upright, puffing and panting, trews stained with dust. Not that I need to say anything. Wulfhere's there to add any words of derision for being an old fucker with which I might have taunted.

Four of Ealdorman Ælhun's men stand guard at the church doorway, but others surround it. Is it a waste of a precious resource? Should they be elsewhere? If we had double the number, then yes, but the ealdorman's correct to be cautious. The enemy might still be within, hiding with the communion wine or in the crypt. They might even have crawled into an open grave.

I turn to the ealdorman, the question on my lips.

'We've checked the two open graves. We've checked those recently closed over as well, to see if someone's buried their way inside. They haven't.' I nod, pleased with his forethought but not enjoying the reminder that Edmund, Eadberht and Siric lie in the newest graves.

Still, we don't need to be mirroring each other's actions. I trust the ealdorman. And he trusts me. With our combined forces, we'll find our bloody enemy.

The door guards bow on seeing me, standing straighter.

'Good men, firm,' the ealdorman confirms as we open the door. It creaks alarmingly on its hinges. I wince as frightened eyes look my way.

I notice those who still live are indeed the young or the old, those with no skill to lift a blade, or no doubt, thought too young to keep the secret. There are some men and women of fighting age as well. But those who survive have grief-stained faces. I swallow against their sorrow. They came here to be bloody protected. That hasn't happened. But, maybe they should have told me more about those with them. We could have kept them apart if we'd known who to suspect.

I eye the oldest of the children, a boy who can't be more than ten winters old. I wish I knew his name. One of the older women holds his hand. Are they related, or does she merely offer him comfort? Priest Wilfrid's there, too. He hurries forward. His face is a mass of ugly bruises, his upper lip thick enough to expose his crooked teeth.

'My lord king,' he expels, fear in his words. 'Are they found?' He looks everywhere. Over my shoulder. Behind him. And then glares at the few survivors. I can see there's a lack of faith. I'm unsurprised.

'Not yet, no. We've come to question those who remain.' I explain. He nods, but his eyes are wild.

'Perhaps you should pray for the dead?' I suggest. His hold on the here and now is thin. Maybe we should remove him from here.

'Of course, my lord king, if that's what you command.' He hurries away, his robe brushing against the wooden floor. I turn to Ealdorman Ælhun.

'I didn't.' I begin, but he shakes his head.

'A man such as him needs to be ordered during such an ordeal. He'll find comfort in his prayers.'

Wærwulf has joined us. He's already going through the men, women, and children who survive. His voice rumbles as he speaks to them. Frightened eyes watch him. I can't believe they'll tell him anything. They might not even know anything. But we need to try.

'Has the interior of the church been searched?' I question the ealdorman. The building isn't elaborate. A long, thin wooden building, built in the style of a hall, only with a narrower end towards its tip. The font is situated there, and it's from where the priest conducts his tedious services. There are a few doorways leading to other sections of the church. Other than that, or hiding beneath the benches or behind the wide wooden pillars holding the roof aloft, I'm unsure where anyone might conceal themselves.

I look at the survivors. If the older group members are truly warriors, they mask their skills better than I ever could. Their arms are weak and frail, their postures either stopped or stick-thin. I don't believe the children are a threat either, but they could be. I don't see the tall woman or the strong woman who said she could work metal. I don't see the short man either. In fact, I'm sure I see many fewer than just the six people we know are dead.

'Yes, the priest showed us even the smallest of hiding places where he keeps the communion wine. There was no one in any of them.'

Wærwulf returns to me much quicker than I expect, as I'm absorbing the ealdorman's words.

'Begga's behind it all,' he offers, unease in his voice. 'The others didn't want her with them. She wasn't supposed to come, but they didn't notice until she was here.'

'And then they said nothing?' I growl, fury flaring, turning to menace those who survive.

'She advised them that Jarl Halfdan had threatened to kill her, and this was the only way she could be sure of surviving. One of the oldsters, Astrid, is her aunt or someone similar. The relationships aren't easy to disentangle. She uses a word I don't know.' I eye the older woman. She's fearful but meek, head bowed as she senses my scrutiny. I wince to see the bruises on her chin and cheeks. Quickly, she hobbles to join the priest, favouring her left leg, taking the boy I watched with her. Some of the others follow.

'She woke to find the others already murdered and tried to prevent Begga from leaving the church but was tripped and battered over the head by someone else. She only revived a short time ago. She needs some assistance. The bruise on the side of her head is huge and egg-shaped.'

'And the others?'

'Know nothing and suspected nothing. Until I spoke with Astrid, they thought you must have ordered the murder of their fellow Christians.'

'Fuck,' I mutter, wincing as the word echoes loudly within the church. Priest Wilfrid pauses his prayers but resumes quickly. I look around. No matter my feelings towards my Lord God, this place should be sacrosanct. The Viking raiders have once more shown an utter lack of contempt for the religious houses of the Mercians. At Repton, they stained the church with their fires and splattered blood on the walls of the church of St Wystan's. I'm uneasy about their success here as well.

I turn and begin to head outside, my gaze everywhere. But, my eyes alight on something above. A small gap in the wall, a window, no doubt intended for some glass, should there ever be enough peace to order the precious commodity. Now, a canvas flaps over the gap, doing its best to keep the wind and the rain from entering the building. But.

I beckon Ealdorman Ælhun to me.

'What do you see?' All of my men look upwards, including Wærwulf.

'They couldn't get up there, surely?' he questions.

'They had a great deal of rope,' I mutter unhappily, 'because they used it to dangle the dead over our ramparts.'

The canvas is twisted. It flaps, but half inside the building and half outside. It must be getting windy.

'They wouldn't be on the roof?' Ealdorman Ælhun queries, but none of us dismisses the notion. It would explain why we can't find the fuckers. It might also explain how they can communicate with their allies beyond the walls of Northampton.

I turn and look at my warriors.

'Who fancies a bloody climb?' I quip. Not one of them looks at me. I'd glower, but it's a long way up. I don't want to be the one to do it. If I fell from such a height, I'd be dead, and so would any of my men who went up there.

'Get some ropes. A lot of ropes,' I announce, unable to tear my eyes from the flapping canvas. It wasn't like that when I was inside the church the other day. I don't recall it ever being like that. It was held down by some means, but now it's not. And I think the bastard Viking raiders are using it. Now, we need to determine how they've accomplished it. We must stop them from communing with our bloody enemies beyond the ramparts. That way, we can keep Northampton safe and avenge the murders that have taken place within my settlement.

The cheeky fuckers. Professing to be Christians and then using our damn church against us.

Chapter Twenty

Not that it's so bloody simple. The rope is brought from wherever it's stored. Great trailing lengths of it, but how we're to do anything with it, I don't know. And who'll do it is another question that remains unanswered. The news from outside is that the Viking raiders continue to enjoy a respite. They stand before the east-facing wall but aren't close enough to be within reach of arrows, spears, or anything else we might think to throw down at the bastards. It's a pity we can't throw the dead bodies, but that would make it even more difficult. It would be as though we'd killed the poor fuckers, and then intended to use them against the rest of the enemy.

'Get Hereman,' I eventually instruct Rudolf. He and Pybba go together. It's better if everyone moves in groups. I suspect the enemy of being on the roof, but we must still be wary until we know that for certain.

Hereman arrives. I look for Rudolf.

'He took my place,' Hereman mutters. Damn the bastard. I know why. He would have been perfect for sending up on the roof. 'What do you want me to do?' his eyebrows are furrowed, his expression perplexed as he stands beside our small group, all of us looking up at the window revealed by the flapping canvas. His head swivels from what we're looking at, and back to me.

'We need to bloody get up there,' I advise him, just as he's saying, 'The bloody thing wasn't flapping before.' Immediately, Hereman understands my thinking.

'Cunning bastards,' he nods respectfully.

'Can you get a spear up there, with a rope attached to it?'

'What good would that do?' His eyebrows are furrowed.

'We need to get up there as well, and that could be the means to do so.'

'Ah,' and he smirks, immediately comprehending why Rudolf was so keen to remain on the rampart in his place. 'I don't know,' he admits. 'It's high, and if we're attaching a damn rope to it, it'll be even harder. Who will you send up? No one will want to go fucking up there.' He's right, but I grunt in reply.

'We need a rope up first,' I muse. I've looked around. I don't even know how the window was formed. Undoubtedly, the building would have been supported in some way to enable it to reach so high. Perhaps they might have left whatever they used when adding the tower. But, whatever they used has either been burned or used elsewhere.

'Isn't there another way?' Hereman complains, testing the weight of the rope and his spear simultaneously now that he's affixed one end of the rope to the spear. The door opens again, all eyes turning towards it as Pybba returns. He's breathing heavily.

'They're bloody up there. I can see them,' he huffs. How he's checked this, I don't want to know. That he's out of breath worries me.

'The six of them. They have a piece of cloth or a banner or something like that. It must be how they're staying in contact. They didn't see me,' he hastens to reassure me before I can berate him for giving away the element of surprise.

'Now we know where they are, we need to get them down. Do we have any bowmen?' I question Ealdorman Ælhun.

'Yes, but getting them at the correct height to aim will be a problem.'

'Can't we use the rampart?'

'I think the enemy will move and hide at this end of the roof, before the tower, and then arrows will be no good. The rampart doesn't run all the way around the walls.'

'Arse,' I exclaim, mindful of where I am and trying not to earn the wrath of my Lord God, even while cursing the damn fools who built the church roof so bloody high. Or, the walls too damn short. Bastards.

'I think I can do it,' Hereman speaks with more confidence, nodding as he does so. 'But I'm not bloody going up there,' he adds immediately. 'It won't hold my weight, or indeed, the weight of most of us.'

My mind turns to Rudolf, the bloody git. But then, he's been left dangling in enough rivers in the last few years to refuse to take any greater risks. I can't blame him.

'Hiltiberht?' I question, wishing I didn't have to, but he has the same youthful slimness of Rudolf.

'He doesn't like heights,' Pybba adds quickly. 'He's more likely to fall and smash his skull open if you order him up there.'

I gaze at Pybba. I could send him, for he has a slimmer build, but he lacks the ability to hold on with both hands. He offers me a smirk. He must be thinking the same. And no doubt he's grateful for it. I consider all of my warriors. None of us are exactly slim or slight.

'We need a child,' I speak aloud. The thought fills me with unease.

'A child will never be able to kill our enemy,' the ealdorman argues.

'Let's see if we can get a rope up there first,' Hereman argues. I nod. He's right. It's bloody frustrating to know where they are and be able to do nothing about it. How those bastards got so high, I really don't know. They must have no fear.

'From in here or outside?'

'In here,' Hereman quickly replies. 'I'd rather not have the bastards taunting me.' His words seem to fill the interior of the church. Again, Priest Wilfrid's prayers are interrupted but begin again quickly.

'Get out the way,' Hereman calls to everyone, especially those who've wandered almost directly beneath the window as though they can see better from there. Frantic feet scramble clear, and then Hereman, with a wistful look at his spear and the attached rope, steps backwards and forwards, closing one eye and then opening them both, only to close one again.

'Aim for the wooden beam,' I advise. The wood up high is locked together, a cross beam or something like that. I know little about building. That's why we have skilled carpenters, but there is a thicker piece of wood up there. No doubt it'll mean something important to the church. If it allows us access to the roof, I'll also heap my bloody praises on it.

'Thank you for stating the fucking obvious,' Hereman growls. I think he'll launch the spear, but instead, he drops his arm.

'I can't do it with everyone watching.' I roll my eyes but turn my back on him, indicating the others should do the same with a frantic hurry-up motion of my hands. It's probably better if we don't watch his failing throws.

A whoosh through the air, followed by a loud clatter and an even louder, 'bollocks,' assures me that Hereman has failed with his first attempt. I clench my fists tight to my side. We need to do this, but who can I send up there when the rope is in place? I suddenly realise that if Hereman does manage to stick the spear in the wood, it doesn't matter if it is a child who scampers up first. All they need to do is secure the rope better, and someone else can go and face our enemy. I don't want to be the one to do it, but if no other bastard will, I'll perform the task. I'll show my men what I'll do for Mercia's security.

After all, it can't be worse than crossing a steep bridge with the River Severn thundering far below. Can it?

Once more, there's a clatter of the spear hitting the wooden floor, but this time Hereman doesn't exclaim in disgust. Instead, a triumphant cry accompanies the return of his spear to the ground.

'I've got it now,' he murmurs happily, retrieving the spear to try once more.

I hear his shuffling feet and someone being roughly moved aside with a squeal of shock, but the attendant clang of iron on the wooden floor doesn't ring through the church.

'You bloody bastard beautiful spear,' Hereman cries instead. I turn to find him grinning widely, the spear quivering far above our heads, the rope dangling just within reach to the ground. We should have used a longer piece of bloody rope.

'Well done, Hereman,' I clap him on the back. He grins, and then it slides from his face just as quickly.

'You're not bloody going up,' he announces even though I've said nothing.

'No, I'm not, but I will be when we've made it more secure.' I realise I'm being watched and meet the eyes of the young boy who was holding Astrid's hand. He gabbles something, and I turn to Wærwulf, although his intention is clear enough to see from the way he points upwards.

'He'll go,' Wærwulf informs me. 'He says he's good at climbing. He used to help his grandfather with their ship before coming to these shores. He was always climbing the sail.'

'Can you tell him I need him to carry another rope up there and secure it tightly for men to use.'

Wærwulf looks resigned but again speaks to the lad. He skips forward, his tear-stained and furious face breaking into a look of fiery determination. Hereman has been coiling a long rope, my intentions evident to him. He's looped it at such a size that it'll fit over the boy's shoulders. Astrid rushes forward, a string of words fleeing from her bruised mouth. I expect her to chastise the boy for offering to help us.

But Wærwulf's face is furrowed as he listens with a growing smile of respect.

'She's instructing him, telling him how to tie the rope to the top, and advising him that he must hold tight and not risk falling, for the floor won't be as soft as the sea, should he loose his grip.'

'So he's bloody fallen before?' I murmur unhappily. Not because I'm disappointed but because he's a brave boy in an enemy land, and still he wants to help. If he's lived through the assassinations last night, I don't want him to be killed here. He came to us for protection. I should like to offer it to him.

'He has, but he always gets back up,' Wærwulf has asked Astrid. She shows no fear, and I take comfort from that.

'What's his name?' I feel I should know this. Wærwulf nods, and asks.

'Knut, after his grandfather.' I see pride on Astrid's face. In that moment, she reminds me of my aunt. Is she forcing the boy to achieve his greatness, as I've been forced? Or is she simply allowing him to see what he could become? I swallow, a thickness in my throat. Without such women in our lives, what would we boys and men become?

Knut picks up the coiled rope, loops it over one shoulder and down his body, and then reaches for the dangling rope. It's too far above his narrow stretching arms, although I see muscles amongst the thin sticks that lead to his shoulders. Hereman bends to lift him, boosting him high enough to grab the trailing end of the rope. With a speed I find dazzling, Knut clambers along the rope, using his hands and his feet to give him enough leverage that it's as though he crawls along the ground, as I've seen small children do. My mouth drops open in shock, while Astrid, watching me and not her grandson, cackles with delight. She mutters something else to Wærwulf, who laughs as well but doesn't tell me what she said. I don't press the point. I probably don't want to know.

The only moment Knut seems to struggle is climbing onto the thick beam high above our heads. Here, he pauses, hanging by little more than his fingers. Then he swings his legs, grabs the beam and hauls himself over it. At that, I expel a breath I didn't know I was holding, while Astrid issues a further torrent of instructions. I'd ask Wærwulf what it all meant, but there's no need. I can see clearly that she's offering advice. Knut's reply drifts down to us, his high voice a counterpart to the void above him. I imagine the enemy can hear him, but provided they don't show their faces in the flapping canvas covering the opening, he should be safe. Hereman stands, another spear in hand, should he need to kill one of the enemy. I don't like to consider the mess it might make on the damn floor.

With the second rope much more securely attached than merely threaded around Hereman's first spear, I think Knut will return to the ground, only he doesn't, moving towards the canvas instead.

'Tell him bloody no,' I order Wærwulf with a bark, although Astrid's already shouting. I realise then that Knut has a flashing blade at his waist. Does the boy mean to kill our enemy alone? I hope not.

'Get him bloody down,' I urge Wærwulf, for Knut isn't listening to his grandmother or Wærwulf. Or indeed, to any of us. Surely the word 'no' can't be that different in his tongue to ours?

Knut doesn't stop. He's almost reached the window.

'Fucking bollocks,' I glower, taking myself to the second rope and testing it in the hope it'll take my weight. It holds firm.

'Shit,' I mutter. Hereman's there as well, trying to grip the rope.

'Stay here, and skewer any of the fuckers,' I urge him, already deciding what I don't need to kill our enemy on the roof. I really don't want my byrnie for it'll be heavy, but I keep it. I dismiss some of my weapons, taking my seax but not my sword. The damn thing will become tangled in the rope.

From above, Knut's shouting something, and Wærwulf's quick to translate, even as I fear to look upwards. I don't want to watch the boy disappear out of the window.

'He says they're all up there, at the far side of the roof, to this side of the tower.'

'Tell him to get the fuck down,' I growl. Wærwulf's words are quick in response. I don't believe he uses my exact terminology. Fuelled by rage and fear for the youngster, I reach up, taking the strain in my arms, and wishing I was as nimble as the young fool above me. I try to mirror his actions, wrapping my legs around the rope, but it doesn't help me. Instead, I'm forced to stretch one arm and then another, pulling myself labouriously upwards. In moments, sweat beads my forehead, and I want to get down. I'm barely above Hereman's height. I don't know how I'll make it to the top, and if I do, I'm not convinced I'll have any strength left with which to fight. But, I've begun this, and I'm not about to look like a fucking arse, giving up when Knut has made it so effortless.

'Hurry the fuck up,' Gardulf calls. I'd give him a mouthful, but I can't. My teeth are gritted, my arms trembling and finally, the top of the rope's coming within sight. Although, how I'm to get myself onto the beam, I don't bloody know.

I catch sight of movement. Knut's almost out of the window.

'Call him bloody back,' I huff, wishing I didn't sound so out of breath.

Up high, I dare not look down. With my back facing the ground, hands wrapped around the rope and then the beam, I pull my legs up, feeling the strain in my belly. They easily grip the beam when I lock my feet around it. Now's the difficult part. Shutting my eyes and taking my chance on a swift prayer to my God, well, why the fuck not when I'm in his house, I haul with all of my might, surprised when I open my eyes and find I'm lying along the beam, chest heaving. I look down and then wish I hadn't. Gardulf's making his way up the rope. It feels like he's a very long way down. He, unlike me, moves quickly and gracefully. He thinks enough to bring another rope as well. In no time, there'll be all of us up here and no one on the ground.

I get to my knees, avoiding the tight and twanging rope that Gardulf's climbing, but I don't stand. I shuffle forward on my hands and knees, the canvas flap assuring me that outside, the wind's getting up. Bloody hell. Could this get any fucking worse?

'Get down,' I reach out and tap Knut on the back of his legs. I don't want to startle him. 'Get down,' I say more softly, pointing down to where Astrid watches on. Knut shakes his head. I could do with Wærwulf beside me to explain why he needs to go to his grandmother. Gardulf has made it to the beam and grapples with the extra rope, while Lyfing's now on the first rope. Knut growls at me, but something catches his eye. He skips past me, with no regard for the length of the fall or the narrowness of the beam, and takes the rope from Gardulf. He has it tied tightly in moments, looping end over end and then letting the rest fall to the ground.

'Well, he made that look bloody easy,' I murmur. Gardulf's eyes are confused, his hands moving as he tries to recreate the action, but now isn't the time to tie bloody ropes. I've got up here. Now, I need to go to the roof and kill our bloody enemy.

It would be much easier if the ground weren't veering alarmingly beneath me. Shit. Sometimes, I really should leave such tasks to my fellow warriors.

With half an eye on Knut, who is at least now back along the beam by the ropes, and Hereman's embedded spear, I pull the stiff canvas entirely free. I'm wary, listening for sounds of my enemy, although how I'm supposed to decipher a usual sound for a thatch roof and an unusual one, I don't know. If they saw Knut, they might be there, waiting for me. If they didn't see Knut, then quite how I'm to climb through the window, I don't know. Surely, I reason, cursing under my breath, there should have been an easier way of doing this.

I hear a shriek and look down, but Ingwald's secured himself on the rope, even if he's slipped down half a horse's length. His hands will burn for that. Poor fucker. The beam quivers as Gardulf comes towards me.

'Hurry up,' he urges me. His face is bleached of all colour. If altercations were supposed to occur on roofs, I'm convinced we'd all have bloody wings.

'I'm doing my best,' I grumble. I know I'm not. I'm all fingers and thumbs. I'm too focused on those down below. I wish I hadn't taken it upon myself to show my men how it's bloody done. I'd curse Rudolf, but it seems he's the one with more than half a thought in his head today.

As confident as I can be that there's no one waiting to impale me from outside, I stand and take a reaching step towards the open window. The wooden planks of the construction are at least almost wide enough for my foot to fit across it widthways. I hold onto the top of the window and then, holding my breath, duck beneath it, my long hair flying into my mouth and eyes so that for a moment, I can't see and can only taste my hair, which needs a decent wash.

I spit it aside, shake my head, and clear my vision. I'm not about to let go. I can feel my legs wobbling alongside my arms. Fuck this. I can see the church roof, the thatch firmly woven together. Others have been this way, and they've left me something. I'm not sure I appreciate it, but it does make the transition from wall to roof easier. Gripping firmly with my left hand, I tug on the dangling rope. It holds firm, but to truly test it, I'll need to add all of my weight.

'Fuck, fuck, bollocks, fuck,' the chant is constant as I count to three and force myself to take the risk. I don't think what will happen if this is how they mean to kill me. It holds, and I swing myself upwards, feet embedded in the thatch, my arms straining once more as I haul myself upwards. Gardulf's head appears through the window. I glimpse it just as I'm cresting the steepness of the sides of the roof and dragging myself onto the only flat part of it. It's narrow, and there's nowhere to hide, but my enemies aren't expecting me. I'm unsurprised. The wind is so loud it wouldn't be possible to hear what's happening below them.

The six Viking raiders are all to the far end, before the tower, using ropes to keep themselves aloft, tied around a spear thrust into the thickest part of the thatch. The rope I've used to get so high has been left dangling. Perhaps they mean to use it to get down, but I don't think so. They have other plans on their minds, evident from the flap of coloured linen Begga waves at her allies beyond the walls. While the lower part of the church roof doesn't entirely overtop the battlements, I manage to spy a collection of my enemy who are watching, far from the site of their attack. They also have a few coloured pieces of linen to wave in return. While one person waves the linens, the others are entirely focused on the corner of Northampton. I know exactly what they're looking at.

'Bastards,' Gardulf joins me, as does Ingwald. The rope's vibrating. More of my warriors are coming.

I eye the distance between my foeman and where I'm standing. It's a perilous long way. We should have brought spears to throw and bows and arrows to skewer them. I need Hereman up here, but he's too heavy and well-built. He'll not make it up the twin ropes.

I gnaw my lips, considering what to do. I didn't think this through. That much is obvious. I should have considered what I'd do when I got here. I should have thought about how I'd get them off the roof. Maybe it would have been better to set fire to it. That would have had them rushing to ground level if they could get down.

I turn and see Ealdorman Ælhun, eyes wide, mouth open, as he watches me from the battlements where he must have retreated to after he saw I was going up the rope. I lift my hand to wave jauntily and regret it as my trews slip on the slick thatch of the roof.

Fists bunched into the thatch, I glare at my enemy. The five men and one woman are oblivious to our arrival, so I have some time to consider. But not much. At some point, one of my men will cry out, or one of the enemy will turn and see us, trying to stand firm on the vantage point. I consider whether these people, like young Knut, are shipmen and women. Are they used to scaling sails? I know I'd be no good at it, even if Astrid thinks the sea is a soft place to land. I don't think it bloody would be.

'What do you intend?' Gardulf whispers to me. I admire him for being able to stand, but wish he wouldn't. I can't have him falling to the ground. I don't want to admit that I'm terrified out of my mind and have fuck all idea.

Ingwald kneels as I do, his face pale, his throat moving as he swallows heavily. I'm glad he's struggling to keep his food down. Behind him, the rope vibrates, but all I can think is where the fuck did our enemy get so much bloody rope from? I didn't realise we had so much of it going to waste inside Northampton. And, if they brought it with them, shouldn't we have found it, or rather, shouldn't Rudolf?

Thinking of him has me looking to Ealdorman Ælhun once more. Rudolf's eyes are wide, his mouth hanging open, his hand on his weapon's belt as though such would be helpful from there. But, the thought of his seax gives me the idea of what we need to do now.

'Cut the ropes,' I advise Gardulf and Ingwald. 'Cut their ropes. We have to hope the fuckers fall to their deaths.'

There is a problem with my suggestion. The spear they're using to anchor themselves is close to them, far along the roof. To get to it, we'll alert them to our presence. The rope I've used to get onto the roof is entirely separate from the one they're using. We'll be the ones under attack. A pity it's not closer to us, but when was anything I needed to accomplish ever fucking easy.

'Here,' Goda joins us. I'm amazed he's here when one of his fingers is missing, but he's more stable than I am. Even here, he's keeping a cool head as he offers a length of rope. 'We've tied it to the projecting beam. If we fall, and we're not too far from it, it might prevent us from hitting the ground with a wet sound.' He speaks in a whisper, a gleam in his eyes that makes him look like a crazy, mad bastard.

I want to refuse. If we're all tied to the rope, then we can all bloody fall down, but I'd rather be tied to something.

'I'll go first,' I announce, reaching for the ends, but Goda shakes his head. 'If you go first, you'll be fourth along the line. If you want to be at the front of the rope, you need to wait for everyone to attach themselves.' This I don't like. The breeze is buffeting me, and the desire to get down is overwhelming. I've underestimated the absolute pleasure of standing on the ground with my two feet. I won't be forgetting in a fucking hurry.

'Get on with it,' I growl. The sense of impending disaster is impossible to ignore. I can't see what the enemy is doing before the walls now, but the coloured banner must mean something.

Ealdorman Ælhun and Rudolf focus on me, so at least, for now, the enemy isn't renewing their attack or trying to sneak through the tunnel. Not that they'd be able to do so. It's heavily guarded.

'Fuck this,' I mutter, finally allowed to secure myself to the rope. I stand unsteadily and loop it around my waist, aware my legs and arms are shaking. Gardulf's next to me. He watches me impatiently. I wish I shared his enthusiasm for the next part of the task.

I turn towards our enemy. Their arrogance drives fire into me. I might not want to be here, but the knowledge that they believe us too stupid to find them spurs me on. I step out, praying my legs stop shaking, and then move the next foot. Our single rope means we all must move as one or risk becoming unbalanced. The others realise quickly. We must look a sight, shuffling one behind the other. How we'll fight when we get to the enemy, I don't know. Although, well, I intend to slice through their ropes and send them falling to the ground. Sooner they landed with the wet sound of breaking bones and exploding body juices than we bloody do.

I count under my breath. One two, one two, moving my legs in time to the count. The enemy is getting closer, the spear which holds their tethers, almost within reach. I force myself not to hurry. The enemy beyond the walls might be able to see us, although the tower should provide some protection. They might even have a means of communicating with these people that they've been discovered. One two. One two. I reach for my seax. The trick will be to cut through all six tethering ropes quickly, before they realise or can do anything to secure their footing. The wind's stronger up here, exposed on all sides. I wobble and clench my arse to prevent myself from falling. It's worse than having the shits and needing a quiet place to find some bloody comfort.

I reach out only to pause. To do this, all my men need to sever one of the ropes. I wait, trying to get them as close as possible without twisting our rope in the enemy tethers. We can't surround it. It's not flush to the top of the thatch but slightly skewed to one side, down the slope.

'Fuck,' I mutter under my breath when Gardulf and Ingwald are as close as possible. I meet their eyes. They instinctively understand my intentions.

'One, two, three,' and we all reach for the closest tether to us. I don't look to see who dangles from the lengths of it. I don't want to know. Neither is it easy to saw through the thick hempen threads with our seaxes. Better if we had a sharp war axe than our bloody seaxes. They might be good for cutting through flesh and sometimes bone, but a bloody rope? That requires something altogether different, and we don't have it.

The vibrations through the tethers must alert our enemy before we're finished. Cries of dismay ripple with the wind. I rely on Goda to shout if the enemy tries to get to us. Hopefully, they'll be more bloody concerned with securing their hold on the thatch.

Part of the tether I'm sawing away at gives, but threads of it still hold. It might be easier to pluck the spear from the thatch that holds it, but it seems well planted. I doubt we'll ever be able to remove it. Not until the thatch is replaced and rethreaded. I don't envy the men and women who can perform such a task with the wind whistling in their ears.

I feel Ingwald's rope fracture in a shudder that works its way from the top of the spear where it's embedded. A shriek of dismay greets the action, but alas, not the cry of a body hitting the hard ground below.

'Hurry the fuck up,' I grimace through my rictus grin. Frustrated, I lift my seax and slash down with the tip. It snags the few remaining strands and gives, the rope springing free with enough force to whip my hand as it passes.

Gardulf does the same. I almost taste success, but Goda's words reach my ear.

'Ware, Coelwulf, ware.' I don't feel it, but I sense it. One of the enemy coming towards me. I turn and slash at one of the remaining ropes but do nothing to spring it free. The tall woman faces me. Begga's face is red with fury. Her lips move, but I can't hear the words. I imagine it well enough as she raises her war axe and flings it towards me. Instinctively, I try to avoid the weapon, only to remember the perilous nature of my footing. Instead, I grip the embedded spear and only shuffle my feet. The war axe twangs against the wood of the spear but does no greater harm before sticking in the thatch. The shriek of rage from Begga reminds me of a raven on the hunt as she fights to retrieve her weapon. I remember then that while she might have a war axe or had a war axe, Rudolf also warned me that she had two seaxes. Soon, she'll remember that as well.

She's not alone in advancing, either. Two others are slowly making their way along the top of the thatched roof: the short man, and one of the others. I don't miss that the short man, Ake, uses the rope to pull himself along. I look down, realise the rope is taut beside me and lash into it. The seax almost has no impact, but then I recall the war axe. With a grunt of effort, I wrench it free and slice through all three remaining tethers. Ake falters, his momentum gone, arms waving in the air as he tries to regain his balance.

A bellow of fury leaves his mouth, but there's nothing he can grip onto. At last, I hear the thud of something heavy hitting the ground. One of the bastards is dead. A ragged cheer greets my actions. I'm glad the Mercians approve of my presence on the bloody roof.

The four of us now focus on our enemy. We wanted the six of them to plunge to their deaths. One of them has done so, but five remain. Begga continues to menace me, seax blades flashing in both hands. She walks with supreme confidence, not looking where she's going, not seeming to notice how high up she is or that one wrong move could have her following Ake to the ground.

I bloody admire her, then. I can't help it. She's as I must appear on the slaughter field. Unhurried. Unworried. Fearless.

The seax strike comes from nowhere. With her eyes fixed on me, she doesn't even notice it hitting her stomach. Her byrnie would absorb the blow from the handle, but somehow, it's the thrown blade that hits her, point first, slipping through the material of the byrnie. There's a cry of fury and other gabbled words, and two men are holding a different coloured piece of cloth aloft. I gaze at the vivid blue, considering what it means, even as Begga surges upwards. Her balance remains finally tipped, but blood leaks from her belly wound.

I growl low, gripping my seax, preparing to strike her. I won't let her wound me, or kill me, or take the life of one of my men. I watch her, not taking my eyes from the steady advance, even as Gardulf shuffles around me to try and reach the waving cloth.

I raise my seax arm to strike out at Begga, only to knock Gardulf with my elbow. He cries out as I grip him to steady his balance. My aim's badly affected. Then she's on me. In the time it's taken me to blink, she's there. I can feel the heat of her fury and the slickness of her blood as I crumble beneath her flung body weight. I hit the rough thatch, the air lost from my body, feeling the tension in the rope that binds me to my allies around my waist as though I'm being sliced in half.

'*Skiderick,*' I growl, struggling to evade her blows. I've managed to keep hold of my seax. I want to use it to batter against her back, but there's something else happening. The tension in the rope increases, pulling uncomfortably at my waist. If I weren't already flattened, I'd fall, I know it. Gardulf's words are incomprehensible. Ingwald's shouting as well, but it's Goda's call that I understand.

'Shit.' We're all slipping down the thatch. I need to win free from my allies.

With Begga pinning me down, I roll to the side, taking her with me, able to see the silver scar on her face, running down her neck and beneath her byrnie, even as I lash out at the rope. I feel it's beginning to fray, the tension abating, but Begga continues to batter me. She should be dying or, better yet, dead, but her flailing limbs still mean to wound me. With another violent strike, the rope gives. I know my warriors will be safe.

'Fucking hell,' I expel. I feel myself starting to slip further now I'm free of the rope. The others might stand a chance, but I'm in the shit. I roll flat on my back, digging my feet into the thatch, burrowing through the layers of it trying to tether myself with my weight and little else.

I don't know what the others are doing. All I can see is the blue, cloud-spotted sky overhead, the sun bright in my eyes. Then Begga rears up, casting me into shadow.

'Die bitch,' I growl, using my seax to stab into her exposed throat, sheeting myself in the maroon of her lifeblood. She bucks once, twice, and flops against me. I almost breathe in relief only for my body to slip once more.

With more luck than skill, I force her additional weight from my body. Begga's wide-eyed expression is unseeing as she rolls free. I watch her lifeless body catch in the thatch for a moment.

'Bloody hell.' I risk it all to kick her free. I slip again, the harsh material digging into my back but doing nothing to stop me from falling.

With both hands on my seax, I dig my feet in and surge upwards, turning as I go, impaling my seax in the thatch, so I have something to keep me aloft. I glance upwards, seeing the horror on the faces of my allies, a cry of warning almost too late. Gardulf's under attack. A man as stringy as him clambers towards him, seax raised, death glinting in his hate-filled eyes.

Ingwald sees the danger. With a skip of speed that almost sees him falling, he and the enemy are embroiled.

'Help me,' I urge Goda, desperate for something more solid to hold than my seax and blood-drenched hands.

Goda clutches the rope around his waist, but the others are still attached. There's nothing for him to throw to me. I eye the trailing ends of some of the other tethers. We didn't sever them close to the spear, but they're out of reach. Gardulf and Ingwald fight the remaining enemy. I hope the others have gone, for I can't see well enough, my gaze exclusively on the threaded thatch which keeps me precariously aloft. I wish there were something to grip onto.

From below and surrounding us, a roar of angry voices reaches my ears. I fear for Ealdorman Ælhun and my other warriors. Has the trap already been sprung? Have we been up here, pissing in the wind, risking our lives, while we're already too late?

'Coelwulf,' I glare at Goda as he calls my name. What does he expect me to fucking do from here?

'Coelwulf,' he calls again, and now I see young Knut, skipping along the roof, another stretch of rope trailing behind him. He hangs motionless in the air, but then the rope's thrown towards me. I grab it with one hand. Test the tautness of it, and content it should take my weight, relinquish my hold on the seax. I want to take the double-headed eagle blade with me, but it must stay here like the spear. With shaking hands and arms, I pull myself upright and then upwards, wrapping my arm around the rope so that I have some leverage should the wind knock me aside.

A shriek of outrage, and a body slips past me, the man who was fighting Ingwald reaching for anything he can grab. His hand misses me but closes around my seax in a move I'd never be lucky enough to replicate. Arm outstretched, he holds on with all his might. I look down, seeing no fear in his eyes. I reach for Begga's axe, hold it one-handed, and fling it at his exposed head. I don't even wince as it cleaves his head in two, his hand slipping and his body sliding inexorably down.

'Fuck me,' Gardulf expels. The original piece of rope holds him and Ingwald together. Goda as well. Knut clings on with nothing but air, but I look around me, breathing and trying to calm my rapidly beating heart.

'What's happening below? Why the cry of battle-hardened warriors?' Then I see why. We're to get no bloody respite, no matter our endeavours. 'Fuck, we need to get down.'

Chapter Twenty-One

The way down is even more perilous than the climb up because I have to look where I'm going, and the ground veers alarmingly beneath me. It doesn't help that I know the enemy is trying to open the tunnel from the inside. We might have killed those on the roof, but it appears there were more of the bastards than just that.

Knut scampers downwards. I can barely watch him as he lowers himself down and through the window. I'd like to descend from the great height in one quick movement, but instead, I have to force myself to clamber through the window, and then along the huge beam and then down the descending rope. All the time, I'm shouting instructions.

'Inform Ealdorman Ælhun the tunnel's threatened.'

'Order Beornstan, Ordheah, Cuthwalh, Oda and Wulfhere to the tunnel.'

'Hereman, get back to the bloody tunnel as well, Gardulf, go with him. And get sodding Rudolf as well.'

I know my words can be heard because every time I speak, there's the sound of hurried footsteps over the wooden floorboards. Knut remains above, his eyes watching everything I do. I almost think he's been told to keep a special watch on me by his grandmother. I don't know whether I like that feeling or not. It's bloody unusual to say the least.

'Get the horses away from the tunnel,' I call as I work hand over hand to descend the rope. I've seen others slide down it. My hands are slick with the blood of the dead woman, so I have to grip it tightly, or I'll land with a thunk.

'Have the main gate reinforced. Get these people inside the hall where they'll be safe.' This I direct to Priest Wilfrid, who's taken to his knees, wailing. What I need right now is to know where every fucker is and that they're safe. I don't need to listen to the distressed priest and his cries to God. Blades will save us, not the benevolence of some bastard God I've never met.

I pause momentarily to savour the feel of the wooden floor beneath my feet, but then I'm rushing from the church. I need to get back to the hidden tunnel and the ramparts.

'My thanks,' I call to Astrid and Knut. She has a smile on her lined face, even as she shouts to her grandson. I look to Wærwulf, but he's impatient to escort me and doesn't seem to listen.

'Order them all to the hall,' I remind him. His voice rumbles away as I surge through the open doorway. The air is filled with dismayed cries, but I don't think they come from my people within Northampton. Especially as I know so many of them are inside the great hall. No, this must be the Viking raiders under Jarl Halfdan. They anticipated a much warmer welcome than they're receiving.

I rush through the streets. More and more of my warriors join me from where they've been seeking the enemy and checking the defences. I know we should be secure. We took advantage of Northampton's weaknesses enough in the past to put defences in place to prevent anything from happening to us.

I'm brought up short before the secret tunnel with the ramparts in sight. There's a heaving mess of fighting, the horses caught up in it all, as their shrill neighs fill the air. 'Bastards,' I glower, watching Haden rear and try to escape.

But I can't see the enemy. Well I can't see a whole host of them as I would expect if the tunnel had fallen, allowing entry from outside. Is this another ruse? Quickly, I scamper up the steep wooden steps to the ramparts, keeping my hand on the rail because I don't wish to risk falling when I've just reacquainted myself with the ground having been dangling so high. Below me is a frenzy of outraged horses and bellowing warriors, mine and Ealdorman Ælhun's. But what's happening beyond the ramparts?

'They came from nowhere,' the ealdorman greets me without preamble. 'Your men and mine quickly prevented them from doing what they wanted.'

My eyes peer over the rampart. I veer back in shock. The number of enemy warriors has more than doubled. They've made it down and through the defensive ditch and now stand, jeering upwards at the turf and mud walls, shields and blades to hand. The broken-down and burned remains of the encampment stretch away into the distance towards the ford, but no one moves amongst the wreckage, which still smokes in the far distance. The fire we started by accident has done a great deal of damage.

I can see Jarl Halfdan, a satisfied smirk on his face, but he doesn't look towards where the tunnel is but to the south of the ramparts. I notice it with a furrowed brow, even as I peer entirely over the rampart. I can't determine if the tunnel has been opened from the outside. I don't think it has. Instead, I eye Jarl Halfdan, who's not looking at the tunnel at all. Indeed, his warriors might have made it through the deep ditch, but they don't congregate below me.

'Has he been doing that long?' I demand from Rudolf, who stands and watches. I thought he was protecting the tunnel, but it seems not.

'What, looking elsewhere? Yes, he has.'

'Why?' I gaze down at the seething mass below me, at the church's thatched roof, clearly visible from here, even the spear obvious against the thatch as I know where to look for it, and then I look down. We thought the tunnel was the target, but what if it isn't? These fuckers have shown themselves eager to climb up high. To make use of rope and take a risk. We've done the same. What if they mean to try our tricks?

'We need to check the wall to the south,' I order the ealdorman and Rudolf. 'Do you have a spare seax?' I question my young warrior. He hands it over without question. Gardulf and Hereman have just rumbled up the steps, but now I turn them, playing the blade on my weapons belt.

'That way,' I point. Hereman understands more quickly than the others.

'This way. Hold the tunnel and the ramparts,' I instruct the ealdorman, unsure if he has the men to do both but relying on his calm and orderly approach to do what he can.

I rush down the steps, holding tightly once more. 'Haden,' I call, hitting the ground heavily. I doubt he'll heed my call, but I'd like him out of there. I'm thundering once more through the streets, back towards the church. I don't have time to mount up. Luckily, there's no one on the streets other than my warriors or those of Ealdorman Ælhun's. I pause close to the main hall and eye the other gate. It's heavily protected. There's no way anyone can enter that way. The bridge has been pulled aside. They could come in a ship and couldn't grab a firm hold on the thin strip of river bank that will be visible.

No, that's not from where the threat comes. I curse myself for a bloody fool, hearing the crash of horse hooves following on behind. Then Knut is beside me, pointing urgently in the direction I'm already going. I round the corner of the church, already anticipating what I'll see, grimacing at the broken remains of those who fell from the height of the church's roof. In the background, Knut's gabbling to Wærwulf.

'My lord,' he calls, ensuring I can hear him, but I don't want to hear it. I want to see it for myself.

There, before me, spread across the turf and mud wall of the rampart, hidden for some time behind the church and other buildings close by, is a huge sail depicting Jarl Halfdan's emblem of a blue wolf. I can see exactly how they intend to use it; above it, one figure already waves towards Jarl Halfdan. This must be the signal he was looking for.

'Fuckers,' I glower as Wærwulf reaches me.

'Knut says,' but his words die on his lips as he looks upwards, seeing exactly what Knut meant to tell him. I don't recognise the person up there as being amongst the Norse Christians seeking refuge amongst us, but I do see Astrid at the bottom of the sail. I think she's trying to cut through it, to have it crumble to the ground, but she's not. I turn to Wærwulf.

'She's trying to tie it down, prevent them from lifting it,' he huffs. This does make more sense.

'Do they have another one on the other side?'

'This is to be lifted over,' Wærwulf explains.

'Get fire,' I urge him, calling my remaining warriors together and hastening to mount Haden who's been following me. I'll get there quicker and be able to accomplish more with Haden.

'Crafty bastards,' I mutter. I can't even curse myself for being a fool because I could never have imagined this. Not in four fucking lifetimes.

Haden eagerly takes my command, my warriors running beside me as we surge to the wall. The walls are high. I don't want to go up there. This is an area where the rampart doesn't extend. I don't know the reason why, perhaps for this very opportunity. I thought I knew everything there was to know about Northampton. I believed I'd ensured it was safe and protected, but now I realise I made an appalling oversight and one that the enemy intends to exploit. We can't allow that to bloody happen.

When I'm as close as I can get, I jump clear from Haden's back, hands outstretched to grab hold of the sail. It lifts just before me, but I have it in my hands well above head height, the stink of damp and grease on it unpleasant. For a moment, it holds firm. I close my eyes willing it to tumble. Only then it does, the ground coming to meet me far too quickly.

I roll with the canvas, attempting to get it beneath me to cushion my fall. The world goes white, and I land, limbs curled tight beneath me, the air knocked from my body. When my eyes open, I can smell burning, the acrid stench making me cough. I lift my arms, and kick my feet, but I'm entirely enclosed, the bitter scent of salt-tinged dampness covering everything.

'Bollocks,' I mutter. I've managed to dismantle the sail, but I also ordered it to be burnt. What if they've set it ablaze, not knowing where I am? I continue to fight, but it's impossible. I'm entirely covered. I can't even sense which way is up any more. Instead, my hand snakes to my seax. I grip it and try to pierce the canvas with it but there's too little room.

'Coelwulf,' I hear my name and open my mouth to respond, but nothing more than a muffled bark erupts. I stab again. The sail seems particularly strong, just like the fucking ropes. These Viking raiders know how to make ropes and sails that will withstand the elements. And a bloody sharp seax blade.

'Here,' I cry, as my name repeats. I hear footsteps coming closer, including the clip-clop sound of hooves. 'Here,' I call again, wincing as hands pat the cloth and finally skewer it with a sharp sword.

I glare up at Wærwulf, who glowers at me.

'Arsehole,' he complains, but the worry on his face is easy to see.

I ease myself free, uncomfortably reminded of the men I killed in their tents earlier. Was that only this morning?

Lurching to my feet, I glare upwards, seeing the sail entirely downed, flames trying to battle against the ingrained dampness and the slick grease that covers it. Higher up, eyes look down at me. Two sets of eyes, familiar from when they begged us to allow them inside Northampton for fear Jarl Halfdan would kill them. They'd do well to get down from there, on the other side of the ramparts surrounding Northampton, for fear I'll be the one to stop their hearts from beating.

'Did we stop them?' I huff, eager to take a deep breath rather than the cloying cloud of grey smoke that drifts close.

'Yes, the sail's down. They won't be using that to get inside Northampton.' That comforts me, but I doubt it will stop our enemy from trying their luck.

I continue to eye the ramparts, unsurprised when the Viking raiders up there bend to show us their arses. Taunting fuckers. A pity we don't have a spear long enough to gut them.

'What now?' Wærwulf queries. I shake my head. I don't know what they'll do next. They thought to gain entry by tricking us and then tricking us again. So far, the focus hasn't been where we've expected it to be. I thought they acted so to confuse us.

'What if they redouble their efforts at the tunnel?' I question, only for a flurry of raised voices to have me mounting up and galloping for the main gate. 'What the fuck now?' I glower. I'd like a moment to recover myself, to regain my breath, to consider what we've managed to avert until now. But I do not have the time.

Haden takes my commands easily, skirting the tight corners with sparks flying from his hooves. I fear he'll fall and break a leg, but I should trust my mount more. He knows his limits much better than I do.

'What is it?' I gasp, looking at the eyes of the men who guard the gate. There are familiar faces, and also some new ones, and the man I spoke to earlier steps forward, jutting his chest out as though determined to be the one to face my wrath.

'Your aunt is on the other side of the bridge.'

'Fuck.' He doesn't need to tell me more. We've disabled the bridge to ensure the enemy can't get inside from that direction.

'Is she alone other than the rest of my warriors?' But I'm already moving to the gate and instructing the men to remove the multiple wooden bars and open it wide. With a sharp crack of protesting wood, I gaze across the expanse of the river and look straight at my aunt and the four men who escorted her north.

'It seems you can't play nicely while I'm away,' she offers with a glint in her eye. She's steely, her horse alert beneath her. 'May we enter, my lord king?' she bows from her saddle. I'm nodding, even though this will be difficult without the bridge.

'Provided you like a swim, then yes,' I reply. I'm looking to my warriors. I can't say that Gyrth, Wulfstan, Ordlaf and Hemming look pleased, but already, they're urging their horses into the fast-flowing current.

I seek Icel amongst them.

'He's not coming,' my aunt confirms, her lips pursed as her horse enters the water. We have a rope to hand should it be needed. I don't think it will be. The animals like a good swim, or so I tell myself as the water rushes up the side of my aunt's dress and my warriors' legs. The water will be bloody cold. It's also fast, just like when we killed the enemy at the ford earlier. I bite my lip, urging them to hurry and be successful.

My aunt's horse surges up the thin lip of the river bank. I'm ready to grab hold should the animal falter. With the others close behind, I escort her through the gate, where she dismounts in a flurry of wet legs and cloaks. She looks around, taking in all that's happening, including the sounds of battle from the other side of Northampton, the smoke wafting through the street and fixes me with a wry smirk.

'It seems you didn't really need to know what I went north to discover from Bishop Burgheard, but if you must know, Jarl Halfdan has made a mistake in trying to overpower the Picts. In his absence, the allies he gave land to revolted against him and allied with King Ricsige. He's here to renew his alliance with the Repton jarls and to claim parts of Mercia for himself, for he has nothing else with which to reward his angry warriors. King Ricsige once more commands much of Northumbria.'

I nod. I admit, I've had my suspicions about Halfdan's arrival. It's better to have them confirmed.

'Icel has taken it upon himself to go to Worcester and help Mercia's warriors protect it. Now, I'll go to the great hall and get dry. I suggest you finish this fight with Jarl Halfdan. It delays you.' And with nothing further, she marches from my presence, even as my bedraggled warriors eye me. It's good to see them, but they're sodden and shivering.

'Get bloody warm,' I call to the four of them. 'Get warm, and don't even think about coming to join the fight. Not unless it's an emergency, which it won't be.' So spoken, I greet them affectionately, pleased to have them back amongst the rest of my men here within Northampton. I wish Icel were here. I can't help fearing he actually means to avoid the battle, not aid Worcester, but I'll wait and see what happens. Mounting once more, I turn Haden towards the tunnel beneath the rampart

What other bloody tricks does Jarl Halfdan plan on playing? I'm sure this won't be the fucking end of it.

Chapter Twenty-Two

But it is.

I can scarcely believe it when Jarl Halfdan begins to retreat, the cries of his warriors reaching my ears as they shout the retreat or groan in disappointment. I watch from the viewpoint, not trusting what I'm seeing, as his force begins to drift away. I survey them beneath the glowing haze of the coming night, unsure whether I understand what I'm seeing. Jarl Halfdan has done little but play tricks on me. Is this merely another one of them?

Those who still live amongst the Christian Norse who are really Jarl Halfdan's warriors put down their weapons as one in front of the tunnel which they've not been able to breach. I can see no signal has been shared between those within and without. The two who meant to lower the sail over the far walls of Northampton have also dispersed. I imagine they're risked jumping from the tall walls having shown the Mercians their arses. I consider whether they still live or not. I hope not, but they'll make the ditch fucking stink if their corpses fester there.

With Ealdorman Ælhun beside me, my aunt joining me once

she's dry and assured the fighting has finished, I stand and watch until I can see nothing. There are no campfires, no lights at all.

'Are they hiding?' I'm grateful Ealdorman Ælhun breaks the heavy silence by asking what I'm thinking.

'Perhaps,' I wish I could say one way or the other.

'Did many die here?' my aunt queries.

'Those amongst the campsite, yes, but not elsewhere.' I've finally remembered my men left at the ford. Ealdorman Ælhun has arranged for reinforcements to be sent to them, and the bridge returned to its normal place now that the threat has evaporated. Better not to send wet horses and men to spend a cold night beneath the stars.

'Get some rest,' I order the ealdorman, stifling my yawn, and dreaming of getting some sleep. Rudolf, Pybba and Hereman keep me company. Wærwulf's talking to Knut and his grandmother. I consider what else they might know about Jarl Halfdan's plans. The remaining Viking raiders, masquerading as Christians, have been imprisoned. The surviving Norse Christians mingle with the people of Northampton. I'm unsure if that will go well.

'He bloody tricked you,' Rudolf's furious now the fight's over and Northampton re-secured.

'He did, yes, just as I've deceived him before.' I can admit when an idea was a good one. I don't like to, but I will. Underestimating my enemy is how they'll bloody triumph.

'Will he bloody do so again?' Rudolf demands. I arch an eyebrow. It's surprising that the other two men allow Rudolf to lead the questioning. Maybe they don't want to be the doubting bastards any more. Perhaps they're tired of being the ones to query my actions.

'Probably.' Again, I don't like to admit that, but it seems highly likely that he will.

'What will you bloody do?'

'What I always do. Be sodding ready for anything,' I murmur. I'm feeling the aches and pains of a day spent riding, fighting, and swinging from a fucking high roof. I'm overjoyed my men and I have lived through it all, but my head itches. There's something not right. I wish I knew what it was.

'Was the whole thing a means of distracting you?' Pybba speaks heavily. I wish he didn't put the words to my uneasy thoughts.

'Potentially,' I agree. I'd like to know how the rest of the Mercian kingdom fares. Is Worcester threatened as Icel seems to believe? Is Torksey, despite my aunt's information to the contrary? Is bloody London? What I wouldn't give for an eye glass that would allow me to see all of these things from this spot in Northampton.

'What will you do now?' Again, it's Pybba that forces me to think about this.

'For now, I mean to stand here all night and watch the bastard enemy,' I growl.

'But then what will you do?' Pybba presses. His stance is belliger-ent. I wish I knew what he was thinking. It's telling that Ealdorman Ælhun and my aunt don't speak.

Rubbing my hand over my beard and mouth, I shake my head.

'I don't know. We were supposed to have a year of peace. I don't think any of us believed that Jarl Halfdan would return. Not with all he gained in Northumbria, alone, and with a third of the effort of taking Repton.'

'We were never going to have peace,' Pybba barks, unheeding that it was my aunt who suggested it. 'It was always a flight of fantasy that the ealdormen and bishops dreamed about achieving.' I nod. I'm inclined to agree with him. In all honesty, I didn't want there to be peace, or at least, I didn't think I did. Now I'm not so sure. Perhaps, on some level, I did crave peace and the time to rebuild. I'm a contrary bastard.

'What about Wessex?'

'I'm not allying with those demented fools,' I round on him.

'That's not what I meant.'

My eyes narrow, and I incline my head, looking at him in a whole new light.

'What did you mean then? Speak plainly. You're as obtuse as Icel.'

'They're already under attack. It would be better if the Viking raiders turned their eyes entirely to the south.'

'How the hell would we achieve that?' I don't like to think of my fellow Saxons being under duress, but perhaps Pybba has half an idea. After all, I've suspected the Wessex king of being in league with the Viking raiders for a long time.

'Well, we can never order a Viking raider to do anything. They don't take kindly to it,' Pybba confirms, a hint of irony touching his words. 'But, if they mean to retrieve Jarl Guthrum, then perhaps they'll see the wealth that Wessex has to offer once more and be reminded that Wessex's king isn't a warrior like you. The Wessex king has paid them off before.'

'Pybba, you're all honeyed words,' I smirk, wishing I could follow along with his idea. But as much as Wessex might direct the Viking raiders towards Mercia, I could never do the same. 'But we can't do that.'

Pybba shrugs. 'Worth a try,' he states.

'Then what?' Rudolf insists, but perhaps Pybba is correct after all.

'I'll think about it,' I confirm, then wave them to silence. I can hear voices from beyond the ramparts. I want to know what they say, and luckily, Wærwulf arrives at that moment, his lips forming words, which I shush.

He nods, not all concerned by being told to shut up, and we stand and listen.

The voices come from far away, or so I think. It's difficult to tell in the darkness. They could be directly beneath us or far away, almost at the river.

I turn to Wærwulf as the sound becomes clearer and clearer. The scowl on his face is telling. Still, we wait. Only when the voices have faded away does he meet my gaze.

'They're still searching for the way in and for their allies within

Northampton. They don't believe they've been captured, despite everything that happened today.'

'Is that it?'

'From what I could hear, yes, and it mirrors what Astrid and Knut have been telling me. Knut heard things he shouldn't, but they've made no sense until now. The intention was to open the tunnel, and if that failed, to use the sail to gain entry and overwhelm us. Jarl Halfdan's determined to take Northampton.'

'Did he say anything else?'

'No. It's a shame we didn't know earlier.'

'Indeed, we'll have to watch the enemy we've captured. They'll no doubt try to escape.'

Ealdorman Ælhun interjects then. 'They're under lock and key,' as though that answers everything.

'But we know that means less than we might hope,' I mutter unhappily. 'Under lock and key isn't as good as dead. But we can't kill them. The enemy already believes we killed some of their number. If we do kill them, then we're as bloody bad as the evil bastards.'

'Then what will you do with them?'

'I think it's time we went to Worcester. I'm sure Jarl Guthrum would welcome seeing some of his allies.'

'What are you thinking?' my aunt questions, her tone severe.

'I'm not thinking,' I counter. 'I find that's when all the bloody problems start.'

I see her nod, a small smile playing on her lips as she acknowledges the truth.

'What of Northampton?' the ealdorman questions.

'I'll leave her to your care. I see no way for the Viking raiders to get inside. They've not managed it yet. Keep the Mercian banner showing. Make them believe I'm here. But I'll take the enemy from here and the Norse Christians as well. It'll be better if Bishop Wærferth has control over their fates. That'll leave you with loyal Mercians to worry about.' Ealdorman Ælhun grunts in agreement, but I can tell he's unhappy in the growing moonlight, revealing the silver in his hair and beard.

I'm not exactly bloody happy, either. I don't want to be led by my enemy. Not any more.

Chapter Twenty-Three

Worcester

It takes six days to reach Worcester from Northampton. Our prisoners are a sullen bunch. The Norse Christians are much more content. I'd like to think the journey is relaxing, but it isn't. Even with my aunt, we're almost outnumbered by the Norse.

'My lord king,' Bishop Wærferth greets me with a wry grin as I dismount outside his hall, having gained entry into Worcester's growing defensive walls.

'Wærferth, you're well?' I manage to offer instead of launching into the many topics I wish to discuss with him. I see Ælfgar and Eadfrith, and offer them a nod of welcome. It's good to know they've arrived safely. Icel's there, too. I can't decipher his expression. He shows no relief that we're here. He stands in a warrior stance. Something's ruffled him.

'I was going to set off to Northampton today. I hear you have some Norse Christians for me.'

'I do. I've brought them with us.' I indicate Knut, Astrid and the other remaining people.

'Not all of them?' he questions, eyeing those bound to horses.

'No, some of them aren't yet keen to relinquish their heathen beliefs,' I offer blandly. He seems to understand despite ignorance regarding everything that happened after Ælfgar and Eadfrith left Northampton. 'Come, let's go somewhere to talk without being overheard.' I step towards him and only then notice Jarl Guthrum, or rather Æthelstan, dressed in penitent grey behind the bishop. I notice he puts his weight on the foot that wasn't wounded.

Guthrum's eyes are keen, taking in his fellow Norse. I wonder what he's thinking. Does he suspect what's happened within Northampton? Did he think Jarl Halfdan would try to rescue him? How could he even have known that Jarl Halfdan had lost his hold on Northumbria unless it happened before the events in Grantabridge? I consider that. There was someone at Grantabridge wearing Jarl Halfdan's wolf emblem. I recall it now.

'My lord, you're comfortable in Worcester,' I acknowledge him with as much warmth as I can muster while my mind is busy thinking.

'I am, King Coelwulf, thank you. I am enjoying the instructions from Bishop Wærferth and his priests and monks.' I notice a gleam of pleasure on the face of Bishop Wærferth. I hope he's not been won over so quickly. 'And these people, who are they?'

'Well,' and I beckon Astrid and the others to my side. 'They also wish to convert and serve Christianity.' I wish I could say they'd run away from the Viking raiders, but that's not necessarily correct. Equally, as they said they came from the ruins of Grantabridge, I would expect Guthrum to know who they are. 'Alas, these others are our prisoners. I've yet to decide what to do with them.'

'So, the Christians are to be made welcome?' Jarl Guthrum asks, a hint of hope in his voice, although his eyes are guarded, and I don't miss that he peers more closely at those in chains.

'Yes. No doubt with your assistance.' I offer with what I hope is a smile on my face. Jarl Guthrum beams, the owl tattoos rippling on his arms as he does so. But I'm busy thinking. Perhaps, bringing the prisoners here was a bad idea. I might have them sent to Gloucester instead. Better to have them away from Guthrum. Admittedly, if I was a Norse bastard, I'd be selling them into slavery. I don't intend on doing that.

'Then we can go to the church?' Jarl Guthrum asks the bishop, like a child seeking permission.

'Perhaps they might be allowed to dismount, eat and drink first,' I suggest.

'Ah, of course.' He moves amongst the others, welcoming them, and I look to Wærwulf, but he shakes his head. The Danish words Jarl Guthrum uses are nothing to worry about. For now. And in the background, the prisoners are being led away from the Christians, so Guthrum has no opportunity to speak with them.

'What have you done to the great Viking raider Jarl Guthrum?' I ask the bishop, determined to make light of my worries.

A pious expression on his face, Wærferth offers me a delighted smile. 'It's not me, but the word of our Lord God.'

'Then he has my most sincere thanks.'

Bishop Wærferth laughs at my wry tone. He beckons me aside from the Norse Christians. Bishop Wærferth's warriors watch the men, and I incline my head towards Kyred. He nods once, looking severe. He's not as pleased by all this as the bishop.

My aunt joins me and Wærferth. The two exchange pleasantries until we're close to the river, the sound of our conversation covered by the rush of the burbling water.

'My lord king, is it true that the jarls mean to rescue Jarl Guthrum? He seems content enough.'

'Too content?' I question. Bishop Wærferth does me the honour of considering the question instead of simply denying it.

'No, not too content at all. He's keen to learn, which surprises me. Even when he sleeps, he's under constant guard but makes no complaint about it.'

'That might be for now. Perhaps it was all set in motion before he realised what baptism meant.'

'That could be correct,' Wærferth admits. He's not alone in eyeing the River Severn running beside us. To the far side, the land held by the bishop is being worked upon by the many labourers. It's a calm scene. Yet none of us can ignore the river or the knowledge that the Viking raiders could use it to get here.

'There's easy access to the sea,' Wærferth admits. 'If they do mean to come this way.'

'And then they'd be able to overrun Mercia from the west, not just the east.'

'Or, they might be satisfied with rescuing Jarl Guthrum and slinking away.'

'When have the Viking raiders ever been content and merely slunk away?' my aunt asks acerbically. At least I don't have to question the bishop.

'So what will you do?'

I fall silent. I'm still far from convinced that my intention is a good one.

'We must convince Jarl Guthrum of one of two things. Either that Mercia is too powerful to fight. After all, Jarl Guthrum is our hostage, and Jarl Halfdan can't crack his way into Northampton even with his people infiltrating the settlement under the guise of converting to Christianity. Or, we must persuade them that there are much easier targets. After all, Mercia is only accessible via rivers. There are,' and I pause, unhappy to be repeating Pybba's words, 'other places that are easier to attack.'

'So we either kill them all, or we let them go to Wessex and Northumbria, as well as the Frankish kingdom?' There's a bite to the bishop's words. I wince to hear it.

'That's about it, yes.'

'Then we'll have to bloody kill them all.' His arms fold while speaking, crossing his narrow chest, chin jutted out.

I watch him from the corner of my eye, also testing my aunt's reaction.

'What about converting them?' the bishop persists. 'You've already brought men and women for me to teach.'

'They're too few, and it would take too bloody long.' A heavy silence falls between us.

'So, do we release Jarl Guthrum or kill him?' My aunt's cold analysis reminds me once more of why she should have been Mercia's king, not me.

'That rather depends.'

'On what?' the bishop's words are resigned.

'On whether he has a part to play in all this. Better to know our enemy, after all.'

Bishop Wærferth shakes his head, lips pursed, only for his eyes to narrow.

'If Jarl Guthrum, or Æthelstan as we call him, returns to his people, he might spread the word of God.' That's not exactly what I'm thinking, but I don't deny it's possible. 'He might look kindly upon Mercia?'

'Or he might be so bloody terrified he never considers coming here again.' But Bishop Wærferth shakes his head at my words.

'No, no, he won't be terrified, but he'll be respectful. He'll admire you for allowing him to live and adopt the new faith. If he wins free, and we must ensure he's forced to win free, then he'll remember that.'

'So we must fight, but not hard enough that he can't escape?' my aunt demands.

I'm nodding. But her face clouds.

'Mercian men might die.'

'They might, yes, but if it gives Mercia the protection she needs, then they've died for their kingdom.'

Ire flashes, and her jaw's rigid. I know she's thinking of Edmund and all we lost to apprehend Jarl Guthrum. But, as so often the case with these bastard Viking raiders, our intentions have been undone by their overwhelming numbers.

'I don't like it,' she expels. 'I don't like it at all. But, it might well achieve much. Still, we don't want the enemy in Worcester.'

'No, we don't,' I admit. 'Or at Kingsholm. We want them as close to the estuary as possible.'

'So, what, you mean to risk Gloucester?'

'I do, yes,' I confess, not liking it. 'We'll take every warrior to protect Gloucester, Kingsholm and Worcester. It's better to have the buggers there rather than so much deeper into Mercia. Better yet to have them think they can trick us and escape with their Christian king.'

'This is very dangerous,' my aunt mutters. I'm unsurprised. It's a huge risk. It's akin to welcoming the enemy into our heartlands with only a limited response. Mercia could be entirely overwhelmed from the east, thanks to Jarl Halfdan, and the west, thanks to Jarls Anwend and Oscetel, if this goes wrong.

'It is,' I confirm. 'Everything to do with these buggers is dangerous. Evidence from the past shows that they're deadly. But, it also reveals they can't hold anything once they win it. They lack the desire to do so. Look at Jarl Halfdan – he's lost Mercia and Northumbria. And, if Jarl Guthrum is convinced of the righteousness of Christianity and Mercia's strength, then he'll believe himself lucky to escape alive. That should, it's to be hoped, convince him to look elsewhere for his next target.'

'You mean to direct him towards kingdoms that would ally with you?' the bishop resumes his complaints.

'I merely mean to direct them away from here. Mercia has no alliance with Northumbria or with Wessex. Not yet. Wessex wants Mercia to fight its battles for it. We can't do that. We must protect Mercia, and only then can we even consider looking elsewhere.'

An uneasy frown settles on his face, but he nods unwillingly.

'Will you inform Wessex?'

'Of what? That Mercia is to be attacked via a ship army, and we mean to lose to it? I don't think so.'

'No, we won't inform Wessex of this,' my aunt announces forcefully. 'I've had enough of Wessex and her tricks. Let's see how she copes when they're turned on her.'

Chapter Twenty-Four

Gloucester

Jarl Guthrum doesn't even quirk an eyebrow when told of the move to another Mercian stronghold. He and his fellow Norse Christians, Knut and Astrid foremost amongst them, are still being watched, but now it's known amongst my warriors that the enemy is to be invited in, our scrutiny has somewhat lapsed. The prisoners are to be taken to Kingsholm.

Our focus is now elsewhere, on the River Severn. Not that the Norse know that. Still, I might have convinced others of the necessity of this deception, but my conviction is waning even as theirs increases.

The journey to Gloucester is undertaken with all the pomp and ceremony to be expected from Mercia's king, his aunt, and retinue travelling together. Bishop Wærferth's fully committed, as is Kyred who brings the bishop's warriors. The monks and priests are joyful. They carry priceless relics with them. I wish they didn't, but we've not been able to tell everyone of the planned deceit. If this goes tits up, I'd rather not feel the wrath of the bloody church as well as my aunt and all those others I'm placing in danger.

I know next to nothing about the Severn estuary or much of the

Severn River other than those elements I've fought over or half-drowned within. Shipmaster Æthelred and his three sons have been enrolled in the scheme. Shipmaster Æthelred eyes me, perhaps drinking in the many wounds I've taken since we last met, wincing at the scar that almost circles my neck and the slice on my arm which is healing well.

'I offer my sympathies for those men you've lost,' he states sincerely, but spoken with a gruffness that has me appreciating he's lost men himself. He knows what it is to be a warrior, yet grief-stricken. I cough the sorrow from my throat.

'My thanks,' I choke, and he does me the honour of involving himself in some aspect of his ship's sail, so I have time to recover myself. I really fucking hate my grief. It strikes when I least expect it. I think myself almost reconciled to it, only to discover that I'm far from over the loss of Edmund, Siric and the others I've also lost.

'What's this half-arsed scheme you've cooked up now?'

I appreciate his acceptance of what I want to do.

'We invite them in. We let them rescue Jarl Guthrum. But we make a bloody good fight of it. They can contend with their jarl then. Bishop Wærferth hopes he'll spread the word of Christianity, but I want him there to counter Jarl Halfdan's influence.'

'So, you mean to sacrifice Gloucester in this half-cocked scheme?'

'Not sacrifice, now. It was hard enough to get the fucking Welsh to rebuild the bridge. I'm not going through that shit again.'

A grin on Shipmaster Æthelred's face, and I wonder what stories he could tell me about the bloody Welsh. Probably enough to have me hating them as much as Edmund. Damn it. Again, he's never far from my mind.

'Tell me, how does the river work? And the estuary? Will they be able to make it this far?'

His face, old, lined, and tanned with the summer sun, furrows in thought.

'Yes, they are ship men. Well, they say they are. If they can navigate the Humber and along the Trent, I see no problem for them here. They might need a guide if the bore's running, but men such as them, well, if they're half as good as they imply, should have no problems with it. So, what do you need from me?'

'I need to know the best way to protect the river to the north of here. Gloucester's one thing, but I won't have them racing along the Severn if this gets fucked up.'

'Aye, my lord king. A wise precaution. Leave it with me. My sons and I know some tricks. And others will work with us as well. You contend with the thieving bastards here, and we'll deal with them after Gloucester.'

'My thanks. You'll be well rewarded.'

'I ask nothing but to know the kingdom's safe. Well, perhaps a ship or two to add to my fleet and with which to scare the bastard Welsh.' He chuckles on leaving me. Even he's pleased at the prospect of the battle to come. I wish I were. No, that's not quite right. I hunger for the coming fight. The small altercation outside and inside Northampton was just that, small. I didn't get to sate my blood rage. That might be a problem. It's one thing to hunger to blood my blade. It's another to pull back enough that we don't kill all the bastards.

I tried to leave my aunt in Worcester, but she was nonplussed.

'I will be there,' she informed me in no uncertain terms. I know where her thoughts took her. At the least, she can keep Kingsholm safe, alongside Werburg and the remainder of my warriors not put into position around Gloucester. That the prisoners will also be within Kingsholm, is suddenly less appealing. Perhaps, I should have allowed them to remain in Northampton. Like horses left over after a victorious fight, I don't truly know what to do with the few men, and two women, who are really traitors.

We have a substantial force. Whether it'll be enough is irrelevant. Jarls Anwend and Oscetel intend to retrieve Jarl Guthrum, or Æthelstan as he now prefers to be called. Self-righteous bastard. They don't plan on taking Gloucester, or so we believe.

'You sure about this?' It's Icel who questions me. I can't say he's enamoured of the idea. His welcome when I arrived in Worcester was far from effusive. Now, we stand side by side, looking down at the rushing water beneath us. I've fought on this bridge spanning the River Severn. I've watched a previous iteration of this bridge burn. I've done too much on a flimsy piece of wood suspended above the rushing tumult below for my liking.

'No. You?' I question him. Of late, I sense a change in Icel. Has he grown weary of fighting for Mercia? Has the loss of Edmund reminded him of all the other men who've given their lives for this cause? After all these years, does he no longer feel the cost is worth it?

I see him fiddling with a cord around his neck. He grips something in his hand, but I can't see what it is. I'd like to ask, but I lack the stones.

'I never am bloody sure about anything you do,' he surprises me by grinning, banishing my bleak thoughts regarding his future. 'But my lord, you always make this work, somehow. I've fought for and beside weak kings and weaker fools and men who were strong and had the strength of a much larger force at their backs than you've ever had. I've stood in the shield wall beside you against men who should have overwhelmed us, and they never have. I might not be sure of anything, but that doesn't matter. I would never have done the bloody things that you do, and so that makes you the better man. No matter what I might say and think. It's time I respected that and accepted who you are and what you've accomplished.'

I don't deny his words with false modesty. This is the most he's ever said to me about his past; for once, it's not wrapped up in a riddle. I respect that. I should bloody value what he's saying to me. Just as he's trying to accord me his regard.

'Fuck off,' I glower, and his deep chuckle seems to dip below the bridge, rise up with the water and come from all around me. Somehow, it's comforting.

'That's my boy,' he grins, slapping my back with the force of two men, knocking me forward. Fuck. I should never underestimate the man he is. My doubts evaporate. If I don't believe this for myself, I can believe it if others do.

'Let's get this shit show underway,' I growl.

'Stay the fuck alive,' he orders me, and now I don't know if that's something I've stolen from him or if he's stolen it from me. I open my mouth to ask a question, some memory tugging inside my mind, but I snap my mouth shut, while Icel mounts Samson and encourages him to the far side of the River Severn with half of my warriors.

Icel has given me confidence this day. I won't ask for more. He's bloody sweated and bled for Mercia. My wants and needs are small compared to that. But, as I watch him, hand on Haden's black and white nose, I realise something I should have appreciated a long time ago. Icel loves me as a son, and I love him as a father, and really, there's no need for anything more to be bloody said.

Chapter Twenty-Five

South of Gloucester

'Well, are they fucking coming or not?' It's Hereman who grumbles. I'm not surprised. The sunny weather has given way to damp summer rain. It's not cold, far from it, but you can only get so wet before you start to get bloody cold. We're exposed to the elements out here, close to the river. All we need now is for the bore to rise, and we'll all be thoroughly miserable.

Jarl Guthrum and his Norse Christians are within Gloucester. Bishop Wærferth has concocted some ceremony to keep them occupied. Whether Jarl Guthrum realises how close he could be to escaping is beyond me. His new piety seems sincere. I'm sure it won't last once he's rescued.

'Fuck knows,' I glower. This all hinges on the bastard jarls coming to rescue Guthrum. For the fourth or fifth time today, I consider whether we've misunderstood their intentions. They seemed content enough to sacrifice him when we got our hands on him. What if this is just another of the tricks Jarl Halfdan decided to play on us? I hope Ealdorman Ælhun is safe within Northampton. I pray the tunnel and rampart keep him and his men protected from whatever might be happening in my absence.

'They're coming,' Rudolf speaks with more confidence. But then, he ventured towards the mouth of the estuary. He's seen the ships. He knows they're there. It's just when they come this way, that's the problem. We thought it would be today, but there's no guarantee. We might all be getting wet for no reason. Hereman's not the only one to be stewing. Haden's not happy, either. He doesn't like the bloody rain. Not that he'd welcome it being hot—contrary beast.

'Tell me what we intend to do again?' Gardulf questions. He's another unconvinced by our actions here. That doesn't bloody surprise me. He wants Jarl Guthrum dead. Fuck. I want Guthrum dead, but it's obvious holding him captive will only create more problems for Mercia. Especially now that Jarl Halfdan has fucked up to the north.

'They know he's here,' I begin.

'How?'

'We allowed some of their scouts to get to Gloucester masquerading as traders two days ago.'

'And we let them bloody out again?'

'Of course we did.' This is a tedious argument. I know he's pissed. I almost wish Icel was here with his overwhelming confidence. It would be preferable to Gardulf and his four hundred questions. He's as bad as Rudolf.

'And then?'

'And then they'll come and bloody rescue him.'

'So why are we here and not inside Gloucester?'

Now, this does seem bloody strange, even to me.

'If we hide within Gloucester. That would give away our intentions and stop us from doing what we're going to do here.'

'But that's where the fight will be?'

'Yes, but also no.'

His evident confusion doesn't surprise me. I'm impressed my warriors haven't asked me more questions. Icel has half the force to the other side of the River Severn. So, I have thirteen men with me. Alongside Rudolf, Gardulf, and Pybba, I also have Wulfhere, Hereman, Wærwulf, Cealwin, Osmod, Beornstan, Eadfrith, Goda, Sæbald and Ordheah. Perhaps I should have sent Gardulf and Hereman with Icel. He'd have shut them up soon enough.

'We want them to take Jarl Guthrum, remember.'

'Yes, so why are you risking the bishop's warriors?'

'I'm not bloody risking them. I need the enemy to not realise I'm here. I can't have them triumph over me. They must take this victory from Mercia but not from me.'

'Fuck me, my lord, you make things bloody complicated,' Gardulf complains.

I feel a broad grin touch my lips.

'Maybe. It's certainly much harder to assure success against us than beat the fuckers into the ground.'

Rudolf laughs at this. Of all of my warriors, he and Icel are the two that truly comprehend what we're doing here in the bloody rain.

'So we're not fighting?'

'Oh, we're bloody fighting,' I counter quickly. 'We'll make this look like a real battle.'

'How will we do that when you want them to win?'

'I only want some of them to reach Gloucester. We can only have a hundred men at most there, two ships worth. The rest, well, we'll pick them off here. And if that doesn't work, we'll hunt them down and kill them that way.'

'So we're going on their ships?'

'Perhaps.'

Silence reigns, well, as silent as it can be when the rain's drumming on the ground, and fourteen horses are nickering in complaint.

'I still don't bloody understand,' Gardulf whines. I shake my head, dislodging water from my helm.

'It's quite simple,' Rudolf jumps in before I open my mouth. 'Two ships out of the fleet are allowed to progress. The others will be stopped. We fight those bastards and then allow those two ships to retreat with Guthrum. We'll kill more of 'em than kill us, and they'll have Jarl Guthrum. They'll take heavy losses, so will be partially successful. They'll have what they want but lose valuable warriors. They'll know Mercia is strong even when King Coelwulf isn't fighting them. The hope is they'll decide to find easier pickings after that.'

Gardulf nods along as Rudolf speaks. I consider why. Does the daft fuck understand because Rudolf's his age? Or is it that, instead of being fucking angry with me about allowing Jarl Guthrum to escape, he's listening to Rudolf's words?

'So, we get to kill more than those within Gloucester?'

'Yes,' I expel a held breath. 'We get to kill 'em all if we want. Only the jarls themselves, if they come, and two ships need to survive.'

'Good,' and he turns away as though that solves everything.

'Why the fuck didn't he accept it when I told him that?' I growl.

Pybba grins. He's sheltering beneath a seal-skin cloak. He's thought of everything. He's not getting wet and miserable.

'The joy of youth,' he choruses. Once more, I'm reminded that I'm not as young as I once was. I mean, I'm not that fucking old. A few creaks and groans. A handful of scars. The odd slit around my throat. I mean, most of them are from the last year. Well, some of them are. I might have others from my misspent youth, an altercation with a hoe, and some bloody stubborn ground.

'They're coming,' the whisper comes from Wærwulf. I risk poking my head clear from the welcome mound we're sheltering behind. I know they can't see us from the river. I had Shipmaster Æthelred check for me when he brought his ship this way. The mound is tall enough that even the horses can't be seen.

In the blink of an eye, I see a host of sails. A growl escapes my throat. The realisation of what's about to happen settles on me as uncomfortably as a coarse blanket. My skin itches. I grip my borrowed seax handle to stop me from scratching at my neck.

There are nine ships. The first two carry Jarl Anwend's one-eyed raven and Guthrum's owl on their sails. The one directly behind it depicts Jarl Oscetel's snake. Of the other six, three are Anwend's and two Oscetel's, with another one using the power of oars and not a sail at all. It's easy to see who's the most powerful jarl when it's so boldly proclaimed. Not for the first time, I consider why Jarl Guthrum is so important to them. I think I'd leave him where he bloody was. He's shown himself to be overconfident and a fucking liability to his allies. But then, I know men can exert a strange control over others. Whatever he has, the others are prepared to fucking die for him.

'Let them come,' I remind my warriors, who grumble and growl. There's no possibility of seeing Icel and the rest of my warriors from here, but if I could, I imagine he'd be cautioning them to the same. This goes against everything we stand for.

I stamp down my fury, like Haden, hitting the ground with my foot and not a hoof. It grounds me and reminds me of all we mean to accomplish. We need the jarls directed elsewhere. We thought we'd rid ourselves of Jarl Halfdan, but the bastard returned. Now, I consider, where are his ships? Has he left them out in the estuary? Have they not made the journey at all? And on that long trip around the bottom of our island, the enemy will have feasted their eyes on the wealth of Wessex and been reminded of how much easier it is to attack and kill their kings than the kings of Mercia. Or so Icel assures me will happen. When he went to Wessex, I don't know, but it's evident he knows it very well.

'Aye, lads, let them come,' Pybba reaffirms. I don't take my eyes from the ships. The emblems on those sails seem to taunt me. I wish I could see the men as more than ants. Only the occasional dull shimmer of iron reminds me that they're lethal ship warriors, determined to rescue their jarl.

'Let them come,' I mutter under my breath. 'Let the fucking bastards come,' but it's more to remind myself than the others. They won't do anything without my orders. It's me I'm worried about.

A hand on my arm and Pybba's understanding eyes greet mine.

'It'll be what it is, lad.'

I nod and once more hunker down behind the mound. There's

still time to wait. While I know the river moves fast, from here, it appears sluggish. We don't need to leave. Not yet. I look down at my trews and tunic. I don't wear my usual clothes. Not that I fight in elaborate clothing, but today, apart from my byrnie, which I wouldn't exchange for anything, these aren't my clothes. They're picked out in brown or green fabric, whatever could be found in the stores at Kingsholm. I'm not to look like a king today. Not, my aunt informed me acerbically, that I ever really look like a king. I heard the dismay in her voice. I had half a mind to tell her that in her apron and rolled sleeves, she hardly looked like the bloody king's aunt, but I knew better than that.

The others are similarly dressed. All emblems of my kingship in the shape of the double-headed eagle have been removed from their clothing and horse harnesses. I don't know when they had the time to have my emblem adorn everything they owned. I thought they'd all been too damn busy fighting for the last year but apparently not. Even bloody Rudolf was made to give up an elaborate piece of Dever's reins. How I'd not seen it before, I have no idea.

Now, we look like plain men, perhaps with no master. We could, I realise, have festooned ourselves in the bishop's colours. But that's not what's at play here. The jarls are to assume I'm still in Northampton. We're an opportunistic bunch who'll thwart the ship attack instead of a coordinated attack. We'll show the bastards that even, allegedly caught unprepared, Mercia possesses the warriors to obliterate them these days. Or so they are to believe.

I've even cast aside my usual sword while my seax remains embedded in the roof of the church at Northampton. Not that my other blades are poor. They're of good construction and a similar weight, but I miss my sword all the same.

The rain finally ceases, the dark clouds driven away by a strong wind blowing inland. Not what we want, or so Shipmaster Æthelred apprised me, sucking his teeth as he did so.

'I think it's bloody time,' Pybba informs me. Somehow, after all the waiting, I feel loath to begin this. But, the smell of smoke on the horizon, faint as it is, assures me that the enemy is about their business, either in Gloucester or close to it. The two lead ships have been allowed past where we mean to stop the others.

'Right, lads,' I stand, stretching my legs and arms, cracking my neck, and reaching for my new seax.

'Let's go and kill some fucking Viking raiders.' A ragged cheer greets my words. We've been waiting a long time for this. Or so it seems.

'Stay the fuck alive,' I order them in a growl.

Chapter Twenty-Six

The ships quickly come into focus. In no time at all, I can see much more than just the emblems on the sails. Catching sight of a gloating face has me hurrying Haden. His hooves fly over the damp ground. I'd rein him in, but we may have left it too late. I should have been paying more bloody attention. We need to reach the ships before more than the lead two can slink their way along the River Severn towards Gloucester. That would undo all of our plans and put the people of Gloucester, including Bishop Wærferth and his monks, at greater risk.

I hope Icel has been more alert.

The thundering hooves bring the attention of first one and then many more of the laughing ship warriors. They're armed but are hardly on their guard. Well, not until they see us. I hear the cries then, and those lounging on the rowing chests hasten to their feet, eyes wild. The cocky bastards thought this was all going to go their way. I see the eyes of someone I know well. Anwend's son. I've not killed him before now, but perhaps this time, we will. Or maybe we won't. The intention here is to convince the Viking raiders of Mercia's battle prowess and have them running for their lives.

I close the cheek straps on my borrowed helm as I rise in the saddle. I don't want him to recognise me.

Furtive movements on the ship have armed warriors ready to counter the attack. The sharp slap of a spear burying itself in the ground ahead assures me they're not all lacking skill and wit, even if I wish they bloody were.

The ships are moving more quickly than I'd like. We've caught up with the first of them, using the power of the sail to drive it inland, the oars stowed aboard. I can't see the lead two ships. It seems, as so often the case, that this collection of ships lacks a cohesive commander. That will work to our advantage.

Now, we need to outstrip them to reach the designated location before they do. This bloody wind will undo our careful planning with how it speeds the ships. That and my own inattention could fuck this up before it's begun.

'Hereman,' I call over my shoulder, but the wet slap of something falling assures me he's already sighted and taken out their observant spear thrower. The howl of the wounded man reaches me later. Provided they have no one else with such good aim, we'll be able to get close enough to attack.

The river bank is filled with summer growth, green cloying weeds close to the flowing water and further away, threatening to tangle with the ships. I hope Haden knows to stay away from them and to watch for any poorly placed holes dug by small animals. Ahead, part of the river bank juts into the water. It's here I intend to board the ships. It's here that Icel should join us in a two-pronged attack. Then we'll move to the next ship. In delaying our arrival here, I've ensured they know of our presence, but that can't be bloody helped now.

Another twang of a thrown weapon, and Haden pulls up short, front hooves kicking, but at least he avoids the spear. I scrabble to stay mounted while Rudolf and Dever veer off to the side with a wild shriek from Rudolf, although Dever takes it in his stride.

'Open your fucking eyes, my lord,' Pybba helpfully shouts.

'They are bloody open,' I retort angrily, bending low over Haden, encouraging him to reach his full speed again. We need to reach the jutting river bank quickly.

The shouts of the enemy echo all around. Some taunt. Others are fearful. I keep my eyes ahead. I see what I've been looking for as we round the bend, and I'm dismounting before Haden can stop. Mud springs up from his hooves, and I slap him aside. He needs to stay out of the way.

The others join me, apart from Hereman and Gardulf, who have another task to complete. I watch them, willing them on.

'Stay the fuck alive,' I growl my oft-repeated reminder to those surrounding me, securing their horses and hoisting weapons to hands. It doesn't make it any less relevant. They variously nod or grunt in agreement, sliding hands through shield straps and testing weapons belts for their blades of choice. Across from us, I see Icel in his battle garb. He looks like a menacing bastard. The sun touches his byrnie, helm and weapons. I wouldn't want to fight the fucker. He offers me a grimace or a grin. I can't tell from here. Perhaps it's even a shake of the head for my tardiness and for the fact Hereman and Gardulf are still labouring up ahead.

Then, the first enemy ship is in position. They realise we've set a trap before they can do anything about it. Sail proudly proclaiming allegiance to Jarl Anwend, and with his son hollering commands to his shipmen, the ship's carried into the rolling mass of snaking rope we previously laid across the narrowest stretch of the river. Gyrth and Hemming have pulled it taut from Icel's side of the river bank. Hereman and Gardulf manage to do the same from our side. I allow myself a grin of triumph. We've not buggered it up. Not yet. The ropes might not hold the ships for long, but it gives us the opportunity we need.

'Now.' With Hereman striding to my right, elbowing Wærwulf aside, who thought to take the honour, and Rudolf to my left, as ever close to Pybba, the rest of my warriors spread out beside us. Gardulf shoulders his way to Hereman. He's grown in confidence since his father's death. Edmund would be bloody proud to watch him now. Pity the fucker didn't allow his son such praise while he lived.

We're a long, thin shield wall with no one behind us but our grazing horses, reins tied tightly above the saddles. Icel and his warriors mirror our actions. The ship stops abruptly with a creak of distressed wood, the speed of the deceleration forcing some onboard to their knees, while the shriek of one man makes me think he's fallen overboard. A wet sound assures me I'm right.

'Fucking arsehole,' Hereman mumbles from beneath his helm, the words are echoing and menacing.

'Now.' With the ship stopped, we move along its side. The river bank's lower here, somewhere liable to flood easily, as evidenced by the boggy ground, just as Shipmaster Æthelred assured me. It caused havoc trying to get the bloody ropes in place and secured. But it's what we need. With a surging step up, bending my body forward to ease the movement, we're on the side of the teetering ship, using the oar holes against them. They've moved most of the shields lining the ship. They hold them in their hands.

I feel the surge of the enemy coming to meet our attack, but they must also counter Icel's offensive from behind them. Do they have the men? I imagine they do, but I doubt they could have anticipated such an attack from both sides of the river.

'Forward,' I bellow. One step, and there's some resistance from our foemen.

'Forward,' I order, Icel doing the same, his word echoing mine. There's more resistance.

'Forward.' The crash of a war axe on my shield assures me we have the enemy at a disadvantage, but they're prepared to fight bloody.

'Attack,' I cry, and my warriors join me in roaring their joy at facing our opponents.

I hold my shield firm and then drop it quickly, a glancing blow on my foeman's shoulder. They don't have their shield wall in place yet. Icel does. I glimpse it between the curve of my shield and Hereman's.

Mercia's warriors attack our enemy down both lengths of the ship even as we strain for balance, the rocking of the captured ship making it difficult to hold any formation.

A bang on my left shoulder, and I'd glower at Pybba, but my attention's elsewhere. Hereman makes a wild strike beside me, his shield bashing into mine, jarring my right shoulder. I snarl. He offers a shouted 'apologies' before resuming his attack. The ship's unsteady beneath us. I have to stand, legs wide, to keep my balance. Any fucker with a spear could slice me in the stones. I try not to think about that. Our adversaries aren't behind us. They're in front.

My foeman's fierce in his resistance. I hold my shield steady, ignoring the twinges from both shoulders and reach over to attempt a blow on any exposed part of his body. My blade glances off something metallic, a blade or a helm. I'm not sure. But not his shield, for my arm can't reach that far.

I don't move my warriors any further forward. It's enough to stand our ground and assault our opponents. I don't want to force my men to fall into the river to the other side when our enemy disintegrates. That's not part of the plan. I've warned them to be bloody careful when it gets to the dirty end of the fighting.

Around us, I hear the cries and thuds of the fight. My seax hand endeavours to find a way through the shields to skewer my foeman. I won't be the last one to draw blood. Not if I can help it. Already, the scent of blood mixes with the dampness of the ship and the sharp bite of men who've been out at sea, scoured by the wind.

A thud on my left shoulder, and I open my mouth to complain to Pybba again, but it's not him. Hastily, I yank the arm of my foeman towards me.

'*Skiderick*,' I glower, pulling and pulling until a squeak of pain assures me the man is at his limit. With a swift movement, I release him and stab into his unprotected underarm, almost backhanded. It's far from comfortable. His shriek of agony and the drum of falling liquid assure me I've skewered him bloody well. The resistance against me falters as the scent of iron and salt fills the air. It's not a solitary occurrence. Hereman grins at me or grimaces, his teeth reddening from where he's bitten his tongue, but the adversary he fights is below his feet. Hereman bends and slashes across his exposed throat, just to ensure he's well and truly fucking dead.

Rudolf and Pybba fight together, as is so often the case, Rudolf acting as Pybba's missing hand while Pybba guards his back. I watch Rudolf, noting the precision of his strokes. The efficient way he kills his opponent using as minimal effort as possible. Fuck. It's like poetry in motion. I allow a swell of pride. I taught him how to do that.

Well, Pybba and Icel might take the acclaim, but it's me Rudolf wishes to emulate. So, they can bugger off.

In front, the enemy shield wall's crumbling, and not just ours, but the one to the other side as well, which Icel fights against. The ship will be ours in no time. I look for Anwend Anwendsson, but I can't see him. No doubt he's already dead—stupid bastard. We let him live once. He shouldn't have taken the risk that we'd do the same again. We'll have to contend with the consequences of that later.

We'll force holes into the ship and allow it to sink. The ropes have it tangled, but if someone with half a mind thought to sever them, it could float free. Removing it later will fall to Shipmaster Æthelred and his sons. I can't do bloody everything. Already, Hereman and Gardulf are busy hacking at the wooden ship's hull. The familiar sound of wood being hewed is incongruous with the gurgles and cries of the wounded and dying.

Shouts of anger and fear thrum through the air as the ship following on behind realises what's happening. The bastards thought to have it all their way. They should have known better. The arrogance astounds me. Have the Mercians taught them nothing throughout the last many summers?

'Is it bloody done?' I call to my warriors, maintaining my hold on the shield. Someone's still fighting, although it's a solitary occurrence.

'Nearly,' Wærwulf growls through gritted teeth.

I do lower my shield, then. The adversary fighting Wærwulf

doesn't know he's beaten. He crashes his war axe against Wærwulf's shield, skipping out of the counterattack and running at him again.

'Get the fuck on with it,' Hereman calls, glancing up from his labours. He's well known for his patience. Sweat beads on his face. His teeth are reddened, but he's not grinned so much since his brother's death. Water's flowing quickly up his legs. The ship will sink soon.

Wærwulf's words are guttural as he speaks to the man in his language. I watch the shudder of realisation flood his foeman's senses. After all, any of us could gut him from the rear, and if not us, then one of Icel's warriors. I meet the older man's eyes. He nods, once satisfied, his nose running with blood, reddening his greying beard. He's wounded, but not badly.

I consider unleashing Cealwin on the still-fighting Viking raider, but shake my head. Wærwulf wouldn't appreciate that. This is his man to kill. I have to hope he accomplishes the task before the ship sinks any lower. Already, I'm moving back to the side of the craft, balancing precariously on the lip of the ship.

With a strangled cry of defiance, the man succumbs. Wærwulf looks up, aware of the scrutiny he's under, breathing more heavily than the rest of us, even Gardulf and Hereman, with their axes.

'There were three of 'em. I didn't just kill one, like you bloody lot.' He spits on the flailing limbs of the dying man and then bends, impaling him to stop the heart from beating.

'What the fuck are you waiting for? This isn't it.' he growls. I find a grin on my face. Wærwulf's a nasty bastard when riled.

'You heard him,' I call to my warriors, noticing who wipes blood or sweat from their brow. 'Let's get to it.' I turn to face the way we've come. The ship's moved almost sideways now, the river's flow trying to turn it away from the restriction of the ropes and threatening us with a quick dunking. Before we can fully scuttle it, as Shipmaster Æthelred assured me it's called, the next vessel careers into it, sail still showing. With a lurch, the ship we're standing on shunts forward, even closer to the tangled mass of ropes blocking the way.

Just in time, I jump back into the rapidly filling ship, the cold bite of the water making me shudder, even as I wince at the sharp snap of fracturing wood.

'Watch out,' I roar at those with Icel, although they're just as alert. Appraising eyes watch the mast as it nears the strung-out rope, being pulled closer and closer until it meets it. The rope acts like a hot knife through butter. The wooden mast teeters, sliced close to the base and then begins to fall back along the length of the ship as the force of the water turns the craft. No longer sideways on. I realise what's going to happen at the same time as the rest of my warriors.

'Get the fuck off,' I roar. If we fall overboard, we'll be buggered. Everything slows down. The mast falling, my warriors scrambling to jump clear now they're not being forced to go one behind the other due to the ship's nose-on position to the river bank. Abruptly, the Viking raiders waiting to meet our attack on the next ship realise they're going to be victims of more than just our sharpened blades. As they run from the falling mast, shrieks and cries of outrage ring above the creak of wood and complaints from my men. The ship, battered and holed, broken and devoid of its warriors, rears out of the water, as though attempting to reach dry land. I struggle for balance, not wanting to release the grip on my blades or shield, or fall into the swell of the river, while water stings my eyes, and I spit aside the taste of dead men.

When the ship finally settles, I turn and glance at our enemy.

'Fuck me,' I muse to Hereman, righting himself beside me, war axe forgotten about in his hand. Our ship's listing now, taking on copious amounts of water, but it's nothing compared to the mess of the craft behind us.

'Bloody bollocks,' Hereman offers, both of us hearing shrieks, cracks, groans and the general wailing of our enemy and their rapidly submerging ship. We stand, ignoring the growing swell of water around our knees, the swirl of abandoned shields and bodies that knock against us, and look at what's happened to those who came directly behind. Some try to make it to the river banks, landing with wet splashes and disappearing from sight. Others reach for wooden chests or even the abandoned oars, somehow thinking the wood will keep them afloat even though they're garbed as warriors. The mast on the sinking ship stands proud while all around goes to shit. I shake my head, astounded by the speed of it all.

'Sometimes, it really seems as though someone's bloody looking out for us,' I muse. Hereman's bark of laughter brings a grin to my blood-splattered face. My warriors shout their own words to one another, exulting in this triumph.

'Bloody hell,' Rudolf hisses, standing upright from where he's been pilfering a floating corpse. Pybba joins him, his face blood-streaked, but otherwise unharmed. I see Icel on the river bank, watching it all with a grin of satisfaction on his old face.

The enemy ship and almost all of its warriors disappear beneath the swirling mass of dark-tinged water with a wet gloop. Bubbles froth in the water, but no one surges from the watery depths. Silence fills the air.

Not that we have time to enjoy the temporary triumph. The ship we stand upon is sinking fast, although not as fast as the submerged ship. We're all encumbered with shields, swords, seaxes, and most worryingly, heavy byrnies. Only the strongest man could swim with so much to weigh him down.

'Get on dry land, you lackwits,' Icel roars from the river bank, breaking the moment of calm success.

'Bloody come on,' I huff, not wanting water up to my arsehole. The wood's turned slick, the contents of the ship, well those that are light enough, bobbing in the water, the corpses as well. I grimace at the bloodied mess. Pybba and Rudolf already pant on the river bank, shields in hand, ready to defend themselves from those still coming on behind.

At the last moment, when I think I'll make it without getting any wetter, the ship lurches alarmingly to the side once more. I reach out, grasping for the river bank. Hereman grabs me, but not before dunking my arse beneath the water.

'At least you're not entirely wet,' Hereman half-heartedly consoles. I shudder, but there's no time to feel sorry for myself.

Two ships are incapacitated, which leaves only five others. I can't imagine it'll be as easy with them. Not now they've seen our tactics.

The next craft teams with enemy warriors. The ship's commander, as Shipmaster Æthelred warned me, is alert to the danger. I watch the man sucking his teeth and eyeing the mess ahead. I can imagine what he's thinking. The two ships who've already passed us without a fight won't be able to escape unless the river is cleared, but does he want to be the one to do it by cleaving a path between the wrecks? I doubt it.

Yet, the men on board encourage him onwards with bellows of fury. No doubt some of their friends have drowned, not exactly an honourable death. They won't be feasting in the afterlife.

'Shields,' I call to my warriors. They nod or grunt or shake water from their hands and prepare for the next assault. I wish my legs and arse were dry, but they're not. The cold's creeping along my feet. I hate having bastard cold feet.

'Steady,' I warn. The Viking raiders are throwing anything and everything at us. A discarded boot thuds against my shield, a broken pot against Hereman's and even the severed hand of one of the dead against Gardulf's shield. As it lands, flecks of blood and flesh rise up into the air.

'They're getting bloody desperate,' Pybba offers, stating the obvious. He's not wrong.

The ship comes to a gradual stop in front of us, just behind the ruins of the other two ships, making use of a huge stone thrown into the water to bring it to a halt. I don't fancy hauling that clear of the water. The ship's commander looks far from happy, but the warriors surge towards us. This part will be on dry land.

'Stand firm,' I urge my warriors. 'We'll fucking kill 'em like we did the others.'

I hear a gabble of words from the enemy, which I think I understand, but Wærwulf provides the translation.

'They mean to attack us. The ship behind will face Icel and the rest of the men.'

'Bollocks,' I glower. We'll be outnumbered, but when has that ever bloody stopped us?

'Hold shields, and then we'll rush them back into the river,' I direct. There's to be no posturing today. I want them dead, and the men we face want us dead. We're not both going to get what we fucking want.

'Forward,' I urge my warriors, shields locked in place. As one, we advance towards the surge of the river. I can hear the gurgling cries of wounded men. I'd pity them, but it's their damn fault. If they'd stayed at home, none of this would have happened.

The ground beneath my feet is quickly tangled with long weeds and the occasional frog that rushes out of the way. I don't blame it. It'll get trampled.

The enemy stream towards us, visible above the rim of our shields.

'Hurry,' I encourage my men. I don't want our adversaries to have the time to form up. I don't even want them to have time to stand upright before we encounter them. I don't get my bloody wish. They're quick. My line of men crashes against their shields. We take the initial advantage, but they're immediately countering us, withstanding the assault.

One voice directs their steps. Not that he's amongst the warriors. His cries come from the ship. Is it one of the jarls or the ship's commander? I don't recognise his voice, but then, he's bellowing like a boar being hunted. It's almost impossible to detect his individual words. Our enemy must be used to it, though. They stand firm against our onslaught. With my seax to hand, I slash and swipe, trying to land a blow on the man who faces me. But, he's a similar height, head covered in a blackened helm, neck protected by iron, and all I do is bring forth sparks along the rim of his helm.

Hereman has more luck. His foe is a man of slight build, for all he fights quickly. I lean aside from the probing blade that tries to gouge me or Hereman. Hereman leans over the shield. I strain to keep my protection in place as he slashes his foeman's upper arms. For a moment, so much red sheets my face that I struggle to see. But the man is down, and Hereman, with all his guile, lowers his shield and stabs the man who faces me as well. A guttural moan from beneath the blackened helm, and his defence intensifies. He's not dead, just wounded.

'*Skiderick*,' I murmur, meeting every one of his frenzied blows with a defence. I want to overwhelm him, but he moves so fast it's impossible. Another takes the place of Hereman's dead warrior, and Hereman absorbs himself back into the shield wall.

I can hear the battle from across the river but can't see it. I hope Icel has the rest of my warriors under firm control. I yearn for him to overwhelm the enemy.

But there's no time to think about that. My foeman is wild. Whatever Hereman did to him, he's gone from a reasoned warrior, determined to win against all odds but careful with his blows, to a man who'll risk it all. I counter his attacks, ducking below the weight of his war axe as he tries to bash my head. I'm grateful for my borrowed helm as a blow glances from it. His swings are wild, his focus either very specific or just bloody lucky. I can't tell.

My shield protects my belly, and I can't move it, wrapped together as it is with Hereman and Pybba's shields. My enemy doesn't have the same problem. His shield moves up and down wherever I think to draw blood. My hand throbs with the force of my thwarted blows. But I don't allow anger to guide my steps.

I'll fucking kill him.

Eventually.

I duck and weave, all the while staying in the same place. When he aims for my head, I tilt to the side. When he aims for my feet, I split them, half a thought that he might realise and slice up, taking my stones with the cut of his blade. And all the time, I'm trying to land a blow of my own. His head is out of reach. The shield protecting him. His shield entirely protects his one arm; the other moves quickly, and

I have to dodge his wild strikes instead of thinking about how to draw blood. It leaves me with only one real option.

Hereman grunts beside me. Pybba holds firm with his shield, shouting instructions to Rudolf to ensure neither is bloodied by the enemy. With more time, Pybba's managed to slide his shield onto his stump so he can stab and slice with his seax.

I look from one to another, in between evading my enemy's blows.

'Hold,' I urge them. They don't indicate that they've heard.

'Fuck it,' I mutter, releasing my grip on the shield, hopeful it will remain in position, and thump to my knees, my feet tingling from the cold, my arse even wetter where it rests on my damp legs. Decisively, I stab forward, my seax opening up my enemy's ankle before he can realise I'm gone from facing him. A gout of blood rushes over the top of his sock, and I've sliced open the other one as well before he even notices the pain. I carve upwards, taking my blade as far up his leg as possible, which isn't far enough to have him bleeding to death, but it nearly bloody is.

A crash on my extended arm as his shield falls has me snatching it back, scrambling upwards, just as my shield begins to tip towards me. I slide my hand into the strap, place my legs, and slash into his abruptly exposed upper chest. He's too slow, at last, to evade my reach.

Foul breath taints the air, the scent of his blood mingling with whatever he had to eat two days ago, his rotten teeth visible, and his mouth opens with a shriek of pain. He must be bleeding from more than one place now. His ankles. His leg. Whatever Hereman did to him.

But he's not about to accept that this is the bloody end.

His frenzied blows come ever faster. A wild strike almost loses Hereman his ear, but I shove him aside at the last moment, my seax weaving with the movements of my foeman, as Hereman grunts and then rights himself. The warrior he faces is a brutal bastard, long greasy hair visible beneath his helm of dull iron. He has no cheek guards, and I can see the red of his sparse beard. He should shave if that's all he can grow.

Another feral slash of the war axe, but I can tell my enemy's losing focus. His wild, lucky blows are becoming weaker and weaker. Behind him, more of the enemy are forming up, keen to try their luck. The two ships have disgorged their men to either side of the river.

I need to finish this. It's time for a new man to die on my bloodied blade.

This time, I wait, doing nothing until an unruly strike wobbles towards my head. With a grimace, I tilt my head to the side, stabbing up with my seax, finally finding a target. There's a small gap between his leather gloves and the protection of his arm rings. While they jangle on his muscled arms, I slash the skin on his wrist and then stab into the open wound. I'd like to sever it, but I have my seax, not my sword, at my disposal. The war axe falters, springing free from his opening hand. I yank on it, pulling it closer and closer, the man's crazed eyes meeting mine, his neck a mess of bloody gore. My seax stabs into it, and he gurgles, the sound wet and guttural.

'*Skiderick*,' I mutter. I'd kick him down, but I can't. Instead, eyes glazing, hand and leg bleeding, face as well, he crashes to the ground, taking his shield with him. The bastard's dead, but he's my enemy's first line of attack.

Now, I need to kill the rest of the arseholes.

Chapter Twenty-Seven

There are more of them than I'd like. There are less of us than they might think. It's just the way I prefer to overwhelm the cocky bastards.

Beneath my feet, the ground's growing slick, and not just with the water from the river. No. The blood of my enemy is feeding the grass. There'll be much more of that before this is over. Hereman's back on his feet. Pybba and Rudolf protect my other side. It feels as though we move as one, for all we're a long line of warriors. We step, and stab, shove and punch. This is the way of the shield wall, and my heart thuds in time to each movement, a rhythmic counterpart to my actions. I don't look up to see how Icel and the rest of my men fare. I know they'll do all they bloody can. Not one of us wants to fall beneath the blade of one of the bastards.

The river's an inviting target. These men have disgorged from their ship to overwhelm us. Now we drive them back towards the surging river. The ships are tangled and broken, bodies abutting pieces of wood wedged into position. It's a grim sight. It makes my heart swell with fucking pride.

Slash and crash. I can smell the water, mangled with the scent of spilt blood, but an opportunity all the same. We've drowned many of them already. Now we need to finish the rest of them.

I remember when we last used this tactic. It didn't go as planned. Now I hope it will. Slash and crash, one step forward, the weight of the enemy tugging on my arm and shoulder. I growl low in my throat. Fucking bastards. I hate them all. It's not going to ensure my victory, though. Hate isn't a weapon. Not at all. Skill. Precision. Hereman's blind good luck. That's what's needed.

Foemen growl and grimace behind their shields. I can hear their rasping words. I don't need to know what they are to understand the intent. Not that it's truly so hard to keep track of what they're being commanded to do.

They mean to overwhelm us. We mean to overwhelm them. I know who'll be victorious. A shudder runs through my lips, my shield hitting me there, somehow making its way past the protection of my chin strap. I taste blood, lick the salt from them, and use it to stir me onwards. Not rage. Never rage. Righteousness, if you will. But really just the belief that these people aren't welcome here. They never have been. Mercia is the land of the Mercians, not the bastard Viking raiders.

Hereman cries out. I glance his way, seeing him dodge the scything action of a blade. I hold my shield steady. He keeps his weapon where it needs to be and then lashes out. More blood fills the air. It rains down on me, adding to my split lip. I don't know what he cut or how he managed to cut them, but the screams of agony assure me another of our enemy's wounded, if not dying. I'd like to think he was dying, but it's never that bloody easy. Find the right place to burst the innards, and a man can die in moments. Find the wrong place, and rage, pain and fury will make him a crazed bastard, just like a wounded stag.

A thudding through my arm, and now my foeman moves against me. I watch his war axe waver above my head, the long wooden handle allowing my opponent to reach right over the shields. I watch it, grimacing with the growing weight on my arm. One means to pull my shield aside; another means to knock me so that my helm blocks my vision.

I growl, focusing on what I can do, not on what they're doing. My seax stabs upwards, and my shield juts forward. I feel the pressure ease from the weight on my shield, but the war axe is still coming. I've done nothing but encounter empty air.

This time, I focus on the war axe, watching the glistening flecks of red blood and tangled hairs on its sharpened edge. I don't know who this arsehole wounded, but I'll repay the bloody kindness. I stab up and up, using the seax as though it were a knife to spear meat. For that's what this is—meat to be speared, but not eaten. I'd gag if forced to do more than taste my enemy's sweat and blood.

A bleat from behind the shield, and my seax finds purchase in the underside of the man's hand. He thought to use the war axe against me, but I've found a space where it curls around the wooden handle, and now blood rains freely. I feel it washing me and jab even further into the hand. It clenches, a shriek of fury from my enemy. I grip it tightly and whip it free. More bloodied rain falling down my helm and towards my mouth, but redirected by my nose guard. My foeman's grip falters.

'Shit. Watch out,' I call, unsure if Hereman will heed my words as my enemy releases his grip on the war axe. It thunders towards my feet and Hereman's. Too close, too close. I feel it travel down my byrnie, my trews, and jump aside at the last possible moment. Looking down, I breathe a harsh breath. Bollocks, that was close. I almost lost my fucking big toe.

I kick the war axe. It's in the way now, but the bloody thing is buried deep, the sharpened metal edges showing clear of the ground.

'Ware, axe at your feet,' I inform Hereman, but his battle cries drown out my words. And the pressure returns to my shield.

'*Skiderick*.' I imagine it's the wounded man, eager to get his revenge on me, hurling his weight against the shield.

'Advance,' the cry comes from Pybba. Gritting my teeth, sweat beading into my eyes, I try to follow his order. We need to get them back to the river, back in the water. The bastards will drown in the morass, weighed down by their equipment. But the arsehole I'm pitched against is having none of it. The shield wall concertinas around me, Pybba moving on, Hereman doing the same.

'Shit,' if it falls apart, it'll be my fault. I'll have no one to blame but myself. I look down. Feet peep beneath my shield, bright socks just about visible as my eye travels along the leg. I need to finish him, and quickly. My eye catches sight of the embedded war axe. I move my seax to my weapons belt, feeling the slickness of the dead on the blade as I do so. With half an eye on my shield, I bend and yank the war axe free. It doesn't want to give, and now the cry of advance rings again, and I'm two steps behind the rest of my warriors.

'*Skiderick,*' I growl, aware the grip on my shield is faltering. I need to finish this.

'*Skiderick,*' I repeat through tight lips, regripping the wooden handle, and thank fuck, the war axe surges free from the sucking ground, bringing with it the stench of damp shit.

Without thought, I haul it behind me and bring it down with a satisfying crunch over my shield and that of my enemy. The pressure immediately eases, and I push forward, the reassuring crack of my shield reconnecting with Pybba and Hereman's ringing through the air.

'About bloody time,' Hereman huffs. My focus is on the dead man beneath me. His helm's askew, covering his eyes, his legs pounding the ground beneath him.

'Are you bloody dead,' I glower. The war axe is impaled in his helm, although no blood spurts. I can just about glimpse the white of his skull.

'You must be bloody dead,' I reassure myself, and then, because no one has yet taken his place, I pull my seax back into my hand and stab him where his heart should beat. 'Now you are,' I mutter. It would be easier if I could see his eyes, but the war axe has skewered the helm in place.

'Stay bloody dead,' I mutter, focusing again on my allies. We're closer to the river bank now. The grasses are longer, obscuring the path and making themselves felt as a trip hazard. Hereman lands heavily on one knee, his shield dipping low. I reach out and stab his enemy, following the action with a punch to the man's chin with the grip of my seax. His eyes close unbidden behind his helm, but they clear quickly. He growls. Hereman regains his feet, and now we both fight him. He stands no chance. Or he shouldn't, but another takes the place of my dead enemy. I can see little more than the ringlets in his beard, although I smell the foul bastard. He's emerged from some hell, stinking of fire and bad ale.

His weapon of choice is what seems to be a two-bladed seax, and both ends glisten with filth and aged copper. He should have cleaned his blade, whatever the fuck it is. He spins it in his hand, taking delight in his skill at such an action, as opposed to trying to kill me. He barely has a hand on the man's shield, who now lies beneath my feet. I lash out, momentarily releasing my grip on the shield to kick it with the flat of my foot. The shield slides into the other warrior's. His antics falter, his hand grabbing but not catching his twirling blade, as I slip my hand back into the shield strap, reaching over the shield with my other hand, catching the side of his neck as he fumbles for the blade. A gaping wound, a rush of blood, and he falls as well, his strange blade landing on his helm with an ineffectual thud, bringing a smirk to my lips.

'Fucking arse,' I glower, amused by his actions. With my shield dipped low, I see the river bank and those who still try to climb ashore while some are eager to retreat.

'Advance,' I order my men. I risk looking along the line, bending backwards to see the rear of my warriors. They've left a trail of dead and dying behind them, but all seem well.

'Advance,' I bellow again. 'Two more steps, and they'll be food for the fish,' I roar. My words are greeted with a bellow of joy, and in two quick forward steps, the sound of men splashing into the water, their curse-filled rage rings through the air.

I suck in a deep breath, thrusting my feet to either side of me.

The kick to my shield sent my foot trembling. It's not a pleasant feeling.

I look down, a reaching hand trying to grip me and pull me into the water.

'I don't fucking think so,' I huff, stamping down, ignoring the jolt in my knee and the sensation of bending in my foot. The man's hand falters, wide eyes meeting mine. I thrust down with my seax, bending low so that I'm almost level with him before skewering him right between the eyes, his helm long since gone, perhaps sinking to the bottom of the river.

I stand, ignoring the ache in my knees and the sensation of my wet trews pulling tight around my calves, and eye the mess of the other side of the river bank. Icel and his warriors take their ease, his gaze meeting mine.

'What bloody took you?' he calls. I growl low in my throat while Hereman chuckles, the tone dark and filled with menace. They'll be having words later.

The two crashed ships are almost entirely submerged, and the next two now have only a skeleton crew on board—no doubt they thought to be victorious – but are now desperately trying to turn, as are two more of the ships. But behind them, another ship is about to ride into the seething, bloodied water. They're more aware than the others.

I can see where they've made preparations, shields overlapping along the ship's side, only shimmering helms visible behind them. I eye the lack of a sail, surprised they use oars, not the wind.

This has been bloody hard, and we're far from finished. But that's never sodding stopped us before.

Chapter Twenty-Eight

'Shields,' I call to my tired warriors. I can see what the bastard enemy is thinking. They can sense our exhaustion. That's not a problem for me. They'll not be giving this much thought despite the evidence of their eyes. What they're seeing are tired men with little or no chance of success. That's going to play to our advantage.

With a nod to Icel, and my warriors on the far bank, I snap my shield into place, Hereman to the right of me, Pybba to the left. We stink. The grass stinks. The river stinks. I'm covered in blood, little of it my own. The cry of the wounded reaches my ears. Some of those shouts are wet with water, and others are wet with the strangled, gargling words of men who'll breathe their last. Eventually.

I fill my body with the stink of what we've accomplished and prepare myself for what we must still do.

'Come on, you bastards,' Hereman rumbles. I can feel his tension beside me. He wants this done. I want this done. We still need to make our way to Gloucester. This element, as hard as it is, is only part of our plan. If Jarl Guthrum is to escape but to realise the might of Mercia, he must see his dead and dying men. He must witness the strength of a rogue band of warriors who align themselves with no one other than Mercia. And he must be bloody fearful.

It's a lot to ask my warriors. It's a great deal to ask of Gloucester, Bishop Wærferth and my aunt. But it's what we're bloody doing. This is my answer to the problem of Jarl Guthrum and his Grantabridge jarls. No more clinging onto Grantabridge or taking Repton or Torksey. No. After this day, they must all look elsewhere. I wouldn't object if they turned their gaze towards Wessex. King Alfred's done fuck all to help Mercia, but plough her women and steal from her. I won't have it. Not again.

I'm waiting to hear the crash of the ship hitting the river bank. A few spears have been flung overhead. A rumble of outrage has erupted from those who see their dead allies. Now, we just need to wait to overwhelm them because we must.

'Now,' it's Hereman who calls the order. I've been watching. Waiting. I think we should wait a moment more, but I won't counter Hereman's order. This is how it works. I order the advance, or another does. It ensures the enemy never truly knows who's in command.

Mindful of the slick ground beneath my feet, I step forward, my foot meeting resistance and then crashing through the rib cage of one of the dead. I gag at the scent of dead flesh and yank my foot clear. Perhaps we should have pulled the dead away, but we didn't. And now they'll serve a purpose. And it's not to soak my boot up to my mid-calf.

Shields locked in place, Hereman breathing evenly, Pybba's breath barely audible, we encounter the enemy again.

They've not disembarked, fucking cowards. They mean for us to fight on their ship. That's not a problem. We've already done that once.

'On three,' Hereman calls. He doesn't need to elaborate. We all know what he means.

'Three.' He bellows.

'Bastard,' Pybba huffs, and I chuckle. Just like Hereman to jump right in.

I step up on the ship's side, feeling it sway and shudder beneath the weight of many more men. My shield before me, I'm tempted to yank away the shield blocking my path. I hear unease amongst the enemy. Not all of them are as staunch in their resolve as they should be.

I lower my shield and smash it against the enemy one. It's lower than a man would hold it now that I'm standing on the ship's side. A rush of air and I jump, just managing to catch myself on the lip of the ship. I'm not alone. The entire boat shudders once more as thirteen men mirror my actions, avoiding the reach of our adversaries blades. They mean to sever our legs: bastards, all of them.

'Fuckers,' Hereman growls, sweeping his shield aside to attack the foeman cowering there. Well, not exactly cowering. I hear the meeting of blades as I hold my shield, ready to protect Hereman, and prepared to attack when needed.

'Bastard,' Hereman huffs, his words tight and spoken through a heaving chest, but I can hear him winning.

'Now,' I holler, and we all drop shields and power forwards. The enemy think their shields will save them. They believe being on the ship will bloody save them. They reason men won't willingly risk their lives, falling into the watery expanse and being sucked down by the current and the weight of their byrnies.

They should have been paying more bloody attention to what we did with the first ship.

My opponent shrieks, the sound strangely garbled, as though he already has some impediment to speaking clearly. I slash across him with my seax, his eyes following the blade, his hands resting on his weapons, a war axe and a seax, but doing nothing to raise them to defend himself. Damn fool.

I reverse my hold, stab into his exposed throat and hear the gurgle of his last breath. I kick him aside.

'Right,' I glower, looking for the next man I mean to kill. But there's no one else for me. The rest of the force is on the other side of the ship, facing Icel and his warriors.

No one even seems to be watching what's happening to their allies across the ship's breadth. But I'm wary. These men aren't fools. Usually. They have some skills.

My fellow warriors join me, our opponents dead or dying, the splash of some hitting the water assuring me they're going to a watery grave. I hope the fish enjoy them.

'Shields,' Pybba calls. We reform our shield wall, the strangled cries of those behind being ignored. If they could attack us from the rear, I might be worried, but most of them are either dead or gutted over their own shields, a testament to the value of that tactic.

'Advance,' Pybba instructs. We make our way across the ship. In some places, my warriors will meet the enemy quickly. For me, it'll take a while as I scramble over upended wooden chests and the mast and the other equipment that stretches down the centre of the ship. I don't know what it's all for. I'm wary, eyes alert to everything as they peer over the rim of my shield. I hold it high enough to mask most of my body and low enough that I can see what I'm doing. I'm suspecting subterfuge. It's been too bloody easy. They must have something else planned.

I'm not alone.

'Just do whatever it is you're bloody going to do,' Hereman huffs. Pybba's muttering to himself. I listen to his words. They echo what I'm thinking.

'In the chests? No too small. In the sail? No, it's furled too tightly. Beneath the ship? A risk too far.' I'm just about to offer my own thoughts when I see something gleaming. A blade, no doubt, erupting from where the sail's furled. I look closer and curse.

'It's not the sail,' I call. ''Ware.' As one, a collection of fifteen enemy warriors fling linen aside. They must have been storing it for trade. It looked like the sail from a distance, but now I realise it's absent. Where the bloody thing is, I don't know, but the fifteen warriors and those who were protecting the far side of the ship, join them, and they're coming towards us. Their faces are hard and stern, and their weapons, where they show, sharpened or blunt, depending on what they want. They look like mean bastards.

'Fuck,' Hereman huffs. Pybba's nodding as though he expected some trick. I'm pleased they've shown their hand so quickly. We still have time to counter what they're doing. They think to overwhelm us. It won't be that fucking easy.

But, I'm wary of the narrowness of the boat. Those to either end will have only a small space to fight in.

'To me,' I bellow instead. We're facing a shield wall, two men deep and stretched along the ship's length. If I can get my warriors to emulate that action, only here, in the centre, we'll be as strong as they are without the risk of my warriors plunging to a watery death. I've lost enough of my warriors. I don't plan on losing more. My thoughts turn to Edmund. He'd approve of this, even if he would have been losing the contents of his belly over the side of the ship.

I sense my men obey me. Not one opens their mouths to bloody argue—a rarity.

Now, the enemy has too many men, and they're all bunching together, trying to find an opponent to fight.

'Now, now,' I mutter. 'One at a time, form an orderly queue.'

My shield meets resistance, Hereman's, Pybba's, Rudolf's and Guthrum's as well. Behind us, the rest of my men are reaching with their blades.

I skip forward, forcing the enemy backwards. They might have hidden beneath dirty pieces of linen that resembled the sail, but they left the mast. With quick steps, the foeman is forced back. Some stumbling, a few realising my intent.

And more than half of them are trapped between my force, with my extra warriors adding their strength to the shield wall and the mast.

'Fuckers,' Hereman growls. He's busy with his blade, smashing and crashing. Behind me, I sense someone duck, and turn, startled, to find one of the enemy already dead, impaled by Wærwulf, blood on his lips. He pulled the man through my legs. I didn't even notice. I stamp down, eager to see if there are more of them down there and feel a shield jut up against mine. I can't see the man who fights me when I whip my head back up to look. I can see the man behind him, though.

I lurch upwards, springing forwards, seax extended to stab him, but he ducks, and I hit nothing but the wood of the mast.

'Fuck,' my hand vibrates with the unexpected hardness of the defence. The shield before me presses against my shield and then my chest. It's tight and uncomfortable with Wærwulf pushing in behind me. Hereman's battling away, his elbow rising and falling. It's all I can do to avoid him hitting me, as his wild strikes are just that, bloody wild.

'Take him,' I order Wærwulf, not enough breath for anything else. He understands. I sense him moving behind me, bending down. His loss of support is felt in the half step back I'm forced to take, legs wide, avoiding my ally, as he hacks at the feet of my short adversary. A gasp of pain, a cry of shock, and the weight against me seems to double. Somehow, the other man has slid his way behind the smaller enemy. Two men threaten me now, and Wærwulf's antics aren't enough to dissuade my short adversary.

'Bollocks,' I huff, refusing to back away any more. With my seax, I bash against the shield, meeting the eyes of the taller man behind the shorter one. He has no shield, using the man before him and his shield. I offer him a smirk and then stab down. I want to slice, but with Hereman beside me, and Wærwulf below me, a stab is all I can manage.

My strike goes wild, but I recover my blade and try again. I can use my reach to hack at the short man. But the taller man is there. His hands get in the way whenever I try to wound my opponent. He moves the smaller man's head forcibly, first one way and then another. There's no rhythm to it.

'Fuck,' I glower, feeling the strain along my shoulders. This was supposed to be done quickly, not slowly. I want the man dead, the Viking raiders defeated, and then I need to get to Gloucester.

The taller man grins, showing me a mouth full of blackened teeth, his tongue uncomfortably long and sharp where it hangs low.

'*Skiderick*,' and I reach across and grip the slippery thing. He gags. I'm not surprised. I wouldn't like to consider what's on my gloves. Shit, mud, grass, water, blood as well. I'm astounded I can keep my grip on it. But I do, somehow. I need more hands. One holds my shield, the other the man's tongue, and my seax. The handle bashes against his nose, threatening to dislodge my hold, and his short ally, my short opponent, keeps butting up against my shield.

'Hereman,' I huff, hoping he'll realise my predicament. I've temporarily stopped my foeman from attacking me, but it'll only be fleeting. Any moment now, he'll think to bite my hand or yank his head to one side. It's not Hereman who assists me.

'Get down,' Wærwulf grunts from behind. I keep my hold on the tongue but lower my head, feeling his weight crashing down behind me. I try to stand tall, to hold myself steady, but the ship lurches at just the wrong fucking moment. I lose my footing, taking Wærwulf, the short man, and myself down, along with the tall man. The smell's disgusting. Fetid water, shit and piss flood my nostrils, although the short man's shield keeps me from plunging my face entirely into it. His legs buck beneath me. I imagine the poor fucker's drowning, but dead is dead. I stay in place. I'm kicked and shoved. I can feel Wærwulf frantically trying to get off me. I feel like a bloody horse, with his legs to either side of my shoulders.

What a bloody mess.

A meaty fist rears up beneath the shield, but it's a last effort from a fading man. I veer aside, taking Wærwulf with me. My dying enemy encounters nothing but air.

'Get up,' Wærwulf orders me, his words filled with a cross between amazement and fury.

'Get off me then,' I glower, and it's only now he seems to sense the problem. I feel him struggling for balance, being shoved from side to side by those who still fight, and then his weight lifts from my shoulders, and first on my knees, and then my feet, I lift my head up to find the tall man skewered by his tongue to the wooden mast, and the short man spread beneath his shield and mine, unmoving.

I glance around, but in the time I've been down, the fight has ended. Those who protected the far side of the ship have encountered my warriors and lie dead or dying. None of them is quite as pinned as the tall man and his snake-like tongue. I eye him, but he's also taken a weeping wound to the neck. His byrnie's blood-sheeted, his face as pale as the missing sail cloth, and I know he's dead, but I didn't truly have much to do with it.

'My thanks,' I offer Wærwulf, my footing firm because the ship's wedged itself against a collection of grasses and the hanging boughs of a tree. We're almost on dry land.

I eye Hereman. He's looking from the dead man to me, a perplexed expression on his face. I catch sight of Icel on the far side of the river, already encouraging his men to mount up because the other ships are running back towards the open sea.

'What the fuck?' Hereman huffs. I understand his confusion, but I'm not sure either.

'Fuck knows. They're dead, though; that's what matters.' I announce, bending to clean my seax on the tunic of one of my foemen. The smell of the ship is growing noxious. Someone's surely shit themselves, perhaps more than one of them.

'Come on,' I huff, swiftly examining my warriors. There are cuts and bruises. Rudolf's nose is running with blood, which he wipes along the sleeve of his tunic, leaving a muddy brown colour along the bright green of the tunic. My aunt won't be pleased about that.

Pybba sports a cut down his left cheek. I don't know how he gained it. It weeps as well, the blood sliding along his neck. I think it looks much worse than it is. The others are in a similar position. Some of them wounded, well, all of them wounded in some way. But now we need to leave.

'Come on,' I urge. 'We've won half the bloody battle,' I call and muted cheers greet my words. I wish I were leading the way but Icel is. Now I need to beat him to Gloucester. Not that this is about who gets to Gloucester first. Only it really bloody is.

With a swift look over my shoulder at the mess we've made and the strewn bodies, including the ships which are either sinking or entirely sunk, I rush to Haden. He offers me a look of disdain down his long black and white nose, almost as though he's thinking, 'You're not riding me looking and stinking like that,' but he lets me mount. I check my warriors, even Osmod mounting up, albeit slowly, and then we're away. Overhead, the cries of black crows flood the air, even the lone cry of an eagle.

They're welcome to our leavings.

The sooner they've picked clean the dead, the less there will be for us to bury. Although, I hope there are some left for Jarl Guthrum to see. He needs to know how powerful Mercia's warriors are, and how lucky he will be to escape with his bloody life.

Chapter Twenty-Nine

We follow a trail of destruction to Gloucester. It's easy to see the two enemy ships have come this way. We warned the people who make their living along the riverbank. They did their best to leave, but it seems the bastards have torched anything that was left behind. Small wooden buildings, used when the ships need to be brought ashore, blaze in the summer air, despite the rain.

'They didn't exactly arrive with bloody stealth,' Gardulf complains at my side. I eye him. He's holding his left arm tight to his body. I can see no sign of blood, but that doesn't mean he's not wounded. Bruises can be even more painful than cuts.

'We didn't exactly bloody want them to,' I counter quickly. Rudolf's strangely quiet. I turn and eye him, confident I don't need to watch Haden's every step. He knows to avoid impediments to our progress.

Rudolf's nose still runs with blood, and his face is too pale for my liking.

'That should have bloody stopped by now,' I call to him, indicating his nose with a tilt of my chin.

'Well, it hasn't,' he scowls. The words are muffled, but I know what he means.

'Shove this up,' Pybba suggests, offering a dirty rag. I wouldn't want to put that up my nose, but Rudolf does so, eager to stop tasting his own blood.

'That wasn't as easy as we thought,' Wærwulf comments sourly. He also has some injuries. Not on his face, but I saw him limp when he mounted. One of his legs, perhaps the right, is hurt. I don't know if he's knocked it or cut it.

'No, but these things bloody rarely are,' Pybba murmurs. He's sitting well in his saddle, Brimman taking his commands easily as he follows Haden.

'We're nearly bloody done,' I assure them. I don't like the idea of allowing Jarl Guthrum to escape, but I know it's for the best. He'll either spread his religious conviction amongst the Norse, or he'll vow never to step foot in Mercia again. That should mean that Wessex or elsewhere, becomes the shiny prize he desires.

I hope it's a combination of the two. I'm eager for him to dismiss Mercia as too mighty for him to overwhelm with force. Mercia and her people will not allow the events of Repton and Torksey to reoccur. No. The Viking raiders need to find themselves another bloody enemy.

I decipher the cries of men and women as they hear our approach, recognising us as Mercia's warriors and not the enemy.

'Peace,' I shout to them, but the single word streams behind me because Haden's speed is too fast. In no time, I can see the bridge over the River Severn and hold out half a hope that Icel won't have reached it yet. I narrow my eyes. I can't bloody see well enough to know one way or another, but I can see smoke over the settlement. Whether Icel and the other half of my warriors have arrived or not, the enemy is there, and they've set fire to something. I hope it's not the fucking bridge. I endured enough getting the bloody Welsh to rebuild it. I won't suffer that again.

As we get closer and closer, I sense my grumbling warriors and fleet-footed horses, forgetting all that's gone before. This battle will be a new one. It's one we need to lose but win, all at the same bloody time. My aunt is here. Bishop Wærferth as well, and as we get even closer, I see the two Viking raider ships we allowed to pass without attacking them at the quayside. Their sails are raised. The emblem of our enemies is easy to see against the bleached linen. One shows Anwend's emblem, the other Guthrum's.

I growl low in my throat.

This was my bloody plan. This was my fucking idea. But now I want nothing more than to kill all of the jarls, and I include Guthrum in that.

'Remember the strategy,' Pybba shouts to me as I allow Haden to pick up pace. Not wanting him to realise I'm reining Haden in because of his caution, I slowly pull him back to join the other horses. I don't look to Pybba. I don't want him to see my suppressed fury.

'Remember the bloody plan,' he reiterates, but I don't think it's directed just at me, even though I lead my warriors.

'We have to let him sodding escape,' Pybba cautions once more. 'He escapes.' No one replies. I sense his gaze on my back.

'Remember the fucking intention,' I call to my men. 'We let him escape. But only just. Wound him. Take a finger. Take an eye. Do whatever you fucking want, but ensure he leaves, or this will have been for fuck all, and we'll be at war with all of the Grantabridge jarls and Jarl Halfdan in the time it takes to shit your last meal from your arsehole.' My words are rough, filled with suppressed fury. I know where I need to direct it.

Gloucester's east gate is open, and we stream inside. I remember when we came here and found the Welsh trying to retreat. I'm reminded of all the other times I've been to Gloucester. All the occasions I've unwillingly prayed at the church, or haggled in the market, or found a tavern to quench my raging thirst. Those days are long gone, but Gloucester's a special place to me. I'll protect it just as I will the rest of Mercia, even if I've enticed the fucking Viking raiders here.

Gloucester's warriors rush towards us. I exchange quick words with them as they take the horses and lead them away. They know what they must do: get the animals to Kingsholm and protect the royal settlement. I won't allow anyone to wound my horse. Not again. I won't permit Kingsholm to be overwhelmed. There are so many risks with what I'm doing. Kingsholm must be held secure. That's where the majority of Gloucester's inhabitants have gone for protection from the events about to unfold here today. My unease that the Viking raider prisoners are also at Kingsholm prickles once more. I should have left them at Worcester. I should have bloody ordered them killed.

Choking on the grey smoke, we walk as one into Gloucester through the open gateway. Smoke billows from the quayside. The crackle of flames can be heard from close to one of the water mills. I hope the bastards haven't torched it. I know how complex the mechanism is to line up and put in place. I don't want the miller to bitch to me about it for the next three years, or however long the memory stays fresh in his mind. He's a grouch of a man but a good one.

Again, a flash of memory has me turning as though to find Edmund beside me, his face filled with fury at finding the bastard Welsh inside the market site. But he's not there. Neither is his horse, or indeed mine. Instead, I catch sight of the Viking raiders ahead.

They've surrounded the long hall that dominates the settlement. Inside, transactions are completed, and law is dispensed, and right now, that's where Jarl Guthrum is being held. He thinks the expedition here was for some other purpose, something religious concerned with the priory, but it wasn't.

'With me,' I urge my men. I amble to a run, feeling every ache in my body. My chest is too tight, my arms too heavy, and my head unsteady. We've already endured a bloody long fight, and we've only just started. I wish Ealdorman Ælhun and his warriors were here, but they're not. I left him at Northampton. Equally, there are fewer men here than there should be on any given day, and especially when facing a Viking raider attack. All we need to do is put up enough of a fight which will enable them to escape.

Easier said than done.

'My lord,' I turn and see Icel emerging from the drifts of smoke at the quayside. I eye him, noticing his greying beard flecked with pink and his broad shoulders. He looks unharmed.

'It's good to bloody see you.'

'A bloody nasty fight,' he mutters, but his lips are thin with determination. I look behind him and see my warriors. Eahric and Ælfgar limp, Lyfing and Ingwald bleed from cuts on their chins, but all fourteen are here. That fills me with renewed resolve.

I turn to my men. I hold the gaze of some of them, including Pybba and Rudolf. Rudolf's nose has stopped weeping, but I doubt it'll ever be straight again. His breathing is nasally, and he winces and coughs. I've half a mind to tell him to get his arse to Kingsholm.

'Don't even think about it,' he reads my mind, and his defiance is fierce. Pybba nods just once. A sign that he's content for Rudolf to continue. Not that any of them would know when they'd reached the limit of their skills. I can hardly argue with him about it. I'm not capable of that either.

'Remember the bastard plan,' I urge my warriors. I see Gardulf gripping his seax. His face is dirty and etched with fury. Hereman's perpetual good humour's missing. This is too personal for the pair of them. It's too bloody personal for me.

'Aye, yes, get on with it,' my warriors growl or call to me, and I feel a smile on my lips as I absorb their desire to stand beside me, no matter what I order them.

'Stay the fuck alive,' I command, and more and more of them meet my eyes. Fire burns within them.

I turn and run. The great hall is smoking, the Viking raiders are attempting to retrieve their lost jarl, and the cries of those fighting reach my ears.

On feet that abruptly feel lighter, I dash towards the fighting. Not to the front door, though. I catch a glimpse of combat inside and hear the shrieks of wood being moved over floorboards but veer aside to the rear of the building. There's another entrance here. Few know of it. It's for the servants, not for the king of bloody Mercia.

The Viking raiders don't notice us, and no one shouts a caution from where they protect their ships on the quayside. The smoke cloaks our passage, not that we're exactly quiet, with shields, byrnies and our weapons. I think this has always been the Viking raiders weakness. The thirst for blood, revenge, and for triumph. It blinds them to anything the Mercians can do to rebuff their attacks. They don't even stop to question where the other ships are. This time, I'm bloody relying on that.

Ahead, emerging from the smoke, I see a figure I don't want to see.

'Aunt,' I glower. She looks at me, taking me in from my feet to my head, in one swoop. She nods, satisfied.

'At last,' she offers, as though I'm late for Mass or the witan and not to deal with the bloody enemy.

'Why are you here?' I huff.

'To show you the entrance.'

'I know my way to the entrance,' I glower, but she shrugs a shoulder. I eye her then, really taking her in, while Icel bends to examine the low doorway. It's not actually that small for people who don't have a warrior's build.

'Why are you wearing a byrnie?' I demand.

'To be safe,' she offers, shrugging again. I open my mouth to argue, but Pybba interjects.

'Come the fuck on, Coelwulf.' More and more of my warriors are making their way inside.

'How many of them?' I ask my aunt.

'Too many, not enough. It doesn't matter. Just do what must be done.' A clatter of a horse's hoof and I look up, expecting to see Tatberht come to take my aunt to Kingsholm, but instead, I meet the gaze of Bishop Wærferth. His clothing is askew, and his face flushed, but I think he wears a bloody byrnie as well. He moves to dismount.

'Don't even think about it,' I caution. 'Either of you. Don't make me leave some of my men here to guard you.' A wounded look crosses the bishop's face. My aunt wears a weapons belt beneath her cloak. When did she get that? I look closer, and my blood runs chill. She has Edmund's sword. Damn her. And damn him—and bloody damn Hereman and Gardulf, who've no doubt known about this all along.

'Of course, nephew,' she demures too quickly, and I don't bloody believe her, not for one moment, but the sound of fighting from inside the long hall draws my attention.

'Hurry up,' Rudolf pokes his bloodied nose back through the door, and there's no time to argue.

'I'll contend with this later,' I inform them. I don't miss the look of relief that passes over their faces. They'll defy me. I know they bloody will. 'I can't be everywhere at once,' I shout over my shoulder, hoping they'll hear the caution and heed it for once.

Inside, it takes a moment for my eyes to adjust to the gloom beneath the eaves of the building. I can sense there's a battle taking place, but I can't see it yet. I grip my shield and seax, prepared for anything, only to be jostled by someone in front of me. For a moment, I'm not sure who it is. But the wild strikes and breadth of his shoulders ensure I realise it's Hereman.

Now I can see more, although smoke billows around the space. Someone's either distributed the fire from the hearth, or something's burning. It's acrid, and I cough. It's not the usual smell of sweet herbs and apple wood. I witness the Viking raiders battling against Bishop Wærferth's warriors. They know what to do, and they're making a good job of it. I also see Jarl Guthrum, protected behind Kyred and the rest of Bishop Wærferth's warriors. Guthrum's face is aglow. I can't tell from watching him whether he wants to bloody escape or not. Unexpectedly, there are also a handful of his fellow Norse Christians beside him. Astrid and young Knut are most prominent. They know my intention. The others don't. I've assured them that they don't need to leave Mercia. I also ordered them not to fight. They didn't listen to me either.

Icel, Pybba, Hereman and Gardulf are absorbing the brunt of the fight. They're slowly moving their way into the room. Our enemy must escape. This pretending is more difficult than just killing the bastards.

The Viking raiders are determined to triumph against us and retrieve Jarl Guthrum. They have enough men to meet our attack, even as they try to overwhelm Kyred. In the press of the small space, I realise it would have been better to stage this outside. Here, it's too cramped and too liable to fall apart.

A blood-curdling cry from a Mercian elicits a judder down my spine. I don't want my warriors to die here, not for bloody this.

'Bloody, come on,' I urge my men, adding my weight to Hereman's back. His furious face turns my way.

'There's nowhere to bloody go,' he growls. 'The bastard floor's on fire, and we'll burn alongside it.'

'Bollocks,' I glower, abruptly appreciating the problem. The stinging smoke is being caused by the bastards trying to burn us out.

'Jump it,' I mutter. But Hereman's shaking his head.

'If you want to lose the hair on your legs, then yes. And probably on your head as well.' Only then do I realise the sharp, caustic stink of the flames is caused by burning hair.

'Bloody hell.' I look around. My warriors have their shields ready and prepared, but it's as though flaming fingers hold us back, pushing us further and further back to the doorway we gained entry through. I look up, eyeing the wooden struts, thinking of our climb inside Northampton's church, but the rafters here are already blackened, and in places, the flames leap up to meet them. They'll be weakened, and we have no time to wrap a rope around them.

'Lay your bloody shields over the flames,' I order my warriors. But Hereman makes no move.

'Lay your bloody shields over the flames,' I repeat, trying to shoulder my way through. Hereman turns to glare at me, Gardulf doing the same.

'They're fucking wet enough,' I remind them of our fight in the river. It's not taken us that long to return to Gloucester that they've dried out.

Hereman lets me through. I glance at the Mercians being overwhelmed and then drop my shield. For the briefest moment, the flames are extinguished before the wood and fabric of the shield start to smoulder. I step over them, not allowing myself to consider what I'm doing. It's either this or work my way to the other entrance and then have the enemy trapped between mine and Kyred's force. I don't want to do that. It'll make it much more difficult to allow the enemy to escape.

I'm over with only a slight singe to my legs. At least my feet are bastard warm again. I bend and bat out the single flame with my damp gloves.

'Hurry up,' I urge my warriors. I'm where I want to be, but I have no shield.

I wait long enough to ensure the others follow my lead and then rush to join the skirmish. Jarl Guthrum's disappeared from view. I don't know if he's been retrieved already by those fighting under his sigil or that of Jarl Anwend's. I can't tell if the enemy is retreating with their quarry. The smoke's too dense to see the main doorway. Instead, I focus on what I can do: reinforce the other warriors fighting on my behalf. Behind me, I hear the fall of shields and the shrieks of my warriors as they forge a path over the flames, but at least they're with me.

Now, we need to end this quickly before Gloucester's main hall is little more than a smoking ruin. Then, when that's done, I can tell my aunt and the bloody bishop exactly what I think of their attempts to join the fight.

That, I realise, will be harder than overpowering the bastard enemy.

Chapter Thirty

Not that it's that bloody easy. Why would it be?

With my warriors reinforcing me, even though I have no shield, I join Kyred and the rest of Bishop Wærferth's warriors in battling the enemy. I can't tell how many of them there are.

I feel the line of fighting warriors redouble their efforts as I link with them. I add my weight and strength to the back of the line of men, hoping no one will cry out and name me as the king. I need to avoid catching Jarl Guthrum's attention. Young Knut smirks at me, as though this is nothing unusual for him. Maybe it isn't. I don't know what sort of life he's led until now. It's not exactly bloody unusual for me, either.

The enemy is led by a man I think I recognise. His deep voice shouts orders. It might be Jarl Anwend. It might be someone who sounds like him. Has he heard about his son's failure? I hope not. I consider where Jarl Oscetel is for none of his ships made it this far.

A sudden opening not far from me, and I'm shoved roughly, almost falling if not for the steadying hand of Astrid. I consider why she's involved in this and stands amongst the skirmishing. She should be elsewhere, looking after her grandson. Although, perhaps this is how she intends to do so.

'My thanks,' I growl, looking at what's caused the disturbance. I can see enemy shields, their tops shimmering with a line of reinforced metal over their edges. They forced my warriors aside, cleaving a space to retrieve Jarl Guthrum from where he still stands behind Kyred and his men. I'm shoved and pushed, squashed and stepped on, but I do nothing other than watch. This is what I bloody wanted. Isn't it?

'Are you sure about this?' the voice is deadly and menacing. I look into the eyes of Astrid and see years of pain and fury in them.

I want to tell her that, no, I'm not bloody sure.

'I can kill him, even now,' she assures me. I notice her finger running over the sharpened spike of her seax blade. It looks deadly. Far sharper than my blade. She could easily pierce Guthrum with that. I'm pleased she stands at my side, not with her fellow Norse.

'I am bloody sure,' I exhale. I watch, as do my warriors, some putting up a show of defiance, although nothing too great. It looks like we're trying, but we're not. It appears that we don't want to allow them to take Jarl Guthrum, but we do. In fact, I'm urging them on. I'm hoping they get him and leave before more of my Mercians are wounded and the great hall is little more but smoke and ash.

At the last possible moment, when I see over the tops of my warriors' heads that Jarl Guthrum senses his imminent escape, young Knut rushes towards him, the shimmer of a blade in his hand catching the flickering firelight. It dances with the promise of shedding blood.

'Bollocks,' I glower, sensing that Astrid has also seen what's happening. She's already left my side, moving with swiftness I think should be beyond her. She has many more winters to her name than my aunt.

'Wait,' I huff, hurrying myself, Wærwulf as alert as I am, for all he stinks of burning leather. I hope it's not serious.

Together, we rush towards the small fight playing out before us.

Jarl Guthrum has no weapon, but his warriors are close to him. They come festooned in byrnies and helms, gleaming with iron and menace, proudly proclaiming his sigil.

'Bollocks,' I huff again. I can see Knut's intention. He wants to kill Jarl Guthrum. As much as I want the bastard dead, he can't die here, in Mercia, seemingly at the hands of the Mercians. That would plunge Mercia back into war with the jarls. It would be a war of attrition with all of the Repton jarls, which could be impossible to win. We need peace. We haven't gained it the way we thought. But we still could. Provided young Knut doesn't kill Jarl Guthrum.

A swirl of smoke fills my vision. I cough and swipe my hand across my eyes, but I still can't see well enough. Pybba has also realised what's happening—his cries to Rudolf ring in the air.

We need to get to Jarl Guthrum, and I can't fucking believe it's because we need to keep him alive.

The cries of the Viking raiders flood my senses, and I follow them, the Mercians under Kyred unaware of what's occurring and staying out of my way as they sway and surge with the shield wall. I fear a blade will skewer me, but it doesn't.

Abruptly, the smoke clears. My mouth drops in surprise.

Ahead, Jarl Guthrum stands, without weapons, facing Knut. Young Knut's face is filled with a cold fury I expect to see on the faces of much older men and women. Astrid's just to my side of Jarl Guthrum, trying to get to her grandson, but the Norse warriors block her path. They surround Jarl Guthrum but only to this side, where the Mercian shield wall has been cleaved in two.

'Bollocks,' I mumble, trying to think of a solution to this problem.

Before I can do anything, Knut launches himself at Jarl Guthrum. He moves quicker than any men sent to rescue the Norse jarl. He rears up before Guthrum, and a slither of blood arches through the air.

'Bollocks,' I expel once more, moving. I have to do something. I had my suspicions about Astrid's intentions towards the jarl. I never thought to question Knut's. I've been a bloody fool.

'With me,' I order Wærwulf, Pybba and Rudolf. I snatch a shield from a Mercian waiting at the rear of the shield wall. His squeak of outrage follows me as I plough into the Norse warriors surrounding Jarl Guthrum. I must reach Knut. I rely on my warriors to follow me.

All I need to do is snatch Knut away from Jarl Guthrum before he kills him.

Outraged cries greet my actions. I duck out of the way of a wild strike with a war axe, grateful for my helm and shield as I bring it up to evade the blow that would have allowed me to see stars. On I go. These few steps make me feel like I've travelled from Torksey to Northampton. I think I'd make that journey bloody quicker.

Jarl Guthrum and Knut have engaged. The jarl looks like a wolf stalking its prey, but Knut's lithe on his feet. He can dodge anything the jarl throws at him. I can hear Guthrum saying something to Knut, but he speaks in his tongue, and with the noise of the fight all around us, I can't detect the words. Does he taunt him?

In sight of the small fight, I feel my feet go from underneath me as someone shoulders their way into me. I lose my balance, tumbling to the floor, knowing enough to drop my borrowed shield and curl into a ball. I feel warriors falling over me as I roll into them. A shriek. A cry. The sound of drawn blades. The scent of terrified men. The dampness of piss floods my nose before I come to a stop, struggling to find my feet, unsure which way round I am.

'Here,' a gruff voice offers me a hand, and I'm on my feet. I look back on the way I've come, and all is chaos. Broad backs and shields block my path. I can't determine what's happening.

'Bollocks,' I exclaim once more, hunting around in the smoke-hazed air for my shield. I need it to stop Knut—but there's a hand on my arm. I turn to meet red-rimmed eyes beneath a dull-black helm.

'They're keeping your identity from the enemy,' I hear Kyred inform me. I nod, then. Swallow the taste of my blood from where I've bitten my tongue, to go with my split lip, and stay beside Kyred. He's bloody right. My men are bloody right. All the same, standing here, allowing events to unfold without me, is too reminiscent of what happened at Repton. I was bound and gagged, and the Viking raider jarls thought to kill me. I relied on Edmund that day and the rest of my warriors. We were victorious. We drove them from Repton and chased them to Torksey. But this is a different day, and everything else has also changed.

Today, we need the enemy to bloody escape.

I concentrate on breathing, on trying to see what's happening. A faint cheer begins, growing louder, and then Pybba's at my side, Wærwulf with him, a squirming Knut in his arms, and a furious Astrid.

I look from one to the other.

'Apologies,' Wærwulf half bows but has to be careful to avoid Knut's bunching fists. He gabbles. His words are far too fast for me to understand.

'My fault,' I mutter, hoping this farce is almost ending.

'Put him down,' I command Wærwulf, but his grip tightens, and even Astrid shoots me a look filled with loathing.

'Right, keep him held tight then,' I mutter, determined to have some semblance of command here. 'Has he escaped?'

'Yes, on his way, even now.'

'Then we follow,' and I beckon my warriors. Wærwulf shakes his head. 'Yes, stay with Knut and Astrid. Take the boy to Kingsholm,' I suggest. Wærwulf nods. His arms bulge against the bucking boy. The resounding slap of Astrid's hand on her grandson's face has me turning back to berate her, but the boy is finally still.

'I'll take him,' she announces, holding out her hands to take the limp form of her grandson into her arms. Wærwulf's indecision is clear to see. He wants to come with me. He also wants to ensure Knut can't interfere further.

'Hand him over,' I order. 'But bloody stay with them.' And with that, I'm following my men and Mercia's warriors through the open doorway and once more onto the roadway that leads towards the quayside. Ahead, I can see the two ships between the smoke and hear the cheering men who believe they've won this. I mean. They have, if

I'm honest. But we're not overwhelmed. And hopefully, none of my warriors are dead. Now, we need to ensure they believe this was all as it bloody seemed.

Jarl Guthrum didn't see me. He can't suspect my involvement. He thinks I'm heading back to Northampton, not here, watching his fellow warriors load him into a ship.

The area is empty. There are the hundred or so Viking raiders and the Mercians. Everyone else shelters away from this fight. I hope my aunt, Bishop Wærferth and Knut can be included in that.

I stay behind the front line of Mercians, eyes alert to what's happening ahead. Once they reach the ships, they need to leave. They'll struggle to get beyond the wrecks of the other crafts, but they must not be allowed to turn north and infiltrate deeper into Mercia. If they even think about it, Shipmaster Æthelred will prevent them.

If they go north, this will have been for nothing, and the jarls will have gained more than they did when they banished King Burgred at Repton.

Everything's happening too slowly. I turn and glimpse the smoke streaming from inside the hall, but already, the fury of the flames has been quenched. It's damp smoke, not the hungry bite of seeking flames. Only then I hear something I'm not expecting. And see something as well.

'What the fuck?' I mumble, watching but not understanding why Wærwulf runs this way. 'What the hell's he doing?' I mutter to no one but me. He's supposed to be going the other way. He should be taking Knut and Astrid to the safety of Kingsholm, keeping the boy and the woman far away from the Viking raiders.

My eyes narrow. Wærwulf's hurrying. Astrid's following on from behind.

'Shit. Rudolf, Pybba, Hereman, Gardulf, to me,' they turn to face me, and I can imagine the surprise on their faces at what's unfolding before us.

Wærwulf runs, and he's being followed. The sound of hoof beats echoes despite the din of the running battle towards the quayside. He shoots glances behind him, even while he grips a bucking Knut tightly. He's not alone. There are others as well. My bloody aunt and Bishop Wærferth. But it's the horses that arrest my attention.

'The fucking bastards,' Gardulf chokes, and I'm with him on that. The horses should be inside Kingsholm's tall walls, protected from everything here. But they're not.

'Stop them,' I bellow. Now, I sense all eyes turning towards the unexpected attack from behind. This wasn't supposed to happen. Our rear should have been protected. I spare a thought for the warriors of Gloucester who had command of Haden and the rest of the horses. I hope they still live. I fear they don't.

The intention of these enemy warriors is clear to see. They mean to steal the horses, and who knows what else they've also grabbed. Have they attacked Kingsholm? Did they know enough to understand it's my stronghold? I'll kill every last fucking one of them.

Rage burbles inside me. I stamp down on it. A wrathful man never won anything without wounding himself.

'On me,' I call to my men, knowing they'll quickly join me. Wærwulf leads my aunt, the bishop, and Astrid back towards the hall. It's the safest location at the moment. This place is about to descend into a bloody battle scene, even more violent than anything that's gone before.

The Viking raiders are gleeful on their horses. I can't honestly believe that Haden has allowed another to mount him. The man who rides him must be far more skilled than most of the bastards I've encountered. Either that or Haden has been wounded. He gallops at speed towards the river, which is so unlike him as well, I must assume there's something at play here that I can't detect.

'How?' Rudolf word hangs unanswered. He's not alone in voicing it.

'Fuck knows,' Hereman glowers.

'We need to bloody intercept them,' I mutter, stating the obvious.

'Send them to the bridge,' Pybba suggests, his breath ragged as he hastens to keep pace.

'How?' Gardulf demands petulantly. The bridge is to the north. The ships to the south and the horses are moving so quickly; they're almost at the ships.

I'm frantically trying to think of ways to prevent the horses from being taken. I can't see enough room for them on the two ships. They undoubtedly thought of using the other crafts as well, but that won't happen. When they realise that, the horses will be hobbled, or killed, anything to prevent us from using them. I'm convinced of that.

Without more thought, I dash towards Haden. I can't think of any other way of forcing him aside. Maybe he'll see me. Hopefully, he'll realise I'm not riding him.

I hear a bellow of rage from Icel as he comprehends my intentions, but it's too late. I've committed now. I'll take my horse back. I'll keep Mercia secure and fuck anyone who suggests my priorities are misdirected.

Bending to the task, I push myself to run faster and faster. With my byrnie and weapons, it's not easy. I have a horse for speed. I need stamina when I face my foes, not the fleetness of a youth. As Rudolf streaks beyond me, I curse him.

'Get back,' I huff, but my words lack force. I doubt they reach his ears. They hardly reach mine.

I can hear more and more of my warriors, their equipment jangling erratically, as we get closer and closer to the horses. The Viking raiders laugh at our efforts from atop our bloody horses. The horses show no intention of slowing, and a trickle of fear tries to make itself heard, but I dismiss it.

This isn't fucking going to happen. Not while I live and breathe.

Rudolf streaks past Haden's galloping charge, aiming for Dever, his arms outstretched. If the enemy were prepared, they'd skewer him with a spear. But, they seem to be lacking such equipment. They have byrnies and weapons belts, but not spears. I'm grateful for that.

Dever's shrill neigh rings loudly as he sees Rudolf. Haden is just ahead of me. I can tell now that his gait's erratic. He's favouring his right rear leg. I can grasp why—a huge gash flaps with his movements. My rage ignites.

'No fucking bastard will wound my damn horse,' I cry. 'Haden,' I bellow, but my horse doesn't hear me. His onward rush continues, sparks flying from his hooves. His eyes are focused only on going forward. I see now that the Viking raider has tied himself to my horse. A gloating look sweeps over me as he rushes past, thinking the battle won and the horse his. But no horse will ever look kindly on a bastard that does that to him. And I know what I need to do.

Struggling for breath, I redouble my speed, feet fleeing beneath me. I swear, I've never run so fucking fast in my entire life. My chest feels fit to burst. With a springing upwards thrust, I'm in the air, grabbing the fucker who has my horse and hauling myself into the saddle behind him.

Haden's wound imprints itself on me, the sight of his innards giving me the strength to go from running to riding in half a heartbeat, my arms grasping the Viking raider before me. I get a mouthful of salt-encrusted hair in my mouth and spit it aside. Only then does he jerk with recognition of what I'm doing.

An incomprehensible stream of words floods from his mouth, half-formed as I punch him in the back so that he bucks forward. I reach for the reins then, not wishing to get any closer to him but appreciating if I don't, the three of us will end up in the River Severn.

I jerk back on the reins, shouting to Haden, trying to make him understand it's me, not the bastard who wounded him, that's now in control, but my foeman jerks backwards. I thought to wind him, but his elbows pummel my chest instead. Already out of breath for a terrifying moment, I choke on his knotted hair, the strength in my arms deserting me.

'*Skiderick*,' I huff. Redoubling my efforts, holding tight to the breath I have inside my body, allowing it to leave only slowly, I nut him on the back of the head. It's not as effective as I'd like. My helm shunts him forward, but the ropes that bind him to Haden's saddle ensure he keeps his seat. He's kicking Haden, encouraging him to gallop faster and faster. My enemy has no fear of the approaching river. Stupid bastard.

Changing tactic, I release the reins, instead reaching for my seax. My hand fumbles for it in my weapons belt. Bent almost doubled, I can't immediately find it. My questing fingers finally alight on it, and I wrench it free, sawing at the thick hemp rope running below Haden's belly. How he allowed this to happen, I've no idea. I wouldn't be allowed to do such to him. For a moment, I think him as traitorous as my enemy, only then I remember his wound. The bastard made him like this. Haden isn't a pliable mount. He shouldn't be forced to bend his head to those who think to overrule him.

With a sharp snap, the right side of the rope comes loose, the man before me battling against me, now realising my intentions. A fast impact to the ground will do much more damage to his head than my head butt.

Again, words stream from his mouth. I can sense that behind us, the number of rushing hooves has diminished. My warriors have rescued some of the horses. Now I need to retrieve Haden and kill this fucker in the process.

A seax appears perilously close to my eyes, but I rely on my helm to keep them safe, transferring my seax to the left hand to also sever the rope there. A hand clamps over mine, trying to stop me. I twist my elbow, evading the reach, but the Viking raider is quick. Immediately he grabs my hand again, and he's fucking strong. Mounted, Haden rushing onwards, the roaring cry of the enemy on the ships encouraging the man to join them, I sense my blade being turned against me. He's taken a risk, using both hands to defeat me while only holding on with half a rope.

Understanding flashes in my mind. A smirk touches my tight cheeks. I lift my right leg. My enemy's forgotten about the rest of my body. He thinks I'll use my seax or my head, but not my legs. Haden's back is narrower here, the shape of my arse not impressed into the saddle, but I trust him all the same. Knee almost as high as my nose, even while I continue to dispute the ownership of my seax, I kick the man hard, once, twice. Down his right side and then into his back. He bucks forwards. And for a moment, I fear he'll keep his balance. I'm lifting my foot to kick him again when I sense his body starting to slide. This is what I need to bloody happen.

The rope gives. He crashes forward against Haden's long neck, forgetting my seax as he scrambles to keep himself upright. Haden's speed is so fast that the ground disappears beneath us in an unending flurry of brown, and not the individual planks that comprise the quayside.

When my enemy goes down, it's going to smash his head to a bloody pulp.

I raise my legs again, slipping forwards into the saddle and the uncomfortable warmth of another man's stinking arse. But, the reins are now trapped beneath his body, and Haden's onward momentum shows no sign of slowing despite my control of him.

'Fucking bollocks,' I expel. I stab into the man's back. He arcs against the flood of pain, but I need him off Haden, as well as dead. He kicks me, his feet stabbing into my lower legs. I growl and think of stabbing them. But no, I need him gone.

Grimacing, I stash my seax and work my hands beneath his sweaty arse. When I'm assured of my grip, I shove him forward over Haden's head. For a moment, he seems to be flying. The river is no more than three horse lengths ahead. I grab the reins, cooing to Haden, and I don't see the man fall. I hear it, though. It's not a wet splashing sound but a crash and thud, followed by a strangled cry of pain.

The bastard.

'Steady boy,' I encourage my horse, running my hand along his sweating neck and gently tugging on the reins so that we veer aside from the river, back towards the rest of my warriors. All of the horses have been retrieved. I drink in the sight of Pybba and Brimman, of Rudolf and Dever, and then I turn back to view the two ships.

They prepare to leave. Their prows face towards the open sea. In my mind, I'm urging them to get on with it. The Mercians have been tested. The longer this continues, the more likely it is that someone will forget their orders and take a shot at Jarl Guthrum, just as Knut attempted to do.

At last, I see the familiar shape on one of the ships. Jarl Guthrum stands at the prow, facing the way he wishes to go and not towards me, his arms raised to either side as though he's a bishop exhorting God on behalf of his fellow Christians. I allow a smile to crack my tight cheeks.

The fucking arse thinks God was behind his release.

He has no bloody idea.

Chapter Thirty-One

I dismount quickly as soon as I sense the immediate danger is past. I need to have words with Knut and my aunt and bloody Bishop Wærferth. But first, I have other priorities.

I begin with my horse. Haden's puffing hard, his long body rising and falling far too violently, even for my foul-tempered animal. I don't run my hand along him, but instead, lead him quickly to a water trough. He needs to drink. Then I need to wipe the sweat from his withers, and then someone must tend to his wound.

I'm aware of others doing the same. As soon as Haden's drunk some water, but not enough to fully sate him, I encourage him aside. Other animals must drink as well.

Gloucester's preternaturally quiet. I miss the cries of the traders busy loading and unloading supplies. I miss the sound of men and women drinking in the tavern—the hum of monks with their prayers from the priory.

Dever takes Haden's place, and I meet Rudolf's gaze. His eyes are flinted. His nose bleeding once more. Fury streams from his tight shoulders, and I can see why. Haden's not the only animal to have been wounded. Good old dependable Dever has a weeping wound on his back leg. It looks nasty.

'See to that,' I urge my young warrior, even checking him for visible signs of injury. Rudolf bleeds from one or two places, most notably on his chin where a blow has cut into his fledgling beard, and of course, his nose from earlier. Other than that, he doesn't limp, favour one side of his body, or wince when he moves.

Content, I turn to the next of my men. Pybba. When he grins at me, a row of blooded teeth greet me, and I grimace. He's hobbling and favouring the right side of his body, although Brimman looks well enough. He nods at me. We've accomplished our task. That doesn't mean we bloody enjoyed it.

'How?' Icel greets me with his gruff voice. I'm already shaking my head, even as I rake him in. He's bloodied, whether it's his own or not, I don't know. On his dark byrnie, it's difficult to see more. He strides with the confidence of a warrior who's taken no wounds.

'I don't know. They must have killed the Gloucester men,' I glower, seeking out others. I need to reassure myself that my warriors still live. I won't lose more men. The last year and a half have lost me more good warriors than I've managed to recruit, and I think of each and every one of them as my friend. A king needs his friends. There are too many fucking enemies as it is.

'How is everyone?' I question. Kyred stands at the quayside with his warriors, looking at the way the two ships have gone. Perhaps, I realise, I should have ordered warriors to watch their retreat. But, I hope that they'll be suitably happy with what they've achieved, for now. Then, when they reach the wrecks and bodies of their comrades, they'll just be bloody pleased to leave without taking greater losses. One man. That's what they've got to show for the deaths of perhaps two hundred.

'We're all still alive,' Icel glowers. I nod, tasting the bitterness of what's happened here today. I'm not happy. I hope it buys Mercia some respite. I'm exhausted, and it's not just my arms and legs. It's inside me as well. I've buried my friend. He died a hideous death. I realise now that I do need to grieve and say my goodbyes. I need to stop looking for him in every battle. I must stop hearing his voice whenever I'm unsure or ask for an opinion. He's bloody dead. And fuck, I miss him.

'Your horses?' I notice then that he doesn't have Samson with him.

'I assume at Kingsholm, as agreed.' He offers, his white eyebrows arched high. It's a question we need answering, although I'm loathe to do so. I peer towards where Kingsholm lies slightly to the north. I hope it's still safe and protected. Now the flames in the great hall have been extinguished, I can't see any other great gouts of flame rising skywards. I don't want to think of what the bastards might have done to my home. The fact that only some of the horses were stolen is strangely reassuring.

Gardulf staggers into view, holding tightly to Kermit. I wince at the livid bruise already showing on his face, his helm cast to one side, and his hair dishevelled. For all my thoughts about Edmund, I'm instantly struck by their similarity. The loss of Edmund will never stop hurting. Not while his son stands before me. I swallow against the bitterness of that realisation. I'll not cast Gardulf out. I can't. He's one of my bloody warriors now.

'Bastard,' he spits, running his hand along Kermit. The horse looks exhausted, even his back seeming to sag beneath some invisible weight. I eye him carefully, and then Icel is there, running his lines hands along the animal's back. He stands abruptly, bright blood showing.

'We need to cauterise this,' he mutters. 'It's a deep wound. The arseholes,' his fury returns in an instant, and he's already striding towards the great hall, his seax to hand. I watch him go. His back is straight, his gait even. He shows no signs of the exhaustion that weighs me down. I might have to ask him about that. I've been fighting for no more than a year and a half. He's been at it his entire life. How does he stay so focused? Does he not simply wish to hide away on some high peak somewhere, using earthworks so ancient most merely think of them as a part of the natural landscape?

Gardulf voices my thoughts. 'I don't know how he fucking does it,' and I realise I'm not the only one grieving. I reach towards him, wanting to embrace him, but he veers away, more skittish than one of the horses. It wounds me, but I understand it. I took the sympathy of these men poorly when my brother died, and not just because my brother and I never saw eye to eye. No. These men grieved and knew I grieved, but I wasn't about to fucking admit it.

Hereman looks up. His face is covered in blood. He looks worse than when Rudolf's nose bled.

'What the hell?' I ask him. 'Where's your damn helm?' I can see no other reason for the flood of blood. Already, I'm moving towards Haden, thinking of extracting a strip of linen to stem the blood, but of course, Haden doesn't have his usual equipment. Instead, I stumble and almost fall over the dead body of one of the Viking raiders. I eye him, and suddenly, everything starts to make sense. The man has no weapons belt. But I know him all the same. He was one of the prisoners from Northampton.

'He was bastard ugly,' I huff, ripping a strip of linen from his green tunic and hurrying towards Hereman, trying not to notice how much effort it takes to do something so simple. Perhaps I should have used my seax.

'Sit down,' I order Hereman, my words so sharp, he obeys without argument. It's so rare, I shudder. Hereman must be mortally wounded. Or maybe he's just as exhausted as I am.

With the linen held high on his forehead, he wipes his eyes clear with a dirty hand and looks at me from blood-shot eyes.

'A blow to the head. The fucker dislodged my helm and followed up with a scything blow to my forehead. It hurts like a bitch.' I nod. More and more of my men are tending to horses or to one another. About now, I could do with my aunt reappearing or Werburg. She's learning fast from my aunt. I have many wounded, although, as I count them, no one has died.

'Everyone's here,' Rudolf announces, trying, and failing to infect his voice with the usual cheekiness masked as helpfulness I would expect from him. Fuck. Even Rudolf's weary of the constant fighting and he's only been at it for as long as me. In fact, it's slightly less time. He's not always killed, as I have.

Sadness infects me once more. My men are weary of this. Fuck, I'm shattered. Icel, and his perpetual desire to defend Mercia, makes him a rare man indeed. Not all of us are built the same.

Icel strides back into view as though I've summoned him, trailing the smell of heated metal with him.

'Hold him,' he growls. I leap to restrain Kermit because Gardulf doesn't immediately realise Icel's intentions.

'Hold, boy, hold,' I urge the beautiful horse, eyes wild with pain. As the blade hits the animal's flesh, a shrill whinny erupts from his curled lips, teeth gnashing towards me as he tries to evade Icel's blade. 'It'll heal, not that you'd think it right now,' I mutter. But the other horses repeat his whinny; even Haden, his head high, neck outstretched, joins in the unusual symphony. I feel a stirring inside me.

My men are weary. My horses are sorely used. We're all fucking tired, and bloody pissed off with the damn Viking raiders. Surely, this time, we've done enough to protect Mercia. We took Jarl Guthrum prisoner, but that was a fuck up. Now, converted and retrieved, can he do more damage to the Viking raiders than our blades can do? Will he, with his ships and shipmen, finally turn towards another foe? I spare a thought for King Alfred, and Wessex. I can't deny that my ploy has been to make the enemy consider attacking Wessex. Is that unfair of me? Not, I realise that I think Alfred would give it even a moment's consideration. He'd happily send the foemen against us. He'd happily ally with us, and then use Mercians to fight Wessex's battles. I know he would. I should feel no remorse, and yet I bloody do.

A sound makes itself heard. A familiar one. I turn, hand reaching for my seax, even while Kermit still strains against his reins, held tightly in my hands. Gardulf has come to join me, restraining his horse from the other side of his head.

I look up, blanching at seeing my aunt riding bloody Jethson. But the animal's quiet beneath her, taking her commands.

'Bloody hell,' I explode. Her face is tight, the lines of her lips in the harsh light revealing to me something I've been trying not to see for most of my life. She's ageing. The winters are lying more and more heavily on her shoulders.

'My lord king,' she glowers. I swallow heavily. She must bring bad news. Why else would she be here and riding Jethson and addressing me as her king?

'Lady Cyneswith,' I incline my head, moving aside from a quietening Kermit. I sense all of my warriors are watching my aunt. We all fear for friends and family inside Kingsholm. The silence stretches, Jethson's eyes widening as he smells the scent of death and fear from the other horses.

'Kingsholm is safe,' she informs me. I want to sigh with relief. But there's something else there. Something I don't want to hear.

'The prisoners escaped with the aid of their allies. Kingsholm itself was protected by the men of Wessex led by Ealdorman Æthelwulf. He seeks your assistance. King Alfred is beleaguered, fearing for his life and his kingship.'

I feel my mouth drop open in shock and horror. I close my eyes. I know what the next words will be, but I don't want to hear them. We're all weary. We're all worn out. We need rest and time to recuperate. The bloody peace accord with the Grantabridge jarls was supposed to give us that. When it didn't, we tried something else.

'King Alfred reminds you of his request for an alliance and asks that you meet him as soon as possible, not in a few weeks. I believe you must accede to his demands on this occasion, or we'll have Viking raiders for neighbours, and Mercia will have no peace.'

The words crash into my mind. I want to deny them. I really

fucking do. But as I watch her, seeing her as the embodiment of Mercia and its kingship, I know she speaks the truth.

Fuck. We need to ride to Wessex.

I don't fucking like it. Not at all.

Cast of Characters

Coelwulf's Warriors

Æthelred – a youngster adopted by Coelwulf's war band

Ælfgar – one of the older members of the war band

Athelstan – killed in the first battle in The Last King

Beornberht – killed in the first battle in The Last King

Beornstan – one of Coelwulf's warriors

Cealwin – one of the older warriors from Kingsholm, first appears in The Last Shield

Coelwulf – King of Mercia, rides **Haden**

Cuthwalh – one of the older warriors from Kingsholm, rides **Aart**

Edmund – rides **Jethson**, was Coelwulf's brother's man until his death. Brother is **Hereman**. Dies in The Last Seven.

Eadberht – one of Coelwulf's warriors. Now dead.

Eadulf – one of Coelwulf's warriors

Eadfrith – one of the older warriors from Kingsholm, first appears in The Last Shield

Eahric – one of Coelwulf's warriors, rides **Storm**

Eoppa – rides **Poppy**, dies in The Last Horse

Gardulf – first appears in The Last Horse – Edmund's son, rides **Kermit**

Goda – one of Coelwulf's warriors, appears from The Last King onwards, rides **Magic**

Gyrth – one of Coelwulf's warriors, appears from The Last King onwards, rides **Keira**

Hemming – son of Beornberht, a young warrior from Kingsholm, rides **Perry**

Hereman – brother of Edmund, rides **Billy**

Hereberht – dies at Torksey, in The Last Warrior.

Hiltiberht – a squire

Ingwald – one of Coelwulf's warriors

Icel – rides **Samson**

Leonath – first appears in The Last Horse, rides **Petre**

Lyfing – one of Coelwulf's warriors

Oda – one of Coelwulf's warriors

Ordheah – one of Coelwulf's warriors

Ordlaf – one of Coelwulf's warriors

Oslac – one of Coelwulf's warriors, dies in The Last King

Osmod – one of the older warriors from Kingsholm, first appears in The Last Shield

Penda – first appears in The Last Horse – Pybba's grandson

Pybba – loses his hand in battle, rides **Brimman**

Penna, his daughter

Beca, his granddaughter

Rudolf – was a squire at the beginning of The Last King, rides **Dever**

Siric – first appears in The Last Horse

Sæbald – injured in The Last King, but returns to action in The Last Horse

Tatberht – first appears in The Last Horse, normally remains at Kingsholm. Rides **Wombel**

Wærwulf – speaks Danish, rides **Cinder**

Wulfstan – one of Coelwulf's warriors, rides **Berg**

Wulfhere – grandson of Tatberht, rides **Stilton**

Wulfred – one of Coelwulf's warriors, rides **Cuthbert.**

The Mercians

Bishop Wærferth of Worcester
  Bishop Deorlaf of Hereford
  Bishop Eadberht of Lichfield
  Bishop Smithwulf of London, dies in The Last Seven
  Bishop Ceobred of Leicester
  Bishop Burgheard of Lindsey
  Ealdorman Beorhtnoth – of western Mercia
  Ealdorman Ælhun – of area around Warwick
  Ealdorman Æthelwold – of Berkshire
  Ealdorman Wulfstan – dies in The Last King
  His son – (fictional) dies in The Last King
  Werburg – (fictional) his daughter
  Ealdorman Beornheard – of eastern Mercia
  Ealdorman Aldred – of eastern Mercia
  Ealdorman Æthelwulf – ealdorman of the Gewisse – sister
is married to Alfred of Wessex
  Lady Cyneswith – Coelwulf's (fictional)Aunt

The Northumbrians

Archbishop Wulfhere of York
  King Ricsige of Northumbria

Viking raiders

Ivarr the Boneless – dies in AD870
  Halfdan – brother of Ivarr (above)
  Guthrum - one of the three leaders at Repton with Halfdan

His sister (fictional), who dies outside Northampton
Oscetel - one of the three leaders at Repton with Halfdan
Anwend – one of the three leaders at Repton with Halfdan
Anwend Anwendsson – his fictional son
Jarl Sigurd – dies in The Last King
His wife (fictional) who dies on the border with the Welsh

The royal family of Mercia

King Burgred of Mercia
  m. **Lady Æthelswith** in AD853 (the sister of King Alfred of Wessex)
  they had no children
  Beornwald – a fictional nephew for King Burgred
  King Wiglaf – ninth-century ruler of Mercia (827-840)
  King Wigstan- ninth-century ruler of Mercia
  King Beorhtwulf – ninth-century ruler of Mercia
  King Coelwulf II– ninth-century ruler of Mercia from AD874 (the main character)
  Coenwulf – his older brother, died 10 years ago (fictional)
  Lady Cyneswith – his aunt (fictional)

The royal family of Wessex

King Alfred of Wessex
  m. **Lady Ealhswith**, a woman of the Mercian royal family in AD864
  Æthelflæd, their older daughter, born c.866
  Edward, their son, born c. 874

Misc.

Wiglaf and Berhtwulf – the names of Coelwulf's aunt's dogs, Lady Cyneswith

Wulfsige – commander of Ealdorman Ælhun's warriors

Kyred – oathsworn man of Bishop Wærferth of Worcester

Turhtredus – Mercian warrior

Begga, Ake, Pedr, Leif, Mundi and Brag - Norse Christians

Astrid and Knut, her grandson – Norse Christians

Places Mentioned

London – **more strictly the twin settlements of Lundenwic** (a market site) **and Londinium** (Roman ruin) **at this time**

Gainsborough, in north-east Mercia.

Northampton, on the River Nene in Mercia.

Grantabridge/Cambridge, in eastern Mercia/East Anglia

Gloucester, on the River Severn, in western Mercia.

Worcester, on the River Severn, in western Mercia.

Hereford, close to the border with Wales, on the River Wye

Repton, important Mercian mausoleum. St Wystan's was the name of royal mausoleum.

Gwent, one of the Welsh kingdoms to share a border with Mercia.

Powys was one of the Welsh kingdoms to share a border with Mercia.

Gwynedd, one of the Welsh kingdoms to share a border with Mercia.

Warwick, in Mercia.

Torksey, in the ancient kingdom of Lindsey, part of Mercia

River Severn, in the west of England

River Trent, runs through Staffordshire, Derbyshire, Nottingham and Lincolnshire and joins the Humber.

River Avon, in Warwickshire

River Thames, runs through London and into Oxfordshire

River Stour, runs from Stourport to Wolverhampton

River Ouse, leads into the Cam/Granta, runs through Bedford (Bed's Ford)

River Nene, runs from Northampton to the Wash

River Welland, runs from Northamptonshire to the Wash

River Granta/Cam, runs from Cambridge to King's Lynn (East Anglia)

River Great Ouse, running from South Northamptonshire to East Anglia

Kingsholm, close to Gloucester, an ancient royal site

The Foss Way, ancient roadway from Lincoln to Exeter

Watling Street, ancient roadway from Chester to London

Icknield Way, ancient roadway from Norfolk to Wiltshire

Ermine Street, ancient roadway from London to Lincoln, and York.

Historical Notes

The events of 875 with regard to Mercia are murky, and little known, let alone understood. The entry in the Anglo Saxon Chronicle (ASC) for 874 has long been taken as implying that Mercia was essentially under the rule of the Viking raider jarls from Repton. Coelwulf, our 'foolish king's thegn,' has been spoken about with derision and even disdain. This narrative strongly supported Wessex as 'the last kingdom,' which follows on with Alfred being left with only the island settlement of Athelney from which he launched a counteroffensive and reclaimed Wessex in the coming years.

Historians are now reinterpreting this 'Wessex-centric' interpretation, and despite the lack of available information, a few facts do perhaps support Mercia's position as far from broken. If the Repton jarls had held on to the settlement, why then did they split, Halfdan going to Northumbria, while the other three men went to Cambridge/Grantabridge? Cambridge would, at the time, have been more a part of the kingdom of the East Angles and not Mercia. Northumbria was an entirely different kingdom as well. It must be questioned why they wouldn't have just remained where they were if they'd overwhelmed Mercia. Why didn't they continue to hold those settlements but had to look elsewhere?

In writing this story of Coelwulf, I'm aware that there was an alliance with Alfred at some point in these years. We don't need to accept that this was Wessex trying to help Mercia, it could equally have been the other way around. If the ASC is correct, then during this year, Wessex was beleaguered, not Mercia. There are no reports of fresh assaults on Mercia.

'Here the raiding army went from Repton, and Halfdan went with some of the raiding-army into Northumbria, and took winter-quarters on the River Tyne...and Guthrum and Oscetel and Anwend, the 3 kings, went from Repton to Cambridge with a great raiding-army, and settled there for a year. And that summer (875) King Alfred went out to sea with a raiding ship-army and fought against 7 ship-loads, and captured one of them and put the others to flight.' ASC (A)875-[874]

'Here the raiding army stole away from the West Saxon army into Wareham. And [876] the king made peace with the raiding-army, and they swore him oaths on the sacred ring, which earlier they would not do to any nation, that they would go quickly from his king-dom; and then under cover of that, they stole away from the army by night – the mounted raiding-army into Exeter.' ASC (A) 876 [875]

The later Alfred-Guthrum treaty is very well-known. But, it need not be the first time that Guthrum had reached an accord with the Saxons. It need not be the only time he was baptised. The above makes the point that the Viking-raiders had never before made a peace accord with 'any nation.' Is the narrative perhaps labouring the point here in favour of Wessex?

Jarl Halfdan is also somewhat difficult to pinpoint. It's been written that he went to Northumbria, divided up the land, and then went to Ireland, but the dates of this are far from certain. Events in Northumbria have, in many ways, been as roundly dismissed as within Mercia. This also plays into the narrative that Wessex was 'the last kingdom.' While I might be fictionalising this period, many historians are looking at events more closely. Mercia, at this time, needs reconsidering. Coelwulf's achievements need reconsidering as well. Arguing that the coin evidence of the Two Emperor issue should be 'dismissed' and that only the words of the Anglo-Saxon Chronicle can be relied upon is circuitous. The ASC said this didn't happen, and so it can't have happened overlooks the intentions behind the writing of the chronicle and the potential for centuries of rewriting. The victor writes history. We shouldn't forget that. And, often, the victor 'rewrites' history as well. A new article about the later reigns of Edmund, Eadred and Eadwig is purposefully looking at erasers in the available ASC using infra-red. We must be suspicious of all we know. For information on the Coelwulf Two Emperor coins please research https://www.ashmolean.org/watlington-hoard and https://www.here fordshirehoard.co.uk/

Indeed, while working on my non-fiction project, I was drawn to this telling statement from the beginning of a charter issued in the early 900s.

'It is known and manifest to all the wise that the words and deeds of men frequently slip from the memory, through the manifold agitations caused by wicked deeds, and as the result of wandering thoughts, unless they are preserved and recalled to mind in the form of words and by the precaution of entrusting them to writing.' S1280 Æthelred and Æthelflæd charter (Online Sawyer).

Mercia was no longer the powerhouse it had been throughout the eighth century, but its contraction may have been widely exaggerated, again, to the detriment of Mercia and the aggrandisement of Wessex. We need only look back at Wessex in earlier years to discover just how much it wished to overwhelm Mercia, starting back in the seventh century when Penda's sister was wed to one of Wessex's kings, only to be cast aside and bring Wessex into war against Mercia. There was no love lost between the two kingdoms, even if marriage alliances had attempted to correct the imbalance or, more likely, serve as a means for one or other to overwhelm the other. The Mercian Network are now seriously looking at just what information can be found to question the long-held views of the era. It will be fascinating to discover what else can be discovered from other written sources, architecture and from examining information that has been somewhat dismissed in the past. As one author frames it, 'Questions of origins [of the Saxon kingdoms] could be answered relatively easily in the nineteenth century, when Bede's edited version of the account of the Anglo-Saxon *adventus* provided by Gildas and entries in the *Anglo-Saxon Chronicle* were taken at face value.' P.13 B Yorke, The Origins of Mercia in Mercia ed. MP Brown and CA Farr. The same applies to the later entries in the Anglo-Saxon Chronicle.

While the meeting of Alfred and Coelwulf was where my fledgling ideas for this series, it has taken much longer for it to actually happen. This is purposefully done. Mercia needs to have its own voice. Alfred needs to be virtually ignored. That said, while biased towards Wessex, the entries we have in the ASC may not tell us everything we need to know about Wessex either. We know much less than we think. We should be wary of any narrative that attempts to 'fix' the period. We simply don't know what we think we know. Wessex was about to be entirely overwhelmed by the Viking raiders. Or so it's written. Events will start to move more into the accepted narrative, but as always, with an eye to what might have really happened as opposed to what we're told happened. Not, I stress, that I necessarily think the intention was to cast Mercia in a bad light. But propaganda is no new thing. It was imperative, by 890, when the ASC was begun, to present Wessex as a shining light for whoever the intended audience of the ASC was. Again, we don't know that with any surety. It might have been a court document. It might have been hidden away in a monastery. It might have been a literary pursuit by someone who simply wished to see if they could copy and then continue the work of Bede. It's not a history as we would recognise it.

And it has been subjected to countless editors in the intervening period. The 'truth' will never be known. We must accept this and continue to explore 'other' scenarios.

Coelwulf's story will continue. Soon.

Meet the Author

I'm an author of historical fiction (Early English, Vikings and the British Isles as a whole before the Norman Conquest) and fantasy (Viking age/dragon-themed), born in the old Mercian kingdom at some point since AD1066. I like to write. You've been warned! My first non-fiction title is also now available.

Find me at mjporterauthor.com. mjporterauthor.blog and @coloursofunison on twitter. I have a monthly newsletter, which can be joined via my website. All subscribers will receive a free ebook short story collection.

https://dashboard.mailerlite.com/forms/699265/105452112446489757/share

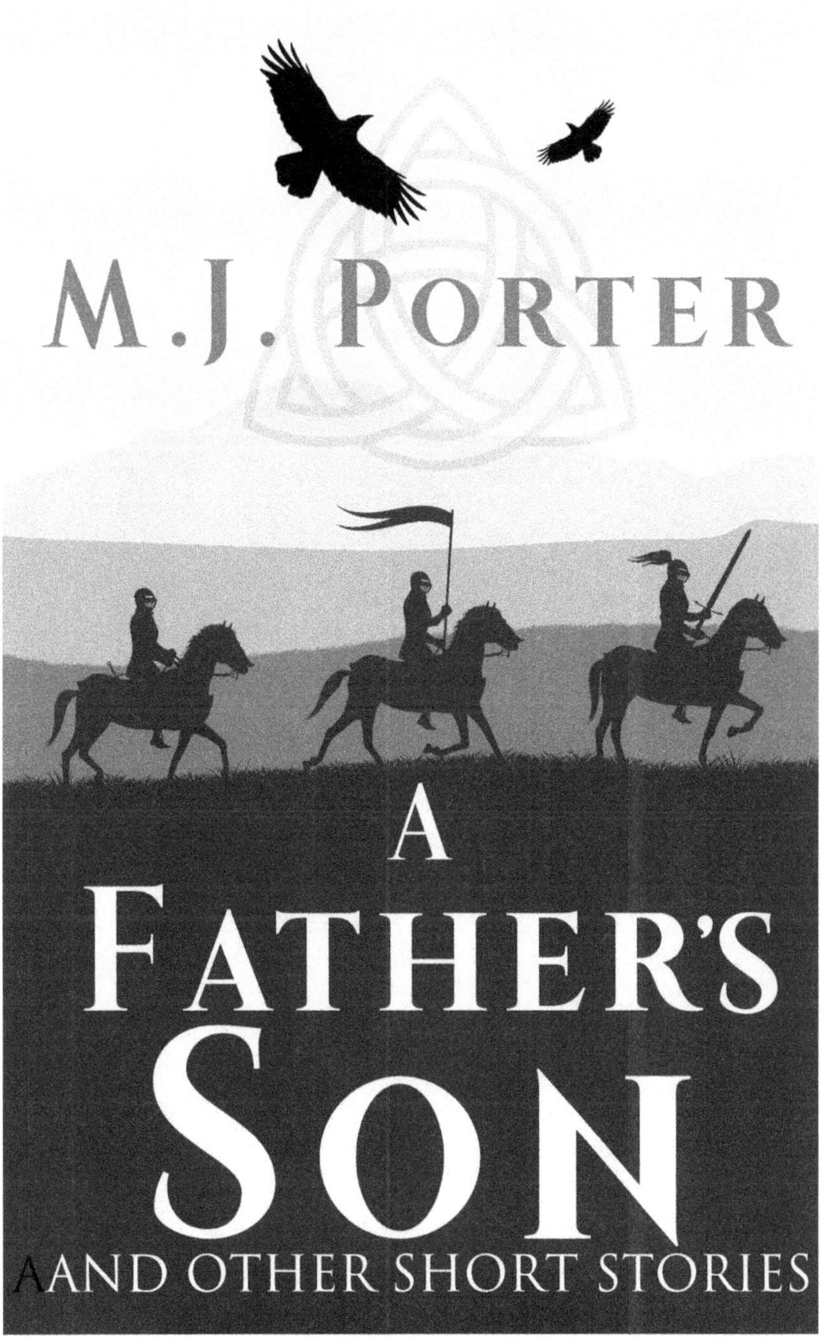

M.J. PORTER

A
FATHER'S
SON
AND OTHER SHORT STORIES

What to read next?

I hope you've enjoyed Coelwulf's newest tale. If you'd like to keep reading about Saxon England, and Mercia in particular, then please consider this series of interconnected titles, which I term 'The Tales of Mercia.'

<u>Gods and Kings (Seventh century)</u>
Pagan Warrior
Pagan King
Warrior King

<u>The Eagle of Mercia Chronicles (Earlier ninth century)</u>
Son of Mercia
Wolf of Mercia
Warrior of Mercia
Eagle of Mercia
Protector of Mercia
Enemies of Mercia

The Lady of Mercia's Daughter (Tenth century)

A Conspiracy of Kings

<u>The Earl of Mercia Series (End of the tenth century)</u>
The Earl of Mercia's Father and subsequent titles (please note, perversely, I began this series first).

Enjoy

Books by M J Porter (in chronological order)

The Last Viking

The Last Alliance

The Tenth Century

The Lady of Mercia's Daughter

A Conspiracy of Kings (the sequel to The Lady of Mercia's Daughter)

Kingmaker

The King's Daughter

Non-fiction title

The Royal Women Who Made England: The Tenth Century in Saxon England

The Brunanburh Series

King of Kings

Kings of War

Clash of Kings

Kings of Conflict

The Mercian Brexit (can be read as a prequel to The First Queen of England)

The First Queen of England (The story of Lady Elfrida) (tenth century England)

The First Queen of England Part 2

The First Queen of England Part 3

The King's Mother (The continuing story of Lady Elfrida)

The Queen Dowager

Once A Queen

The Earls of Mercia

The Earl of Mercia's Father

The Danish King's Enemy

Swein: The Danish King (side story)

Northman Part 1

Northman Part 2

Cnut: The Conqueror (full-length side story)

Wulfstan: An Anglo-Saxon Thegn (side story)

The King's Earl

The Earl of Mercia

The English Earl

The Earl's King

Viking King

The English King

The King's Brother

Lady Estrid (a novel of eleventh-century Denmark)

Fantasy

<u>The Dragon of Unison</u>

Hidden Dragon

Dragon Gone

Dragon Alone

Dragon Ally

Dragon Lost

Dragon Bond

<u>As JE Porter</u>

The Innkeeper (standalone)

<u>20th Century Mystery</u>

The Custard Corpses – a delicious 1940s mystery (audio book now available)

The Automobile Assassination (sequel to The Custard Corpses)

Cragside – a 1930s murder mystery (standalone)

Acknowledgments

Once more, I must thank you, my readers, for taking this journey with me into the past. Writing about Coelwulf, Haden and the men, women and horses who make up this cast of characters is an absolute pleasure, and I feel really honoured that you, my readers, want to read about their exploits. It has been an absolute delight to finally return to this series, and I will be writing more this year (indeed, I already am.)

Thank you to my cheerleaders, EP, AP, MP, JC, MC, ST, CS, and AM. And to Shaun, my cover designer. I will never allow us to not find a new colour for the covers for this series.

You won't need to wait as long for Coelwulf to reappear this time, I promise.